Hell Ship to Kuma

Barge Girl

By Calvin Clements

Introduction by
Timothy J. Lockhart

Stark House Press • Eureka California

HELL SHIP TO KUMA / BARGE GIRL

Published by Stark House Press
1315 H Street
Eureka, CA 95501, USA
griffinskye3@sbcglobal.net
www.starkhousepress.com

ISBN-13: 978-1-951473-46-4

Cover design by Jeff Vorzimmer, ¡caliente!design, Austin, Texas
Book design by Mark Shepard, shepgraphics.com
Proofreading by Bill Kelly
Cover art by Tom Lovell

First Stark House Press Edition: August 2021

HELL SHIP TO KUMA

Johnny Roper should be captain of his own ship by now, but bad luck seems to follow him around. He's forced to hire on as bridge officer on the *Wanderer*, a rusty old freighter with a dubious crew, to get back on his feet. The engineer is a drug addict, the mate a coward, the second mate a thief… and the captain, Murdock, a sadistic bully. Their mission is to pick up freight on Kuma. But as Roper soon finds out, they have a passenger on board—Karen Gorman has been hired by Kuma's big boss, Da-Chong, as an entertainer on the island. Roper should have known better than to sign on, because the Wanderer is a hell ship headed for disaster.

BARGE GIRL

The first time tug captain Joe Baski sees Stella she's standing on a coal barge, hanging up her washing. The way the sunlight shines through her tight dress, Baski knows right off he's going to have to meet her. But he quickly finds out that Stella—raised on the New York East Side, looking for a way out—married an older guy named Murk. Undaunted, Baski seduces the blond beauty. That's when his troubles begin. Because a near-fatal accident involving Murk arouses the attention of Delancy, the local cop, and more importantly, the insurance claimer, Coletti. Colleti says the accident is Baski's fault, that he had been planning murder. And in his heart, Baski knows that Colleti might be very close to right.

The Stormy Seas of Calvin Clements

By Timothy J. Lockhart

The sea—vast, eternal, and often stormy—has always been fascinating to writers. From Homer to Shakespeare to Melville, the sea has been a setting, part of the plot, and sometimes even a character. Writers such as Jack London and Joseph Conrad and the American Charles Williams wrote some of their best books about the sea and the people who sail on it—or die in it. And all four of the novels by Calvin J. Clements, Sr., are set largely on the water.

Perhaps because he led a colorful, even hazardous, life before he turned to writing, Clements had an unusual ability to infuse his fiction with scenes of thrilling action and deadly danger that ring true to the reader. His protagonists are tough men hardened by long service afloat, and Clements shows us with authentic details how such men handle themselves, their crew members, and their ships in life-threatening situations.

Clements's novels are the two here, *Hell Ship to Kuma* (1954) and *Barge Girl* (1953), plus *Satan Takes the Helm* (1952) and *Dark Night of Love* (1956). Gold Medal originally published the first three and Popular Library the fourth. Stark House Press reprinted *Helm* as a Black Gat book in 2020. *Dark Night* has yet to be reprinted, but used copies are available at reasonable prices.

Clements was born in New Jersey on February 14, 1915. He attended high school for only one year, joining the Navy when he was 16, perhaps because of the Great Depression. He served for several years in the Philippines and pre-communist China, and his experiences there strongly influenced *Helm* and *Kuma*. After leaving the Navy, Clements did a short stint as a prison guard and then joined the New York City Fire Department, from which he retired after 20 years of piloting fireboats. His intimate knowledge of the waters around New York deeply informs both *Barge Girl* and *Dark Night*.

While working on fireboats, Clements began writing seriously and over the next several years was able to publish his four novels along with stories in magazines such as *Collier's* and the *Saturday Evening Post*. But in 1959, perhaps drawn by Hollywood money, as Fitzgerald, Faulkner, and other writers had been before him, Clements switched from print publication to screenwriting. He began earning credits on popular TV shows such as *Desilu Playhouse*, *Alcoa Hour*, *Alfred Hitchcock*, and *Dr. Kildare*.

That period is well known as the golden age of the TV Western, and Clements soon became identified with that genre, churning out scripts for *Have Gun, Will Travel*; *How the West Was Won*; and, most notably, *Gunsmoke*, for which he wrote 39 episodes. He also wrote film scripts, one of his best being the classic Western *Firecreek* starring James Stewart and Henry Fonda. As a result of his prolific TV and film writing, Clements received an award from the Western Writers of America and was inducted into the Cowboy Hall of Fame.

Clements died of cancer in Tarzana, California, on March 11, 1997, at the age of 82. He was survived by his wife, Agnes, three children, and four grandchildren. Both the *Los Angeles Times* and *Variety* ran his obituary. The University of Oregon holds some of his papers, including scripts for several TV programs (particularly *Gunsmoke* and *The Rifleman*) and the screenplay for *Firecreek*.

As evidenced by the scope and success of his work, Clements was an imaginative and talented writer, and the two novels reprinted here reflect those qualities. They are quite different: whereas *Kuma* is a dark Far East adventure story, *Barge Girl* is a somewhat lighter U.S.-set romantic drama. What the novels have in common is interesting characters, realistic settings, and sturdy prose.

The protagonist of *Kuma* is John Roper, a former merchant-ship captain reduced, three years after "being broken from a top berth in the States," to taking a mate's job in Saigon aboard the tramp steamer *Wanderer*. The ship is an old, rusty Chinese-built freighter with "slave pits" previously used to transport African, Chinese, and Indian workers to South African mines. Although the time period is not specified, the third-person narration mentions that "[t]wo years before, Roper had been one of the few captains volunteering to transport refugees out of Shanghai down the Whangpoo River under Red artillery fire," so the story is set in about 1951.

Wanderer operates on both sides of the law, sometimes transporting legitimate freight but often shipping "salvaged" and stolen goods. As Roper joins her crew, she is about to leave to pick up such goods at

Kuma, a fictional "remote jungle island" possibly in Indonesia. Kuma is a primitive place ruled by a man named Da-chong, an urbane but ruthless Chinese crime boss.

Wanderer's fearsome owner and skipper is Ephraim Murdock, an Ahab-like tyrant who rules his ship with the "Bible on Sunday" but a "heavy hand" the rest of the time. Roper's fellow mate Djerf, a former Dutch Navy officer discharged for cowardice during World War II, tells him that Murdock is a man who "hires only the unwanted, a man who derives pleasure from the degradation of others." Indeed, at a ship's dinner Murdock tells Roper that Djerf is "yellow," that a fellow mate is a thief, a former captain busted for stealing some of his ship's cargo, and that the ship's engineer is a drug addict who "lives on the needle"—all this with the men sitting there at the table.

Despite his repulsive personality, Murdock is married, and his wife, Kim, is along for the voyage. The only other woman on board is a passenger, Karen Gorman, a curvaceous, copper-haired, green-eyed entertainer who has made the questionable decision to act as Da-chong's "tid-bit" for a time in return for a generous paycheck. Karen says she is only going to dance for Da-chong, but Roper knows better and thinks she does too.

Much of the conflict in the novel comes from Murdock's unsuccessful attempts to dominate Roper, to remind him that he is a mere mate, not the ship's captain he once was. But the reader gradually learns the truth about Roper's downfall: he saved his burning ship after the drunken chief officer panicked and set off the abandon-ship signal. Three people died in the fire, however, and his gun-butt blow to the officer's head might have caused the man's death—but not before he testified against Roper.

Murdock is more successful at dominating the rest of his crew members. Having mentioned, in a skillful bit of foreshadowing, *Wanderer*'s slave pits early on, Clements later shows Murdock visiting them. The crew knows that Murdock's wife and Djerf ran away together and that Murdock sent native trackers after them. Thus, the crew members wonder whether he has imprisoned Kim and her lover in the dark, dank, rat-infested slave pits or is merely pretending to have done so to keep the crew afraid of him—an effective if horrifying technique in either case.

Clements shows us what it is like to command a ship and how exercising command changes a person. He writes that Roper "hated trivial problems or emotional ones. The habit of command had given him a dislike of being maneuvered into a position calling for a retraction or explanation of his words—a snobbish habit, he was ready to admit, but one he could do little with."

The action rises to a crescendo with a fierce storm at sea and then a fierce fight aboard ship. Throughout the novel Clements paints realistic pictures of people, places, and events. For example:

> Through the rain could be seen the dense shoreline of Sumatra, the flanks of a cove reaching out to embrace them. As they continued on, drifting with engines stopped, the light picked up a nook of the cove that had been cleared somewhat of trees. There Roper saw the dark ragged outlines of a wharf running parallel to the shore, and faintly visible was a wide path leading from the wharf into the jungle, a path bordered by stunted mango trees with hanging vines blowing wildly in the rain. Suddenly, as if a signal had been given, wavering torches appeared on the path and shadowy forms began flitting across the clearing to gather on the wharf.

Hell Ship to Kuma would be a better novel if there were some backstory to explain what made Murdock such a tyrant and if the relationship between Roper and Karen had developed more slowly and more realistically. Also, some of the characters, Da-chong in particular, are stereotypes by today's standards. But the novel is a page-turning adventure story with a good balance of character development and driving action. A reader who ships out with *Wanderer* and her captain and crew is in for one hell of an entertaining voyage.

Barge Girl moves more slowly but also reaches a satisfying conclusion. The novel is the story of Joe Baski, captain of the tugboat *Hackett Junior*, which in the 1950s tows barges in the waters around New York City, and Stella Murk, the pretty young wife of Albert Murk, an old, fat barge "captain," or watchman.

Baski's dream is to finish building a 50-foot motor cruiser, a twin to the yacht-turned-patrol boat on which he served as quartermaster during World War II, and then charter her in the Florida Keys and the Bahamas. Baski, the novel's narrator, thinks, "To me, the ultimate goal in anyone's life should be ownership of a cabin cruiser large enough for coastwise travel, large enough so you can move away from the river and bays if you have the urge." Stella's dream, after she gets to know Baski, becomes leaving her unappealing husband and sailing away with him.

But of course complications abound. The chief one is that because Murk agreed to marry Stella when she was pregnant by another man, Stella now thinks, despite having miscarried, that she owes him loyalty if not love. Then, in an interesting reversal of James M. Cain's "murder for money—and lust" plot in *The Postman Always Rings Twice*, Clements has the accident-prone Murk experience two mishaps that could easily be construed as attempts by Baski and Stella to kill him.

The first—Murk's failing in his dangerous trick of jumping from dock to barge—gets Lieutenant Delaney, a "harbor dick," involved in the story. Baski knows Delaney to be a square, straight-shooting cop but also "a stickler for pinning a rap where it was supposed to be pinned." It also brings in an insurance investigator named Coletti, "a dark little man with a razor-thin mustache above razor-thin lips," who appears in "a checked suit, a pale maroon sport shirt, and a porkpie hat." Coletti's "only purpose in this life" is to close his indemnity cases "with the suckers signing for peanuts," and he "never, *never*" pays off on a shaky claim.

As Baski tries to persuade Stella to divorce Murk and sail away with him, Delaney and Coletti try to figure out whether Baski is a murderer. That he has already painted the name "Stella B."—B for Baski—on his boat's stern convinces Coletti that he is. "The next time you work something out like this," Coletti tells him, "don't get ahead of yourself and christen your boat with the name of your intended until she's a widow."

Perhaps realizing that his plot is a bit thin, Clements introduces some titillating elements to hold the reader's interest. For example, after temporarily despairing of being able to persuade Stella to leave Murk, Baski encounters the moneyed "Gold Dust twins," Babs and Toni, who introduce him to marijuana and ménages à trois. When he awakes from their days-long "reefer party," Baski finds himself in bed with Toni and then sees Babs in a chair: "She was snoring. She wore exactly what Toni was wearing, nothing."

Barge Girl is not as exciting as *Hell Ship to Kuma*, but Baski and Stella are likeable characters, and the cat-and-mouse game among them, Delaney, and Coletti makes the novel, especially its second half, a compelling read. One senses that in writing *Barge Girl* Clements was trying to produce something other than the typical love-triangle crime novel.

Clements's shift from novels to scripts was undoubtedly good for the screen. We can only speculate what he might have achieved had he stuck with fiction. But at least we can savor the four novels he did write, and now, with this volume, we have a fine new edition of two of them.

—April 2021
Norfolk, VA

Timothy J. Lockhart is a lawyer and former U.S. Navy officer who worked with the CIA, DIA, and Office of Naval Intelligence. Author of the novels *Smith* (2017), *Pirates* (2019), *A Certain Man's Daughter* (2021), and *Unlucky Money* (scheduled for 2022), all from Stark House Press, he lives in Norfolk, Virginia, with his wife and daughter and sails the waters of Hampton Roads and the Chesapeake Bay.

Hell Ship to Kuma
By Calvin Clements

Chapter One

The woman came out of the bathroom toweling her hair, her sun-browned figure, slightly on the plump side but not unshapely, still dripping with bath water.

"Mix me a drink, Johnny boy. If there's any ice left, make it a long one." She continued ruffling her hair with the towel, her arching bosom quivering in rhythm to the movements of her hands.

The man in shirt sleeves sitting by the open window did not rise to comply with her request for a drink. He watched with annoyance the beads of moisture gliding down her body, to darken the rug at her bare feet.

"This heat," said the woman. "This damned heat. Never a letup." She threw back her head, shaking her hair loose, permitting it to fall in blue-black folds across her naked shoulders. "Really gets you, doesn't it?"

Irritably he stirred in the chair, a big, deep-chested man in his thirties, his hard, square-cut features glistening with sweat. There was a brooding quality in his gray eyes as he looked across at the woman, the grim lines etched about his firm mouth deepening as he watched her combing her fingers through her hair, head back and eyes closed. He was aware that the humidity of the bathroom made drying almost impossible, but still he found himself increasingly annoyed by this unrestrained display of nudity.

However, everything was annoying him these days.

He went back to gazing through the open window, his eyes following the maze of rooftops to the distant fringe of junk masts curving through the city. Farther north, where the Saigon River elbowed into view, he saw the clumsy junks themselves, competing for river space with weary freighters and rust-streaked river steamers. An ancient stern-wheeler getting under way was belching dense smoke. The steamer's churning wake as it moved slowly upstream served as a reminder that everything hadn't stopped dead in its tracks, even if he had.

"How about that drink, Johnny boy?"

She was drying her back by holding the towel firmly behind her and moving her body caressingly against it. She was an attractive woman, dark-eyed, her wide pleasant features rather too full to be classified as pretty. She seemed oblivious of the suggestive motion of her undulating hips as she looked across the room at him, silently questioning his delay in making the drink.

"Why the hell don't you do that in the bathroom?" he said abruptly, his voice low, but hard and strident; it was a voice that would carry with little effort from the bridge of a ship to the lower decks.

The woman stopped her toweling. She looked surprised. "You can't get dry in there. It's too sticky."

"Leave the door open."

"Why can't I stand here? I don't see—"

"Because the bathroom is the place for what you're doing."

She arched her brow quizzically, half-smiling now and not taking his words too seriously. "My, we're really in a mood today, Captain Roper. What brought this on?"

"Nothing brought anything on," he snapped. "Just stop acting like a tramp, that's all!" Instantly he knew it had been the wrong thing to say. Their relationship—no more complicated than the brass four-poster over by the wall—added a significance to the word "tramp" he had not intended.

She was staring at him with lips parted. Quickly she draped the towel in front of her, as if suddenly aware of her nakedness. She reached for her underclothing on the bed. Silently she turned and went into the bathroom, a touch of comedy and pathos in her awkward attempt to use the towel as a shield across her buttocks.

The door closed sharply behind her.

Roper swore softly, not so much as an abstract apology but rather as an indication of his further annoyance. In a few minutes she would come out and either speak overly lightly to show she understood his remark had not been pointed, or say nothing, either way forcing an apology from him. He hated trivial problems or emotional ones. The habit of command had given him a dislike of being maneuvered into a position calling for a retraction or explanation of his words—a snobbish habit, he was ready to admit, but one he could do little with.

Moodily he watched the rickshaws hurrying by in the narrow street below; an old man with baskets of produce hung from poles across his bent shoulders was trying to cross the street ahead of one oncoming vehicle. The rickshaw slowed and veered, not soon enough. It sideswiped the farmer as he tried to hobble out of the way and sent him sprawling. Potatoes and gourds tumbled from the baskets, rolling across the cobblestones and into the filth of the gutter, and a group of young boys appeared as if from nowhere. They grabbed for vegetables on the run, shouting excitedly to one another, grinning back at the old man angrily struggling to his feet.

The inevitable arm-waving and threatening gestures between the farmer and rickshaw driver began, and their singsong screechings drifted up to Roper in the muggy air. He viewed the antics of the two unamused, with a kind of detached pity. Everybody sweating out a rat race to fill empty bellies.

Not everybody, though, he reflected. Just the slobs; like the two below, and the kids who had stolen some of the produce. Like Flo and himself. All sweating it out. And to what purpose?

The question was left unanswered as the bathroom door opened behind him.

"Johnny ..."

"Yes?"

"You're not forgetting your appointment with Vanderkeke?"

He shook his head without turning. "There's time. He's dropping by below for lunch. At noon, he said."

The door closed softly, and he immediately regretted not having spoken some word of apology. She had been expecting it. Why the devil couldn't he unbend, loosen up a bit when a soft word was called for?

He lit a cigarette, his eyes wandering again to the activity on the distant river, to a squat, dirty freighter already heavy in the water but with more barges being warped under swinging booms and dipping cargo nets. Within an hour she'd be leaving, he reflected, slipping her moorings on the flood. Before nightfall there'd be the clean smell of the sea, the feel of open water.

The mere thought brought an ache deep within him. Three years ago he would have disdained a second glance at an overloaded freighter on the move, contemptuous of the dangerous practice for the sake of a few extra dollars. But a brief three years could make a difference in a man's perspective, he had come to learn. Now he'd be willing to overlook more than a submerged Plimsoll mark if he could change places with this freighter's skipper. A damn sight more.

"I had your uniform coat cleaned, Johnny."

She came out of the bathroom wearing a green silk robe, the towel wrapped around her head turban fashion. She smiled uncertainly at him, then moved over to the closet. "I'll get it."

She brought the coat to him, holding it from habit as he slipped his arms into the sleeves. He examined the tarnished gold on the sleeves absently, keeping his tone casual as he said, "If anybody's the tramp around here, it's me, Flo. I suppose you know that."

Instantly her mood lightened. She laughed at him and went up on tiptoe to brush her lips against his chin. "Strictly high-class, Johnny boy. Both of us. High on class, low on luck. Did Vanderkeke say what kind of position he had for you?"

"Just that it was an opening." He slowly buttoned his coat, thinking about it. "There's a rumor he's buying two new packets and looking for skippers well acquainted with the Islands. I thought he hinted one of the berths would be mine. In a way, though, it wouldn't add. Not good business to put a discredited skipper over those native crews. They're underpaid and always restless, quick to sense shaky authority."

"You," she said, frowning at him, "are not discredited. Stop using that horrid word. You still have your license."

He shrugged. "There's nothing so irreparable as being broken from a top berth in the States. Unless you want to settle for half pay on a tramp, your ticket's pretty much ornamental after that."

"Maybe," she said, "you want to borrow this towel."

He smiled in spite of himself. "I guess it does sound like that."

"That's better," she said. "You look positively beautiful when you smile. Have you enough money to take Vanderkeke to lunch?"

"I'll get along. Hsing will take a chit for it."

She shook her head. "Better use cash. You'll want to make an impression." She went over to the dresser by the bed and picked up her purse. "And I want no arguments this time."

He didn't offer any. He stood ill at ease, as usual, as he watched her take out a few bills, a tiny furrow appearing between her eyes as she weighed her personal needs for the day. In the six months they had been living together this same scene had become an all too frequent one, but it had been at her suggestion that he had stopped taking temporary berths and had begun haunting the Dutch shipping offices for permanent employment, a move that quickly left him without funds. Keeping up an appearance, of course, was necessary. She insisted on helping out, and he was always uncomfortable in the knowledge that she worked as a hostess in a cheap cabaret, her salary not easily earned.

"You're a sucker, Flo." He pocketed the fold of bills she handed him.

She understood and smiled. She reached up to adjust his tie. "It's only money, Johnny boy."

"If I wasn't around you could be banking some of it. For that ticket back to the States."

She brushed imaginary lint from his coat. "There's time for that."

"You keeping track of this dough?"

"And adding six per cent." She kissed him lightly and patted his cheek. "Run along now. If Vanderkeke is downstairs now, he'll be wondering what kind of a shipmaster you are to keep an owner waiting."

There was nothing pretentious about the dining room of the Internationale. A circular bar divided the tables, and above the bar a four-bladed fan revolved monotonously, ruffling streamers of fly paper hanging from the low ceiling and stirring beer-scented air. From the side walls a jaundice-colored paint was peeling, partly eradicating verse in both lipstick and pencil. At one table two English sailors were shaking dice for drinks, their eyes following the rolling cubes. At another table a Chinese merchant was wolfing down a large platter of eggs, using chunks of black bread to catch the yellow yolk dripping from the corners of his loose mouth and then shoveling the bread between his lips without ceasing to chew. Nearby, a heavy-set balding man and a buxom woman, apparently tourists, were watching the merchant's performance with fascination.

"Special occasion, Hsing?"

The aged white-coated Chinese who had been carving a roasted turkey smiled amiably as he set the knife down. He carefully wiped his hands on his apron and removed the gold-rimmed glasses, which lent him a scholarly appearance. "This is your own Thanksgiving holiday, Captain. Had you forgotten?"

The days had been all one and the same for some time. Roper ordered bourbon and water.

"But lunch first, no? If you will be seated at a table—"

"I'll have the bourbon now, Hsing."

Hsing's nearsighted eyes frowned his disapproval of drinking before lunch, but he reached beneath the bar for the special brand he reserved for his favorite customers. Two years before, Roper had been one of the few captains volunteering to transport refugees out of Shanghai down the Whangpoo River under Red artillery fire. Hsing, with a deep love for his homeland and his people, had never forgotten this. He always served Roper the best he had, never mentioned the mounting tab for food and drink.

"Why not eat now, Captain?" He poured Roper the drink, filling the tumbler only halfway. "In a short while the tables will be crowded, to say nothing of the condition of this bird."

"Lunching with Vanderkeke," Roper explained. "He'll be dropping by any minute."

Hsing's yellow face wrinkled into a frown and he shook his head.

"He was here earlier," Hsing said. From beneath the bar he brought up a small white envelope and placed it gently near Roper's hand. "You will not like what is in here. It refers you to Kiwong Stevadoring, for the position of checker."

Roper stared incredulously at the envelope. An offer of dock employment, where ships' officers, the boozers and the misfits, were hired by the day and at little better than coolie pay, approached a contemptuous gesture.

"But what about the packets?" Roper asked slowly, still stunned by what was tantamount to a passing handout. "Didn't he mention my working for *him*, for *his* line?"

Hsing passed a cloth over the bar in obvious embarrassment. "I spoke of that, as soon as he mentioned Kiwong. He seemed surprised you expected a packet position. He explained why it could never be, but two words are sufficient: no face."

Roper drew a deep breath, struggling to conceal his anger. It was the truth, but it hurt. No face. Not enough to satisfy the Dutch, that is. On stinking tramps, yes. But he was attempting to move out of his class.

Out of his class! A Dutch packet limping in and out of nearby ports.

He wanted to laugh, but suddenly there was an ache in his throat. Three years of temporary berths, short-hauling among these islands on filthy Portuguese and Chinese boats, had built within him a hard bitter core of frustration. Now it seemed ready to rise and strangle him.

"I had thought," Hsing said, busy at the turkey again, skillfully partitioning the wing, "to tell you after lunch. Bad news is always more digestible after one dines."

"Is Fazio still doing business from the waterfront?"

The Chinese halted his carving. Slowly he set the knife down, his slanted eyes peering soberly over his glasses. "Such employment is not for you, Captain. Tomorrow, perhaps, you will view this rebuff in a different light. Tomorrow—"

"I can do without a sermon," Roper said. "Is Fazio still working out of his old place or isn't he?"

Hsing sighed. He picked up his carving knife. "Does an octopus change its lair when its tentacles reach ten thousand miles?"

Abruptly Roper turned from the bar, at the door scowling aside the sore-eyed beggar holding forth a withered hand. He walked out into the glaring sunlight of the street, ignoring the rickshaw coolie starting toward him. Turning eastward, he moved through the hot smells of the street, his bitterness mounting. Maybe Vanderkeke was right. Maybe he hadn't been marking time these past months, but had actually been descending his own private ladder to a point where he was now being thought of in terms of a handout.

Checker! One bale, two bales ...

He laughed shortly, striding faster, feeling for the first time in three years a buoyancy, as a man might when shedding a burden.

The burden of respectability, perhaps.

Chapter Two

Fazio settled back in the wicker chair and thoughtfully chewed on the yellow cigar. His narrowed black eyes briefly idled over Roper, who stood in front of the paper-littered desk.

"I've got something open," Fazio said, "but I'm wondering if you'll fill the bill." He took the cigar from his thin mouth, turned his head, and spat a sliver of wet tobacco in the direction of a filing cabinet.

"If it's a berth, I can handle it," Roper said. "From the top down."

Alfonso Fazio carefully probed between two yellowed teeth with a dirty fingernail. He was a little man with a dark triangular face. Through the open window behind him came the hustling early-day sounds of the river, the screech of a block, the groans of a laboring winch mingling with the quick snorts of a Diesel tug. From below the window rose the wailing chant of a street vendor.

"You can handle it, Roper. You've got toughness and savvy, and a good background. Big question is, will you play along all the way if I place you? Where will you draw the line and leave me looking foolish for hiring you?"

"Opium. Anything on that level."

Fazio's dark features contracted into a grimace. "The junk racket's a sucker game today." He rolled the cigar between his lips. "Roper, you turned me down flat some time ago when I approached you with an opening. A busted officer in these parts weighing how clean a buck might be hands me a laugh, but it also makes me cautious when he makes a switch. What gives? Because your rear end is damn near coming through those britches you're wearing?"

Roper placed his hands flat on the desk and leaned forward. "I didn't come up here to have my nose rubbed in it," he said. "I'm looking for more than a routine berth at more than a routine salary. You still running a placement bureau on the side, or aren't you? If you aren't, let's cut this short."

Unruffled, the swarthy shipping agent smiled cordially through a haze of cigar smoke. "Point I was trying to make, Roper, will you rear back once a buck is in your pocket? If you're ready to thumb your nose at the world, no reservations, you're my man."

"I'm ready to do a job on a ship. What cargoes she handles is something I don't intend to worry about."

Fazio thought about it a moment. "That's good enough for me." He straightened in his chair, briskly drawing a memo pad toward him. "I worry about two things at this desk. Is the man capable, and will he keep his mouth shut if and when he decides to quit? Tougher combination to get hold of than you might think. A man busted from a skipper's berth, though, I'll always talk to. My fee is six hundred for the introduction."

"Gold?"

"What else?"

"That's a lot of dough."

Fazio paused, glancing up. "Nothing penny-ante in this job, Roper. Six hundred is cheap."

"I'll have to send it to you."

The agent went back to writing the note. "The *Wanderer* puts into Saigon every three or four months. Pay me first time in." He glanced up again, grinding the cigar to one side of his mouth: "She's owned and skippered by Ephraim Murdock. Ever hear of him?"

"Can't recall that I have."

Fazio took the cigar from his mouth, half-smiling at the hot ash. "Guess you never heard of the cobra business he pulled on a haul from Bombay to Shanghai?"

Roper said he hadn't. It was hot in the tiny, dusty office and he was beginning to sweat. He wished Fazio would get on with the letter of introduction.

"As the story goes—and there's quite a few vouching for it—some fifteen or twenty years ago he happened to be transporting animals from India to Shanghai. Before he left Bombay a large box was secured on the fo'c'sle, all hands being warned of the good-sized cobra that was in it. Well, the first night out the box was found with its cover off and no sign of the snake. For two days the hands were put to hunting it, searching the ship from stem to stern. No dice. It was nine days to Shanghai, and everywhere the hands would walk they'd be looking behind them and shying from dark corners. At nights none of them slept more than two winks, making out the slightest sound to be this deadly reptile crawling across the deck on its belly." Fazio chuckled. "It's a good bet, of course, the box had been empty from the start."

Roper could well picture the sleepless nights of the frightened crew. He saw nothing funny in the situation.

Fazio continued his writing. "He's a tough bird to get along with, Roper. You'll have to be on your toes."

"I've worked for characters before."

The agent's brow lifted as he blotted the memo pad. "Might call him that. He's from the old school: Bible on Sunday, heavy hand the rest of the —" A knock on the door interrupted him.

"It's open!" Fazio growled.

The dark slender man who came limping across the room wore neatly pressed sun tans, a black tie, and a ship's officer's cap bearing the marking of a mate. Beneath the cap visor his features were smooth, lean, and high-boned, almost classically handsome. Obviously he was part native, some mixture of Javanese, Roper guessed.

He placed a heavy Manila envelope on Fazio's desk, and then stood waiting and silent, ignoring Roper.

Fazio ripped the envelope open. Without looking up he tilted his head at Roper in an offhand introduction. "Djerf, Captain Roper. Mr. Djerf is a mate aboard the *Wanderer*, Roper."

Djerf turned and shook Roper's extended hand. He did it mechanically, without any show of pleasure or displeasure, his slightly slanted eyes roving briefly over Roper's face. There was a certain military bearing to the man's appearance that did not escape Roper. He found it incongruous with the mental image he had formed of Murdock's officers.

"Is Murdock ready to pick up Da-chong's cargo?" Fazio asked. Carefully he was counting a thick sheaf of British pound notes he had removed from the envelope.

Djerf nodded. In a soft voice, carrying a trace of Dutch, he said, "But he asks assurance that Da-chong will have a full load. The last time there was not quite a thousand tons. Captain Murdock wants your guarantee that there is at least double that amount waiting at Kuma."

Fazio ceased his counting, glancing up peevishly. "How the hell can I guarantee anything like that? If Da-chong says he's ready for a pickup, he's ready. It's got to move off that island when he wants it to move, or he'll get another shipper. Tell Murdock I'm in the middle here on that— and making damn little out of it."

"I think he feels the goods at Kuma must be in greater bulk to continue disposing of it at—" Djerf hesitated, not looking directly at Roper, but quite obviously wondering if he was speaking too freely in a stranger's presence.

Fazio dismissed the mate's caution with a wave of the bank notes in his hand. "You're telling me nothing that I don't already know. But Da-chong wants a pickup and I've got to supply it or lose out there. Tell Murdock the quantity is a matter to take up with the Chink when he reaches the island. I have nothing to do with that. Nothing at all."

"He also inquires on the matter of a mate. We will need the man aboard Wednesday at the latest, preferably tomorrow morning."

Fazio carelessly shoved aside the bank notes and drew the memo pad toward him. "I'm giving Captain Roper an introduction to Murdock." He studied the top sheet a moment, tore it off, and folded it into an envelope.

He handed the envelope to Roper. "Might be wise to spend a few minutes with Djerf before he returns to the *Wanderer*. Some pointers from him might save you from stubbing your toe. Right, Djerf?"

Djerf nodded. His smooth dark features betrayed no surprise that a shipmaster was filling a mate's berth. He turned and limped over to the door.

Roper started to follow.

"By the way, Roper." Fazio was leaning back in the chair, one foot thrown carelessly up on the desk. "I'm always ready to invest a few dollars in any master with a head on his shoulders and fifty per cent of the charter money in his pocket. Good skippers worth backing are not too easy to find, so maybe I'll settle for less than fifty, maybe thirty. Think you might be interested sometime in the future? Say, after you've been with Murdock a while and have a stake?"

"Something to think about."

"Do that. And keep your eye on the mark, Roper. It's good advice to the helmsman, but also applies to a man who has a destination in mind. Don't get sidetracked by any Boy Scout impulses. Incidentally, Murdock has the last word on hiring you. But just tell him you were broken in the States for killing your first mate and you'll have no trouble."

Fazio shrugged his thin shoulders at Roper's hardening expression. "How else can I put it? Frankly, I can't think of any better reference than that for where you're heading."

Roper found the *Wanderer's* mate waiting at the curb below, watching trucks and bullock carts rumble by in a continuous stream. More out of sociability than a desire for a drink, Roper suggested that they go to a bar. Djerf refused.

"From the customs wharf I can point out the *Wanderer*, if you care to walk there."

They crossed the street to the bulkhead line, Roper annoyed with the other's curtness but saying nothing. Moving in the shadows cast by high prows of freighters and the jib booms of sailing vessels extending far over the street, they finally picked their way through ships' stores strewn before the first customs shed. Avoiding darting Hi-lows working on the multicolored drums of chemicals stacked there, they turned out onto the crowded wharf. Here groups of coal-black natives wearing loincloths and smelling of fish and garlic were loading a river steamer. The perspiring natives—apparently Maos from the hills—worked quickly and efficiently, their lean muscular backs glistening as they tiered brown bags of flour into cargo nets.

Halting near the natives, Djerf stepped up on the stringpiece, shading his eyes against the white glare of the sun as he squinted across the river.

"By the east embankment, Mr. Roper. I believe you might call it— Is eyesore the word?"

Roper instantly agreed it was the word. Across the water, blending in with the muddy bank and the battered junks anchored off the channel, he saw a lone freighter squatting low in the water, her sides a solid scab of rust. In the distance she was small and ugly, not a sign of paint from waterline to the smoke-grimed stack. To Roper's eye, she looked Chinese built. Her bridge was oversized and placed too far aft, and on the fantail a small structure resembling a watchman's shanty looked as if it had been thrown up on second thought to balance her lines. The odd rake to her stack, tilting forward, apparently storm-damaged, gave the vessel the grotesque appearance of one that traveled backward.

"She's a mess," Roper agreed. "Fazio spoke of stubbing my toe. Perhaps you can give me a brief run-down on what to expect aboard."

Djerf beckoned to a water taxi cruising along the pier-head line. As the boat turned in sharply he answered Roper's question, speaking slowly, as if carefully choosing his words.

"Aboard the *Wanderer* you can expect to meet a man who hires only the unwanted, a man who derives pleasure from the degradation of others. What more is there to know? When you board the *Wanderer*, Mr. Roper, leave your manhood behind. Then you will not stub your toe." He moved over and descended the wooden ladder on the face of the wharf into the waiting boat. He sat on the stern thwart, not looking back as the boat shot out onto the river and headed for the east bank and the *Wanderer*.

As Roper walked back to the hotel his mind dwelt on Flo. As the *Wanderer* seldom worked this far north, he would not be seeing her too frequently—if ever again. There was much he owed this woman in addition to the small sums she had advanced him from time to time. Her companionship, the stability of mind her presence offered during the past months were intangibles he could not repay. What could he offer as a parting gift?

The answer came to his mind when he spoke to Hsing, informing the Chinaman he would be leaving port on the *Wanderer*. Hsing himself sent a boy out to purchase the steamship ticket to San Francisco, after unhesitatingly agreeing to advance the necessary amount.

It was after midnight when Flo returned to the room. The well-scuffed leather suitcase of Roper's on the bed immediately caught her eye. "Congratulations seem to be in order," she said, standing at the door smiling. "Is it still Captain Roper, or was Vanderkeke silly enough to put somebody over you?"

"It's only a mate's berth," Roper said. He moved over to the table and began mixing a whisky and soda for her. "And it's not on one of Vanderkeke's boats. She's the *Wanderer*. A tramp."

She closed the door, looking uncertain. "I don't think I've heard of her. Does she use Saigon as her home port?"

Roper shook his head. "Most of her work is south."

"Oh." Her expression sobered as she understood the meaning.

Roper avoided her eyes as he stirred a bit of soda into the glass. He did not particularly regret that their relationship was coming to an end. Physical ties are fragile things, and he hoped she would understand that it had been inevitable that they should go separate ways.

He held the drink out to her and she absently took it, removing the low-brimmed felt hat from her head with her other hand and dropping it onto the bed. She looked tired, the shadows beneath her eyes accentuated by the naked light overhead.

"That means you won't be coming back?" she asked.

"Be quite a few months," he said. He stood there awkwardly. He was thinking a parting note would have been easier, and despised himself for the thought.

She went over to the window and stood there looking out into the darkness. "Funny it never occurred to me you might sail away and be gone longer than a few weeks each time."

"Flo—"

"It's all right, Johnny. Really it is."

They undressed in the dark, in silence, and when she crept in beside him he made no attempt to touch her. For a long while they were silent, her warm thigh slightly touching his. He gazed up at the path of starlight reflected along the dark ceiling, and at last he said, "Flo?"

"Yes, Johnny?"

"There's a steamer ticket on the bureau."

"I saw it. Thank you, Johnny."

"You're to outfit yourself and bill Hsing. You're going home in style. That's something you've wanted, isn't it?"

For several moments she was silent. Then she said, "I'm not going home, Johnny. I know I've often spoken of saving for that ticket, but I was just kidding myself, setting a goal to shoot for, you might say. If we can't look forward to something, then there's no point in living, is there?"

"Why stay? There's more for you at home."

"It's easier out here, Johnny. I don't know how to explain it, but it's easier."

"It just seems easier, Flo. Being white, you have the illusion of being somebody here without fighting for it. But it's only an illusion." He wanted to speak of the white prostitutes in the back alleys who also were driven to the Islands in their youth by frustration, but he kept silent.

"Think about it, Flo."

"I will, Johnny. Good night." She turned on her side, facing the wall.

He continued gazing up at the half-light playing across the ceiling. In the morning she would make her choice: Use the ticket or cash it. Once it was cashed, she was lost. She would never go back. It was too easy to continue drifting in the Islands, satisfying physical needs and pretending you were living. After a short time there would be another man in his place and she would believe herself in love again. That too was needed in the pretense of living.

He woke to the dirty light of dawn creeping through the window. Quietly he rose and went into the bathroom. He shaved and washed and put on his uniform. When he was ready to leave he stood by the bed looking down at her. She was still asleep, her face to the wall, the thin blanket drawn up to her shoulders, her dark hair tousled across her cheek. He didn't wake her.

As he walked down the stairs he found himself thankful that a final farewell had been avoided. And then he remembered she was a light sleeper and probably had pretended sleep, knowing their parting would be an awkward one, wanting to spare him.

Hsing was not in the bar and so he walked out into the graying street and turned in the direction of the waterfront. The eastern sky was heavy with lowering storm clouds. They lay ahead of him, cold and motionless, as if brooding over the freighter that waited for him on the river.

Chapter Three

A strong smell of green tea and rancid galley odors greeted Roper as his sampan bumped against the *Wanderer's* gangway. He spun a silver dollar back to the sculling boy and stepped across, shouldering his bag as he mounted wooden steps worn and shiny through long use.

At the top of the gangway he stood a moment, surveying the *Wanderer's* decks.

The freighter had been secured for sea, her booms cradled and her deck gear well lashed. Near the galley door a naked coolie squatted by a slop bucket, warding off green flies with one hand and pawing through the garbage with the other. Farther aft, leaning back against the engine-room hatch, a stocky Negro in oil-stained coveralls was apparently taking a breather from his duties below. He sucked reflectively on a stained cigarette, his black eyes on the bleak skies overhead. He glanced once Roper's way, flicked his cigarette over the side, and disappeared down the hatch. There was no one else on deck.

So what did you expect, Roper thought—a brass band?

He walked toward the bridgehouse, noting the deterioration of the deck plates, the yellow scale and deep pits in the steel. In the combing around number-two hold, a jagged opening, where the rust had completely eaten through, was backed with planking. He paused to study this, speculating on how thin the hull of the *Wanderer* might be. If it were anything like this, the vessel was not long for the open seas.

"Mr. Roper, I take it?"

A round, florid little man with a stubby corncob tucked into the side of his mouth was descending the bridge ladder. He wore jeans, a soiled T shirt, and a slouch cap under which tufts of reddish hair showed. He removed the pipe from his mouth as he reached the deck and held out his hand, his sun-wrinkled eyes smiling.

"I'm Appley. Djerf said we could expect you. That combing will give you an idea why we don't scale this bucket of rust—we're afraid to."

"It would be asking for trouble," Roper agreed. He shook the other's hand, finding it big and surprisingly firm. He spoke of the absence of personnel, and Appley shrugged.

"Few sleeping it off, few still ashore. We don't carry many hands. Five topside and three down below. In port we fill in with beggars like that." He nodded to the coolie still squatting by the slop bucket near the galley door. "Seen the Old Man yet?"

"No. Is he aboard?"

"You'll find him starboard, second door. Take your hat off and say sir." Appley grinned, the lines at the corners of his cheerful eyes deepening. "I'll take that bag and put it in the vacant stateroom on the port side."

Roper nodded his thanks. He headed for the starboard passageway, reflecting that Appley, with his free and easy manner, was an entirely different caliber of man than Djerf; at least, the fact that he was sailing under Murdock didn't seem to worry him as it did Djerf.

In the starboard companionway he knocked on the cabin door. An unintelligible growl answered him.

Roper opened the door and stepped across the kick plate. The cabin was a narrow, low-ceilinged room smelling of stale clothing, poorly illuminated by two gloomy shafts of light slanting from the twin ports. A roll-top desk was in the center of the room and above it swung an unlighted oil lamp, chained to the overhead. In one corner, near the head of a wooden bunk, was an ancient overstuffed chair, some magazines scattered on the floor before it. In another corner stood an enameled washstand badly chipped, the mirror over it grimy and flyspecked. A brass clock, barometer, and chronometer, brightly polished, formed a triangle on the side wall.

All this Roper saw in a glance. Then his attention was riveted to the man sitting behind the desk and glaring across at him, a powerful heavy-boned man wearing a faded blue coat and a visored cap. Beneath the visor was a hard-muscled leathery face, with deepset eyes that were yellow in color and strangely alive.

"Close that goddamn door when you enter this room, mister!" Murdock's order was a snarl, the tight thin line above his jutting jaw barely moving.

Roper obediently swung the door shut. He approached the desk, removing from his pocket his letter of introduction.

"From Fazio?" Murdock continued glaring, his strange yellow eyes flickering darkly, as if behind each pupil burned an oil lamp with a defective wick. His shirt was opened at the throat, revealing black hair lying in damp, greasy ringlets.

Roper nodded in reply to the question and held the envelope out. "John Roper, formerly of the—"

"I didn't ask your name, mister!" Murdock's lips remained thin, as if compressed with anger. "I asked if you were from Fazio."

Roper said he was. He continued holding the envelope out, wondering if Murdock was always this surly. "Ship's officer, mister?"

Roper looked his surprise. "Yes, of course."

"Then you've no doubt had experience in addressing the master of a vessel?" Murdock said, his sarcasm heavy. He settled back, the chair creaking under his weight.

"Sorry, *sir*."

"Let's have the letter, mister!"

Roper handed it over. Ripping open the envelope, Murdock glanced briefly at the contents and tossed it aside.

"Roper, maybe you know I own this vessel. Now that isn't important. But I'm master of it, and that is. You'll remember that: I'm *master*. Don't ever forget it. Instead of salary, we pay quarterly bonuses. You'll get only a half share for the first quarter, full after that." Murdock broke off, his eyes flicking to one side of the room.

Roper glanced in that direction. Beneath the washstand in the corner the sloping head of a gray rat was emerging from a water-pipe opening. It crept into the room, lean and hungry, its tiny bright eyes fastened on an object on the floor several feet from the washstand.

When Roper started to comment Murdock motioned him to silence. "I'll be sole judge of the amount due you," he said, his eyes fixed on the stealthily moving rat. "But the accounting will be fair, the books open to each man's inspection." He paused again, his hand moving beneath his coat.

The rat had warily edged farther into the room, creeping toward what Roper now recognized as a large piece of moldy cheese. What followed next was too quick for his eye to follow.

There was a movement of Murdock's hand. A blur of light streaked from his fingers, flashing across the room. Immediately the rat leaped high in the air, squealing, tumbling onto its back with its feet convulsively clawing the air. Imbedded in its side a thin-bladed knife quivered.

Dumfounded at first at the speed and accuracy with which the knife had been handled, Roper felt only disgust when he saw the glitter of satisfaction in Murdock's eyes. He understood, now, that the cheese had been placed there for the exact purpose of luring the rat within range of Murdock's knife.

Murdock reached for the ship's log. "Remove that thing, Roper. Toss it over the side."

Roper frowned over at the rat, now lying still. "I'll send a hand in with a bucket."

"You'll find I don't repeat my orders." Murdock studied the log, his voice thinning. "I said remove it."

To Roper, the simple act of disposing of a rat was nothing. He had performed dirtier jobs in the past. But he saw this as nothing more than a deliberate and calculated humbling, and his anger rose. Abruptly he turned and walked over to where the rat lay. He removed a handkerchief from his pocket and picked the rat up by the hind legs. With all thoughts of working on the *Wanderer* gone, he wheeled back to the desk, his temper completely taking over.

Murdock's head was still bowed over the log, seemingly engrossed in the pages, when the bloody carcass of the rat was flopped across the desk, the scabbed belly less than a foot from his nose.

"Perhaps you're a little confused on what berth I'm filling!" snapped Roper. "Were you looking for a mate or a flunky?"

Murdock stared at the rat, his taut lips whitening. Then his head slowly lifted, his yellow eyes filling with rage. His voice was a whisper, and a muscle trembled along his leathery jaw.

"Welcome aboard, mister. Appley's somewhere about. He'll see you settled. That's all—for the present."

Roper bit back a reply refusing the berth. He was under no illusion that his brashness would be forgotten, but as long as Murdock knew where he stood, there was no reason why he should not remain aboard and perform the job he was capable of.

He turned and walked out, feeling Murdock's eyes upon him until the door closed between them.

The stateroom on the port wing to which Appley led him contained the minimum of furnishings, a maple bunk, a bureau, and a straight chair. Near the door a porcelain washstand was perched atop green-molded piping, and above the cracked shaving mirror a two-year-old calendar depicted a voluptuous blonde having trouble with her garter. Littering the bare floor were cigarette butts and scraps of paper.

A large cockroach crawled wearily across the top of the bureau. Appley brushed it to the floor and stepped on it.

"It's not much, Roper, but it'll have to do until we reach Kuma. We drop our passenger there. She has the inboard room across from you—a bit larger than this one, with a stall shower, yet. There's also a spring bunk in there that isn't too hard to take."

Roper was frankly surprised that the freighter would carry a passenger, especially a woman.

"We don't ordinarily," Appley admitted, filling his corncob from a leather pouch, "but every once in a while Da-chong—he's the boy who runs the show at Kuma—has Fazio send down a tidbit. This one's really table fare, stacked up to here. Murdock hates like the devil to carry these trollops. Can't stand a so-called woman of sin. Not much he can do about it, though. How did you make out with him, by the way?"

Roper dogged back the ports for ventilation. He decided not to mention the rat episode. "He certainly doesn't want any doubts as to who's boss of this vessel."

"He likes that understood," Appley agreed. "He's the most egotistical son-of-a-bitch that ever walked a bridge deck. Never insult him, or cast any reflection on his character. You'll get to hate the sight of his ugly face, Roper, but don't ever show it. He stores the slightest affront away in his mind and rams it back a hundredfold when you least expect it."

Roper idly inspected a bureau drawer, wondering what Appley would say if he knew Murdock had already been given something to store away. "Just ignoring him, I suppose, is the best bet."

"Respectfully, Roper. Ignore him respectfully." The mate had half opened the door. He closed it and took the pipe from his mouth. "I don't usually hand out this much advice, Roper, but I think you got booted around enough in the *Victorian* deal. Read about it in the China Press," he explained, noting Roper's surprised look. "The write-up interested me because I knew your chief officer a number of years back. Barnes was a lush then, no more business being on a bridge than a gook steward. But while I was following the case I sort of got the notion East-West Transport used you as a handy scapegoat when they held you responsible for his actions after he died. They had to hang the bad publicity somewhere, and you were it. About sums it up, doesn't it?"

"Just about."

"Barnes was nearing time to be pensioned off, I remember."

"Year or so to go."

Appley shook his head. "Pretty tough thing to break a man working on a year. Can't say I blame you for carrying him. But in a way the company was at fault for assigning him to a freighter-passenger like the *Victorian*. If they had used their heads they would have buried him on one of the banana runs."

Roper lit a cigarette to cover his dislike of the subject. "You were speaking of advice?"

Appley took this in stride. "It's about Murdock's wife. Guess you know she rides with us?"

"Didn't even know he was married."

"Hard to believe anyone would have him, I know, but she's in the adjoining room. Largest outside the dining room, so she puts up there. Point is, Roper, Kim keeps pretty much to herself, but when you bump into her, treat her like a queen. She's part Burmese, and Murdock's sensitive about the color line—when it affects him, I mean." He indicated Roper's bag. "I've some stores to check below while you're getting squared away, but I'll be topside in ten minutes or so to show you the bridge layout. One thing more: Plug those pipe openings under the sink unless you want company at night. Those damn rats prowl the staterooms since Murdock started baiting his."

After Appley left, Roper arranged his few belongings in the bureau. He carefully examined the mattress and blankets on the bunk, and was pleased to find them apparently free of vermin. He was in the process of making the bunk when the girl appeared at his door.

"My room reeks," she said. "Can anything be done about it?"

Roper slowly straightened, hard put to conceal his surprise. The tall, slender, well-poised girl standing in the doorway and looking inquiringly at him was nothing like the image he had formed of Da-chong's "tidbit." She was indeed shapely, as Appley had said, but no cheap attempt had been made to accent the soft curve of her hips or the swell of her bosom in the simple white sleeveless dress she wore. Crisply starched, it buttoned up the front, modestly terminating at the neck in a Peter

Pan collar. She wore no jewelry.

In white high heels she stood almost as tall as Roper, a deeply tanned girl, her close-cropped hair a burnished bronze, her eyes sea green. Dark natural brows and a hint of freckles across the bridge of her nose gave her an appealing tomboy look, full wide lips vouching for her complete femininity. She was a wholesome and strikingly attractive woman.

"Now that we've gone through that," she said, leaning back against the jam of the door and folding her tanned aims, "perhaps you can do something about my room."

Roper took a second glance at her eyes then. They were cold and hard, staring back with insolence.

Well, he thought, it had to show up somewhere.

He said, "What seems to be the trouble over there?"

"It stinks," she answered, "like everything else aboard this boat. I've never seen anything so dirty." She surveyed the shabbiness of his room. "Perhaps everyone else is used to living in filth, but I'm not."

Roper bristled at the implication in her words. He felt like pointedly telling her there were different kinds of dirt, and some did not wash off. But he said nothing, striding past her and across the passageway into the other room. Here he detected the clinging odor of insecticide. He went over and opened the ports.

"I tried to do that but I couldn't budge them." She had followed him into the room and stood watching him chain the ports back. "But I wonder if that will do much good. Even the furniture smells of whatever it is."

"It's a chemical spray. Keeps out rats, roaches, and mosquitoes."

He noted the room and furnishings were quite an improvement over his own temporary quarters. A faded Oriental rug covered the floor, faded and well worn, but still a rug. There was also a club chair in surprisingly good condition, and a small secretary over against the wall. The bunk, though no larger than his present one, had the springs that Appley had mentioned, and a night table off its head was graced by a pottery lamp. Through a connecting doorway standing ajar he caught a glimpse of a shower and a fairly modern washstand.

"There was nothing personal in my remarks, you know," she said when he started to leave. "I've simply been angry ever since I came aboard and saw the accommodations." She smiled, her green eyes warming a trifle. "I'm Karen Gorman. You're one of the mates, aren't you?"

Roper nodded shortly, still annoyed despite her apology. "Anything else I can do for you?"

At his brusque tone her eyes lost their warmth. "I'll let you know if there is, thank you."

Without comment he went out on deck, chiding himself for letting a common chippy get under his skin.

A light rain was misting the river. He stood at the rail several minutes and watched a French liner pass less than a hundred yards away, her high bow still under the control of a laboring tug. Inbound, passing abreast almost simultaneously, was a small freighter, her gray hull and white-enameled bridge house spotless. On her buff stack, red, white, and green bands identified her as one of the Sumatra Export vessels, a subsidiary of East-West, Roper's former employer. Just briefly, as he watched the gray-hulled vessel disappear up the river, he reflected on the pride he once had of being part of the cleanest and trimmest fleet in Pacific waters, of commanding the seventeen-thousand-ton *Victorian*, its largest and most profitable vessel. But now there was no particular feeling of bitterness with these thoughts. Three years could be a long time.

At the galley he was watching an elderly Chinese split the carcass of a pig dangling from a hook when the sound of voices drew him to the rail again. A sampan had come alongside and was discharging five passengers, three Chinese and two Negroes. The Chinese were naked from the waist up, slightly built men with shaven heads and flat stoic faces. There were raw scars at the sides of the head of one of them, where his ears should have been. The Negroes were dressed in whites, both men tall and lean. They preceded the coolies up the gangway, an arrogance in their bearing, as if they held some rank aboard.

Appley appeared at the rail beside Roper. "These black boys are the second and third assistant engineers."

"Any white men in the crew, besides officers?"

"One. A limey. He's the bosun." Appley spat over the side in disgust. "Keep your mouth shut around him. He's Murdock's third ear, backing into a mate's berth, he hopes. He takes the wheel on Murdock's watches and gives him the lowdown on the day's doings." Appley poked his pipe aft. "By God, it's a fancy piece of baggage that Chinaman is getting."

Karen Gorman was strolling toward the fantail, the lithe movement of her hips visible beneath the belted green slicker she was wearing. When she stopped and turned to watch a bumboat sculling by, the river breeze tousled her copper hair, blowing it in attractive disarray across her smooth cheek.

"She doesn't look it, does she?" Roper said.

Appley caught his meaning. "Well, in a way she isn't. None of them are the common flophouse variety. Fazio gets them through a theatrical booking agency. When he spots a good dish performing in one of the clubs, he simply checks if she's available at two thousand a month for three or four months. He doesn't spell it out, but he doesn't have to at that pay. They're all ready to show a lively stern, never fear."

On the bridge Roper once again met Djerf. He was busy in the chartroom, marking in the weekly corrections of buoy changes. He greeted Roper with his usual reserved manner, and their conversation was limited mostly to the weather, Appley taking no part at all. After acquainting himself with the bridge controls, Roper again followed Appley below to the well deck, while the mate explained that there was no animosity between himself and Djerf, that Djerf was simply a man who lived within a world of his own, rejecting every friendly advance.

"Of course, he's had his troubles," Appley commented. "But haven't we all? Incidentally, there's dinner in the cabin tonight. You attend dinners whether you want to or not. Generally they take place once a month. See you then. Seven-thirty."

Roper was tidying his room with a helping hand from a coolie when a short chunky man swaggered in without knocking. An oily-skinned individual with quick eyes and a fixed smile revealing stumps of blackened teeth, he introduced himself as Brown, the bosun.

"Pleasure to 'ave you aboard, Mr. Roper," he said, nodding approval. "Always 'appy to see another white man. Never tell when the Old Man'll fill in with another Chink, or a 'alf-breed like that chicken-livered Djerf." He scowled over at the coolie gathering his bucket, mop, and insecticides together. "'Ere, you! Get a move on an' give Cookie a 'and with 'is pans!"

Hastening to comply, the Chinese stumbled over the bucket, upsetting it and spilling its entire contents on the floor. With a curse Brown leaped over and delivered a savage kick at the man's haunches as he bent to right the bucket. The coolie sprawled in the slop, yelping with pain.

Roper's actions were prompt and instinctive. He moved over, grasped the bosun by the back of his slippery neck, and hustled him over to the door. He flung him out into the passageway with enough force to send him crashing into the opposite bulkhead.

More dazed by the sudden action than hurt, Brown turned, his jaw gaping. "'Ere, Mr. Roper—"

"In the future," Roper said, his tone normal, "you knock on the door before you walk in. Better yet, wait until you're told to come in. And I'm advising you not to kick a man again who's working under my direct orders. Is that understood?"

Brown blinked uncertainly a moment before he managed a weak ingratiating smile. "Sure, Mr. Roper. I ain't taking no authority away from a mate. Jus' these bloody buggers got to be kept in their places. You know 'ow it is, sir—" The closing door cut him off.

Six bells aroused Roper from a half sleep: seven o'clock by his watch. It was twilight when he finished dressing and went out on deck. The rain had stopped, but the darkening sky was still swollen with storm clouds. Traffic on the river had thinned to an occasional sampan taxiing passengers to the ships at anchor, and a large seagoing junk passing by, its patched sails raised to catch the night breeze. On the junk's stern four coolies were bent over a sculling oar, working it to and fro in unison, their plaintive chants drifting across the water. Far off, in the southern section of the city, a soft crimson glow reflected against the low-hanging sky told of cabarets opening for business. As Roper watched the lights deepening into a blood-red glare, he thought of Flo, and he hoped she was not there, but on a liner already at sea.

He was lighting a cigarette when a thin, sandy-haired man wearing black-rimmed glasses came hurrying up the deck, his coat half on. He looked worried, then relieved when he saw Roper standing at the rail.

"Oh, I thought I was late. You're Mr. Roper, aren't you? I'm Fisher, the engineer." Nervously he shook Roper's hand, the thick lenses of his glasses giving him a harassed expression. "Have you the time, Mr. Roper?"

"Just seven-thirty now. Do we go in or wait for an invite?"

"No invite, Mr. Roper. It's understood. Well understood." He headed for the starboard wing, fumbling with his tie.

Roper started to follow when he noticed the girl passenger standing farther aft, half concealed in the shadow of a ventilator. She was leaning back against it, her arms folded, watching the lights across the river. In the darkness he saw the soft contour of her face, the curve of her throat. He couldn't see her eyes.

They'd be ice, he thought; chips of green ice.

He flipped his cigarette over the side and followed Fisher down the companionway.

Chapter Four

"And how do you find your quarters, Mr. Roper? To your liking?"

Roper shrugged noncommittally. He was sitting beside Fisher, facing Appley and Djerf. At the head of the table Murdock drew spoonfuls of soup noisily between his lips, nothing in his attitude toward Roper indicating that he intended to remember the rat incident.

Two candles mounted in silver holders lighted the hard oak dining table, the light softly gleaming on heavy silverware. Pretension ended here, abruptly. Except for two battered servers against the bulkheads and a nondescript green carpet of indeterminable age covering the floor, there were no furnishings beyond the dining table and chairs. Above each server hung a charcoal sketch of a sailing vessel, but these only helped to accent the yellowing enamel of the bulkhead walls.

It was a dismal, cheerless dining room, but not surprising to Roper after the slovenly cabin office. His only surprise on entering the room was Murdock's wife.

She seemed hardly more than a child, a delicately built girl with a small oval face framed by jet-black hair drawn back to the nape of her neck. Her slanted eyes were dark, as inscrutable as Djerf's as she quietly sat at the other end of the table from Murdock, seldom looking up from the plate before her. She wore a white cotton dress, sleeveless, a rose pinned between the soft outlines of small breasts.

Throughout the meal—eaten in silence by each man—Roper's eyes often strayed to the girl, and he wondered whatever had persuaded her to become Murdock's wife. That she'd had good breeding was evident by her delicate handling of knife and fork. Once Roper broke the silence at the table by asking her whether the seasonal rough weather in these waters disturbed her.

"Kim was raised in a fishing village, Roper."

Murdock answered for his wife without raising his eyes from his plate or removing from his mouth the pork-chop bone he was sucking clean. He dropped the bone onto his plate, not bothering to wipe the grease from his lips as he seized another chop from the nearby platter. "Spent half her life on small boats rolling a damn sight more than a freighter. Eat while things are hot. Do your talking later."

Kim smiled gently at Roper, as if understanding his question had been one of politeness. "Once in a great while I am bothered," she answered, her accent barely noticeable.

Roper remained silent for the rest of the meal, taking the hint from Appley, who had looked up to shake his head. It was plain Murdock disliked talking while eating—possibly because his mouth was so continuously stuffed with food that he was unable to engage in speech himself. Boiled potatoes were shoved whole into his mouth, his heavy jaw working only a brief moment before he ripped the meat from a fresh chop and sucked clean the bone. He ate with his mouth half opened, breathing heavily, his elbows propped on the table. Several times he paused in his chewing to belch, then continued eating as gustily as ever, his eyes always on his food.

Murdock was not wearing his cap, and it had been something of a shock to Roper to see the ugly cleft running diagonally across the bald crown of his head. There was not only an actual depression of the skullcap, but also a dark ragged scar, the kind that would forever appear to have never quite healed. With head bared, he was a most thoroughly repulsive-looking man.

When the aged cook cleared away the dishes and served the coffee, Murdock took out a cigar and cleared his throat. As if this were a signal, his wife rose, smiled graciously at the men, and left the room.

"You've met all hands, Mr. Roper...." Murdock lit the cigar, shook the match out, and looked at Roper through a haze of smoke. He settled back, loosening his belt a notch. "You know their names, but that's not enough. You should know more about the man you work with, his shortcomings."

Roper noticed the restlessness of the other officers at Murdock's words. Appley's eyes dropped to his coffee. He made a pretense of stirring it. Fisher looked nervously toward the door as if he wished to be elsewhere. Djerf seemed to cringe inwardly as he gazed down at his cup.

Murdock drew on his cigar, his yellow eyes moving about the table as if to view each man's reactions. He leaned forward, tilting his ash off on a saucer. "Take, for an example, Mr. Djerf. An efficient man, Mr. Djerf. Knows his job well. But efficient does not always mean dependable. In a tight spot you may find yourself jumping in and taking over for our efficient Mr. Djerf."

Roper was completely at sea as to Murdock's meaning, but Djerf's narrow features were growing pale. He was shrinking visibly in his chair.

"Mr. Djerf is yellow," Murdock said, his eyes steadily on his mate. "He has a wide yellow streak running clear down to his behind. Until the war broke out he was what you might call a promising young officer in the Dutch navy. Where was it they found you hiding, Djerf, when your ship was under fire?"

There was total silence in the room. Djerf's hands were beneath the table, but it was evident to everyone they were clenched together. His face was rigid, his skin bone yellow.

Murdock's tone was distinctly mocking, his heavy features bland. "Come, Mr. Djerf. Where was it you were found hiding when they took a count?"

Appley continued to study his coffee, idly turning the cup in the saucer. Fisher was also finding items to study on the table. Roper could only look at Murdock in disgust.

Djerf's voice was barely audible. "In the refrigerator," he whispered. He took a deep breath and lifted his eyes miserably to Roper, who immediately looked away.

"In the refrigerator," Murdock repeated, with a chuckle. "I can just see it. Hightailing it into the refrigerator. I still don't understand why they didn't hang you instead of giving you the boot."

His amused eyes turned to Appley. "You'll find Mr. Appley a different type, Roper. His trouble comes from love of money, anybody's money. As captain of a Venezuelan tanker he discovered it profitable to put into a Mexican port and sell two or three per cent of the gasoline he carried. How many trips, Appley, before they found you were making more profit than they were?"

Appley grinned cheerfully. "Just ten. A nice racket, but they caught on too fast. Another year of it and I'd have retired."

Murdock sucked on his cigar. "A coward and a thief. A coward is not to be trusted with responsibility or a thief with money. That brings us to Mr. Fisher."

Fisher had removed his glasses and was wiping them with a napkin, his eyes watering as he gazed nervously about the table. "Captain, this is ... I mean, is this necessary? Surely we can, er, dispense with ..."

"Mr. Fisher's weakness is a common one out here," Murdock continued, as if Fisher had not even spoken. "He uses the needle. Or let's say he lives on the needle. You'll find him dependable and conscientious. He has to be. Where else would he find a job paying enough to keep him supplied with the stuff? Someday he'll throw himself into the sea, but until that time he will earn his pay by running the most economical engine room in the East. Three Madagascar blacks taking care of the watches; ever hear of that before, Roper?"

Roper replied he hadn't. He wished he could rise and excuse himself, but he knew that the others were waiting for their cue from Murdock.

"A hophead," Murdock said. He smiled at Fisher, who was cleaning his glasses with great concentration. "A hophead, a coward, and a thief. All cut adrift in the States. Derelicts snagged by the *Wanderer*. Just as you were, Mr. Roper."

Prepared for questioning to bring out the details of his smashed career, Roper received only a brief, thin smile as Murdock crushed out his cigar. "So much for that," he went on. "Our passenger will take her meals in her room. The more she stays in there, the better I'll like it. I don't have to tell you to keep your mouths shut around her. We buy cargo, we sell it; and that's sufficient information when she sees us loading and unloading." He pushed back his chair and rose. "We haul out of here at three-thirty. That deckload off Cape Jacques I want aboard before dawn. Mr. Roper will pull the twelve-to-fours, relieving me. That's all." He strode from the room, his exit reminding Roper of a presiding magistrate taking leave of a humble and silent court.

Later, on the wing of the bridge, Appley joined Roper in a good-night smoke and answered a few questions on Roper's mind. The freighter's main business, he explained, was done at Kuma. Partly surrounded by reef ledges, the island was given a wide berth by shipping, and this suited Da-chong fine.

"He's the sole owner, runs the place like a feudal overlord. Nobody seems to know why it belongs to him and I guess neither the Dutch nor the English thought a jungle island in that section of the Indian Ocean was worth enough to argue about. Some twenty years ago Da-chong brought in a boatload of his countrymen and now he runs just about the biggest piracy and pilferage depot in the Southeast. Incidentally, you owe your berth to that Chink. He sent word a few weeks ago to show up with a larger crew if we wanted to be counted in on a big deal being cooked up. To show some compliance, Murdock settled for a third bridge officer."

"He's certainly playing it close, running so short-handed. You must find it tough going in heavy weather."

"We do. But we're streamlined for profit. Murdock's words, not mine. How did you like that little summary at the table tonight?"

"Pretty dirty," Roper said, lighting a cigarette and watching coolies setting up cots on the fantail. "How come I was neglected?"

Appley snorted. "He's too smart to dig into that. The *Victorian* case got quite a spread in the shipping news, so you can bet he knows all about it. But it's his way not to bring up any part of a man's past if it shows him up in a good light. You were busted and that's all he wants to think about."

Appley removed the pipe from his mouth, grimacing as if it had turned sour. "He gets his kicks out of misery. If he stayed awake nights figuring ways to make people hate him he couldn't do a better job. Once he held up Fisher's pay. Damn near drove him out of his mind wondering if he was going to be able to stock up before pulling out of port ..." He paused, glancing down at the forepeak.

Roper also looked down, and saw the dark form of Murdock pacing the forecastle, the tip of his cigar glowing red in the darkness. Occasionally he halted to turn and face the port passageway.

"The picture of the impatient bridegroom," Appley whispered with a chuckle. "Been married over a year, but Kim is a girl afflicted with some woman trouble. At least, that's her story to him. Can't say I blame her."

Murdock had moved out of their vision. Very faintly they heard his knock on a door below. After a moment's silence there was a murmur of voices. The murmur ceased. The door closed and Murdock reappeared, puffing on his cigar. He finally threw the cigar into the river and walked off in the direction of his cabin.

Appley chuckled again. "Kim has just told him she's not feeling too well again. Someday he'll break down the door to see for himself."

"Why did she marry him? Money?"

"She and her family were refugees, just a skip and a jump ahead of the Red ax when Murdock threw the folks some dough to take off. Leaving their daughter behind, of course." He knocked his pipe into the palm of his hand. "I think you'll get along fine with us, Roper. Thicken that skin a bit and you'll get along fine. I manage by playing the clown, letting nothing bother me. At least, I try not to let it show. I'll say good night now. Drop into my room if anything ever troubles you."

Roper woke to the sound of two bells being struck off. Instinctively he knew it was not this that had awakened him. He lay still for a moment, hearing the soft sucking of the ebb against the side, the hum of a generator somewhere in the bowels of the ship. Two spears of moonlight slanted from the ports over his bunk. Turning his head, he saw bathed in the light a long black rat.

The rat was motionless, boldly watching him.

Roper swore. He was reaching for a shoe when a murmur of voices came to him through the bulkhead separating Kim's room from his. He recognized her voice and was aware it was this that had awakened him. Then another voice, that of a man, low and indistinct, came through the wall. It did not sound like Murdock's voice.

This fact made Roper pause, the shoe in his hand. But the man's voice remained low, fading after a few minutes into silence.

Roper turned his attention to the rat, still crouching on the floor. It retreated a step with his movement. Either Djerf or Appley, he thought, taking aim with the shoe. And under Murdock's very nose.

Or had Murdock gone ashore for a few hours? It was inconceivable that anyone would chance being discovered in his wife's room.

The shoe caught the rat in the side, knocking it over. It bounded up and scurried across the room to disappear into the shadows beneath the washstand.

Roper reached for his trousers at the head of the bunk and started to remove the cigarettes from the pocket when he heard a faint murmur from Kim's room again. His curiosity greater than his feeling of guilt at playing the eavesdropper, he leaned over and pressed his ear to the bulkhead. The soft sobs of the girl came to him. Then the man spoke again, muttering what seemed to be incoherent words of love.

It was Djerf.

Roper settled back on the bunk, smoking thoughtfully, wondering if the two in the next room were aware that this room was now occupied. If they were, they certainly had great faith in his ability to mind his own business. And for a coward, Djerf was taking quite a chance. As attractive as Kim was, it seemed hardly possible that a transient affair, something to be quickly forgotten, would make him dare Murdock's wrath.

Roper got up and started dressing as the ship's bell began striking again. Across the room two specks of amber peered from beneath the washstand. He hurled his other shoe and the specks disappeared.

A few minutes later he was sharing a pot of coffee with Appley in the galley. Thinking again of Djerf's boldness in entering Kim's room, he asked if by any chance Murdock had left the ship.

"Some last-minute business ashore," Appley said. He blew into his coffee. "What do you think of the setup on our tub of rust now, Roper?"

"Everything considered, a bit on the weird side." He added, "Quite a strong undercurrent aboard."

He watched Appley's expression for signs of any knowledge of the affair between Djerf and Murdock's wife, but the mate simply nodded, interpreting the remark another way. "It does seem everybody is pulling against everybody else. As for the weird side of things, you ain't seen nothin' yet, as the man says. I have yet to see twenty-four hours being logged without something popping up.... What made you ask if Murdock left the ship?"

"Just curious."

Chapter Five

The *Wanderer* slipped her moorings three hours before dawn. With the first faint streaks of gray appearing on the eastern horizon, she lay off Cape Jacques with four seagoing junks being warped alongside.

They were huge vessels, swarming with coolies, their decks stacked high with crated goods. The one being tied to the forecastle carried a white man, a small plump Frenchman who stood on the foredeck apart from the Chinese. Frequently he lifted a handkerchief to the waxed mustache beneath his nostrils. The act was not solely a disdaining gesture, for from the junks rose the sour odor of unwashed bodies and, more pungent, that of garlic and urine, even drifting up to Roper, high in the bridge wing of the *Wanderer*.

He had the watch, so he remained there while Appley and Djerf directed the loading. Djerf had mounted a large crate that had come aboard and was quietly directing the movement of the cargo slings.

Appley was hopping about on the first junk, freely kicking the crew into hustling the crates into position for the slings. Occasionally Murdock would come from his cabin, growling a directive for more speed.

When the sun lifted above the horizon in a blazing sphere, dappling the sea with gold and crimson, Murdock came out to remain on deck. He finally joined Roper on the bridge, with one junk yet to be unloaded.

"Keep a sharp lookout," he growled. "Anything from the north that looks like a gunboat, sing out!"

Roper moved out on the wing with a pair of binoculars, as he had been doing repeatedly. He scanned the northern area again. With the exception of a group of fishing trawlers working their way around the cape, there was nothing. He reported so to Murdock, who stood near the ladder, watching the activity on the well deck below.

Murdock grunted acknowledgment. He wore his peaked cap pulled low over his heavy brow. He hadn't shaved, and the stubble was thick on his jaw.

He turned suddenly, glaring. "I don't like people staring at me, mister!" He pointed down at three cases being swung in over the side. "Go down and make a check on their contents. You'll find a chop mark on each case. Get the corresponding bills from Appley."

Roper had been guessing as to what type of cargo had to be delivered in such a furtive manner, and he found his guesses to be correct. Appley passed him three sheets from the clip board, and while Brown and a coolie broke open the cases, he checked off the goods inside. It was obviously all pilferage. Each case contained dozens of individual items that would hardly be handled by any one manufacturer. In the first case the items ranged from cartons of American cigarettes to boxes of nylon hosiery. The other cases held the same diversification of goods: bottles of champagne, blankets, a pair of Winchester rifles, surgical instruments, cheap pocket watches of a German make, a half-dozen portable radios, ballet slippers.

Murdock growled his disgust when he viewed the ballet slippers. Roper reported several items that were on the invoices but not in the crates, and Murdock strode over to the side, angrily gesturing to the Frenchman in the junk.

"Come aboard!" he shouted down. "Make a proper accounting or take this stuff and shove it!"

For over an hour Murdock argued with the Frenchman in an attempt to revalue the two hundred cases of goods being secured on the *Wanderer's* decks. Other cases selected at random were opened and checked against their invoices. Some were as stated, others were short 5 to 10 per cent of their declared contents. Murdock demanded a 10-per-cent rebate.

In the midst of the haggling, Karen Gorman came strolling out from her room, wearing white shorts and a halter. A rainbow-colored shawl was pinned about her shoulders, covering most of the halter, but the sight of smooth brown legs, shapely hips, and a head of auburn hair capturing the sunlight brought all business to an immediate halt.

Seemingly unaware of the attention she was commanding, she started picking her way aft between the cases on deck, apparently with thoughts of sunning herself on the stern. The Frenchman was the first to recover. He moved forward, smiling, fingering his mustache. Murdock's rasping voice stopped him. "Miss Gorman, go to your room! When we are under way you may have the freedom of the decks."

She halted, glancing back at him, puzzled. "I'm sure I won't be in your way, Captain."

The Frenchman performed a little bow, his dark eyes traveling down her long legs. "As if mademoiselle could be in anyone's way."

Murdock shouldered him aside. "Miss Gorman," he growled, "you will go to your room until loading is completed!"

She drew herself up at his brusque tone. "Do you realize I have been cooped up in that stuffy room the entire night? After all, Captain, I *am* a paying passenger, and as long as I don't interfere with your work, I can't see why—"

"Mr. Roper, escort Miss Gorman to her room!" Murdock's head edged forward, his flinty eyes on the girl. "And advise her a lock can be snapped on her door to keep her there if necessary!"

Roper was descending the bridge ladder, but before he reached the deck the girl had turned on her heels and marched back to the passageway. He followed, walking into her room behind her.

She swung around, facing him, her green eyes frosty.

"It is quite unnecessary—"

"Miss Gorman," he interrupted, "where the devil do you think you are? On a Cook's tour? There's no promenade or sun deck on this vessel, no swimming pool. There is absolutely no place where a woman with three ounces of sense would loll half naked under the eyes of a dozen men."

"That doesn't seem to be your captain's objection," she snapped, placing her hands on her hips. "I would like to know what harm it would have done to go back where no one was working."

There would have been no harm, he knew, except that Murdock wanted no outsider listening to the bargaining. It would not take long for even someone unacquainted with ship loading to realize that the transaction was not legitimate.

"I felt like a damn fool being ordered to my room," she continued. "And I don't think taking a walk was unreasonable on my part. All right, maybe my costume wasn't the right choice with so many men outside. But frankly, after the sleepless night I had, all I cared about was fresh air. You, I noticed, had your door open to keep from suffocating. Well, I think you'll agree an open door is out of the question in my case."

Roper candidly eyed her trim figure, silently agreeing. He also saw the awkwardness of her position aboard. "Lying to in a tropic river is always uncomfortable," he said. "But I'll arrange it so you'll have little trouble the rest of the trip. We'll put air scoops in here, give you some ventilation when the boat is moving. However, Miss Gorman, I'd advise you to obey the Captain when he orders you off deck. If a lock were snapped on your door you'd be permitted out only an hour or two daily."

"He wouldn't dare!" Her voice faltered. "My Lord, you'd think I were a prisoner aboard instead of a passenger."

Roper shrugged. "Don't press him too far. I'll have those scoops sent in right away." He had the door opened when he turned, looking back. "By the way—"

She had removed the shawl from her shoulders and was reaching for cigarettes on the bureau. Although the restraining halter was by no means skimpy, it failed to conceal the swell of her mature bosom.

She tapped a cigarette on the back of her hand, looking at him, her dark brow lifting. "Yes?"

"I was going to say, if you do leave your door open, I'm sure you'll be all right. I'm right across from you, and I'm a light sleeper."

She continued looking at him, slowly tapping the cigarette on the back of her hand.

"Thank you, Mr. Roper. I'll keep it closed."

He went out, shrugging off her answer, but carrying a subtle and pleasing scent with him.

On deck he ordered a man to break out the air scoops he had promised. He saw the Frenchman surlily accepting a roll of bills from Murdock, bitterly complaining of a small margin for profit. Murdock told him he could sell elsewhere next time.

As the lines were being cast off, Appley came up to relieve Roper on the bridge.

"Frenchie's pretty sore, but this stuff was lying ashore a good month and it's a sure bet the gang watching it was no more honest than those who originally stole it." Appley chuckled. "Pilferers pilfering the pilferage, you might call it. We're in quite a game."

"Where are we taking it?"

"Southwest coast of Sumatra. It's on our way to Kuma, so the profit from this deckload is clear velvet." Murdock's harsh voice from the lower deck, dripping with sarcasm, cut him off. "Mr. Appley, would it inconvenience you to get this vessel under way?"

Unruffled, Appley winked at Roper and moved over to the engine-room telegraph. "He's really in a good mood over that ten-per-cent rebate. The Frenchie will be cursing him in Saigon, and there's nothing Murdock likes better than having his name kicked around. Better go down and give Djerf a hand securing those cases, Roper, before Murdock tells you to. Djerf's not too handy with deck work. None of these Navy boys are."

At noon Murdock called all officers to the bridge for a monthly briefing of the *Wanderer's* accounts. Roper learned this was routine every thirty days, to inform the men who received shares exactly how the *Wanderer* stood in the matter of profits. That Murdock was strictly fair in his accounting, 40 per cent of the net being divided among them, was not too surprising, according to Appley's way of thinking. Who, he asked, would put up with Murdock unless he were well repaid?

In the wheelhouse Murdock had scarcely opened the account ledger and begun reading the transactions when Roper's eyes, from force of habit, swept the sea ahead. At first glance it appeared normal, the sea smooth, a deep blue carpet fading gradually as it merged with the distant haze of the horizon. Then his gaze picked up a faint patch of gray in the waters a scant hundred yards ahead of the vessel. Its shape was oblong, darker near its center, as if here it lay closer to the surface. It did not move, as a whale would for an oncoming vessel; nor did it change color, a trick of the sunlight on a school of minute marine life. Motionless and ominous, it lay dead ahead.

"Submerged junk!" Roper roared, leaping to the engine-room telegraph and yanking the handle back to full astern. *"Dead ahead!"*

Murdock spun around. He quickly recognized what lay ahead, the grave danger that an overturned and water-logged junk lying just beneath the surface offered. To all purposes it was a fifty-ton battering ram awaiting them. "Full right!" he shouted to Brown, who was at the wheel. "Spin it, damn you! Spin it!"

Even as the bosun started to turn the wheel, and the freighter began trembling under the emergency stern action of her screw, Roper saw the uselessness of the move. They weren't going to stop in time, nor could they entirely avoid being struck. Turning the freighter would simply present her port side in an invitation to be opened like a rusty tin can. Even the glancing blow would rip those deteriorating plates apart, tearing through the hull with ridiculous ease.

Murdock also saw this. So did Appley and Djerf. Murdock's features were drained of color. Appley was watching the junk apathetically, resigned to the aged vessel's certain doom. Djerf's face was gaunt with fear, his hands gripping a window sill to brace himself for the shock.

All this was registered in Roper's mind in the split second between Murdock's order for the right wheel and Brown's compliance. In another split second he saw the junk bearing down closer now, presenting its sled stern to the freighter, the lightening grayish color indicating an increasing depth of water. He reached out and prevented Brown from turning the wheel further.

"Swing it midships!" he ordered tersely.

"'Ere, Mr. Roper! The Captain—"

With a sweep of his arm Roper hurled the bosun aside. He spun the wheel back to amidships, then a little to port, bringing the vessel back on its original course, aiming straight for the junk. Although their speed was being cut in half by the wildly shaking screw, the submerged junk was now less than fifty feet away. They would hit at better than three knots.

Murdock had started toward the wheel when Roper had flung Brown aside, but he stopped short just as suddenly when he saw what Roper was basing his actions on.

They loomed over the capsized junk, its long ramplike stern becoming plainly visible in the water. They struck, hard enough to throw all men off balance, but with no rending or plate-splitting crash. The *Wanderer* skidded up the slime-crusted ramp on the knife edge of her own keel, rising several feet before her weight shoved the junk down. She heeled slightly as she slipped off. Slowly she drifted to a halt.

Roper leaned weakly against the wheel, watching the huge junk now bobbing harmlessly by. From the moment it had been first sighted until they struck, only seconds had elapsed, but in that brief time the fate of the vessel had been weighed. His own sharp eye, and an element of luck, had saved the *Wanderer's* presence in these seas from being marked only by an oil slick floating on the water.

Murdock was the first to break the silence. In a crisp voice he ordered Appley and Djerf to check for damage, although it was apparent the freighter suffered nothing more than a good shaking up. Brown was ordered below to send up his relief.

When they were alone, Murdock wheeled on Roper scowling. "Since when, mister, do you cancel out an order in the Captain's presence?"

Taken aback by the question, Roper stared at Murdock. "There was hardly time—"

"It was six of one to half a dozen of the other whether we took it on the bow or let it bounce off our side, but in the future, Roper, you let me do the maneuvering when I'm up here! Got that?"

Roper quietly turned back to the wheel. He knew full well that Murdock understood the junk would not have "bounced," and that for a few seconds he had given his ship up for lost.

Murdock tilted back his cap, the sweat still in evidence on his brow. He left the window he had been standing by and began pacing the wheelhouse, walking behind Roper, out of his line of vision.

"Maybe that's been your trouble, mister. Take too much on yourself. Like beating your mate to death at the boatfalls."

Roper swung around. "I didn't beat him to death!" he barked angrily. "The man was an alcoholic! He died from drink." He broke off when he saw the amusement in Murdock's yellow eyes, understanding that he was being deliberately goaded.

Murdock reached over to the engine-room telegraph, pushing it to full ahead. "Course is two-forty-one. Keep your eye on the mark, mister."

Roper turned back to the wheel again, controlling his anger. The order to keep his eye on the mark reminded him to look farther ahead than the wheel he was standing behind, to keep his own future in view.

"You've got a lot to learn," Murdock continued, once again pacing the wheelhouse and keeping behind Roper. "And you'll get to know your place aboard or you'll be walking the beach again. You're only a mate. Get that in your head, Roper. You're no longer in an elegant cabin with no more on your mind than which passenger you'll be asking to your dinner table. You're only a mate—with a lot to learn. Any man that'd burn three passengers to death with the seas smoothing has plenty to learn. Wouldn't you say?"

Roper drew a deep breath, tightening his grip on the wheel. Hold it, he thought. If the others can take it, so can you. He kept his eyes rigidly on the binnacle mark.

Murdock halted directly behind him, standing there a moment. "I think it might be an idea to stay on the wheel during the rest of this watch. Give you a chance to think over your position aboard." He waited several moments for Roper's reaction. When none was forthcoming, he walked off the bridge.

Roper loosened his sweating grip on the wheel. The fact that for the first time in ten years he was performing a seaman's duties bothered him less than the old wound reopened by Murdock, the reference to his actions when he was in command of the *Victorian*. He had schooled himself to block the humiliating details from his mind, but now, with his attention divided between the broad reaches of the sea ahead and the compass bearing, his thoughts drifted back to that wild night off the stormy California coast, the leaping tongues of fire that had spread through the engine room and the mad senseless scramble for the lifeboats when the drunken Barnes set off the abandon-ship signal.

Roper had never blamed the passengers for their testimony against him. To them, in their panicked minds, he was not the symbol of authority who would see them to safety, but a confused man who brutally swung a gun butt, denying them what, to a layman, was something synonymous with safety: the lifeboats. They had huddled on the smoke-filled deck and watched in disbelief as he drove his crew back below to fight the spreading fire. He must have seemed a madman when he drove them, in turn, to their staterooms, but uppermost in his mind was the long odds of lifeboats surviving in the thundering seas. And while he attempted to bring order among crew and passengers, the fire gained rapid headway when it should have been easily confined to the engine room. Exploding drums of oil had billowed smoke and flame up ladders and then into passageways where he was herding passengers.

Three lives had been lost.

And if that were not enough to answer for, a trick of the weather had suddenly smoothed the high seas, cementing each passenger's opinion that the lifeboats would have been safe.

It was Barnes's testimony from a hospital bed that had aroused public opinion against him. Whether the mate's mind was still liquor-fogged, and he actually thought his statements the truth, or whether he was simply frightened at the tragedy he had caused remained an unanswered question. Whatever his reason, Barnes, with his last few breaths, maintained it was Roper who ordered the lifeboats swung out and then couldn't make up his mind—confirming the passengers' testimony that the shipmaster had been completely bewildered.

The board of inquiry had discharged the case, the old-time sea captains skeptical of much of the passengers' testimony. Besides, Barnes was not an unfamiliar figure to them, so they gave little weight to his words in the final disposition.

But publicity can have devastating effects. With East-West deriving one quarter of its revenue from passenger service, a stockholders' meeting saw Roper promptly ousted from his position in the name of public relations. No thought was given to the fact that other shipping companies would take this as a cue and keep their doors closed to him. With a few words men and women who knew nothing of ships or personnel kicked out from under him fifteen years of fighting his way up the ladder to a master's berth.

Good morning, Captain Roper....

Coffee, Captain, sir....

Yes, indeed, Captain, all secured below....

"'Ere, Roper, the Old Man says get back on the course! 'Ead's swingin', 'e says, an' maybe I'd better show you 'ow to 'andle a wheel!"

Roper snapped back to the present, automatically bringing his wheel over to compensate for his drifting head "Brown ..." He spoke without turning, knowing the bosun was standing at the door with a satisfied smirk on his grubby face. "Brown," he said, "what'll you bet I don't knock your teeth down your throat before we reach Sumatra?"

No answer came from Brown. The wheelhouse door closed, silently and respectfully.

Chapter Six

Fisher was repairing a generator, the parts scattered about on the floor plates of the ill-lighted engine room. His glasses were off and he peered in Roper's direction, nervously, it seemed, until he was able to recognize the visitor.

"Just getting acquainted with the vessel," Roper said. "Mind?"

"Not at all, not at all." Hurriedly Fisher rose, wiping his hands with a scrap of cotton waste. He felt in his overall breast pocket for his glasses. "Not much to see, Mr. Roper. What's here is in pretty sad shape, but Murdock keeps putting me off on replacements."

It was in worse than sad shape, to Roper's eye. Everywhere there were rust and grease, on both bulkheads and panels, the sweating skin of the ship a scabby dark brown. The Diesels themselves had not a speck of chrome or metal showing clean. Even the floor plates were so neglected that Roper found it difficult to walk without slipping. In the rear of the engine room he saw a cot, beside it a steel clothing locker.

With embarrassment Fisher explained he slept there in order to keep an eye on his assistants.

"Don't tell me you can't leave this place at all?"

Fisher smiled, further embarrassed. "It's best if I stay below while we're under way. I've taught the men how to lubricate and answer the telegraph promptly, but they never seem to understand they should get some sleep in the daytime, so as not to doze off at night. Good boys, though. They try."

"But tend strictly to engineering duties."

Fisher understood his meaning and shrugged. "They're being paid so little Murdock ordered their sole duty to be watches. With repairs being left up to me, plus supervising on the watches, I haven't been able to do any cleaning. I started to at one time, but it was such a job trying to keep up I let it go. Here comes Makote. The hat he's wearing and twenty dollars a month is the net Murdock pays for my first assistant. Good man."

The short stocky Negro that Roper had seen when he had first come aboard was descending the ladder. He reached the floor plates, gave a polite, almost condescending nod to Roper, and began moving about, critically inspecting gauges. He was stripped to the waist, his brown belly protruding over his belt. But what made his appearance ridiculous was the peaked hat on his head. It was a ship's officer's cap, but with a wide silver band above the visor and gold winged insignia above that.

"He's quite proud of that hat," Fisher said, smiling. "They all are. Murdock saves a good thousand a month by calling them engineers."

"He saves it by having you do four men's work, you mean."

Fisher shrugged. "It's not too bad. I have ample free time when we're in port." He accompanied Roper over to the ladder. "Those remarks of Murdock's last night ..." He removed his spectacles and studied them, ill at ease. "You see, I'm not too ... Well, it's just that I'm, er, ill, you might say. I don't want you to think you're working with a ..." He paused again, fumbling with his glasses awkwardly.

Realizing that Fisher, like many other addicts, sought an excuse for the habit, Roper was no less embarrassed than the engineer. "I'll have a talk with Murdock," he said.

"See what we can do about putting a hand or two down here occasionally."

Fisher's weak eyes widened with alarm. "No, no, you musn't do that, Mr. Roper. I appreciate your concern, but you musn't suggest making any changes down here. He might think I ... Well, it just wouldn't do."

Roper understood. Uppermost in Fisher's mind was his job, his constant need for substantial sums of money. Narcotics purchased through illegal channels are never cheap. He took his leave of Fisher, feeling sorry for the engineer in his predicament.

Throughout the rest of the afternoon, while the *Wanderer* steadily cut a wake southward through the South China Sea, Roper wandered through the ship, familiarizing himself with the interior. He visited the shanty-like housing aft and found a ladder there inside descending deep into the stern. Using a flashlight, he felt his way down, presently standing on steel floor plates and breathing the musty smell of a compartment long unused.

It was a large compartment, the deck in the rear rising slightly to meet the horseshoe curve of the stern. Except for a small kitchen table and straight wooden chair, both overturned and heavily coated with dust, it was empty. Then Roper's light revealed something he had come across several times in the past on Chinese-built freighters, something that had always filled him with revulsion: slave pits.

There were twelve of them built into the compartment flooring. Each no larger than an oversized bilge section, with the individual floor plates slid back as if for inspection, they gave the impression of so many coffins lying side by side. All contained arm and leg irons, long unused, scabbed with rust. Pools of oily water lay in the bottom of each.

Although he had never seen slave pits put to use, Roper knew they were standard equipment almost half a century before on Far Eastern ships. Their purpose was to provide vessels with additional revenue in transporting Negroes, Indians, and even Chinese to South African ports, where they were signed to terms of labor in mining compounds. It went without saying that any human chained in these coffins of filth and rust with only a bucket of water and a few pounds of meat would go through indescribable torment; for in most cases the floor plates would be in place and cargo stored on top to evade detection by government vessels. For each man thus sealed in, the world held nothing but foul darkness, the groans of his companions, and the constant scurrying of rats.

At the dinner table Roper mentioned the after compartment to Appley, and asked if Murdock had ever engaged in the slave trade.

Appley shook his head. "He has better sense than that. They were in when he bought this vessel. They say he used the compartment one time as a place for meditation, visiting it nightly with his Bible. That's right," he said, noting Roper's expression. "He still reads the Good Book. You'll catch him at it once in a while in his cabin. Maybe he's trying to figure out how much he'll owe on the day of reckoning, but he actually reads it."

"He strikes me," Roper said, "as a man who's never got past the first—"

"I'd say Kuma is self-sustaining," Appley interrupted, inclining his head a fraction in the direction of the doorway. "This Da-chong is quite an organizer. About half the people on the island are farmers, raising cows, pigs, chickens, tending to rice paddies, and so on. They even grow peppers. Oh, Mr. Brown...."

Appley's red cheeks creased with a smile as Brown sat down beside him and reached for a platter of potatoes. "Conference with the Captain again, Mr. Brown?"

Brown swelled with self-importance. "We 'ad a little chat, we did. About the work, 'ow them little bloody buggers don't pull their load." He broke off and eyed Appley with suspicion. "'Ow do you know we were talking? You were up on the bridge, you were."

"Your nose," Appley said. He helped himself to a slice of cold ham.

"Eh?"

Appley turned in his seat. He gently placed the tip of his finger on the bosun's nose. "The brown spot, right here."

Brown rubbed the tip of his nose, frowning his puzzlement. He looked at his finger. "I don't see—" He got the point then and glared at Appley.

"Funny bugger, you are!"

"Someday," Appley said, shoving a piece of ham into his mouth, "you're going to lose that. Your nose, I mean. Besides, it's the most unlikely place to find a mate's berth I know of."

Brown got to his feet, his grubby face quivering with anger. "I don't 'ave to take that!"

"Of course you don't," Appley said pleasantly. "But you will. And if you thought I could promote you into a stateroom, you'd crawl under this table and kiss each one of my little toes."

Brown went over to the door cursing. He slammed it shut behind him.

Appley grinned at Roper. "That's the one thing he won't carry to the cabin, that somebody called him a brown nose. He's afraid Murdock would agree."

"I hope you're not going to chase me?"

Roper turned at the sound of her voice. The moonlight revealed her standing near the ladder, attired casually in slacks and a sweater, awaiting his permission to enter the bridge.

He gave it grudgingly, expecting to be in for the usual line of trite passenger chatter. But she surprised him by moving out on the opposite wing, well away from him, remaining there lounging against the weatherboard and smoking. For twenty minutes he paced the port wing, occasionally entering the wheelhouse to check on the helmsman. Finally, reflecting that his studied indifference to the girl's presence was somewhat childish, he moved out onto the starboard wing to join her.

"Room more comfortable with those scoops installed?"

"Much more, thank you." She threw her cigarette away and turned and faced him, leaning back with her elbows on the rail, the position bringing into prominence the outline of her breasts beneath the sweater.

"Thank you, also," she said, "for coming over here and speaking to me. For a while I thought you'd be giving me the same treatment as the others are. I'm beginning to wonder if they suspect I have the plague."

"It's hardly that bad, Miss Gorman. It just seems that way. You have a lot of time on your hands, and everyone else has duties to perform."

"That's not what I mean," she said. "Not at all. When I do meet someone on deck, they go out of their way to avoid even saying hello. I've seen even Mrs. Murdock go out of her way to avoid meeting me. Why?"

Has the Captain ordered everyone to ignore me?"

Substantially, that had been Murdock's order, to guard against her gathering too much knowledge of their true business. To answer her question truthfully would only provoke another.

"We're not too sociable a group, I suppose, from a passenger's standpoint. Have you ever traveled on a freighter before?"

"Well, no," she admitted. "At least, I've never been the sole passenger. Most of my traveling has been on those little packets, island-hopping to various engagements." She smiled at him, smoothing her breeze-swept hair from her bronzed cheek. "Perhaps I'd been anticipating a relaxing voyage when I shouldn't have."

Roper found himself wondering how so attractive and personable a woman as this one could be lured to Kuma. It certainly was none of his business, but he decided to clear up the point that had been bothering him: Did she realize what she was getting into?

"I can't understand, Miss Gorman, why you have to travel to Kuma for employment. You can tell me it's none of my affair—which it isn't— but a girl as attractive as you must find plenty of work in the city clubs. I don't think you've been starving, or that you're likely to, so you can't feel that you were forced into accepting this job."

She tilted her head, acknowledging this. "No, I'm not starving. But if you're thinking entertainers out here are well paid, you're mistaken. Oh, the big names are, yes. But for me, and others like me, the pay is only high by Far Eastern standards. Do you know what I've saved in two years after hotels and traveling expenses? Don't laugh, now. One hundred dollars."

She took cigarettes from her pocket and removed one, her tone bitter as she continued. "One place will pay two hundred dollars a week. My, such a lot of money! I'm really quite rich. Then I'm idle for three weeks before my agent places me in Hong Kong, say, and I'm borrowing the fare from him. No, I haven't starved, Mr. Roper, and I probably won't for quite a while. But if ever anybody trod an endless belt, it's an entertainer traveling the Oriental circuit. I'm stepping off that belt."

Roper struck a match, cupping his hands against the breeze that swept over the bridge. She bent forward, her lovely features revealed in the flare of the match a moment, then she withdrew, inhaling deeply, taking the cigarette from her mouth.

"Yes, I'm stepping off. But I don't intend to go back with what I started, which was nothing. If someone is willing to pay well for private entertainment, I see no reason for refusing it." She waited for him to speak. "Don't you agree?"

He shrugged. "Suppose it all depends on your point of view. You simply didn't look the type."

"What type?" she asked quietly.

He answered the question with another. "What type of girl would go to an island like Kuma as somebody's private property for several months?"

"I'm an entertainer. I go where there's a demand for my services."

Irritably he said, "A buck's a buck, is that it? Even one lying in the gutter?"

Her voice grew cold as she straightened. "I don't like that remark, Mr. Roper. At least, not from you. Where do you come off preaching? Speaking of types, you don't look the kind of man that would be associating with the cutthroats this ship evidently carries. But looks are deceiving, aren't they, Mr. Roper?" She walked off without waiting for an answer.

Roper couldn't have thought of one at the moment, anyway.

The stowaway was discovered early the next morning. Appley had ordered the lifeboats aired, and when the canvas was pulled back from Number Two, Brown came up with a handful of black hair belonging to a struggling dark-skinned girl in her twenties.

Appley groaned when he saw the girl. "Here we go again. Murdock hates stowaways," he explained to Roper. "About twice a year a hand who should know better slips one aboard. Murdock really blows his top when he discovers them. Hates to think he's been had for a free trip south, I guess. This one'll be lucky if he doesn't hand her a life jacket and toss her over the side. Brown, call the Captain!"

The girl stood barefooted on the deck, perfectly at ease, undisturbed by her discovery. She had a heavy figure, wide hips and high full breasts emphasized by a tight fitting cheap print dress. She pushed her disheveled hair away from her broad features, her black slanting eyes saucily returning the smiles of the Chinese hands who were gathering and clucking in approval. Her profession was only too obvious by her manner.

When Murdock came out on deck his heavy face was grim. Slowly he approached the girl, his hands jammed into his coat pockets. He stood and studied her closely for a moment.

"This bucket is turning into a goddamn floating cat house," he growled. "You! Savvy English?"

Under his smoldering gaze the girl's saucy expression faded. It was replaced by an eagerness to please. "Un'erstan' Anglish ve'y good. French, better."

"Who brought you aboard?" Just briefly her eyes left Murdock, as if to search among the coolies, who had drawn back and were no longer smiling in Murdock's presence. She recovered and looked innocently at Murdock.

"I come myself."

Murdock's slap caught her high across the cheek. She stumbled back, her left cheek reddening with the imprint of his big hand. Brown, who had been standing behind her, grinned and roughly pushed her forward again.

"Point out the man who brought you aboard," Murdock said evenly.

Defiance crept into the girl's eyes as she massaged her injured cheek. She spat on the deck with deliberation, then folded her arms across her large bosom. "I come aboard alone."

A knife appeared in Murdock's hand, the blade flashing in the sunlight as he hefted the weight of it. He motioned to the earless coolie standing among the hands. "Slit the end of her tongue," he ordered. "Let's see if that will loosen it."

Appley's elbow nudged into Roper's ribs as he muttered, "You'll have the same knife in your belly, mate, without a tear shed aboard. Hold your place if this turns out to be nasty."

The girl had paled. She took one agonizing look at the scarred man approaching, then violently shook her head. "It is he!" She pointed to a vacant-faced coolie, who immediately shrank back.

Murdock barely glanced at the man. He nodded to Brown. "She'll pay half her passage by working in the galley. Get her in there at sunrise. See that she stays there until dark." His eyes traveled over the girl's ample proportions. "She'll bunk in the fo'c'sle, working the other half off at night. The duties, she will perform there will be identical with those she has performed ashore."

At first Roper couldn't believe Murdock was serious. But Brown was grinning widely, his quick eyes greedily dropping to the girl's heavy flanks in anticipation.

"What are you waiting for?" Murdock snapped at Brown. "Get the slut out of my sight! Put her into the galley and see that she stays there."

There was no fight in the girl as Brown pushed her forward. Murdock turned and looked at Roper. "You don't like my decision, evidently?"

Although Roper's disgust with such a perverted method of handling a female stowaway must have been reflected in his expression, he did not voice any comment. He doubted if the girl herself was thinking of her situation as a difficult one.

Murdock's eyes drifted over to the coolie the girl had pointed out. "Once before," he said slowly, "I promised the man that again brought aboard a stowaway reason to remember it. I make no idle promises." He began walking toward the coolie, still speaking, but now in a Cantonese dialect.

The coolie cowered, fright filling his narrow eyes as Murdock closed in. Before he could move back, Murdock's knee came up swiftly, smashing into the man's groin, Murdock's full weight ruthlessly behind the forward lunge. The coolie made no sound. His mouth opened, his skin turning the color of yellow wax. He started to crumple when Murdock launched his punch.

It caught the man on the bridge of the nose, smashing it to a pulp. In rapid succession, before he could fall, Murdock drove his fists twice more into the blood-splattered face. He was striding off to his cabin before the unconscious coolie hit the deck.

Roper swore softly. He saw the necessity for strict discipline in their business, but felt Murdock was a man who derived enjoyment from delivering a beating.

Appley motioned to the men standing about to take the unconscious hand below. At first they refused to move, coolies and engine-room blacks all watching with sullen hatred in their eyes as Murdock disappeared down the companionway. They moved to comply when the mate repeated his order.

"Someday," Appley growled, "the bastard will get his. I want to be on hand when he gets taken down a peg. I won't laugh in his face; I admit I wouldn't have the nerve. I just want to be there to see it."

Roper saw both Karen Gorman and Kim standing near the rail. Apparently they had witnessed the entire affair from there. Karen was plainly shocked by Murdock's callous actions. Kim's young features wore no expression beyond a trace of sadness. She turned her head, looking up at the wing where Djerf was standing. Their eyes met, held momentarily; then she turned away to her room.

Perhaps, Roper thought, Murdock might be taken down a peg sooner than Appley expected. And it might come from an unexpected direction—if these two meant more to each other than bed partners.

He had a hunch they did.

Chapter Seven

There is an endless monotony in tropical weather at sea, a sameness in heat and sweat and sun glare; but aboard the *Wanderer* monotony was broken when they entered the Malacca Straits and Murdock discovered a dozen cases of goods had been broken into during the night hours.

Immediately guessing that the object of the search had been the bottles of champagne, Murdock had Brown muster every coolie aft onto the fantail, with orders for them to stay there until the guilty men were produced. For six hours, without water or any protective covering from the scorching tropic sun, the men squatted miserably on the fantail, watching their captain sauntering back and forth on the bridge. Finally, after a consultation among themselves, one left the fantail and reported to Brown.

It was apparent to Roper that this man standing humbly before Murdock had been chosen to shoulder the guilt, that it had required more than one man to open so many cases silently. But Murdock seemed satisfied, almost pleased that they had decided to let one man bear the blame. He promptly ordered the man into the crow's nest. Twenty-four hours later it required four men and a bosun's chair to bring down his unconscious body, his neck and shoulders so badly burned from the sun that Appley and Roper had to treat and bandage the entire area.

"He'll be up and around in a few days," Appley said, "but I'm wondering who's going to be next to step out of line. Every damn time somebody goes off on the wrong foot and gets Murdock started, it seems we get a couple of more things that have him blowing his top. I'm hoping it isn't you, mate. Maybe you'd better slow your time with that girl on those twelve-to-fours. Murdock's been watching that, and I can tell you he don't like it."

"She's up there for air," Roper said. "We hardly say three words during the whole time."

This was the truth. Although Karen Gorman again appeared during his watch, their relationship was maintained on a stiff and formal basis. She kept mainly to herself, though Roper thought he detected in that independence some uneasiness, as if she were beginning to realize the freighter was a small world of its own with no redress from its master.

But it was the stowaway that caused the next furor on board.

From the morning she had been discovered hiding in the lifeboat and ordered quartered in the forecastle, little was seen of her. At sundown she was sent forward, forbidden to be on deck, and during the daylight hours she was strictly confined to the galley, kept there by a glowering Brown, who refused her any free time. It was well known that his disgruntlement stemmed from the fact that she had quickly taken charge in the forecastle, ruling the roost there and proportioning her favors when and to whom she saw fit. Brown was not so favored. When he went out of his way to see that the cook saved the dirtiest jobs for her, she pleaded with Murdock to intercede. He refused. Angrily she kept after him, and whenever he passed by the galley, her loud and profane screechings could be heard all over the ship.

Roper did not witness the incident. It was after the evening meal and he was taking his usual nap in preparation for the midnight watch. The screams woke him.

He hurriedly dressed and went on deck. In the darkness he rubbed his eyes in disbelief.

A single cargo light spotlighted the scene. The stowaway was bound, face to the mainmast, her dress crumpled in a heap about her ankles, her brown body writhing under a lashing being administered by Brown. A makeshift cat composed of several knotted ropes whistled as it arched through the air, making an ugly slapping sound as it whipped across the girl's naked back. From thighs to shoulders thin dark welts were appearing with each sweep of the rope ends.

The coolie hands and engine-room blacks were grouped together, grinning at the howling girl dancing in pain.

It took Roper only a moment to get over the shock of what he saw, and another to leap over and cut the girl down. She slumped in his arms, moaning, smelling of cheap perfume and sweat.

"Lend a hand!" he growled to two of the hands. "Take this woman below."

Relieved of his burden, Roper swung on Brown, only to see Murdock moving out from the shadow of the companionway ladder.

"Roper, you just stepped out of line!" Murdock's face was livid, his yellow eyes flickering with rage. Across his right cheek were several deep scratches, as if he had been raked by fingernails. Later Roper learned that the girl had flown at him when he again refused to lighten her work.

Roper stood his ground under Murdock's anger. "I think you're the one who's out of bounds," he said. "Even stowaways have rights."

"Do they, now!" Murdock's mouth snapped shut as he took a half step forward. He halted, breathing deeply, as if it were costing him a great effort to regain self-control. "Roper, your services are needed this trip. Perhaps we'll need you as badly as you need us. But the fact that we have no way of replacing you doesn't mean you've been handed a license to run this ship! Cross me once more—just once more, Roper— and I'll give you a taste of the cat and set you on the beach with your pay forfeited. Perhaps an eight-hour watch will give you more time to think over your position aboard. Get up there and relieve Appley."

Brown began edging forward, as if hoping that Roper would refuse. He had obviously been enjoying his task, and there was now a look in his shifty eyes that said he hoped the entertainment would continue.

Roper turned away, knowing it would be madness to refuse. He was approaching the bridge ladder when Karen came striding out of the passageway, tying a robe about her. Her eyes glinted angrily.

Roper wheeled and caught her arm. "Where do you think you're going?"

"I'm going to ask to have that girl moved into my room, where she can be given some attention! Of all the beastly things I've ever seen—"

"Get back in your room," Roper said curtly. "Get back and mind your own business."

She tried to pull her arm free of his grip. "I just want to ask if that girl can—"

Roper pushed her back into the passageway. "If you don't want to be confined to your room for the rest of the trip, get in there and keep quiet!"

She managed to control herself. "I don't think there's anything that would be beneath that man!"

"There isn't. And don't you try testing him."

Appley had witnessed Roper's intervention from the bridge wing. "Looks like he's really bent on reaching Kuma with a decent-sized bridge staff, Roper, but like he said, the next step out of line will sure be your last. You'd better learn to say, 'Yes, sir,' and 'No, sir,' and think three times before you open your mouth for anything else. So the hussy stays off her back a while, so what? Will she be any the worse for it? We're about running par for a trip, mate, so any time you see something you don't like, start counting the dollars you'll be getting at bonus time. Always helps."

To Roper a double trick was something any bridge officer could take in stride. But he hadn't counted on Murdock's presence through four hours of it. His look of surprise brought a growl from Murdock when he came up on the bridge.

"You're not up here to relieve me of my watch, but to learn that I'm the master aboard, Roper. No one profits from punishment aboard this ship."

Roper casually moved out onto the wing without replying. He doubted very much that Murdock's sadistic nature had not benefited from the girl's beating. Feeling a greater repugnance than ever toward Murdock, he wanted as little to do with him as possible. But Murdock appeared on the wing a few moments later, standing a few feet from him.

Roper kept his eyes forward, on the rise and fall of the freighter's bow as it cut a foaming trough in the sea. The wind had freshened, stirring white caps barely visible in the darkness ahead.

"We'll be picking up Great Channel by morning, Roper. Ever been through there?"

"Once."

"We'll be cutting the Point close to save time. I'm making allowance for the set, but if it stiffens out of the southeast, change your course two or three degrees. Pass the word to Djerf at four." He took a cigar from his pocket. "Still thinking about that girl?"

"My opinion still stands," Roper said.

"And that was?" He bit off one end of the cigar and spat to leeward.

"I gave it to you before and it earned me an extra watch.'"

Murdock turned, his heavy jaw tightening. "You trying to tell me that chippy has her rights? Well, she hasn't, and neither has anyone else the moment they try to get something for nothing! When you take something from anybody, you must pay. The offended can demand and exact payment. That's one of the basic concepts of the Bible."

Roper refused to question this statement or even to comment on it. He had no desire to get into a religious discussion with Murdock.

"You don't agree with me?" The glow of Murdock's cigar momentarily lighted the raw scratches on his cheek. His eyes were fastened on Roper.

"I haven't given it much thought."

The cigar tilted from Murdock's broad face as he scanned the dark overcast sky. "Roper, I spoke once before of your station aboard this ship. I'm not going to speak of it again. Maybe you think you're permitted a certain leeway because of your former rank. You're not. I reserve for myself the right to punish anyone aboard for crimes or breaches of discipline. And I'll punish as I see fit. I advise you to take that statement seriously."

He turned and went into the wheelhouse, and he stayed there the rest of his watch. Promptly at midnight he went below.

Djerf came up early to relieve Roper. Generally he had little to say, listening to routine orders and course changes without comment, but this night he engaged in small talk. He spoke of the ultimate disposition of the deckload they were carrying, how the Bushmen at Sumatra would resell it piecemeal to fishing boats for distribution throughout a hundred different ports. But while he was speaking of these things it was apparent he had something else on his mind. Soon he acknowledged this.

"I do not intend to burden you with a problem, Mr. Roper, or ask for advice. It is simply ..." He glanced toward the wheelhouse, where the helmsman was faintly outlined in the soft glow from the binnacle. "It is simply," he said more softly, as if gauging the distance his voice might carry, "I must settle my mind on a certain thing. I ... I..."

He turned away suddenly, gripping the railing with both hands, facing the darkness ahead. His voice choking, he went on. "Mr. Roper, what makes a coward? If this minute you told me that tomorrow morning I would remain asleep, never to awake, I would not care. Here, this minute, you could ask if I would give my life for her and I would say yes. And it would be the truth. What is it, then, that controls my body when I am faced with danger? What rises in me like a sickness when Murdock raises his voice to me? Is it the injury to my leg, the year of suffering I underwent when it was crushed in a typhoon? Perhaps. But the very thought of what Murdock will be saying when he learns we are gone—"

Djerf turned, the dark light of the moon reflecting a haunted quality in his eyes. He studied his clenched hands before him. "In Saigon we were to leave together when Murdock sent for me to come to his cabin. It was only to deliver some money to Fazio, but before I learned that fact I became so ill I vomited in my room. I was barely able to walk into the cabin. But now the time draws near when I cannot hesitate. Murdock will not be put off any longer in his marital rights. When we lay off Kuma Island, Appley is to vacate his room and a connecting doorway will give Murdock a suite on that side. It follows that she and Murdock will then live together as man and wife. She claims she will kill herself first. I believe her. Mr. Roper, I firmly believe her."

Roper lit a cigarette, his guard rising. He disliked sharing Djerf's confidence, for he felt the less he knew of any plans concerning Kim's future, the better off he would be. He saw the explosive elements in the situation and wanted to remain far in the background. He would be clashing with Murdock enough without interfering in his private life.

"She and her family were among the refugees driven from northern Laos," Djerf continued, when Roper remained silent. "It is not difficult to understand her acceptance of Murdock at the time. If a man quotes from the Bible, you are apt to ignore outward appearance when in search of a sanctuary. You do not refuse a tattered life ring when drowning for fear the interior of the ring is in worse condition than its covering. Sometimes there is no choice. But within three months after their marriage she forced Murdock to give her a separate room. Her illness was not all pretense. She became violently sick at the thought of his touching her. He is ... he is not the same as other men. From pain and degradation comes his pleasure. For him there is no beauty in a woman."

Djerf braced himself as the ship rolled. "For quite a few months she was permitted to go ashore unescorted. Perhaps Murdock sensed that ashore she was not alone, for recently he ordered Brown to escort her wherever she went. Her room then became the one place we could talk. We were certain you overheard us together that night I visited her room, and it is for that reason I am now speaking to you."

Roper flipped his cigarette over the side, watching the wind carry the sparks astern. "Djerf, I always mind my own business. If that's been worrying you, ease your mind. I haven't spoken of it to anyone."

Djerf slowly nodded. "We both felt we had nothing to fear from you, Mr. Roper. However, I am relieved with your assurance. If you had accidently dropped a word ..." He drew a breath and seemed to hold it. "Last night I dreamed Murdock knew, that he was waiting for our next move. The thought that he might know, that he might be waiting for us to make that first move, is a horrible one. Because we must make that move, Mr. Roper. We *must*. Can you understand that?"

The relieving helmsman coming up the ladder reminded Djerf how long he had been talking. Without waiting for an answer, he bade Roper good night, and made his way into the chartroom.

As Roper went down the ladder he found himself in sympathy with the predicament Djerf and Kim found themselves in, but at the same time he was aware he must treat it impersonally. To be caught in the middle of what amounted to nothing more than the old triangle would be foolish on his part.

Below in the passageway Roper saw a thin rectangle of light coming from beneath Karen Gorman's door. He hesitated there a moment. She knew he was relieved each morning at four, and the light from her room seemed to be an open invitation. With another woman Roper would have taken this invitation at face value, and acted accordingly. With this girl he wasn't too sure.

She answered his knock immediately.

When he entered she was sitting in the club chair, a book in her lap. She still wore the robe she'd had on earlier.

"I was hoping you'd drop in." She closed the book and straightened her robe.

"Really? Why?" He shut the door and removed his cap, inhaling a faint fragrance of perfume as he moved into the room.

"Won't you sit down?" She indicated the bunk, which had not been slept in.

He sat down, resting his elbows on his knees, whirling his cap, watching her light a cigarette, and seeing an elegance in the simple gesture.

She brushed back a wisp of copper hair from a tanned cheek, the smoke drifting from her red mouth. "Sounds brazen, doesn't it? But you're the only one aboard I can talk to. I suppose I want to be reassured that I'm still living in a civilized world after all that's been going on."

"You've got nothing to fear, Miss Gorman."

"Karen." She arched her brow, smiling. "If you don't think that's too informal."

"Karen." He nodded, wondering why he had felt she would be any different from the others. "You have nothing to fear, Karen. Nothing that happens on board concerns you or will hurt you in any way. That is, if you stay out of the way."

"After what happened to that girl tonight, I wondered just how safe I was. That was a horrid thing he did to her."

"It was, and that's why I wanted you to keep out of it. Murdock is capable of anything when he's riled up. Particularly when he dislikes someone." He stopped, not wanting to explain Murdock's antagonism toward women of loose morals.

"And he dislikes me?"

Roper shrugged. "Women in general, I think."

She turned in the chair, drawing her feet up and tucking the robe under them. "Do you? Dislike women?"

"Not at all. What makes you ask?"

"That chip on your shoulder. Or should I say in your eyes? And don't tell me it isn't there. Not that I minded, Mr. Roper...." She paused and looked at him.

"John. Mostly it's been Johnny."

"Not that I minded it, Johnny. It's better than the leers I've been getting from some. But now that it's brought up, I wonder at it. You always appear ready to eat anyone who looks sideways at you."

Roper smiled. "I'm not that bad." He thought about it as he fished for a cigarette. "I suppose when you get knocked down a few times it shows."

She tilted her head at him reflectively. "You look the bouncy type to me. I don't think you'd ever stay down for long."

"It's been three years. Long enough."

"Three years? I'll bet you were hit low."

It was an invitation to talk, and Roper, much to his surprise, found himself giving details of his background, the early age at which he had entered the forecastle, his self-denial of frills and pleasures as he set for himself the goal of mastering a vessel under the great East-West Transport flag. As he talked he was aware of a most comfortable feeling sitting there with this attractive girl curled up in an armchair and listening so attentively, and sometimes tilting her head in sympathy as he slowly went over his last voyage on the *Victorian*.

"But couldn't you get a job ashore? I mean, rather than come out here and mix with the kind of riffraff who run ships like this one?"

He shook his head, lighting a fresh cigarette. "You don't put fifteen years behind you that easily. I'd never be satisfied ashore. I'd feel I'd been beaten. I haven't been. For a while I thought I'd be satisfied just to be back on top again, a master's berth. But now I want more."

He drew on the cigarette, forgetting the girl for the moment, his voice harsher than he intended. "By God, I'll be paid for these three years. I'll be master again, and this time it will be my own ship. Sooner or later I'll run my own house flag over a freighter being snugged into the Embarcadero. And there's not a damn thing going to stand in my way!"

"And you won't care how you get it?" Her sea-green eyes were level as she looked across at him. "You won't care if you'll be stepping on people?"

He continued smoking, not answering the question.

"I don't think you mean what you say, Johnny. If this position aboard means so much in getting a fresh start, you certainly were quick to jeopardize it earlier this evening."

He admitted that was true. "I can't stand to see anyone hurt who doesn't deserve it."

"I'll bet you're really a softie, Johnny Roper." Her tone was light and she was smiling at him with her cheeks dimpling, her teeth white against her sun-browned face.

Roper became aware of the subtle scent again, the utter desirableness of this girl curled so childlike in the chair. The fact that she was for sale provoked a sudden anger.

"Karen, we've touched on this subject before, but exactly what are you going to Kuma for?"

"Two thousand dollars a month. Good reason?"

"And what are you going to do for two thousand dollars a month? Or shouldn't I ask?"

"Why shouldn't you ask?" The familiar frost began to gather in her eyes. "I'm a dancer. I intend to dance in Kuma."

He shook his head slowly at her. "Karen, somebody is being taken for a ride. And I don't think it's Da-chong. What makes you think a man will pay such a salary to watch a girl dance?"

"What makes you think he won't? A rich man can afford the whim of having entertainment brought to him."

"By God, Karen, you're a ninny if you believe—" Roper paused, feeling suddenly he was playing the fool. An entertainer kicking around the Orient knew the score. Why should she deliberately smear herself black? Why admit to him she intended trading on her feminine talents, the sky the limit? Maybe she'd done plenty of small-scale trading already, and was moving into a field calling for higher fees.

"You were about to say?" Her eyes were as cold as they had been the day Roper had first seen her.

"Forget it," he said, getting up. "I've got a bad habit of trying to straighten people out."

"You believe I need straightening?"

He looked down at her. "No, I don't think you do, Karen. You're as cool and levelheaded as they come. I think you know exactly what you're doing, including the exact price you're going to ask ... shall we say, for services not called for in your contract?"

Her reaction was so different from what Roper expected he instantly regretted his words. She had been looking up at him, listening with a storm gathering in her eyes. He had looked for an outburst, but she suddenly reddened, the storm disappearing. She lowered her eyes guiltily, slowly rising from the chair.

"Perhaps we'd better say good night, Mr. Roper."

Roper reached out, pulled her to him roughly. He placed his lips against hers, brutally forcing her head back, his arms holding her supple body tightly against his.

For several moments she made no effort to resist, permitting their lips to cling. Then her hands moved up to his cheeks, gently pushing his head away. Her eyes were devoid of expression as her lips moved to form a smile, the familiar inviting smile seen in alleys and side streets the world over.

"I don't think you can afford it, Mr. Roper. So why tease yourself?"

He flushed and released her, knowing she was attempting to strike back at him. Well, he had left himself wide open. He picked up his hat from the bunk, turned, and went over to the door.

"It was an enjoyable talk, Miss Gorman. Good night."

She inclined her head. "Good night, Mr. Roper. I also enjoyed it—up to a certain point."

In his room Roper lay awake for a long while, staring at the pale reflection of the sea wavering across the overhead. A shame, he thought. A damn shame. A beautiful and intelligent girl. But give her a year or two and there would be nothing left but a cynical hardness.

He fell asleep thinking of her.

Chapter Eight

Sunday morning the freighter made her entrance into the Indian Ocean, turning her bow southward for the jungled belly of Sumatra, where her deckload was to be disposed of. Despite the steady drizzle drumming on the decks, eight bells saw Brown announcing all hands topside for Sunday services.

Roper and the other officers wore oilskins, standing in a small group to one side, away from the coolie deck hands and engine-room blacks, who appeared bored even before the services had started. Kim and Karen took positions in the shelter of the companionway, Karen disdainfully moving aside as Murdock strode by her with a Bible under his arm.

With Brown directly behind him and holding a dripping umbrella over his head, the picture the *Wanderer's* master presented was an odd one as he mounted the number-two hatch. He reminded Roper of an Egyptian galley master being tended by a slave. Murdock, he reflected, would have felt at home in those days.

For several moments Murdock gazed over the small assemblage before him. Then he opened the Bible in his hands, bowed his head, and began reading in low tones, his voice almost inaudible in the steady rain sweeping the deck.

Although no student of the Bible, Roper recognized the reading as the Sermon on the Mount. Appley, standing beside him, nudged him with an elbow. "That's all he ever reads," he whispered. "Probably feels like God doing it."

At the end of the reading Murdock leisurely closed the Bible, glanced once at the coolies and blacks standing wet and miserable near the rail, and walked off to his cabin.

Roper was watching Karen, her hands in her slicker pockets, leaning back against the bulkhead. She was staring apathetically across the rain-drenched sea, her young features melancholy. Her eyes moved and met Roper's. Expression unchanging, she straightened and strolled away to her room.

Gusts of rain swept out from the darkness ahead, rattling the wheelhouse windows. They had bypassed their true destination as a precaution against spotters along the coast and were now backtracking into Sumatra without lights to unload their pilfered goods. Murdock stood behind the helmsman, eying the compass closely. On both sides of the freighter a lead was being swung, and it was on the depths of water being sung out that he was navigating. It was ticklish business, for they were within two miles of the coast, with the heavy rain cutting visibility to fifty feet. Time and again he ordered a course change, but never more than a degree. At the chart board Djerf carefully checked each depth against their heading, his smooth dark face a study of concentration in the faint light of the desk lamp.

Almost an hour passed before Roper was ordered to use the searchlight.

The light slicing through gusts of rain revealed Murdock's accurate judgment. Through the rain could be seen the dense shoreline of Sumatra, the flanks of a cove reaching out to embrace them. As they continued on, drifting with engines stopped, the light picked up a nook of the cove that had been cleared somewhat of trees. There Roper saw the dark ragged outlines of a wharf running parallel to the shore, and faintly visible was a wide path leading from the wharf into the jungle, a path bordered by stunted mango trees with hanging vines blowing wildly in the rain. Suddenly, as if a signal had been given, wavering torches appeared on the path and shadowy forms began flitting across the clearing to gather on the wharf.

With the freighter cautiously nudging into the berth, its deck lights switched on, Roper found himself gazing down on several dozen grinning blacks with welted faces, their nostrils pierced with bones. Most of them were men, tall and lean, wearing little more than loincloths. The few women were also scantily dressed, naked from the waist up. They crowded around the lowering gangway, a scent of coconut oil drifting up from their glistening bodies.

"These are the boys who do the lugging," Appley explained. "Papa Joe does the buying. Over there; the one carrying the cashbox."

Appley was referring to an ancient stooped man with a tiny wrinkled earth-colored face, moving up the gangway. Large gold rings pierced the lobes of his ears, and a smaller one hung from his nostrils. In his bony arms he carried a small metal box. When he reached the head of the gangway he bowed his black skull to Murdock, scraping his bare feet on the steel deck in obeisance.

Murdock bowed in return and indicated a chair placed near the companionway. A canopy had been stretched across this part of the deck. Here the pricing and buying would be done.

For an hour Roper watched cases being opened and spread out for Papa Joe's inspection, while the old man's narrowed eyes shuttled between the goods and the abacus on his lap. The first case sold for a total of fifty-five British pounds and was swung off the ship; the second went for fifty-seven pounds. There was little dispute; Murdock and the old man had previously agreed on one fourth the value of the approximate retail price.

Karen came out on deck shortly after the buying had started. She looked with sleepy wonderment at the scene, apparently having slept through the maneuvering and mooring, which had been done quietly. Without taking his eyes off the goods being opened, Murdock ordered her back to her room. "Damn," he growled, watching cartons of cigarettes being opened under the awning. "We'll be here a week if he runs a fine comb over everything."

Murdock moved over, indicating the sealed cartons. Since they were sealed, he argued, they must contain the proper amount. The old black displayed naked gums in smiling his agreement, but he didn't rescind his order. His men continued opening the cartons.

It took three days to complete the buying. During that time there was little work to be done, and all hands were given the freedom of an area extending several hundred yards back to a shallow creek curving through the jungle. Here, along one bank of the creek, a dozen thatched huts had been constructed years before for the use of the *Wanderer's* crew during their stays. Actually the place served as a mart where the natives traded raw homemade liquor and young giggling girls to the crew for money, clothing, and cigarettes. Liquor and women were a combination likely to cause trouble, and so to ensure peaceful negotiations it was routine for the deck officers to maintain watches along the creek. They stood their regular four-hour tricks, using for quarters an old wooden bungalow erected on poles on the opposite bank. It was comfortable enough, divided into two large rooms containing metal beds and straw mattresses, and tables and chairs of cane. Only one room was put to use by the officers; the other, by custom, was kept in reserve for Murdock's wife, should she desire a stationary bed for a change. However, she remained on the ship, as did Murdock, Fisher, and Karen. Karen had been refused outright any freedom of the shore.

Neither Roper, Appley, nor Djerf had much time for leisure ashore. In addition to their watches, they were constantly being routed from bed by belligerent blacks, demanding they make good on debts rashly incurred by drunken members of the crew who had made wild promises when their pockets became emptied. Fights over the girls became numerous, and the second night Brown was carried back to the ship with his jaw opened to the bone.

Murdock performed the stitching, pouring alcohol over the wound in generous quantities. He snarled the blubbering bosun into silence.

"Next time you'll know better! You're well paid to help run this ship and I'll not have you or any other white lose face for us with Papa Joe.

Now get up and go back there with Roper. Walking the creek may cool you off!"

When Appley appeared at the creek the third evening, asking Roper if he had seen Djerf, he simply shook his head, attaching no significance to the question. Later, after midnight, when Roper was drinking on the veranda of the bungalow, Appley returned.

The mate lowered himself wearily into a cane-bottomed chair, reaching for the bottle on the table. "Hasn't shown up yet?"

"No. He may be on the ship."

"Searched it. From stem to stern. No sign of him. Her, either."

"Her?"

"Murdock's wife."

Roper put down his glass thoughtfully. He had forgotten about those two and their planning. "They're gone, eh?"

"Well, we've looked—" Appley's mouth hung open. "Gone? Together, you mean? I'll be damned! And you sound like you knew this was coming."

Roper admitted he had suspected the pair would make a break sooner or later. That they elected to cross remote jungle territory, though, came as a surprise.

Appley settled back in the chair, shaking his head as if unable to believe he could have been kept in the dark on such a thing. "So that's why he kept putting up with Murdock; just biding his time to make off with his wife. Good God, this calls for a drink!" He helped himself to a long one straight from the bottle. "Question now is," he said, wiping his lips on his sleeve, "who's going to tell Murdock? I'm going to love watching his face, but the telling I don't think I'm up to."

No one had to tell Murdock. As soon as Appley and Roper reported aboard and stated that Djerf was not to be found, he guessed the truth. He guessed it as he stood on the rain-slicked well deck, staring at each of his two mates and Brown. He breathed heavily, the lines taut about his thin mouth. A hard flickering light began glowing in his yellow eyes.

"They've gone together." He clenched his fists, half raised them. "That's it, isn't it? They've gone off together. They've always been together, haven't they? Even on my ship?"

Appley shrugged helplessly. "It amazes me. I still can't believe it."

"You lie!" Murdock took a half step toward him, the muscles along his jaw coiling into tight knots. "You ..." His eyes flashed to Roper. "You've all known about this! You've known and you've been laughing at me! Watched me turn from her door night after night, didn't you? And you were laughing—laughing while he ... while he was ..."

He took another step forward, his huge hands opening and closing. "You saw him go into her room all this while. You said nothing. My own officers! You knew and you said nothing. It's true, isn't it? Tell me!" he shouted. "Tell me it's true, damn you!"

Roper and Appley remained discreetly silent. To one side, repacking the last of the cases that had been sold to Papa Joe, were four of the Bushmen. They had stopped working, also silent, curiously watching Murdock's antics. Whatever possessed Brown at that moment to step forward, Roper didn't know. Perhaps the bosun saw in Djerf's absence a chance for the vacant mate's berth. Perhaps, unwisely, he thought Murdock would favor the one removing any vestige of doubt concerning his wife's infidelity.

"It's something, Captain, sir, a man don't talk about, 'e don't." Brown fingered the bandage along his jaw, shaking his head sadly. "Always knew a thing 'r two was going on, but it's something a man don't talk about. You know 'ow it is, Captain."

Murdock's head inched forward, his chin dropping until it rested on his chest. His eyes were cold yellow slits as they pinned Brown.

"You saw them together?"

"Aye, an' more than once." Brown nodded. "One night I peeped through the port, I did. And there they were, 'er an' 'im. On the bunk."

Murdock's left hand shot out. He grasped the bosun's throat, cutting off his words. With his right hand he drove two smashing punches in rapid succession straight against Brown's bandaged jaw. As the bosun went limp, arms dangling lifelessly, a third punch skidded off Brown's temple.

What probably saved his life was the seepage of blood through the bandage along his jaw. Murdock stared at it, his fist raised. With a curse he flung Brown aside. The bosun's body bounced against the bulwark before sprawling to the deck to lie there inert.

Neither Appley nor Roper moved. Murdock glared balefully at them, as if he hoped they would try to go to Brown's aid. Muttering under his breath, he began pacing the deck, glowering toward the jungle each time he turned. It began raining again, as it had been, intermittently, for three days, blowing in from seaward and pelting the deck. Black water flowed noisily in the gutters. Murdock continued his pacing, his muttering becoming louder.

"Laughing at me! For a year, laughing at me!" He wheeled about and stared at the Bushmen, who were cautiously whispering among themselves. "You men! Tell Papa Joe I want a tracker! Tracker, savvy? Chop, chop after man and woman, much money if bring back. Tracker, goddamnit, *tracker!*" he roared.

It took almost a full minute for the men to understand what was wanted. When they did, and when they also understood there would be a reward for bringing back the two runaways, they rushed over to the gangway and disappeared down the steps, jostling one another.

Murdock resumed his pacing. He caught sight of Appley and Roper, still standing there in the rain.

"Get off this ship," he whispered. His mouth twisted in a hard line as he turned and faced them. "Get off this ship! It doesn't move until they return!"

Before the mates had reached the bottom of the gangway, Murdock was leaning over the rail, shrieking at them. "I'll give you something to laugh at! You and the rest of that scum!" His strange eyes blazed down as he gripped the rail and leaned over farther. "We'll see how long you go on laughing! We'll see!"

The sound of the cabin door slamming came to the two men as they walked across the clearing. They entered the footpath leading to the creek, sloshing through mud almost ankle-deep, the rain beating down steadily upon them.

"He's truly flipped it," Appley said. "And he's going to get worse the more he keeps thinking of all the waiting he's done for that ripe bud to get over whatever she's supposed to have had. He's right in figuring plenty of people will be laughing. Those who hate him will build the story up: the mate and the Captain's wife at it while said captain takes a cold shower to cool off. Oh, will they build that one up! You can be sure he'll try to give them something else to talk about. Right now you can bet that's on his mind: repairing his reputation as the top— Something wrong?"

Roper had halted, remembering the girl was still aboard. "In Murdock's present frame of mind, maybe our passenger would be better off in the bungalow."

"Leave her where she is," Appley said, wiping the warm rain water from his face. "He won't handle the merchandise. He won't want to rub Da-chong the wrong way."

Despite himself, Roper found it a bitter thing to hear Karen Gorman spoken of as a piece of property. But that she was nothing more than that couldn't be denied. He blocked her from his mind as they prodded on toward the creek. He thought of the *Wanderer's* delay here. For every day the freighter lay in the cove, a loss on the books would be incurred. That was important to him. All-important. For he wanted the *Wanderer* to have a good year, good enough so he could walk off the gangway with enough charter money to satisfy Fazio. In his mind was a time schedule to be adhered to. One year with Murdock. One with Fazio, perhaps two. Then his own ship. That was his goal, and neither Murdock, Djerf, nor any of their problems must interfere. Nor Karen Gorman.

Keep the eye strictly on the mark.

Fisher came into the bungalow several hours before dawn, waking Roper and Appley. He eyed them nervously. "I think he's crazy. I think he's just plain crazy."

"What's he doing now?" Appley sleepily reached for his pipe on the floor.

"Chased me out of the engine room. I had to cut off all the motors."

"No lights aboard?"

"Not a one." He saw Roper's questioning look. "He chased Miss Gorman off, too. I put her up in the next room."

Roper began dressing, weary from a restless night of rain and insects, but his mind suddenly eased at the knowledge that the girl was off the ship and close by.

"Brown's in Djerf's room. Quite ill." Fisher nodded to the bottle on the table. "That's what Murdock's been doing all night. Drinking. The cook locked himself in the galley. He's afraid to come out, and you can hardly blame him."

"What about the other girl, the stowaway?" Appley got up and helped himself to the bottle.

"He sent her to Papa Joe with one of the natives. He's not taking her any farther." Nervously Fisher passed a hand through his damp hair, looking at Appley tilting the bottle to his lips. "He made me leave before I could get my things. I couldn't go below to bring anything with me."

Appley gazed at the label on the bottle. He said nothing.

Roper moved over and looked out the blinds at the incessant rain sweeping through the jungle night like tiny silver arrows.

"Not a thing," Fisher said. What sounded like a suppressed sob lingered in his throat. "He wouldn't let me get my things."

Roper watched the rain. It was one hell of a world, when you thought about it.

So why think about it?

He lit a cigarette and went out onto the veranda. In the east, above the line of dark jungle foliage, the sky had perceptibly lightened, the false dawn casting a ghostlike dimness across the row of thatch huts on the bank of the rain-swollen creek. Restlessly he threw his cigarette away, watching it expire in the muddy ground. He moved along the veranda and found himself standing before the rattan blinds serving as a door to the room Karen was in.

"You can come in, Johnny. I'm still awake."

She was lying on a narrow bed at the far side of the room, her figure barely discernible in the murky light penciling through the blinds at the window beside her. At first glance he thought she was nude. But a faint rustle of silk as she turned dispelled this tantalizing illusion.

"Believe it or not, Johnny, I'll take a place like this any day in preference to a dry stateroom with that man around. I heard everything that went on on deck, and when everyone began leaving the ship I couldn't pack my bag fast enough. I would've died if he had told me to go back to my room."

"You're getting a pretty rough deal for a passenger." He took a chair midway across the room, straddling it.

"He's really in a mood, isn't he? What do you think is going to come of all this, Johnny?"

"Hard to say. Silly business, tying a ship up this way. That's one drawback to a skipper's carrying his wife along. He's too apt to confuse his personal affairs with ship's business."

"Would you simply sail off if your wife left you the same way?"

"Without a second thought."

"I guess you would, at that. You're quite the cool and calculating man, Johnny Roper."

"I want nothing that isn't freely given—particularly from a woman." He lit a cigarette, the flare of the match revealing red hair tousled against the pillow, her green eyes looking across at him. He blew the match out, still seeing in the sudden darkness the silken contours of firm breasts and long tapering legs.

"Know something, Johnny? I'm beginning to ask myself if I'm just a little less smart than I've thought. I'm becoming afraid. More afraid, I think, than I've ever been in my life."

"You don't have to be," he said, feeling a sudden dryness in his throat. "Murdock has nothing personal against you. I doubt if he knows you're alive except for the times he sees you."

"I don't mean Murdock. I'm not afraid of him. Well, not too much, anyway. But when we reach Kuma, perhaps I'll be meeting someone like him, someone who ... well, someone a little uncivilized."

"Seems to me, Karen, you're skipper of your own ship. If you don't like where you're going, you just don't go. I don't think it would cost much to get passage on a fishing boat down the coast. There'll be a good many of them in here soon, I understand."

"Where would I go, Johnny?"

"Kendaponga's not too far. You could get a steamer from there."

"I mean where could I go from there?"

"Where do you want to go?"

"Home, perhaps."

"So?"

"But not the way I came."

He drew on his cigarette, finding it tasteless as a faint fragrance persisted in his nostrils. In the gloom of the room he couldn't see her expression, barely detecting the smooth olive lines of her face, the gentle rise and fall of her breasts.

"I'm really beat up financially, Johnny. Even owing for my passage. There's no turning back. I'm not even sure I'd want to if I could. In that way, I think we're somewhat the same. Neither of us is willing to feed on crumbs when a full-course dinner is within reach. We might struggle with our consciences for a while, but I think that's only a sham, a stall for time while we're gathering enough nerve to take the step."

He didn't reply. Outside, the rain had changed its tempo, blowing against the thatched sides of the house in quick furious blasts. The sound seemed to isolate them from the world, giving him a sharp awareness of the woman only a few feet away. He got to his feet, sensing that she was watching him, sensing in her silence a kindred awareness of their being so completely, so utterly alone.

He moved over and stood looking down at her. He waited then for her to speak. One coy word would have broken the spell, erected a barrier. She remained silent.

He dropped to his knees beside her.

"You're a lonely man, aren't you, Johnny?" she whispered, her arms reaching to enfold him. "So terribly lonely."

He buried his mouth against the warm smoothness of her throat, his whole being alive to the need for this woman. She trembled under his hands. "Johnny ... Johnny...."

Hungrily her mouth sought his, with no submissiveness, but meeting him on equal terms. She arched to him, her arms tightly about his neck, her kisses demanding. The sound of the rain blowing through the jungle was lost in his name as she murmured it, her warm breath against his.

"Now we're arguing in circles again, Karen. O.K. We'll put it this way. There's no reason for both of us to dirty ourselves. I'll do what's got to be done to give us a start. A year at the most on this freighter, another with Fazio—"

"While I'm waiting?"

"Damnit, Karen, that can't be helped! I've got to go on. I'm fed up living in hall rooms, scratching on shipping-office doors. This freighter is the answer to that. I've got to go on with it."

"Johnny, a hundred things could come between us in the time I'm waiting. Not in the way I feel about you, or even in the way you feel about me. But out here, in the business you're in, in the things you'll be doing, the dangers ... Johnny, it just wouldn't work out. I wish I could believe that it could, but I know it wouldn't."

He got up and began dressing, feeling it futile to argue any longer. He couldn't blame her for refusing to relinquish her independence for the uncertain future he was offering. His present course was studded with shoals, any one of which could leave her stranded, and as badly off as before, should she tie herself to him.

She sat up on the bed, tucking her feet under her and rearranging her gown. "Angry, Johnny?"

"No. Not angry." He lit two cigarettes and handed her one. He sat down beside her. "You know that I love you, Karen. Doesn't come easy, saying that. New line for me."

"Oh, Johnny ..." She drew against him, linking her arm through his, nuzzling her nose against his cheek. "Johnny, darling, it's taking all my will power to act rational, to keep from agreeing to anything you say. But if we parted now, Johnny—if I allowed you to ship me off somewhere to wait—I have the feeling we'd never see each other again. Be truthful now: Don't you feel the same?"

He did, but he got up without answering and moved to the door, where the dreary dawn was beginning to show through. "So what's it to be, Karen?" He turned swiftly, his voice harsh. "Been fun? Good-by?"

Quietly she looked over at him. "Does any woman in love want it that way? Johnny, I'm willing to take that fishing boat you spoke of, take it up the coast or anywhere else. But you'd have to be with me."

"That's impossible!"

"I suppose it is. Then I'll have to go on to Kuma."

"And what happens there?"

"I don't like the way you ask that, Johnny."

"You reword it!" he snapped. "Tie a fancy ribbon on it. But what happens at Kuma?"

Her head steadied defiantly, her eyes glinting in the half-light. "Let me answer you this way: How long have you been out here, Johnny? Three years? Well, so have I. And you couldn't take it during those three years, could you? Well, neither could I. So far, the only difference between us is that you've already sold yourself. I'm not condemning you, Johnny, but you grew sick of being kicked around and put yourself on the block. Well, I haven't sold myself—yet. That's right. I said yet." Her lips began trembling. "Now let me tell you something. Things can be just as rough on a woman—so rough she can make up her mind to compromise while she still has part of her self-respect left. Lose all your self-respect and you never regain it. That's a bitter truth, but it is the truth. The smart ones compromise. To put it bluntly, they offer what they can at the highest price and the shortest length of time. Yes, I've heard of Dachong. I've known one of the girls who returned from Kuma. And only one thing impressed me: Nothing showed except the well-tailored clothes she bought, and the diamond clip she could never have hoped to see except in a jeweler's window before she went to Kuma. All right. I've said it. I'm out to get all I can while I still have the chance. And I'll ask you not to condemn me."

He stood looking at her, fuming at the helplessness of his position. "Karen, you state a case for yourself. But it's one that can be shot full of holes. When I'm through in these waters I'll be measured by what I have, not by what I've done."

"The fine distinction between a man and a woman." She nodded. "But, Johnny, I don't intend to walk around with a sign hung on me."

"You won't have to, Karen. Believe me, none of them ever need a sign hung on them."

He went out before she could answer. A pleasant episode, no harm done, he thought. No promises, no ties. Think of it that way.

If he could.

The recall to the *Wanderer* came eight days later. Everyone was happy to leave the creek huts. The crew, finally running out of funds and no longer able to buy either women or liquor, needed little coaxing to return to dry quarters. Neither did Appley or Roper. Both were tired from a continuous patrolling of the creek, preventing the hands from foolishly slipping off into the interior in search of females, who were no longer in evidence now that the crew had hardly pocket change between them.

The relationship between Roper and Karen had remained on a speaking basis, but no more. He did not again bring up the subject of her leaving the freighter, for he had no argument to offer against leaving with her. None except his firm resolve to complete what he started out to do. He sensed that he might once again become physically close to her if he desired, but that now their relationship would be only on a physical level. And he had no wish to cheapen the bond between them, however intangible it was at the moment.

Little was seen of Fisher during the entire eight days. He had not stayed in the bungalow with Roper and Appley, but had occupied a vacant hut across the creek. Several times Roper had seen him emerge from the hut, violently trembling, being sick among the foliage. Once, on the third day, Roper had visited the hut and found him sitting on a bamboo mat discolored with dark patches of dried betel juice. He was turning his glasses over and over in his hands, gazing vacantly at them.

He appeared embarrassed when Roper sat down beside him. "I've made quite a spectacle of myself these last few days, Mr. Roper. Quite a spectacle."

"Look, Fisher, I don't know much about—about the stuff. But can't you ..." Roper hesitated again, wondering how to put it.

Fisher faintly smiled. "Can't I break the habit?" He removed a handkerchief from his pocket and slowly cleaned the lenses of his glasses. "This time I have no choice. I didn't mention this, but Murdock went down to my locker and removed what I had before I left. It'll be weeks before we reach a port where I can get any more." He paused, as if contemplating what that span of time would mean to him. "You know, Mr. Roper," he finally went on, "I have a family in the States. Wife and a boy. Well, the boy's really a man now. A fine man. Be graduating from law school soon. I've always managed to send enough home to see to that much."

"Putting your pay to good use." Roper said his opinion of the engineer rising.

Fisher sighed, shaking his head. "I could have done more for them. Much more for my wife. A good women, Mr. Roper. A wonderful woman." He continued cleaning his glasses absently. "They wonder why I don't come home. I can't, of course. They ... they don't know about me, and I don't want them to know. If I were home for any length of time they'd be bound to guess the truth."

He put his glasses on and adjusted them. "Mr. Roper, how can it be fought? I don't drink or smoke. Would that help?"

Roper honestly didn't know, and said so.

Fisher turned to him. "I've got to do without it, Mr. Roper. Murdock has it, so I've got to do without it. Perhaps that's the answer. If I just can't get it, perhaps the craving will die. And if it does ..." His voice dropped to a whisper. "Mr. Roper, if it does I'll go home. They want me to. They keep saying so in the letters. We were very close, you know. The three of us. Affectionate family. Affectionate," he repeated, as if savoring the word. "Yes, indeed. And both quite proud of me at one time. Well, they still are, as a matter of fact. That's why I've stayed away. No matter what happens, I don't want them to know what a weakling I am." He smiled sadly. "That's what I call giving oneself the benefit of the doubt: weakling. Murdock was more precise in his definition."

"I wouldn't worry about Murdock," Roper said. "In many ways he's a small man. Smaller than any of us. Fisher, would it help if you came back to the bungalow? We'd like to have you."

Fisher fumbled with his glasses again, obviously embarrassed. "I appreciate your thought, Mr. Roper. But for a time I'd better stay here." Awkwardly he added, "I'm a sight when I become ill. I shall, you know. Quite often."

Roper patted the other's shoulder and got up. "Drop over then when you feel like it. Papa Joe sent us a roasted ham. Be a change for you from those dry sandwiches they send over from the ship."

Brown was not a well man when he mounted the steps of the veranda to announce that the *Wanderer* was to put to sea. His eyes were feverish and the side of his jaw, covered with a blood-encrusted bandage, was swollen.

He got no sympathy from Appley. "Maybe when your jaw rots you'll think twice before opening it again," he said. "Did those boys ever come back with news of Djerf or Kim?"

Brown didn't know. He had been confined to Djerf's room, racked by a fever from his infected jaw. He had been fed by the cook.

"Could 'ear 'im walkin' the deck the 'ole time. Cursin' the cook back into the galley every time 'e set a foot out. Grubtime 'e could serve meals, but at night 'e made 'im stay in the galley."

"Then no one else is aboard?"

He shook his head. "Jus' Murdock an' Cookie...." His bloodshot eyes narrowed. "Blimy, the stern! The lock on the stern!"

Brown looked from Roper to Appley with his mouth opening. "There's a padlock on the stern 'ousing. A padlock." He stupidly shook his head. "There never was a padlock on the 'ousing before. Was there, now?" he asked Appley.

The mate gazed off across the creek, where the Chinese and engine-room blacks were straggling toward the path leading to the wharf. To Roper he said, "Better tell the girl to pack."

Appley descended the veranda steps, leaving Brown's question unanswered as he started back to the ship.

Chapter Nine

Molten copper flamed on the western horizon, the wisps of clouds above it reflecting the fading sunlight. Overhead in the dusky sky gulls glided in a follow-the-leader pattern, sweeping across the bridge of the freighter as it moved through the cobalt sea. Fluttering uncertainly after the gulls was a green pigeon, a stray from the receding shores of Sumatra.

"I've seen them die by the thousands," Roper said, nodding up at the pigeon. He moved in beside Karen, who was leaning back against the weatherboard with folded arms. "When they follow a ship out too far, they occasionally get caught in a heavy squall and are driven into the sea. Terrible thing to watch. They scream like humans when they find they're going under."

Karen said nothing. A jacket about her slim shoulders against the night air, she gazed morosely down at the forepeak watch, whose head was sleepily nodding at the horizon.

"All right," Roper said gruffly. "So he's padlocked the stern. Does it mean he's got them in chains back there? Who saw them come aboard? No one. Let's be sensible about this."

"Then why did he lock that door back there? That doesn't make sense."

"Face, Miss Gorman." Appley came out of the chartroom. "Face, and that damn ego of his," he continued, lowering his voice. "It well suits his purpose to have the crew believing he's got them aft and maybe torturing them. In fact, right this minute he's enjoying the state of mind he knows you and the others are in."

Karen shivered as she drew the jacket closer about her. "Last night I couldn't sleep for thinking about it. But if it is a farce, he can't keep it up indefinitely. The truth would have to come out sooner or later, wouldn't it?"

"The point is, the truth doesn't have to come out." Appley accented his words with the stem of his pipe. "When that compartment is opened, who will say two bodies were not disposed of after a time of torment? He knows Djerf and Kim would be in fear of him wherever they went and unlikely to use their true names. So with no one to point a finger and say, 'Here are the man and woman who put one over on Murdock,' there's no one to say they aren't dead, that Murdock didn't get his revenge. Follow his reasoning? A feeble attempt to save face, yes, but island legends have been woven from thinner stuff. That visit to the stern with his Bible last night was all part of the act, miss; all part of the act."

Roper was also positive Murdock was pulling a childish bluff to save face. If the Bushmen had brought the two runaways back, he was sure the word would have been quickly passed along the creek. There was not a shred of evidence that two people had been forcibly brought aboard—despite the fact that there was talk by the hands of muffled screams heard the first night under way. Roper knew this talk was nonsense and nothing else. He was on watch that night and had seen the shadowy figure of Murdock pass along the well deck, Bible in hand, on his way aft. He had seen him enter the housing, and during the short time he was in the stern Roper had heard nothing. Certainly no screaming.

But rumors from the forecastle grew as Murdock's nightly visits to the stern continued, and with the coolie deck hands' acceptance of a man and woman astern, at the mercy of Murdock, a kind of tension settled over the vessel. Scarcely a man set foot on the main deck who did not glance aft at the housing, some merely curious, others plainly sobered by what the padlock symbolized. Murdock never verified, by word or action, the crew's fears. A distinct change had come over him since the vessel had got under way. He was quiet. He seldom spoke to anyone. When on deck he would walk thoughtfully about, a cigar clamped in his mouth, his yellow eyes directed seaward, never at an individual. His attitude was that of a well-satisfied and untroubled being.

Once he lapsed into his brutal ways, but even this was done in a quiet manner. It was the fourth day out and the freighter's engines had developed overheated bearings. They were forced to lie to while Fisher labored through the entire night and then into the next day.

Now it was common knowledge on the ship that Fisher was making a determined effort to break the narcotic habit. True, he had no choice, since Murdock had taken his supply, but he was doing everything in his power to obtain mastery over his body. He admitted to Roper that food sickened him, but he forced himself to eat in an attempt to keep something in his stomach. He took up smoking, literally eating cigarettes every waking hour. The tremendous effort he was exerting was evident many times at night, when he would be found topside, doubled over with abdominal cramps, hands gripping the railing, his body soaked with sweat. Although two weeks was too short a time to break such a deep-rooted craving, Fisher had confided in Roper that it now did not seem as impossible as it once had. He was able to sleep for longer periods of time, and where once he would have writhed helplessly in pain on waking, he was now able to rise with relatively small discomfort.

When Murdock called Fisher to the bridge after he had completed his engine-room repairs, he handed Fisher a small oilskin packet.

Fisher looked at the packet as if dazed. "I—I ..." He moistened his lips. "Captain, I don't need this."

"Throw it over the side, then," Murdock said quietly. "It's your property, not mine." He turned and strolled over to the weatherboard, as if the matter were closed.

Helplessly Fisher gazed at Murdock's broad back a moment, then he slowly looked down again at what he held in his hands. His hands began trembling.

Roper, standing nearby with a sextant, calmly reached over and removed the packet from Fisher's hands. He sent it skimming far out over the waters.

Murdock stiffened at the action, but he did not turn, nor did he speak until Fisher had left the bridge. Then he removed a cigar from his pocket and began examining it.

"Roper," he said, "there are just so many lines in a ledger. Then an account is reckoned. Maybe you've got the idea I'm in the habit of doing a bit of erasing now and then. I'm not. But you'll have to be shown, I'm afraid. That will be my pleasure, Mr. Roper. On the day of reckoning it will be my pleasure."

He walked off without once glancing Roper's way.

With the passing of the fifth day, as they made their way westward, only a few of the crew remained of the opinion that Murdock actually had prisoners in the stern. Quite rapidly the men began to feel foolish on being so easily taken in, Karen included. The disbelief now stemmed from the fact that although Murdock could still be seen making his way aft nightly, he carried nothing with him but his Bible—no food or water. How long, it was asked, could anyone survive without food or water? Food, of course, could be done without for a time. Hardly water.

Among the few still believing the stern occupied, Brown was unshaken in his belief that Djerf and Kim were aboard. He had been temporarily elevated to the rank of mate, and when relieving Roper on watch he would speak of the prisoners aft as if their presence there were a proven fact. He would point out that the *Wanderer* had left Sumatra after only an eight-day delay, that the Bushmen would not have returned so swiftly with empty hands; they would have continued searching longer for a reward in hard cash.

"Murdock probably didn't even wait for them to return," Roper observed. "No one saw them come back, and the more I think of it, the more I doubt that Murdock wanted to catch up with them at all."

Brown shook his head, immediately wincing and touching his hand gingerly to his still bandaged jaw. "'E wanted them back. Can be bloody sure of that. Sailed with the bugger long enough to know 'im."

"How's the jaw coming along?" Roper's ear had caught a slight sound on the bridge ladder.

"Like a blasted toothache at night," Brown answered bitterly. "'E didn't 'ave to do it, 'e didn't. 'E won't even give me Djerf's berth, neither. 'Temporary,' 'e says. I know what's in 'is mind, all right. The blasted money. 'E just don't want to cut me in for a full mate's—" He broke off abruptly, his frightened eyes darting over Roper's shoulder.

Murdock was standing in the wing, gazing ahead into the night.

"Roper," he said, "I've been waiting for you below. If you're finished listening to Mr. Brown's complaints, there's some business to be discussed in my cabin."

Below in the cabin Murdock motioned Roper into the chair by his desk. Then he sat down behind it, snapping on the lamp. From a lower drawer he pulled out a thick sheaf of papers. "We lie off the outer barrier at Kuma, Roper, in case you still don't know the routine there. Junks will load us. You're going in with me to assist in the purchasing, a second pair of eyes. Damn well need them, dealing with this Chinaman. I'm going to rely on you to keep a sharp eye peeled for signs of damage to crates, and for jungle rot or corrosion on any type of instrument or machinery. Now this list here"—he tapped the papers with his finger—"is pretty complete and up to date. It reflects the wholesale price of just about every commodity traded in these parts. We're buying at one-third wholesale and selling at two-thirds. That's our spread. We have to be on our toes not to narrow that. We'll accept no jewelry or anything that might have been a personal belonging. No matter how cheap the price, it might turn out expensive if it's ever traced."

He pushed the papers toward Roper. "Take these with you. The prices quoted are for reference only. We'll get the stuff as cheap as possible. But study the list so he knows he's dealing with businessmen. Save a lot of bargaining, fiddling around."

Roper took the papers, folded and slipped them into his pocket.

"As a point of information, Roper ..." Murdock leaned back in his chair, away from the circle of light thrown by the desk lamp. His expression was obscured by shadows. "As a point of information, what's your opinion regarding a master's right to punish those breaking a law aboard?"

"Depends on what law is broken."

Murdock nodded his agreement. He placed his hands on the desk; as if by a sleight-of-hand trick, a thin-bladed bone-handled knife appeared between them. A bead of light traveled along the edge of the blade as he slowly turned it. "In any event, the formula 'hold for authorities' might be safely followed, don't you think?"

Roper watched the play of light along the well-honed edge, wondering what lay behind Murdock's words. Djerf and Kim had violated no law for which they could legally be detained by a shipmaster. And what authority could they be turned over to? The answer here, of course, was that no such thing was intended if they actually had been apprehended and brought back.

He still didn't believe any such thing had taken place.

"Five days," Murdock murmured. He deftly flipped the knife. It hit the desk, the point imbedded and quivering under the desk light.

Suddenly Roper understood that Murdock was attempting to feel him out, to probe the extent to which he was disturbed by the mystery of the padlock. He wondered if a question or two might settle the mystery.

"When a member of the crew is held," Roper said, "he's entitled to food and water. Otherwise, he'd die." With frankness he went on, "If you expect anyone to believe that Djerf is being held in a pit aft after five days, you're mistaken. Forty-eight hours of this climate will dry a man up."

"Or a woman?" Murdock leaned forward, elbows on the desk, the light falling across his heavy face. "You forgot the woman, Roper."

"Or a woman," he acknowledged. "Neither one could exist without food or water."

Murdock slowly nodded, his lips pursed and eyes suddenly thoughtful. "Food and water are needed, true. Especially the water. Now, where would we get water aft, Roper? Suppose you were ..." He pulled the blade from the desk and examined the tip. "Suppose you were Djerf, Roper, and say you wanted to live. Let's say there was something you had to live for—right beside you. Where would *you* get the water?"

"I wouldn't know." Roper rose to his feet. "If you don't mind, I'll—"

"You wouldn't know? Why, Roper, in this climate you just spoke of you could lick the sweat from the plates. You wouldn't get much water, but it'd always be there, and you'd stay alive—if you liked living enough." He felt the tip of the blade, picking at it with his fingernail. "Your lips would swell, Roper, maybe tear from the rust on that steel, but you'd stay alive. And I guess your teeth might roughen up a bit, trying to get more than a few drops of water at a time when there just isn't any. But you'd stay alive, Roper." He flipped the blade into the desk again, his yellow eyes lifting to Roper. "You'd be living, *both* of you! Living and wishing you had the nerve to stop drinking so you could die."

Roper was suddenly aware that his shirt was dampened with sweat. The very thought that a man and woman might be chained in a pit these five days and existing on beads of moisture was rapidly turning his stomach.

"For food, Roper, there's always the rats. They'd be bound to be attracted. Of course, you'd probably have to be more than five days without food to go for something like that. Say seven. Or eight. Think a rat would look appetizing after—"

Roper closed the door on the rest of it. Another entry Murdock could make in his ledger, but he didn't care. For a moment he stood in the companionway, feeling the night wind drying his moist face, fighting for control of his feelings. He had an overpowering urge to go aft and smash the lock on that housing, but he controlled this also as reason took hold.

He entered Appley's stateroom without knocking. The chubby mate was sitting on his bunk, holding a shoe in one hand.

"You look like hell," Appley observed, pulling on the shoe.

"I feel like it." Roper dropped into a chair and stretched his legs out. Briefly he began relating what had been said in the cabin.

Appley took a bottle and glasses from his bureau. He washed the glasses at the small washstand.

"So he's getting under your skin?" Appley poured a generous quantity of liquor into each glass. "Don't you know he enjoys seeing anybody sweat? He's in there now, chuckling to himself over putting one under your guard."

Roper toyed with the glass. "Probably he is. Appley, what would you do if you knew for certain a pit was occupied?"

Appley tossed his drink down. "Not a damned thing. That's why you're going in to Kuma with him, and not me. He knows that lock won't be touched with me aboard."

He banged his glass on the table for emphasis. "Only one thing is on my mind, Roper: buying those goods, transporting 'em back to Java waters, and getting rid of 'em at a good profit. If you think I'm ready to start a rhubarb on this ship or give Murdock a hot foot in any way, you're mistaken. And I'm not letting you start one, either!" He snapped the last out, glaring at Roper.

Roper pushed his glass aside and got up. "I didn't intend to start anything. I was just curious to know if you had any conscience left."

Appley refilled his glass, his mouth narrowing as he looked up. "Maybe I have more than you think. Maybe I'm paying for each buck I put into my pocket. Goddamnit, man, sit down and finish your drink so we can part still talking to each other! Have you thought of the larger cut you'll be getting when we tally up? We're hoping for a hundred grand from Kuma, net. With one less to divide it among, your share will be fatter."

Roper accepted the glass Appley pushed across. "You've got Djerf's share square-rooted in with ours pretty fast. When did you figure that out?"

Appley's red cheeks creased into a grin. "That night I heard he beat it. Look, Roper, forget the stern. I'll lay you a hundred to one that place is empty. Hell, knowing Murdock's tricky ways, I'll make it a thousand to one. Now what do you say we finish this bottle?"

"That I'm in the mood to do."

She answered his knock by opening her door, but she didn't move aside. Her attitude was not a belligerent one, rather one of restraint, something she had been practicing from the night they had reached their impasse.

"We'll be getting in sometime tomorrow morning," he said. "Thought you'd like to know."

"Thank you, Johnny. Will you be going ashore?"

"I'll be there during the time the *Wanderer* will be buying. Week, maybe."

"A week?" Her voice faltered as she looked at him, her eyes betraying a chagrin at something she had not counted on: his presence during even a portion of her employment. "Well ..." She smiled tentatively. "Be nice having you around, even for a while."

It wouldn't, of course; he saw her embarrassment. "It's not too late to back out, Karen. Remain aboard if you wish and return with us. Once we weigh anchor and leave, there won't be any choice. We're the only steamer putting in to Kuma, you know."

"Yes, I know. But I've always managed to take care of myself. Besides, I'm afraid there isn't much choice now. Not when you think about it."

There wasn't. And he'd done plenty of thinking about it. Both of them were trapped—not physically, but by their own momentum toward a common goal. Neither of them could turn back. Not only would it be conceding defeat, but there was nothing to turn back to.

At dawn the *Wanderer* dropped its anchor to the lee of a deserted atoll, a strip of wild scrub looking lonely and forlorn in the wide rolling sea. Driftwood littered a sloping sandy beach. The atoll was less than a mile long, and not more than several hundred yards at its widest point. A single tree stood in its center, long dead, its limbs twisted and naked. Apparently a wind-blown seed had found its way here and fought to maturity before final surrender.

East of the atoll a small purple mound was emerging from the sea haze, the island soon silhouetted against a brightening horizon. And from that direction, within an hour of the freighter's anchoring, two dark specks appeared; the triangular sails of outrigger canoes taking shape slowly.

The canoes came up, beating to windward, manned by young slant-eyed men with bodies burned to the color of mahogany. They grinned and shouted a welcome to the *Wanderer's* crew along the rail, exchanging ribald remarks with some of the deck hands who had stripped in preparation for swimming off the atoll.

Karen and Murdock boarded one of the canoes, which immediately put out. It was left up to Roper to see to the luggage; and when he finally descended the Jacob's ladder into the second outrigger, the first canoe was lost to sight in the distance.

Tacking under the *Wanderer's* stern, the outrigger heeled over in the smooth sea and then headed eastward toward the island. Roper settled back, his thoughts moving ahead, to the business at Kuma. If the deal there ran to a hundred thousand net profit, as Appley predicted, then at the end of the first quarter he should have a sizable check, enough to be well on his way.

He tried not to think of the slave pits in the *Wanderer's* stern.

Chapter Ten

As they approached the island, skirting ominous avenues of dark green appearing in the water, the sail was lowered and stowed; the boys took to their paddles, cautiously feeling their way through the last of the treacherous barrier, crusted coral growths that could be seen lying below the surface like wind-swept dunes. Once through, the outrigger was sent skimming parallel to a palm-fringed beach, a picturesque spot of pink sand in the brilliant sunlight and dark foliage stirring lazily in the background. Beyond the trees low hills sloped gently into the interior of the island, all having streaks of green and gold that Roper recognized as terraced rice fields.

When they left the beach behind, rounding a breakwater of boulders jutting from the shore, a small fishing village sprang into view. It lay huddled in a deep cove where rotted piles and bamboo planking served as quays to more than a dozen fishing junks tied there. Stilted houses of thatch stood high on the mudbanks, and back in small clearings half-naked men in loincloths were busy repairing fishing traps, some stretching sails of matting between trees for drying and patching. A group of naked children engaged in a mud-slinging contest as they ran back and forth under a clothesline bright with sarongs. A large buxom woman wearing what appeared to be a white nightdress captured one of the children and upended him across her knee. The vigorous smacks of her palm against the bare bottom came clearly across the water.

Roper did not join in the laughter of the two boatmen. He was speechlessly gazing at a heavily laden freighter all but concealed in the left pocket of the cove. From stem to stern the vessel had been covered with matting, brush, and palms. Even her masts were well covered; they looked like two tall trees bearing skimpy branches. The ship was camouflaged most heavily across her decks, apparently to hide her from above. Her stack looked like an enormously fat clump of palms rising from an impenetrable area of island growth. Near the top of the stack, despite its covering of palms, the red, white, and green circles of East-

West Transport were visible.

Roper was dazed for the moment at the implications of the vessel's presence here. Certainly his former firm could not be engaged in handling pirated goods. Or could it?

When he asked what the vessel was doing there, the boatmen simply exchanged glances and shrugged. Either they did not know or they did not feel free to talk.

Roper settled back again, grimly reflecting that there was much that did not show up in a shipping company's annual report.

Outside the cove the shoreline became rocky and dense with jungle growth, but only for a few hundred yards. A jungle-bowered inlet appeared as the canoe turned into the shore, a high-banked opening quickly widening into a lagoon choked with mangroves and twisting vines. The pungent smell of fungus lay heavy in the air here. Fat tropical rats scurried about in the dreary surroundings, unmolested by mottled crocodiles, which watched with eyes the widening ripples of the canoe's wake.

From the lagoon they entered a tree-shaded canal with frond-roofed bamboo houses along its banks. A group of native women, all wearing sarongs of vivid colors and operating hand looms beneath a lean-to of palms, stared curiously as they went by. Before the last house, a handsome full-bodied girl was bathing. She stood naked with both feet in a wooden tub, soaping her face and neck, her eyes squeezed shut against the lather. She became aware of the presence of the outrigger only when the two boys laughingly shouted approval of the fine view they were afforded. She simply turned her back, a single lazy movement of her hips expressing her disdain.

The village proper was heralded by a faint sour odor peculiar to native junks. From the darkness of the canal the outrigger suddenly burst out onto another lagoon, one of tremendous size and crowded with twin-masted seagoing junks. Perhaps a mile at its widest point, it had every appearance of a thriving deep-water harbor. Low warehouse sheds occupied its banks. From the sheds stilted wharves jutted over the water, and native crews were busy unloading crates and bales from junks tied there. Oxcarts piled high with goods lumbered from the wharves to the sheds along the shore, young boys using switches to keep the animals moving. Beyond the wharves and sheds were scores of small houses, all roofed with mats or fronds, and farther back, above the thick foliage of the forest, the tiled eaves of a pagoda could be seen glinting in the sunlight.

The outrigger made for one of the wharves and Roper then caught sight of a white man in loose-fitting ducks who stood by a jeep apparently waiting for them. He was a thin man in his forties, gray and partly bald. Repeatedly he wiped the perspiration that shone from his high forehead with a red bandanna. He came forward as the canoe drew alongside the wharf and extended a helping hand to Roper.

"The others went up to the house," he said, his breath emitting a strong odor of native wine. "I thought I'd stay behind as a welcoming committee. Griffith. M.D. Leave the bags. I'll have a boy take care of them later."

Griffith looked the typical island lush. His cheeks were sunken from lack of nourishment, the flesh puffy beneath listless eyes. A network of tiny veins crept down his thin nose, giving it an unsightly raw look. There was nothing in his appearance to inspire confidence in a patient, and it was obvious why he sought a medical practice on a remote jungle island. On the mainland he would be hard pressed gathering enough fees to satisfy the unquenchable thirst of an alcoholic.

They drove off the wharf and turned down a rutted road where women squatted outside small thatched houses tending cooking fires. Chickens roosted drowsily in the frond roofs of some of the houses they passed, while goats and fat hump-backed heifers freely grazed off the road.

They continued through the village, the jungle closing in as the houses became fewer. Patches of sunlight dappled the road ahead, a strong odor of manure drifting into the car as they crossed a plank bridge into a thinning forest. Then they were driving parallel to a clearing stretching several miles to the sloping terraced hills Roper had seen from the sea.

"These are the farms," Griffith explained. "It took more than three years to clear and cultivate them. Quite a job."

"Many whites on the island?" Roper asked.

"At the present time, one besides myself. Chap named Hock. An American. He's captain of the *Equatian Star*, that freighter you probably saw on the way in."

"Here to give Murdock some competition?"

Griffith shook his head. He moved the wheel to bypass two children digging a hole in the center of the road with their hands. "He's here on other business. It will concern Murdock's ship, so you'll hear about it later."

Within five minutes Griffith turned off into a side road dividing several wooden shacks and two elevated water tanks on steel tripods. A few hundred feet beyond, a wide-spreading house came into view, a rambling, timber-roofed bungalow with extending wings connected by a common veranda. Constructed of a bluish fieldstone, it was set back from the jungle road by a sloping stone terrace lavished with tall palms and hanging vines, and small circular beds of colorful flowers.

On the terrace, Murdock and two men sat at a table, tall glasses at hand, a white-coated boy standing silently a few feet away. One of the men, a fat heavy-jowled Chinese, was wearing nothing but a bright purple loincloth and sandals. The other man was a Westerner, a blunt-jawed, swarthy man with a long hooked nose dividing the thin black mustache he wore. A visored cap sat jauntily on his head. When he threw back his head, laughing at something the Chinese said, his teeth flashed white under the black mustache.

Murdock was taking no part in the conversation. He was sitting in shirt sleeves, sifting through papers lying before him, frowning with concentration as he made notations.

"When you're talking to Da-chong," Griffith said, pulling up and parking alongside another jeep, "don't forget he's respected on this island as top boy. He may look a little comical, but he's absolute authority here. Smile at the wrong moment and you'll be *persona non grata*. The other man is Hock."

Roper glanced up at the house again, looking in vain for signs of Karen. She was not in sight, but he was rather relieved to see other females about. On the veranda an aged woman dozed in a wicker rocker. A dog lay panting at her feet. Nearby a naked child sat on a step, absorbed in manipulating the arms of a rag calico doll. In the left wing three young girls were sitting on a porch swing, engaged in needlework on a cloth spread across their laps.

Lounging on the railing and watching the girls were two muscular Chinese. They were tall men with broad, high-boned features. Both wore light-brown trousers, cut off unevenly below the knees, black leather belts about their waists holding sheath knives.

Griffith verified their Mongol origin as they walked up the terrace. "Da-chong uses them as bodyguards. Ugly boys when they go into action. All muscle, no brains. Never know when to stop."

Only Da-chong rose in greeting as Griffith and Roper approached. An immense flabby-breasted man with cropped head and smooth bland features, he shook Roper's hand, his piglike fleshy eyes smiling with politeness as he asked in precise English if the voyage to the island had been a pleasant one.

Roper replied it had been. The fat Chinese, his navel protruding over the loincloth, reminded him of an oversized Kewpie doll wearing diapers.

Hock briefly nodded, not bothering to rise. There was a perpetual smile on his thin lips, an arrogant set to his hawklike features. He had the look of a man both ruthless and confident, perfectly cast for an island adventurer.

Murdock continued with his computations, not so much as glancing upward in recognition of Roper's presence.

"Will you sit down, Mr. Roper? Doctor?" Da-chong heavily seated himself, his belly quivering. He beckoned the boy over. "I suppose you are anxious to look over what we have for you in the harbor?" He directed his words to Murdock while indicating to the houseboy that drinks were to be brought.

"I am," Murdock grunted. "As soon as possible. We'll get some of it moving tonight."

The broad yellow features reflected surprise. "Tonight? Come, come, Captain. You owe Mr. Roper at least one day of relaxation. An evening of entertainment has already been planned, with our Miss Gorman performing."

Murdock tossed aside his pencil. "I want the first junks out tonight. We've got commitments north and can't afford to waste time."

Apparently well accustomed to Murdock's domineering traits, Da-chong scratched a fold of his belly thoughtfully. "Suppose, Captain, we settle on an item in bulk, something that will require many hours in the transporting but that we can quickly reach a price agreement on. Lead. In twenty-five-pound ingots. Two hundred tons of it." He looked questioningly at Murdock. "Shall we make that the first to go out and thus leave us free for this evening?"

Murdock's eyes strayed over the papers before him. "Two and a half cents a pound?"

Da-chong gazed at the drink in his hand. "Agreed. I will give orders for it to move out immediately."

Roper nodded his thanks to the boy placing a drink before him, puzzled at Da-chong's immediate acceptance of Murdock's figure. Lead at fifty dollars a ton was a bargain. Murdock should get at least a hundred and twenty, a fourteen-thousand-dollar profit on his first item.

"Well, that was fast," Hock said. He tipped his cap farther back on his dark head and smoothed his mustache. "Suppose we do a little talking on this other thing?"

"Ah, yes. The *Equatian Star*...." Da-chong settled back, beaming across at Murdock, his manner indicating that he was about to make an announcement of some import. "Captain, what would you say if I told you that we shall be richer by several millions in gold within a few short months?"

Murdock was unimpressed. He lit up a cigar and blew the match out.

"I'll settle for cargos that have little identity left. When you speak of millions, it means somebody's been hurt bad enough to keep the wires hot in every consulate in the East."

Da-chong continued beaming. "Very true. But only when they *realize* they have been hurt. You will recall, Captain, the drop in tin prices about a year ago, the subsequent decline in the shipments of the metal to America. Naturally the warehouses north soon became full." His fleshy smile was transferred to Hock. "The Captain is not a man to permit opportunity to slip through his fingers. He foresaw shipments in bulk and a discreet inquiry found its way to me. What would you say, Captain Murdock, if someone offered to place a freighter with two thousand tons of tin in its holds into your hands? Would you listen?"

Two thousand tons of tin at a dollar a pound added up to four million dollars. The scope of such a theft dazed Roper. Murdock sucked on his cigar.

"It was not a simple matter of sailing the vessel to Kuma and handing it over," Da-chong continued. "However, anticipating a large shipment on his vessel, Captain Hock contacted me, and between us we worked out a foolproof plan. Our first step was gradually to replace his native crew with men from Kuma. This was performed easily enough, except for the officers. But even here Captain Hock had a free hand, and eventually the *Equatian Star* was manned solely with Kuma men. A few months ago Malayan Smelting sold its entire stock and promised immediate delivery."

Roper listened to the Chinese relating how Hock, with all holds full of tin and cargos of lesser value, had sailed eastward toward the States, but at an opportune time had circled to the south and radioed that a fire had broken out in the holds and was out of control. After a suitable interval he radioed again that he was abandoning ship. Of course, he had done no such thing. He had changed his course for Kuma. From a recent Hong Kong paper it had been learned that the *Equatian Star* was written off as a total loss by the home office. The fact that none of its crew had been picked up was considered unfortunate, but not uncommon in a locality where open lifeboats were subject to drenching squalls capable of broaching the much larger junks.

When the tin was removed to the island, the *Equatian Star* would be taken into deep water and scuttled. Ship, men, and tin would have disappeared without a trace.

"You're going to have the *Wanderer* dispose of this tin?" Murdock asked, frowning at his cigar.

"Exactly. On her next trip she will carry the tin out. We have already arranged for a buyer at Shanghai. The price will be ten per cent over the current market quotation. You will be paid in gold, on which we may also expect a premium. One quarter of this you may keep."

One million dollars for Murdock! The thought that almost half of that amount would be divided among the *Wanderer's* officers was breathtaking to Roper. Well over a hundred thousand dollars in his own pocket. The gimmick, of course, was that the tin would go into Communist hands. This he didn't like, though he knew Murdock would have no compunctions regarding the buyer.

Murdock continued smoking his cigar, unperturbed, on the surface, at least, by the fantastic sum being offered as his share. "Ships," he said, "are frequently stopped in northern waters. Suppose the cargo is recognized?"

"That's our only risk," Hock answered. "But the profit—"

"*My* risk," Murdock corrected. "Why not dispose of it in small amounts, fifty, a hundred tons at a time? And through our usual outlets?"

"No good." Hock shook his head. "That would take two years, and I don't care to stick around that long to collect." He scowled at Murdock. "Hell, if you're afraid to handle it, we'll get somebody else."

Murdock regarded him coolly. "Go right ahead. Damn if I'll start getting greedy at this stage of the game. Just because you're in a hurry to collect is no reason to take unnecessary chances. That's what you're asking me to do. How do you know, Hock, this plan wasn't seen through when you radioed you were abandoning ship? Farfetched? Maybe. Maybe not. But we have no guarantee they're not waiting for a sucker play, counting on the entire load going north within a few months after the *Star* has been given up for lost. Turn into a glutton and we may damn well choke on too big a bite. I'll handle the tin, but on my terms. To hell with the premium. We'll siphon it through the islands with our other stuff. It's the best way. It's the *only* way I'll be counted in."

"It looks like we'll be counting you out," Hock said.

But Da-chong was impressed with this argument. "Perhaps, gentlemen, we can work out a compromise—interest Fazio or someone in buying Captain Hock's share. Disposing of it slowly might not be such a bad idea. Yes, that does sound more feasible. But we will talk of it later." He glanced with disapproval at Griffith, who was beckoning the boy to refill his glass. "Doctor, would you see Mr. Roper to his room? I'm sure he wishes to freshen up."

Griffith got to his feet, rather unsteadily. He was sweating freely, his coat dampened at the armpits "Damned malaria," he growled. He breathed heavily through his nostrils, making a soft whistling sound as he leaned on the table for support.

Hock chuckled. "First time I heard that malaria came in bottles."

The doctor attempted to draw himself up with dignity. His dislike of Hock was quite evident as he replied that in his case, alcohol effectively lessened the attacks. Beckoning to Roper, he moved toward the house.

Chapter Eleven

He found her in a room in the right wing, a high-ceilinged room with walls and floor of stone masonry, and a single window overlooking the jungle road where the jeeps were parked. A fiber mat covered the floor. The furnishings were similar to those in his own room, dainty Chippendale pieces awkwardly incongruous in these tropical surroundings; Roper hazarded a guess that they were all once part of a cargo from a luckless steamer waylaid by Da-chong's associates.

She was studying her reflection in a wide-mirrored vanity when he entered. A diaphanous skirt whirled about her slender ankles as she turned with a smile.

"How do you like it, Johnny?" She spread her arms wide, inviting his inspection.

Her costume was too elaborate to be authentic Balinese, but it came close to it, and was both colorful and picturesque. The headdress, a sunburst crown of reddish gold, blended exquisitely with the copper of her hair, vividly highlighting her green eyes and crimson lips. Golden winged epaulets adorned her shoulders, and these were laced into the upper part of her costume, a heavy woven cloth, also of reddish gold, which gave the illusion of metallic mesh. Her midriff was bare. About her waist a wide gold belt supported the transparent skirt, through which the seductive curve of her hips was faintly visible. Her slippers, also of gold, were spurred with tiny jeweled wings.

"Well?" She continued smiling, awaiting his answer. "I'm wearing flesh-colored tights, in case you're wondering."

"Very striking." He knew it was requiring an effort on her part to play this straight, a dancer displaying a costume to a friend, leaving unspoken the ugliness ahead.

She turned again to study her costume in the vanity mirror. "There's five hundred dollars invested here. I'll dazzle them with gold, if not talent."

He went along. "What does the getup symbolize? Some Balinese character?"

"Yes. The dance comes from Balinese folklore. A young girl saddened by her lover's death. She wishes to fly to the heavens to join him. But I hope they don't expect too much. Frankly, I consider myself a mediocre dancer. Well, more than that, perhaps, but nothing sensational. I depend on a darkened room and colored spotlights playing over this costume to gain the proper effect, and an orchestra to carry the mood. No matter how talented a performer is, she needs some fanfare. They tell me there'll be no special lighting, only a single guitar. Dancing to homemade rhythm and straight lighting has me worried a little."

"Cut it!" He was across the room and gripping her shoulders, keeping her facing the mirror, glaring at her reflection. "Neither that outfit you're wearing nor any dance you interpret is going to appeal to anyone around here! And you know it. What comes after the teaser? Tell me, Karen...." His fingers bit cruelly into her shoulders. "After the appetizer, what are you dishing out?"

She looked at her own reflection calmly. "Johnny, you'd better go."

"There's a name for what you're going to do!" he snarled, twisting her around to face him. "Or maybe there isn't. You're a clever girl. Maybe if the price is right, you'll show them a few tricks they haven't seen."

Her slap caught him across the cheek.

Roper stepped back away from her. In the same moment Murdock walked into the room.

"Aren't you poaching on private property, mister?" Murdock bit this out past the stump of the cigar in his mouth, while stonily taking in Karen's costume from head to foot. "Get down to the wharves, Roper, and check the lead that Chink was so quick to sell. Look over the other stuff, too. Raise hell if there's anything being slipped over on us. Let them see they have to contend with two of us.... What the devil's the costume for?" he asked Karen.

It was a good question, Roper thought, as he walked out without speaking; a damn good question. She needed that costume as much as he needed two heads.

Cargo lights formed a series of pale amber cones down the length of the wharf, touching the high-sterned junks tied there. From the darkness of the lagoon, where the shadows of other junks could be seen being sculled into position for loading, disembodied voices drifted across the water, the laughter of a woman, the cry of an infant, the faint and distant squawk of a parrot from the jungle across the lagoon.

Roper left the jeep on the road and walked down to where a chain of coolies were passing oblong bars of lead from a shed out to the wharf. He glanced at the lead and saw nothing amiss. Each bar was the usual size, and the weight could easily be verified by weighing at random.

A strong odor of creosote and decayed wood greeted him as he made his way onto the wharf to where a thin, round-shouldered lad was checking the ingots against a sheaf of papers. The tally boy, one foot resting on a cleat, the papers on his knee, was completely absorbed in his figures.

"Is this the first load?" Roper tilted his head at the junk alongside, where the lead was being deposited in neat even rows.

The boy straightened, gawking at Roper as if he were a ghost. Then his slanted eyes darted to the line of coolies. He seemed rather relieved at what he saw. He looked down at his tally sheet again, scratching his cropped head with a pencil.

"Number-one load." He nodded. A thin hand motioned to the other manned junks on the water. "All go out tonight. One goddamn quick job! Yes?" His even white teeth flashed in a forced smile, strengthening Roper's feeling there was something wrong somewhere.

Walking off the wharf, ignoring a dog sniffing at his heels, Roper strolled over to the shed from which the lead was being passed. He moved inside its dimly lighted interior.

Piled high near the door were bales of sheeted rubber. Farther on were miscellaneous crates, most of them of Japanese origin, according to their chop marks. He walked past these toward two neat pyramids of lead. Back in the gloom of the shed, in an unlighted section, he saw more pyramids of lead—but not so neat in appearance. The ingots looked as if they had been thrown haphazardly into piles.

Roper recognized the reason for the careless stacking A quick glance showed that fully half of the metal was not in its original shape, but had been on a ship apparently gutted by fire. Some of the bars had melted together, others were merely round lumps. It was strictly in the salvage class, material difficult to handle and difficult to market. A goodly discount would be demanded at the other end.

He left the shed, striding rapidly back onto the wharf, where the tally boy seemed deeply engrossed in his figures.

"When you reach the salvage you have inside," Roper snapped, "you can stop loading! I want an exact count of untouched bars sent up to the house and a duplicate sent to the ship. Anything clean you can send out. Anything touched by fire—*touched*, mind you—will not be accepted."

"Some difficulties, Mr. Roper?"

Da-chong was waddling down the wharf, his fat cheeks creased in a bland smile. He wore a long green sport shirt that draped over his massive belly and concealed the loincloth. He had the appearance of a man who had forgotten to put on the lower part of his pajamas. His sandals made slapping sounds against the wharf planking as he approached.

Walking in back of Da-chong were his two Mongols, casting fierce glances at the coolies scurrying aside, as if emphasizing the prestige of their position.

"We bought commercial lead," growled Roper. "Not stuff that would be discounted fifty per cent down the line."

The folds of fat imprisoning Da-chong's small black eyes expanded, as if in surprise. "But I thought Murdock had knowledge of the condition, that he had inspected the warehouses this afternoon. He offered two and a half cents a pound so quickly, I immediately took it for granted he had examined the lead and thought a quarter was a fair over-all price. The current quotation, I believe, is ten cents a pound, is it not?"

Roper went along with the face-saving exit being made. "Looks like a misunderstanding all around."

The Chinaman bowed, the palms of his hands and fingertips meeting. "Which it was. We can arrive at a new figure. Come, Mr. Roper, let us briefly go over the merchandise in a few other sheds. It will give you an idea of what we have."

For the better part of an hour Roper examined cargos in the warehouses amounting to over three thousand tons. Almost every conceivable item that could be found in Asiatic bottoms was sectioned off inside the sheds. From bags of cloves and amber sheets of rubber, neatly baled, and huge quantities of carpets that required half the floor space of a single shed, the cargos worked down to such items as cast-iron potbellied stoves, commodes, brass piping, and nails.

By a section containing several hundred spools of Manila line, Da-chong smilingly recounted to Roper an incident off Timor, an adventure he had personally taken part in.

"She was a French packet, fogbound in a reef passage while on her way to Bali. This rope we took from her holds, quite a profitable take from so small a vessel. But our true prize was the sport offered by a dozen quite refined ladies on a holiday from their finishing school. Can you picture each young mademoiselle's chagrin on learning they were not so original in their choice of a suitable hiding place for jewelry? Such squealing, Mr. Roper, you have never heard."

"Suppose we go back to the house," Roper said abruptly, immediately losing interest in a mental tabulation of the value of the Manila line.

The Chinese gave him a side glance. "The hour is late, true. I will send your jeep back and we can ride together."

On the way back Roper sat silently in the rear of the car beside Da-chong, morosely occupied with the thought that he was hardly better than the thieves who had outraged that packet and its passengers. The little tale brought home forcefully to him the fact that he wasn't simply buying cargos and then taking part in the resale, but that he was wallowing in slime. Karen's point that nothing she was engaged in was as low as the trade he was following was certainly well taken.

The hell with thinking about it, he decided. Get the job done, then forget about it. A few years from now it will only be a memory.

Hock laughingly swung the girl onto his lap. "Live it, Roper!" he drunkenly shouted across the table. "You too Murdock. Hell, this ain't a wake!"

Da-chong smiled tolerantly as he patted his thick lips with a napkin. "Every man to his own taste." He picked up a wine bottle and leaned across Griffith to refill Murdock's glass, "I think the Captain and Mr. Roper are waiting to see our Miss Gorman perform."

Whether Murdock, who was helping himself to another portion of chicken, was waiting or not was a question. But it had been the only reason Roper had not excused himself and left the room long before. Immediately after the dinner had been served, a clap of Da-chong's hands had brought two girl dancers into the room. Totally lacking in talent, they more than offset this by a wild abandonment to the strumming of a mandolin by a small boy sitting cross-legged in one corner of the room. The girls, wearing only waist-high sarongs and leis of wild orchids, were in a constant fit of giggling over Hock's boisterous comparison of their proportions as they contorted themselves in front of the table, attempting some semblance of rhythm. Under Hock's encouragement, the sarongs were quickly discarded.

The room itself seemed to have been constructed for just such orgies prepared by Da-chong for visitors. Tall mirrors on three walls were angled so as to cast a dozen reflections of the writhing girls. Between the mirrors were crude murals depicting men and women in various love acts. The floor was covered with a black velvet rug, except in the very center of the room, where a large square mirror had been inlaid and left uncovered. The dining table around which the men sat was on a dais, so that the mirror on the floor could be clearly seen.

The two Mongols, always near their master, stood near the draped doorway. Muscular arms folded, they seemed almost overcome by boredom as they carelessly leaned back on either side of the door. No doubt they had witnessed many scenes of greater debauchery than this. The boy sitting in the corner seemed to have been well acclimated also. Frowning in concentration, he watched the dancing girls, his fingers flitting rapidly across the strings of the mandolin. He seemed seriously interested in maintaining some co-ordination between the music and the girls.

Griffith was oblivious of everything but the wine at the table. He was in shirt sleeves, his armpits darkened with perspiration, his head sleepily nodding at the wine bottle before him. At times his filmed eyes would lift to watch Hock as he attempted to seize a dancer wheeling within reach, but his only interest was in the liquor he was consuming.

When the two girls had completed their dance, they donned their sarongs and permitted Hock to encircle their waists and drag them to a sitting position at his feet. Brazenly he fondled their sweating bodies.

At a signal from Da-chong one of his guards drew aside the drapes at the door. Karen entered after a brief moment. A blue satin robe covered her costume, but the overhead lighting caught the sunburst crown on her head and it blazed like a golden torch.

She was quite correct in telling Roper earlier that no matter how talented a performer is, some fanfare must create a mood or a good part of the act may be left in the dressing room. An entrance is necessary; so is a proper setting. But beyond a glance at the bright overhead lighting and a brief start at seeing the two half-nude girls sitting at Hock's feet, she retained her professional composure. Handing her robe to one of the Mongols, she nodded ever so slightly to the boy with the mandolin. His fingers touched the strings.

Closing her eyes, Karen brought her palms together, fingers upward touching her small chin. For a moment she stood there motionless, her eyes closed, a golden-haired queen in prayer. Then her head slowly moved to one side, halting, then to the other side in even rhythmic movements emulating the Hindu temple dancer. She swayed, her feet moved, and she was suddenly whirling about the floor, her transparent skirt flaring to her thighs. Abruptly she halted at the far side of the room, head thrown back, hips moving perceptibly, teasing, the sway of her lithe body before an imaginary figure there implying both anguished supplication and a seductive willingness to offer herself as a sacrifice. As she curtsied away, bowing low, then rising on tiptoe to whirl the length of the room, a kaleidoscope of gold, swirling silk and long flashing legs, it did seem as if her winged slippers were about to rise from the floor.

But mainly it was a routine dance, its counterpart seen by Roper many times—and completely anticlimactic following the lewd dancing of the two girls who were sitting at Hock's feet and smugly watching the performance.

Hock's anticipation when Karen had begun her dance quickly changed to puzzlement, then annoyance as he saw she was avoiding the floor mirror. At his grumblings Da-chong leaned forward, his whisper carrying to Roper.

"One must be patient, Captain. In a week's time you will see the gleam of golden skin in place of cloth. We must not frighten our pretty bird while the *Wanderer* is still here. Once the choice of leaving is removed, the professional ladies become more receptive to overtures, and quite inventive under the stimulus of hard cash."

Hock growled his dissatisfaction with any waiting. He reached for one of the girls sitting at his feet. She laughingly screamed a protest as he undid her sarong and sent it sailing out over the floor.

Karen immediately froze at the sight of the nude girl squirming on Hock's lap. For several moments she appeared to waver between continuing with her dance and speaking out. She saw that Murdock had stopped his eating and was watching her indecision with a contemptuous smile. Then her eyes met Roper's cold look. Suddenly she began reddening.

The Chinese waved a fat hand. "Continue, my dear."

"Continue?" She took in Hock's drunken pawing of the brown-skinned girl with a look of disgust. "Not with *that* going on."

"Something tells me you drew a blank this time," Hock muttered to Da-chong.

Belching loudly over his wine, Griffith peered out at Karen as if seeing her for the first time. "Morals," he wheezed, "are like a breath of fresh air, but sometimes as brief. Go home, young lady. Go quickly."

Karen had put on her robe. She tied it, looking with distaste at Hock, fully absorbed now with his giggling playmate. "Shall I return later?"

Da-chong frowned, fingering his yellow jowls. "My dear lady, I do not think you have the right to select the time or place for your performance. That, I believe, can be left up to me."

"It's impossible to dance under these conditions," Karen replied firmly.

Perhaps, in the past, similar stubbornness had come from girls brought to the island and had been ruthlessly dealt with, because the two Mongols immediately left the doorway and moved a few steps toward Karen, their eyes on Da-chong as if anticipating an order. The young boy squatting in the corner put aside his mandolin, his small round eyes fixed intently on Karen.

"Then I take it," Da-chong said silkily, gazing at his fingertips, "you wish to cancel our contract?"

Karen hesitated. Now that she was faced with the ultimatum, the struggle going on in her mind was plain to Roper. Fervently he hoped his presence would influence her decision.

"I suppose," Karen said wearily, "there's nothing left to do but cancel our arrangement." Suddenly she saw the sly smirks Hock's girls were giving her. Uneasily she glanced at the Mongols. "I'll leave on the *Wanderer*, if you have no objection."

Murdock leaned toward Da-chong, his lips barely moving as he whispered something. The Chinese gently nodded. He gazed at Karen, tapping the tips of his fingers together thoughtfully.

"I have no objections," he said finally. "None at all."

Karen's relief was as evident as the disappointment creeping over each islander's face in the room. Even Hock shot the Chinese a frown. Murdock was lighting a cigar, his face inscrutable.

"However," Da-chong continued, "there is the matter of your passage here. I trust you are able to settle that before you leave?"

"Why, yes. I—" She hesitated. "How much would that be?"

"Five hundred dollars."

Why not five thousand? Roper thought, seeing the trap being opened. Murdock would back up any amount stated.

Karen was dumfounded, but only for a moment. "Five hundred dollars! For being cooped up on that smelly ship? For being ordered about like a common coolie? I ..." She calmed down. "I haven't that much money, no more than a hundred dollars. I'll have to send the balance when I can."

Da-chong examined his fingernails again. "I am afraid that will not do. I am certain you have good intentions of repayment, but the most excellent of intentions oft go astray when the creditor is some distance away. I must ask for payment before you leave the island."

"But I haven't *got* the money!"

"The only alternative, Miss Gorman, would be to continue to perform for us. Shall we say a two-week period to settle the debt?"

Karen immediately protested, pointing out that the *Wanderer* was leaving in a few days and would not return for several months. "What am I to do for that length of time? I could be working somewhere instead, earning several times the amount I owe."

"Which would be no guarantee I would be paid." He shook his head. "I am afraid ..." He pursed his fat lips and frowned, gazing at the headdress she wore. "Those garments have been skillfully made," he mused. "Perhaps if you leave them here ... Yes, I believe I might accept them in lieu of payment. You will be free to redeem them at any time, of course."

Karen looked uncertain, as if expecting trickery. "If you're willing to hold them, I'm sure it's all right with me."

Da-chong waved a gracious hand. "Leave them he my dear. We will consider the debt settled." He nodded to the two Mongols. "You may pass them the garments."

"Pass them—" She didn't get it, but everyone else did. The two bodyguards and the girls were grinning broadly. Even the boy sitting in the corner tittered his appreciation of the joke. Softly Roper swore.

Hock's leer and the smile of satisfaction appearing on Murdock's face erased all doubt from Karen's mind of what was required of her. Lamely, and superfluously, she asked, "You mean disrobe? Now? *Here?*"

Quite gravely Da-chong nodded. "Your costume would hardly satisfy the debt otherwise. Presented to me now, it would increase immeasurably in value. But the choice is yours, Miss Gorman."

Karen's tanned cheeks were crimson, her green eyes reflecting the fresh struggle going on in her mind. To disrobe in front of these men, though humiliating, was not so unthinkable as the idea of remaining on the island for several months. There was no guarantee there would not be more than mere humiliation during the months she was waiting for passage. Nor was there any guarantee she would not be giving performances under more degrading conditions during the next two weeks. She glanced at Roper helplessly.

He was sitting tight-lipped, muscles tense, locked in his seat by a whisper of advice from Griffith. "Easy, my friend," the doctor had warned, his voice thick but low. "Stick your neck out and off it comes. If you want this over your dead body, you will be obliged—and quickly."

Silently Roper cursed Murdock and the fat Chinese for their unsavory sense of humor. It became more of a struggle to remain seated when something of scorn crept into Karen's eyes. However, it was only common sense to heed the doctor's warning. At best, he would be ordered back to the ship, solving nothing for Karen.

Resigned that Roper would make no move to defend her, she turned her scorn on Da-chong, who wore a bemused expression. Looking neither left nor right, she gently lifted the sunburst crown from her head and handed it back to one of the Mongols. She removed her sandals next, pushing them aside with a bare foot. Hesitating only a moment, her eyes lowered, she then unfastened the meshlike gold jacket, unzipping it down the bodice. She opened it wide, her face turning a bright scarlet as her unrestrained breasts came boldly into view.

Hock emitted a long whistle as he leaned forward. "Damn if you're not getting your money's worth!"

Da-chong said nothing. He was watching Karen's face, and the quiet smile on his lips told of his enjoyment at the girl's discomfort. Murdock also seemed to be enjoying the indignity being suffered rather than Karen's charms. He puffed on his cigar contentedly as Karen, with quick movements, unfastened both the gold belt and the diaphanous skirt.

She handed these over, eyes still lowered. The flesh-colored panties followed, peeled down over her smooth hips. She stepped out of these, standing naked under Hock's greedy eyes and Da-chong's smile of approval.

"Satisfied?" Her voice trembled with fury as she stood straight and poised, hands at her sides.

Da-chong permitted his eyes to move slowly down golden figure. "Miss Gorman, there is no reason for a woman such as you to leave here penniless."

"Pig!" She spat the word at him. "At the moment I can't think of any creature you resemble more!" She turned, grabbed her robe from the man at her left before he had time to stop her, flung it about her, and strode over to the door, disappearing through the drapes.

Da-chong settled back in his chair, his thoughts masked with his usual bland smile. "Our young lady will leave on the *Wanderer* as promised. But she forgets one thing. Her return passage has yet to be paid for. By heaven we will get a higher price for this return ticket. We shall see if Miss Gorman becomes so free with insults when we puncture her pride."

Roper stood up, his blood boiling with rage at the helplessness of his position. "I'll take care of the return passage."

"With what?" Murdock snapped. He glared up from the table. "Are you forgetting you're a guest in this house?"

Da-chong's black eyes moved in their fleshly pockets to study Roper. "I feel most obligated for the young lady's passage, Mr. Roper. We'll arrange to send her out on a junk—the last to leave. That would be three or four days hence, I believe."

Not trusting his voice to reply, Roper pushed aside his chair. He walked from the room, feeling the strained silence behind him.

Chapter Twelve

By noon of the following day over six hundred tons of cargo had moved through the lagoons out to the freighter, the inspection of the goods and supervision of loading left in Roper's hands. He worked swiftly, driving the wharf gangs without letup in an effort to cut the *Wanderer's* stay at Kuma. He did little quibbling when the quality of the goods differed from the approved lists being sent down from the house. To see Karen safely aboard the *Wanderer* in as short a time as possible was his main concern.

Repeatedly his thoughts drifted to the disrobing act she had been forced to go through. As often as he told himself he should have interfered, the simple truth was that he would have been unceremoniously shipped back to the freighter that very night, leaving her still in Da-chong's hands. That she had refused to speak to him this morning nettled him; apparently she had forgotten that she was necessarily on her own, that as an emissary from the *Wanderer* he was quite expendable should he step out of line.

And still a big question was what retaliation Da-chong would take against the girl, the price she would be paying for her return ticket. Griffith had assured him she would be in no personal danger, but to be prepared for something more subtle in the way of public humiliation. Just in what manner it would come the doctor didn't know. He held little hope that the incident would be forgotten.

Overcast skies and ominous swarms of flies buzzing across the wharves foreshadowed the storm warning brought in by Brown during the afternoon. He came in riding the foredeck of a returning junk, unkempt as usual, still wearing the dirty bandage on his jaw.

"Blow movin' in. Be 'ere by mornin', Appley says."

Which meant loading would be suspended shortly. Roper cursed the luck. The sooner the freighter had this cargo aboard, the sooner Karen could leave.

"I'll send word along to Murdock," Roper said. "How are things going out there?"

"Right enough. Comin' in I seen a freighter being towed through them reefs by junks. Blasted job they were 'aving, 'olding 'er off the breakers."

That would be the *Equatian Star*. Evidently Hock was taking no chances on having the tin ship wrenched from her moorings to pile up on the shore or founder on the reefs. If such a thing occurred, it would be a tremendous operation, not only to remove the tin, but to dispose of the vessel properly. So long as the freighter was above water, even its wreckage, it would always be a threat to the island's security.

Before Brown stepped back aboard the junk, his remark that Appley had passed along an order from Murdock for all hands to keep out of the shaft alley while at anchor focused Roper's thoughts on the *Wanderer's* padlocked stern. From the shaft alley, of course, a person could hear anything that went on in that after compartment when the engines were silent. Ordering it out of bounds meant that Murdock was still playing his little game to the hilt.

If it *was* a game.

Getting as bad as Brown, Roper thought. Nobody but a lunatic would keep two people in chains this long without food or water. How close to lunacy Murdock approached he didn't ask himself. He was quickly discovering that a man willing to travel the road he was on could not question himself too much without getting some self-condemning answers.

During the afternoon three more junks were sent out. On one were the huge coils of Manila line taken from the French packet Da-chong had joked about, and it was during this loading that all business was terminated when a ripple of excitement swept across the wharves.

The tally boy at Roper's side gleefully explained that Da-chong had sent word the monthly trials were to be held this same night.

"Big damn fine time!" he said, tossing his clip board aside. "All come. Eat, drink, laugh. Ha-ha!" He peeled his lips back, idiotically flashing his teeth as if to illustrate what was to take place.

Gradually Roper elicited from him the fact that a large court was held once a month, with Da-chong acting as magistrate to settle disputes and problems and deal out punishment to those accused of crimes. Most of the crimes were in the category of minor offenses and no one took them too seriously; the penalties Da-chong imposed were treated more or less as a sport for the people. Apparently it was taken by all as a festive occasion, with food and drink in abundance.

Roper swore loudly and fluently at the sight of the wharf being rapidly emptied of laborers. Another delay. Even the junk alongside was being deserted, despite the fact that another hour would see her loaded. Following the men jumping down from the junk was an old woman with swollen legs, a canvas stool under her arm. She was hobbling along as fast as her painful legs would carry her.

"Everybody out to the ball park," Roper muttered. He reached out and grabbed the tally boy by the shoulders as he started away. "Where the hell are you going?"

"One damn big fine time."

"Get a half dozen of these monkeys back here or I promise you Da-chong will have one damn fine time peeling your hide! I want this line loaded and out in an hour!"

Sullenly the boy hesitated. Then he turned and trotted up the wharf, shouting to the coolies straggling along the road. After much coaxing, five of them returned, scowling over at Roper as they shuffled to their junk. Darkness had enveloped the waterfront area before this last vessel had been dispatched for the evening. Roper restored the smile on the tally boy's face by offering him a ride to the house.

When twenty minutes later he pulled the jeep off the road, parking it by a mule cart at the side of the house, the scene on the terrace was that of a huge clambake. Stone ovens had already been set up, the smell of wood smoke mingling with that of spitted meats. From bullock carts still arriving on the road, halves of beef, hams, fowls, and other assorted foods were being deposited by the fires. Chickens were taken from crates, slaughtered, dressed, and spitted so rapidly that the fires hissed and sputtered with the flow of warm blood. Cradles along the road held barrels of wines. Girls tended the spigots, filling bottles and jugs and carrying them to tables set up on the terrace.

The feasting had been going on for some time. Perhaps two hundred people, including many children, were gathered in groups between the cooking fires. Those not lending a hand in the preparations were squatting in circles, eating and talking at the same time.

Da-chong sat on the veranda in a large wicker chair with a high padded back rest. He wore a green sarong all but concealed by his massive belly resting on fleshy thighs. With his pudgy hands on his knees and his round face fixed in a benevolent smile as he looked out on the crowd, he reminded Roper of a throned Buddha.

Below the veranda, to one side of the steps, a half-dozen chairs had been placed for the house guests. Only Karen, Murdock, and Griffith were seated there. Hock evidently was still busy getting his ship into deep water.

When Roper reported the storm warning brought in by Brown, Murdock grunted and took the cigar from his mouth.

"Got the report this morning on the house radio. We'll be pulling out tonight and ride it out off the barrier. This is a special show for our benefit, so sit down and act like you're enjoying yourself."

Why Karen should be accepting Da-chong's hospitality puzzled Roper as he took a chair between Griffith and the girl.

"O.K.," he said, when she coolly avoided meeting his glance. "So I'm not a knight in shining armor. You were the one who could take care of yourself, remember?"

She turned icy eyes on him. "You might have offered to advance the money. Were you afraid to speak up?"

"One, I didn't have the money. Two, it wouldn't have been accepted. Three, I'm not on this island to antagonize the man responsible for most of the *Wanderer's* business."

"Number three is most important, I suppose?"

"It is," Roper said, matching her coolness. "And you look far from the outraged maiden at the moment, sitting here like a guest of honor. You two kiss and make up?"

"Your humor kills me. I was escorted here, not invited." His suspicions immediately aroused as to Da-chong's motive, Roper turned to Griffith. "When do these so-called trials start?"

"Later. We'll have some amateur performances first, in tribute to His Majesty."

"You sound like you're not exactly one of his admirers."

"My presence near him, Roper, indicates tolerance, not affection." The doctor returned to his wine.

Roper watched two youths, mildly protesting, being pushed from the crowd to the middle of the terrace, where room was made for them. Mandolins were slung about their mahogany shoulders. Sheepishly they approached within a few feet of the veranda steps. Da-chong nodded an encouraging smile. The boys picked an off-key tune on the strings and began singing a Chinese ballad, softly at first, then louder as they gained confidence. Roper was relieved when they finished and took the perfunctory applause with elaborate bows. They were followed by a woman singing a mournful piece without benefit of music.

A juggler came on next. Clumsily inept with five rubber balls, he was ignored by the crowd. Drunken cries for service brought girls running with fresh jugs and bottles for all.

When the juggler had completed his act, receiving halfhearted acclaim, a signal from Da-chong indicated that he was ready to sit and judge grievances and listen to complaints. The first cases were three married couples seeking divorces, the petitioners meekly standing before the steps and each stating his or her reason for wishing a divorce. As Da-chong solemnly weighed the merits of the petitions, Griffith interpreted to Roper the decisions, with side comments of his own.

"One couple is childless. They're to return in ninety days after thinking it over further. The other two have children. No divorce. That's not too surprising. Our judge is a strict believer in children's welfare first, the parents' second. One of his few virtues."

These domestic cases held little amusement for the crowd. They hardly listened as they continued drinking and chatting among themselves. A wife-beating case was more to their liking. With Griffith interpreting, Roper learned that the woman was asked with what she had been beaten, and when she replied that it had been with her husband's fist, Da-chong, quite straight-faced, ordered the man to use nothing larger than a cane switch in the future.

The crowd shouted approval at this. The husband wearily smiled his thanks at Da-chong and followed his crestfallen wife from the circle.

Then a fat woman came forth with an old man. The old man was the complainant: He had tattooed a dragon on the woman's shoulder, and had not been paid for his work. In turn, and quite violently, the woman stated the job had not been performed to her liking.

"This one," Griffith said, opening his coat wide and accepting a fresh glass of wine from one of the serving girls, "thinks more of a dollar than her right arm. He'll make short work of her."

But Da-chong seemed in no hurry to decide the case. He began questioning the tattooing artist, then the woman. Carefully he examined the work on her large shoulder. When he finished his inspection he sat back, rubbing his big belly thoughtfully. Briefly his glance strayed to Karen, who was watching the scene with indifference. To the woman he finally said he saw nothing wrong in the work performed. He ordered immediate payment. She mournfully held out empty hands, indicating that she was incapable of paying.

Da-chong rose to his feet and spoke in a stern voice. "He's accusing her of victimizing the old man. Says a fitting punishment would be—"

Griffith's interpretation was lost in the roar of laughter from the crowd. The woman, now blinking in surprise, was retreating from the veranda steps, looking about her as if for escape. She stumbled over a wine barrel being rolled onto the terrace by several of the girl waitresses, who were snickering in appreciation of the verdict.

Although the punishment was not severe in the physical sense, it was an outrageous humiliation of the woman's person. Within seconds she had been dragged protestingly across the barrel, her sarong pulled up over her head, and her immense buttocks laid upon by a half-dozen switches in the hands of as many men and women. The switches were passed from hand to hand, to anyone wishing to take part.

When the woman was released, she rose and limped away, the spectators drunkenly jeering at her tears. They quieted only when Da-chong stood and held up his hands for attention. When he began speaking in rapid Chinese, his tone and flamboyant gestures resembled those of a small-town politician.

Griffith suddenly leaned closer to Roper, his voice tightening in a tense whisper. "He's saying he has also been victimized. By the white girl. Says he has brought her here but she refuses to dance ... obligated to pay her passage ... receiving nothing in return. Says he will leave it up to his people what punishment she should have."

Immediately Roper saw the precedent set up in treating the fat woman so outrageously.

Roper leaped to his feet as the crowd clamored for the same treatment for Karen. They too were on their feet, surging forward, their fever mounting at the prospect of seeing this beautiful white woman being treated in such a fashion.

Karen, not understanding the words, but fully aware that she was involved in something unpleasant, turned pale as several men began closing in, brandishing the switches used on the fat woman. As Karen got up from her chair a big-eared lout padded forward, grabbed her skirt, and had it pulled up as high as her thighs before Roper flung him aside.

Momentarily the crowd hung back, all eyes swinging to Roper as he strode over to the steps.

"I thought each person was permitted a hearing," Roper angrily snapped to Da-chong.

The Chinese wore his usual unctuous smile, but deep in the black button eyes a glint appeared. "Every person is due a hearing, Mr. Roper. Very true. We shall listen to our Miss Gorman."

"What offense is she accused of? She has already paid for her passage here. You yourself stated she settled that debt to your satisfaction!" Roper half addressed this to those in the crowd who understood English, believing Da-chong would not risk losing face by publicly ordering an unjust punishment.

The Chinese bowed his assent. "However, Mr. Roper, I have arranged for her return passage. Her refusal to comply with her contract still leaves her in my debt. Any offer of reimbursement by you does not change the intentions of the accused."

It was not Roper's intention to offer reimbursement. He had been wondering if there had been any exchange of money between Murdock and Da-chong at all. The more he thought of it, the more logical it seemed that Karen's passage, or that of any of the girls the *Wanderer* had transported to the island, was an accommodation on Murdock's part. Would such a trivial sum be mentioned by either man when their deals ran into the hundreds of thousands?

"It has already been paid," Roper said, playing his hunch. "But not by you. The girl was carried gratis, the expense borne by the *Wanderer's* officers, who share in its profit. The small cost of her passage was paid by me, by the other mates, and by Captain Murdock here. There is no entry on the ship's book of any money for her passage. If she is in debt, it is to the *Wanderer* and not to you."

It was a clear score. Murdock had started to rise from his chair, his face hardening. He stopped and settled back slowly at Roper's words, biting down on his cigar. On the steps of the veranda Da-chong continued smiling, his eyes flickering to the waiting and impatient throng. His indecision was plain to see. Much as he desired to see Karen humiliated, some semblance of justice had to be preserved here.

It was the crowd that took the reins from his hands.

People began pressing forward with murmurs of anger at being cheated of this once-in-a-lifetime spectacle. A word from Da-chong would no doubt have stopped them, but none came. Smiling slyly down at Roper at this face-saving victory, the Chinese lifted his shoulders helplessly.

"It seems as if I am no longer the judge," he said gently.

That was all the revelers needed. They surged forward again with yells and laughter.

Roper, who had done his share of dock fighting, didn't wait for them to close in and render him helpless for lack of room. Instinctively he charged forward, smashing out with his fists, the suddenness of his attack driving them back from Karen. One man, gaunt and bucktoothed, who had attempted to tear at Karen's clothing, reeled about with the blood gushing from his smashed mouth; another held the side of his head, dancing about and yelping with pain.

A screeching woman flew at Roper, her long nails reaching to rake his face. Without any compunction he side-stepped and drove his fist into her stomach. She sat down on the stone terrace, eyes popping, her mouth opening in a bewildered expression. A boy came diving through the air in a football tackle. He collided with Roper's upraised knee and was sent back sprawling.

A bull-necked man came stepping across the fallen boy, grinning at Roper. He was hairy and barrel-chested. In his right hand was a cargo hook. He advanced slowly, holding the hook at arm's length behind him, ready for the wide curving slash of the longshore fighter.

No word came from the veranda steps to halt the affair.

The finale, Roper thought. What was there to lose? He leaped at the man before the hook could be brought around, slamming his foot directly into the big coolie's groin. The man doubled up with a groan. Roper grasped him about the nape of the neck, pushed his head down farther. With all the strength he could muster he brought his knee up, releasing the man's head simultaneously. There was a sharp cracking sound. The man flew backward as if mechanically propelled. He hit the ground heavily and lay there, his head rolling limply to one side at a grotesque angle. Fluid began trickling from his ear to form a dark spreading pool on the gray stone.

Even before Griffith reached the man it was known he was dead.

For the crowd the party was over. They began edging back from the lifeless man, their eyes worriedly shifting from Roper and Karen up to Da-chong. Here was something not on the program, something that must be placed in the hands of a higher authority.

As far as Roper was concerned, it was difficult to evoke regrets over the death of a cutthroat, particularly when the longshoring hook lying by his side had been meant to rip through his face and perhaps pluck out an eye. He stood breathing hard, watching Griffith examining the man. His only thought was for his own safety and Karen's.

Behind him he could hear Murdock softly swearing.

When Griffith rose from his knees, pronouncing the man dead, Da-chong heavily descended the steps. He stood beside the body, his narrowed eyes slanted sideways, taking in Roper and Karen with a look of undisguised hatred.

"Your misplaced gallantry, Mr. Roper, will cost you dearly."

"I would say," Griffith interrupted, "that Roper's role was forced on him by your inability to control the court spectators." He straightened his shoulders, buttoning his coat with some dignity. "Clearly this was a case of self-defense, and protecting a defendant whom you were about to admit was not guilty."

"You drunken sot!" Da-chong whispered, his heavy jowls quivering. "When will you stop interfering—" He broke off, suddenly aware that his people were listening attentively, and that his decision must be logical.

A sudden gust of wind blew up from the road, carrying swirling dust across the veranda. Reminded of the coming storm, Roper saw the opportunity for seizing the initiative from the Chinese. A wrong word here, an apology, could be taken as an admission of guilt, and would offer an excuse for holding Karen and himself for a trial that might be little better than the farce he had just witnessed.

"I presume," Roper said, "you'll want nothing further from Miss Gorman." He turned to Murdock, who was sullenly chewing on his cigar. "I'll head for the ship, Captain. When this wind rises those reefs will be impassable. If our passage is blocked, Appley will have a devil of a time riding it out alone."

Without waiting for an answer, Roper took Karen's arm. He guided her through the crowd, the natives reluctantly falling back. Reaching the jeep on the road, he helped Karen into it, then slid behind the wheel. Knowing one word from Da-chong could snatch the girl from him, he hardly drew a breath until he had pulled the jeep around and was headed down the dirt road in the direction of the village.

Karen finally sighed and relaxed back in her seat. "That was certainly close, Johnny. Getting away like this is almost too good to be true."

"What makes you think we're getting away? He doesn't have to throw any bars around us. In case you're feeling optimistic about the future, start debating with yourself how I'll stand with Murdock now. If he considers my services essential after this storm, we'll climb out of this. If he doesn't, your guess is as good as mine."

Timidly she touched his arm. "I've certainly fouled things up for you. I'm sorry. Really, Johnny, I'm—"

"Stop apologizing for acting like a human being," he said sharply. "I'd rather be on shaky ground than thinking of you playing tiddlywinks with Fat Boy. Let's worry about first things first. I can sail freighters, but it's even money I can capsize an outrigger in those reefs without half trying."

As if anticipating the difficulty they would have, Griffith drove up to the wharf shortly after them. The tally boy was with him.

"Expect to operate that yourself?" Griffith nodded to the outrigger Roper had pulled up to the wharf. "The boy here will take you out." He drew Roper aside, out of hearing of Karen, who was being helped into the stern of the boat by the youth.

"I suppose you know, Roper, these people will expect Da-chong to even the score. But not publicly. There will be no more of this trial business. As a judge here, Da-chong prides himself on making proper decisions and righting wrongs. It would be a loss of face and prestige if he attempted to railroad you and the girl into some harm. But at the same time he will be expected to come out on top in an underhanded way."

"If we're found floating head down among the reefs he saves face, is that it? Everybody occasionally gets a cramp while swimming?"

"Something of that sort. Exactly what his intentions are I don't know, but he's back there with Murdock discussing a meeting when the seas smooth. I understand he intends to board the tin ship tonight with his two boys, going alongside the *Wanderer* when weather permits. Take it from me, that young lady will find herself in the cabin of the *Star* and meekly attempting to placate Da-chong if she wishes to leave the island. Need I tell you she would have to develop a lively imagination to please a man who has seen it all?"

Roper held out his hand. "That's a bridge we'll have to cross later, Doctor. Thanks for your help at the house. I hope you're not in any trouble because of it?"

Griffith's thin features moved into a tired smile as he shook hands. "After a certain point, Roper, trouble is only a word. Good luck to you."

During the ride through the lagoon, Roper discussed the coming showdown with Karen at some length. With Murdock the law on the *Wanderer* and Da-chong supreme on the island, they were sandwiched between two immovable and ruthless forces. What they could do Roper hadn't the slightest idea. Neither had she.

But being confused as to which way he should turn was nothing new, Roper reflected. In the past weeks he had felt like a man stumbling around in the dark, never certain of himself. Slowly but surely he had been losing the power of quick decision, of prompt action. If decay of character was a requisite to success in this underworld of shipping, he was certainly on his way.

Why waste time analyzing it? he thought. The tide's still running and you'll drift with it whether you want to or not.

Chapter Thirteen

Within minutes of Murdock's return to the ship, the *Wanderer* weighed anchor in a frothy wind-blown sea, taking up a position several miles westward with just enough way to hold her head into the weather. As the wind strengthened, billowing seas soared high with crests foaming, driving yawning troughs down the length of the vessel. Lightning flickered overhead, and in the brief illuminating flashes of the gathering storm glimpses were had of the *Equatian Star*.

She was scarcely five miles away, riding low to the water, a long dark shape, ominous in Roper's eyes in view of the grim silence from Murdock. No hint had come as to his intentions. The hope that all might be forgiven was quickly squelched by Appley when they began rigging grab lines along the forecastle.

The mate had suddenly interrupted Roper's account of the island episode.

"I'll give it to you straight, Roper. I shouldn't, but here it is. Your ass is in a sling. Both you and the Gorman girl won't be with us once we get back to normal here. From now on, Murdock's policy is no passengers, and that's what you're both going to be when this wind dies—passengers."

"You get that from him?"

Appley spat sea water from his mouth, yanking on the line they were working. "Bastard tells me confidential-like, figuring I'll put you wise. He *wants* you to know, wants to watch you sweat. You're like the man in the boat with one oar, can't do nothing but flounder around. But it's your mess, chum, so don't look for any help from me."

He looked across the deck, where Brown and two coolies were doubling boom lashings. "Make sure of the lashings there, Brown!"

"Doin' it, doin' it! This 'ere damn shackle's bent!"

"Strap it with wire, then." Appley looked back at Roper. "It's all yours, mate. Take it from there."

Take it from there! Roper smiled as he walked down the sloping deck. Take what? There wasn't a damn thing he could do but sweat it out, like that man in the boat. Only he didn't even have the comfort of an oar.

Well, anyway, there it was. Nice and clean, with no loose ends.

Despite the certainty that they were now definitely out on a precarious limb, it was with a peculiar sense of freedom that he entered Karen's room. She was lying on her bunk, eyes closed, the back of one hand resting on her forehead. Her eyes lifted miserably to Roper.

"Quite a sailor," she said, attempting a feeble smile. "Now I know what people mean when they say they'd just as soon die and get it over with."

"Nobody feels good in weather like this. The toughest sailor gets a bit rocky after a while."

"Even you?"

"Even me."

"I don't believe it." She half sat up on the bunk and shook her head as she regarded the soiled condition of the green linen dress she had been wearing.

"And I haven't a thing to change into. Do you think they'll send my things out later?"

"I doubt it." He told her what Appley had said. "I'm being written out of the books here. Which means we'll both be guests of our fat friend."

"Hmm." She closed her eyes. "I don't feel seasick anymore—just sick." She opened her eyes and regarded him. "You look sort of—well, funny. As if you're not worried."

He lit a cigarette and sat down beside her. "I'm worried about what happens to you. For myself I can't seem to work up too much interest."

"Down to stay this time?"

"I haven't even thought about it."

"You mean you're just going to quit? Give up? Allow yourself to be pushed around without a fight?"

He smiled wryly at the smoke trailing from the tip of his cigarette. "Who do you want me to fight? The crews of two ships?"

She sat up and swung her feet onto the floor. "I've always pictured you as capable of doing it—when we first met, I mean. Of course, the picture's been fading a bit."

"You can pick the oddest time for sarcasm, Miss Gorman."

"Sorry, Johnny. I didn't really mean that." She tucked her arm through his and sighed, staring at the floor. "Johnny, I'm a jerk. It's my fault, the position we're in. I've cost you the chance of making a great deal of money."

"That's not important," he said. "In fact, funny as it may sound, it seemed like a weight lifted from my shoulders the moment I understood I'd never see a penny of Murdock's money. I guess I've been kidding myself all along that I could pocket a buck and forget in time where it came from, but—" He stopped speaking when he saw she had begun crying softly, still holding his arm, her head bowed against his shoulder.

"Oh, Johnny, I'm losing my nerve. I'm afraid, so afraid."

"Karen...." Roughly he pulled her to him. "Damnit, stop that blubbering." He forced her chin up and kissed her mouth. "We're in a spot, but one thing I promise you: There'll be broken heads when the showdown comes. By God, it'll cost them—"

She clung to him fiercely, her arms tight around him, her mouth again seeking his. "Johnny," she whispered, "will there ever come a time when there'll be nothing on our minds but us?" Again her lips met his hungrily.

"The condemned eating a hearty meal?" he asked harshly, pulling back suddenly. "Is it like that with you?"

"No, Johnny, no," she murmured. "It's not that."

"Damn right, it's not! There's no condemned in this room!"

"I know, darling, I know. You're stronger than any of them. I'm not the least bit afraid now."

"If you understand that, it's all right. Don't ask me how, but no one is stepping on us."

Her hand cupped his mouth. "Darling, just put your arms around me. When you hold me tight I know nothing can hurt us."

The wind rattled the door as a gust beat down the Passageway. From the decks came the reverberations of sea wash, the moan of the wind. Gradually the sounds merged and seemed to dissolve in the far distance.

The swollen sky hung low, a gray-black mass stirring descending plumes of smokelike vapor. Like ragged entrails they hovered over the arching sea, caressing each mountainous wave that rolled in to explode on the *Wanderer's* trembling bow. She rode to the wind as she bore the brunt of the assaults, staggering under the pounding but lifting her head high each time to the shriek of the wind.

To hold the ship off the broaching seas required delicate balance, and each man's mind was occupied with nothing but this. Through the night and into the next day two officers were required at all times on the bridge, one at the wheel, the other commanding, in an incessant battle to hold the weather off their quarter in the shifting winds, to guard against the treachery of yawning troughs.

Roper, standing his watches with Brown, was no less zealous in his duties than he had been in the past. There were heavy stakes in keeping this vessel afloat, for he couldn't imagine a more awkward position for Karen and himself than to be pulled from the sea by Da-chong, Hock, and Company.

As bad as their position was, they still had a ship beneath them, a period of grace. What he could do or accomplish during this time he didn't know. His promise that there would be broken heads when the showdown came was one he intended to keep, but it would hardly change the final outcome. His vow, despite what Karen thought, would be nothing more than a futile gesture of defiance—and juvenile, he admitted—unless something more concrete than violence were thought of.

Fragments of courses he might follow flashed through his mind. Most persistent was the possibility of taking command of the *Wanderer*, but he dismissed it as idiotic. Murdock would have to be disposed of bodily, also Appley and Brown. Even assuming he might control the engine room by swinging Fisher and the blacks to his side, to wind up in command of a working deck force was as certainly in the realm of pure fancy.

Finally he was forced to thrust aside his personal problem as the storm reached its peak in the late-morning hours and tremendous waves began a steady bombardment against the freighter. Plainly worried, Murdock put in frequent appearances on the bridge at this time. Toward midday, when a series of roaring combers buried the forecastle, sending green water waist-high down the decks, a forward boom began shaking in its cradle. It brought Murdock stomping into the wheelhouse.

Water dripping from his visor, he glared across at Brown at the wheel. "You secure that boom properly?"

"Sure, Cap'n."

"It won't break loose?" His tone was as hostile as his eyes.

Brown hesitated. He squinted down at the boom, now shivering under the pull of frothy waters boiling across the deck. There was a play of at least several inches in that boom; it had been a sloppy job of lashing.

Characteristically, Brown's answer was one calculated to appease Murdock's temper rather than to be truthful. "She's secure 'nough, Cap'n. Did a good job, I did."

"Hop down and double it again!" Murdock motioned for Roper to take the wheel.

Brown hesitated, uneasily eying the forecastle as it was darkened by the crest of another wave. Brown didn't have to be told that a five-ton boom breaking loose in this sea would instantly crush everything in its path, sweeping the deck clean of any man working in the vicinity.

"What are you waiting for?" Murdock rapped out. "If she's lashed as secure as you say, what are you afraid of?"

A sense of foreboding came to Roper minutes later as he watched Brown and two of the coolies straddling the boom with the sea washing about them. They had taken several turns about the coupling with wire rope, but the quivering play in the boom hadn't ceased. Suddenly Roper saw that this play was aggravated from the other end, at the swivel coupling, opposite the end where the men were working. The cause was a broken lashing, concealed by a large clump of seaweed left there by a receding sea.

"That aft end is wearing loose!" Roper told Murdock tersely. He began swinging the spokes of the wheel past his chest, with the intention of taking the brunt of the sea away from the men below. "If she breaks off, they haven't a chance down there!"

Murdock swung a cold eye toward him. "Steady! The fool tended that lashing personally. Let him take the consequences if he can't manage it. Damn if I'll chance a plate buffeted open because of his stupidity."

His eyes followed a cloud of spray lifting along the port side. Immediately it was followed by the crash of a comber off that quarter, another cloud of spray lifting high and sweeping up from astern. Following the pattern of the tropical twister, the wind had shifted to their port quarter. The sudden shift accomplished exactly what Roper had intended, bringing relief to the men on the forecastle.

"Ease her around, mister! Head her in again," Murdock ordered.

Roper held the wheel over, permitting the head to fall off further. "Give them five minutes, at least."

Murdock's blow came without warning, catching Roper behind the ear and sending him staggering back across the wheelhouse. He crashed into the chart desk and fell to his knees, momentarily stunned.

Murdock rapidly spun the wheel back. "By God, it'll be a pleasure to teach you what obedience means! Get down below with Brown, mister!"

Seized by rage at this callous disregard for life, Roper got to his feet. He started for Murdock when a sound stayed him, a low-pitched rumble, audible even above the wind and thud of the sea against their side. Roper turned, freezing instantly at what he saw.

Less than a hundred yards to port a thin black rigid line had appeared in the gray mist being blown across the raging waters. Thickening as it approached, it remained inflexible, the yawning chasm opening before it deepening as it came on.

Murdock was already hurrying the wheel the opposite way, frantically trying to present his stern to the weather. The very thing he had wanted to avoid was now happening because of his disregard for human safety. In turning the vessel 150 degrees to face the wind, instead of the 20 or 30 degrees to take it astern and relieve Brown and his men from danger, he had been swinging the beam of the vessel broad to this tremendous comber building up.

It was on them immediately, before the freighter could respond sufficiently to the helm. The trough opening before it yawned the entire length of the vessel, a black canyon in cascading motion. Below on the forecastle Brown and the coolies had flung themselves on a lifeline as they heard the express-train roar reaching a crescendo.

Holding tightly to the desk, Roper had the sensation of being on a rapidly falling elevator. The vessel heeled as she dropped. The solid curling wall of water loomed over them, swooping down. The vessel was halted in its descent with a splitting crash that buckled Roper's legs. Then the comber hit. It was as if a deafening clap of thunder had exploded inside the wheelhouse, wrenching Roper's hands from the desk and flinging him against the forward bulkhead, his face smashing against the window.

For a long moment, half dazed, he held onto the sill, trying to clear his head. Slowly vision returned, and through the window he saw a solid block of water covering the forecastle, the decks submerged, the *Wanderer* lying quietly, as if debating whether or not to succumb to the shattering blows she had received. After an eternity, it seemed, trembling and shaking, she slowly rose from the sea, a torrent of water running down her decks.

To Roper's amazement the three men on the forecastle were still there, their heads and shoulders visible above the thrashing waters. But his astonishment that they had not been swept overboard was short-lived.

As the waters receded all three men slowly bowed low, until they were bent double over the boom. Lying crosswise on the forecastle, the freed boom held the men against the knife edge of the hatch, their upper bodies almost completely severed by the tremendous weight of the boom. They were facing in the direction of the bridge and there was a macabre touch as they hung over the boom with heads bowed, as if paying final homage to Murdock.

Perhaps with merciful judgment the boom rolled free of the hatch as a smaller wave broke with a rush across the forecastle. The three bodies disappeared, a tangle of arms and legs, the lifeless face of Brown showing blackened stumps of teeth in a ghastly grin as he was swept over the side.

Although Roper, from the first moment he had boarded the ship, had despised the little bosun, he and the coolies were seamen, all entitled to a shipmaster's responsible actions. Bitter at the senseless disregard of human life, he turned to Murdock, who was at the engine-room phone.

"You knew the condition of that boom before you sent them down! Why didn't you warn them to strap that after end first?"

Murdock swore at the silent instrument. "Get below, Roper, and find out our damage! We'll take your questions up later—if we're still afloat!"

Knowing that further comment was useless now, Roper went below. On the way down he saw that the damage to deck gear had been extensive. Debris was everywhere, line, pieces of wood, wire cable, and even kitchen utensils floating about. Huge gaps showed in the starboard railing, where sections were torn away by the sea. Their number-one lifeboat lay aft, splintered against the housing. Karen was just emerging from the passageway; he ordered back to her room.

"Is it bad, Johnny?" she asked quietly.

"Don't know yet. Stay clear of the deck in case there's a follow-up."

In the engine room, at first glance, damage was beyond repair. All along the port side buckled plates were spewing water, some with ragged edges revealed. Most of them were merely sprung, trickles of water flowing down the rusted skin. Appley was there, helping Fisher and the blacks bring up cement, lumber, and mattresses for shoring. All the men wore the same grim expression of concern.

Appley gave Roper a quick summary. "Damn pumps! Working about fifty per cent efficient! Maybe hold, maybe not. No breaks forward and aft, just here. Get Brown down here, and some of those coolies."

"Brown's gone. Washed over with two of the others." Roper didn't wait for questions to follow Appley's raised brow. "We carry a collision mat?"

"One for'ard."

Roper raced topside. With the aid of the cook and two coolies he managed to run the mat over the worst of the break. It was ineffective as a seal but would serve to ease the pounding against the damaged plates. He also put into operation a hand billy.

From that moment on, no one slept. No one had time to. The freighter continued taking on water despite the shoring. At midnight the water showing above the floor plates in the engine room finally remained at a constant level, but if the weather worsened or if the ancient pumps gave out, as they showed signs of doing, they would have to take to the lifeboats.

"Which means," Roper told Karen, "we'd be picked up by Hock's ship."

"How nice. I can't think of any place I'd rather not be."

"We'll wind up aboard there anyway if things go according to Murdock's plans. I'll be damned if I know how I'm going to prevent it."

"You'll think of something."

He wished he had as much faith in himself.

Chapter Fourteen

Morning found the intensity of the storm diminishing, and for the first time the *Wanderer's* pumps, still working in fits and starts, began discharging more water than that which seeped into her. High waves continued to spill across the bow, but the terrible pounding of rolling troughs that had threatened to broach the freighter had ceased. She rode into the weather with only spray slicking her well deck, occasionally lurching as a gust of wind heeled her.

The *Equatian Star* had apparently fared better during the night. She was less than five miles to port, silhouetted against the muddy dawn. Along the curving bow could be seen dark patches where the seas had scaled her, but beyond that the heavily laden vessel appeared undamaged.

After a hurried breakfast Roper and Appley set to work clearing the *Wanderer's* decks of debris. They jettisoned the splintered lifeboat aft and began rigging wire cable where the buffeting waters had stripped off the railing. They were working on the last break when Appley mentioned the fantail housing.

"Looks like the sea's done what everyone's hankered to do." He wearily wiped the sea water from his red face and nodded toward the stern.

Roper glanced in that direction and saw that the force with which the lifeboat had been flung against the housing door had smashed the padlock. It dangled to one side, useless. He had almost forgotten about the stern, and now, suddenly, he saw this too as a victory for Murdock. Whereas Murdock sought to eliminate every shred of self-respect from the men under him, he still remained the untouchable. The one thing that could have pierced his armor he had effectively blunted by simply locking a door. Childish as the bluff started out to be, it would enhance his reputation with the passing of time—at least enhance the reputation he sought.

Roper cast an eye toward the bridge. Murdock's thick shoulders could be seen above the curtain board, outlined against the lightening sky. He was hunched forward, gazing at the sloping seas, his only movements slight inclinations of his head at times to the helmsman, ordering a change of a degree or two to compensate for the wind.

"We've got enough trouble on our hands without starting more," Appley growled, when he became aware of Roper's thoughts. "Grab hold here and keep your mind clear of funny ideas."

Roper took in the slack of the cable Appley was securing to the stanchion, his eyes straying back to the broken padlock. Once a new lock was put on, the opportunity to visit the pits would be lost. In the space of two minutes the riddle could be settled. A few brief moments and he could have the satisfaction of knowing Murdock for the fraud he was.

He wondered if that knowledge could in some way be used to his advantage.

Appley was scowling. "Will you forget it? Start thinking about what you're going to do when that tin ship comes alongside."

"I don't suppose I could depend on some support from you when she does come alongside?"

"You're supposing right."

Murdock, coming down the deck, cut him off. Despite the weary lines in his unshaven face, his voice was crisp and commanding. "Take over the bridge, Appley! You, Roper, get a light and check those forward compartments. Watch closely for signs of vertical cracks. Report to me in my cabin." He turned away, swaying for balance on the slanting deck as he walked to his cabin.

Fisher, his black gang, and the deck coolies lent to him were in the final stages of shoring when Roper entered the engine room. The framing had long been completed, with cement still being poured in by the men working in ankle-deep water. It was a good job of shoring and would form an effective second skin, but Fisher was skeptical of their ability to perform as well elsewhere in the ship if the need arose.

"Materials," he said, wiping cement dust from his sweaty face. "We just don't have them. Cost money, you know."

"How are the forward plates? Have you been up there?"

"Not for several hours."

"Suppose we take a look." They went forward, examining plates on the way. In the forecastle there were signs of weakening seams, and Fisher looked doubtful.

"What the devil can I use up here?"

"We carry a burning outfit? I'm thinking of strip bracing, timber it for added support."

"Well, yes. We might try that."

"Fisher, I wanted to get you up this way to talk to you alone." Roper hesitated. "I shouldn't even ask this. The odds are stacked so much against me you'd be a fool to agree. But I need help, Fisher, if I'm to get Miss Gorman and myself north in one piece. I suppose you know I'll be excess baggage once this wind dies. With a few men on my side, your blacks, say, and you, Murdock might have to oppose any rough stuff from Da-chong. If you four were up on deck when the Star ties alongside and showed yourselves to be on my side, it might work. You may be fired when we reach port, but he could hardly get rid of his engineering force at sea."

Fisher removed his glasses and gently shook his head. "That wouldn't work, Mr. Roper. I'd like to help you if I can. But the blacks are capable of manning the engine room, after a fashion. One stern look from Murdock and they would obediently go below. For myself, I don't care. This is my last trip under Murdock. We'll come topside if you wish, but the blacks taking over my duties would be the outcome, I'm sure."

"You're right," Roper admitted. "I'm clutching at straws. It would be a useless move. Thanks anyway. I'll have Appley stick our tail to the wind until you're finished here."

When he informed Appley of the need to bring the vessel about, the mate handed him the binoculars he had been using. "She's breaking up in the east."

Roper didn't need the glasses to see this. Eastward, the *Equatian Star* could be seen riding more gently in the sea, and the island beyond it, with its palms waving in the wind, was no longer dropping from view with the rolling waves. The sky had lifted from the sea, and although it was still dark and ragged, a drifting patch of milky haze hovered on the horizon. The wind was blowing across the freighter in dying gasps now, the spray lifting from the waves not quite reaching the *Wanderer's* decks. An hour might see the sun above them. An hour's grace.

"Finish your inspection below?"

"Not quite. I'm having a look-see aft."

Appley swore. "Damnit, man, why make more trouble for yourself?"

"Worried about my skin?"

"Might put it that way. If he catches you—"

Roper snorted. "Why not come out with it? I'll tell you what you're worried about. That bank account of yours. You want it to keep growing. And it won't if we find that Djerf and that girl were actually aft all this time without food or water. Because then you'd have to quit this berth. If you found out they were being tortured back there, even *you* couldn't stomach it."

Appley considered this, his webbed eyes studying the pipe he removed from his pocket. "That the way you figure it, eh? Well, maybe you hit it right; what I don't know I don't have to think about."

"Could you take it, Appley, if you found they had been back there all this time? Give me a straight answer. Could you?"

Appley jammed his hands into his coat pockets, his plump face darkening with anger. "Let's drop it, Roper! If you'll notice, I pay strict attention to my own business. Maybe you could take a page from my book."

Roper walked away, swinging down from the bridge. He moved aft along the deserted deck. With only Appley in view, giving him a glowering glance from the bridge wing, he opened the housing door and slipped inside.

His flashlight cut through the darkness, picking up the ladder slanting into the stern. Quietly he descended the ladder and in a few seconds was standing on the floor plates below, the familiar smell of mold and rusted steel in his nostrils. He swept the light about, moving the beam over the curve of the stern, across the overturned kitchen table and chair, both still thickly coated with dust. Then the beam flicked into each of the coffin-like pits fouled with moisture and rust.

They were all empty.

An iron bar leaned against the port skin, something he did not remember seeing there before; but except for the muffled sound of the sea wash and the vibrating thud of the propeller as it churned into the weather, nothing had changed in the compartment.

Well, there it was, he thought. The padlock had been entirely a face-saving device on Murdock's part.

He started for the ladder when a draft of air suddenly swept down into the compartment. The metal door above clanged shut, a heavy step sounding.

Roper switched out the light, silently swearing when he realized that the coming about of the vessel would have instantly roused Murdock from his cabin. Had he been seen entering the housing?

In the darkness he felt his way back to the overturned table, silently crouched down behind it. If he hadn't been seen, Murdock's purpose here might be to inspect the effects of the rolling sea against the counter. If that were so, he certainly couldn't avoid discovery. But suppose he *were* discovered? What difference did it really make? Maybe a deal could be made for his silence.

Murdock's heavy figure came into view, his thick legs carefully feeling for each step as they descended the ladder. He was carrying a lantern, the common oil type having a smoke-stained glass, which filled the interior of the stern with wavering shadows.

"It's a little early today for a sermon, but I thought I'd see how you're taking the rough passage." Murdock's tone was mocking as he moved over to the port side and set the lantern down on the flooring.

Unable to grasp his meaning, believing at first the words were meant for him, that his presence was known, Roper grew nauseous when Murdock spoke again—and the meaning of the iron bar lying against the ship's skin became clear.

Far from being carelessly placed, Roper now saw it was wedged over a plate—a plate covering one of the pits. He had missed this one because he had not counted the pits, but had shone his light into the open ones, never imagining Murdock to be inhuman enough to seal a pit if he actually had imprisoned Djerf and Kim.

One pit had been sealed—*and occupied.*

"Got enough of her yet, Djerf? Or is she still making excuses?" Murdock laughed, his voice ringing hollowly in the compartment above the threshing of the screw and the sound of the sea slapping against the hull. As if this visit to the pits had rejuvenated him, all weariness had been erased from his features. His eyes were alive, glowing as he looked down at the plate beneath his feet, his lips curled into an ugly smile.

"Nine days now, my lovebirds. Nine days with your mouths against those rusted plates. You might say that's the bitter cup you're drinking from. How does it taste after the sweet?"

Roper rose unsteadily to his feet, a wave of revulsion sweeping over him at the thought that he too shared a moral guilt in this ghastly act. What other misery would have been left in his wake before he had reached the top under Murdock and Fazio?

He moved out from behind the table, kicking the chair aside. Murdock turned with the sound, staring dumfounded. In the feeble light of the lantern his bearded face appeared colorless, as if suddenly drained of blood. Slowly he recovered, his mouth closing in a thinning line.

"So you've disobeyed my orders, Roper!" His hand slipped inside his coat. "Did you come to free them? Or were you just curious as to what they might look like?"

It was an effort for Roper to speak. "Murdock, you're a madman. Get back from that plate!"

Murdock's hand came away from his coat. He held the knife low, the thin blade tilting upward. He smiled as Roper halted. "No heroics this time, Roper? Are you starting to think of yourself for a change?" He motioned with the knife. "All right, lift it!" Murdock backed a step off the plate, his yellow eyes suddenly pulsating. "Lift it, Roper. Yesterday they were alive, at least one. I heard stirring. Today I'm not so sure. There seems to be a slight odor. Come to think of it, maybe the stirring yesterday was the rats."

Any doubt Roper had of Murdock's insanity was now wiped out as he looked at the man's strange eyes, glowing in obvious enjoyment of the situation.

"They wanted to be together, Roper. They are. Chances are, though, they tired of one another fast. Lift the plate, Mr. Roper! Or haven't you the nerve?"

With a snarl Roper leaped forward, hurling the iron bar clattering to one side. He inserted his fingers in the grip holes, heaved upward and to one side, sliding the plate partly off.

He stared at what he saw, horror slowly being etched deep in his brain.

The two rats poised for flight on Kim's small bosom stared back at him a fleeting second. They scampered off, running down Djerf's lifeless arm around the girl.

The rats had been there for some time.

"They've paid, Roper. And it was only right they should." Murdock was looking down at the pit, unmoved by what he saw. "The book says, 'An eye for an eye, a tooth for a tooth'; to a man who reads and understands, it means your illicit pleasures also must be paid for."

"You bastard!" Roper's voice was thick with rage as he straightened. "Do you think you can hide behind that God-fearing routine? You'll fry in hell, Murdock! You'll fry in hell, and I hope there's a special torment for you down there!"

"That," Murdock said evenly, "is something for the future. At the present time we're aboard a ship, *my* ship, and you've disobeyed my orders." He broke off, listening, his head tilted.

Suddenly Roper realized, too, that their voices had been the only sounds in the compartment. There was no sound from the shaft alley, and the steady pulsing from the engines had ceased. Very faintly, from above, came the sounds of voices, of a winch in operation.

Murdock smiled thinly. "It appears the *Star* has come alongside. You might be interested to know, Roper, a little party has been planned, with you and that chippy topside sitting as guests of honor. But I think Da-chong is making a mistake wanting you around. I know I'd enjoy the kind of performance she's going to be persuaded to do if I didn't have to worry about you. Too unpredictable for peace of mind, Mr. Roper. You're too un—" Murdock lunged with the knife, his arm shooting out to its full length.

Roper jumped back, twisting aside. Not soon enough. The blade sliced through his coat and belt, cutting across his stomach muscles. It felt as though a hot poker had been placed against his middle.

Murdock swore as he tried to withdraw the knife for another thrust. It was caught fast, held by Roper's belt. In attempting to wrench it free, he inadvertently pulled Roper toward him in the same moment Roper gathered all his strength and aimed a pile-driving punch.

The punch connected squarely with Murdock's face, the jar of it traveling into Roper's shoulder.

Murdock stumbled back, blood streaming from his smashed nose, his eyes fogged. The knife was in his hand.

In the same instant Roper started to close in, Murdock recovered sufficiently to flip the blade into position for throwing. He backed away quickly, breathing hard, spitting blood and measuring the distance.

"Hold it, mister!"

Roper's halt was involuntary. He was suddenly aware of the warm flow down his legs, of an accompanying weakness from the slash across his middle. How deeply the blade had bitten he couldn't tell, but the fact that he was losing blood and might pass out completely, leaving Karen to face Da-chong alone, filled him with panic.

Murdock was grinning, his mouth a wide red smear from the flow of blood oozing from his pulped nose. "Did you ever see the Chink use a bull whip tipped with lead, Roper?" He poised the blade of the knife between thumb and forefinger. He slowly raised his arm. "Lead, Roper, a scorching tip of lead. She'll dance this time, my friend. She'll dance in the cabin of the *Star* with the whip undressing her."

"Djerf!"

Murdock's head jerked in the direction of the pit. Roper leaped forward. He scooped the lantern off the floor and swung it in a single overhand motion before the other could recover from the ruse. It smashed full in Murdock's face, the glass splintering, the light going out.

The compartment was in darkness for only an instant. Murdock's scream and the ignition of oil that had splattered his head and face came at the same time. He jumped about, beating at the flames frantically, roaring threats amid howls of pain.

Roper swung into action. He picked up the iron bar from the flooring, stepped in, and swung it savagely across the back of Murdock's neck.

Murdock uttered not a sound. He stumbled forward a few feet, his hands dropping limply to his sides. He toppled face forward, the last of the flames licking at his collar expiring as he crashed full length across the floor plates.

Dizzily Roper reeled about in the darkness, his legs two rubber stilts requiring an effort to control. There was a faint smell of burned hair and cooked flesh in the compartment that further sickened him. He fell against the bulkhead and stayed there a moment, resting, collecting himself.

When he felt sufficiently recovered he took the flashlight from his pocket, switched it on, and moved over to examine Murdock. He found him to be still breathing, his brutal face a mask of blood. Traces of glass glinted in the blood.

Roper set the light on the flooring, its beam directed across one of the pits. He grasped Murdock by the coat collar, dragged him to the pit, and rolled him in.

It did not occur to Roper that no more fitting punishment could be found than letting Murdock taste the slime and darkness to which he had sentenced Djerf and Kim. He simply needed a place to keep Murdock immobilized, and a slave pit answered the purpose.

He worked as quickly as his strength permitted, still in fear that the blood he had lost would render him helpless. He no longer felt the pain of the slash he had taken. Excitement gripped him, a scent of victory. With Murdock out of the way, he could see a glimmer of hope of extricating Karen and himself from an impossible situation. In effect, he had neutralized the *Wanderer*, at least temporarily, and he was no longer standing between two ruthless forces.

The steel plate that fitted over the pit was heavy, weighing some fifty pounds. Roper slid it into its grooves, panting from the effort.

"Roper...." Murdock's glazed eyes had opened, filling instantly with an insane fear as he saw the plate moving up past his chest. "Roper! My God, Roper, the rats! The rats!" he screamed, as the plate moved on, cutting off his view. "The rats!"

Roper laughed harshly as he stood up and stamped on the plate. "They won't touch you, Murdock! They won't touch their own kind!"

Rapidly he lifted other plates from nearby pits and dropped them crashing on the one over Murdock. Not until he had loaded three hundred pounds over Murdock did he stop. He laughed again as he heard the little frantic sounds Murdock was making. The sound of his own laugh sobered him. It had an insane ring that frightened him.

He picked up his light, flashed it around, found what he was looking for: Murdock's knife, lying nearby, half submerged in the oily water of a pit. He picked it up and slipped it inside his waist, ignoring the jolt of pain. There was an elation flowing through his veins, an elation hardly justified by the idiotic plan he was putting together. He didn't permit himself time to think out too many details, or weigh the chances for success or failure. It was too fantastic, too insane to think about. He mounted the ladder slowly, conserving his strength, hearing a voice on deck. No. It came from the *Equatian Star*. Da-chong's voice.

The bastard, he thought. The dirty bastard. Maybe I'll cut his throat, anyway.

He laughed again and went up the ladder hand over hand.

Chapter Fifteen

A canvas deck chair on the *Equatian Star's* tarp-covered after hold supported the corpulent form of Da-chong. He sat in the hot sunlight, big hands happily linked around his wrinkled belly, the sweat rolling from him like grease from an animal being basted. He was watching his two Mongols escorting a struggling Karen from beneath the *Wanderer's* companionway, his black eyes benignly smiling over folds of flesh at the girl's futile efforts. He failed to see Roper vault the rails of the locked ships, turning his head only when Roper leaped up on the hatch where he sat and slid behind his chair.

"Ah. Our gallant friend. We have been wondering where—" His words were choked off by Roper's left arm as it slid across his throat and wrenched his head back.

Swiftly, before the Chinese could recover from his shock, Roper placed the point of the knife under the yellow jowls, alongside the windpipe, puncturing the flabby flesh with the tip of the blade. He held the knife firmly as a trickle of blood issued forth.

"Drop your hands!" Roper snapped. "Drop 'em or I'll butcher you!"

Da-chong slowly lowered his trembling hands until they rested on his thick thighs. He sat rigid, his feet flat on the tarp; a tremor shook him.

Roper slightly relaxed his hold. The Chinese blew and sucked in his breath explosively. "On the grave of my ancestors, Roper," he panted, "I swear—"

"One move and you'll be an ancestor yourself!" Roper growled. "I'm hoping you make that move! How many men are below?"

"By heaven, Roper, you will broil across a spit." He stiffened as the knife bit deeper. "Three!"

As if the decks of the *Wanderer* and the *Star* were huge theatrical props, and the occupants actors, collectively looking to their director for a cue, all activity had ceased. A dozen heads turned toward the hatch. High on the bridge wing of the *Star*, Hock was leaning on the railing with folded arms, his cap tilted back on his dark head, eyes narrowed in a frown, the smoke curling from the stub of a cigarette hanging from his lips. On the *Wanderer*, Appley, in the act of descending from the bridge, was clinging to the handrails and gaping across, one foot on a step, the other not quite touching the next lower one. Below him, still in the companionway, the two Mongols wore the puzzled expressions of men gazing at something beyond their comprehension. The coolie hands on either ship—six on the *Star*, as counted by Roper the moment he had stepped from the housing—had all been engaged in securing the fenders lying between the ships and making fast the lines that held them together. They too were all frozen in the same gawking position.

The only ones not immediately looking Roper's way were Fisher and his three blacks. Fisher was sitting dejectedly on the deck near the engine-room hatch, his back propped against the combing. One side of his jaw was swollen out of proportion, an ugly bruise shading the cheekbone. His assistants were gathered around him, all gazing down with pained sympathy. Apparently Fisher had attempted some show of resistance to the manhandling of Karen.

Only a fleeting second passed before the Mongols in the companionway remembered their primary function. With a shout they released Karen and scampered across the *Wanderer's* deck, heading for the railing. They came on the run, drawing their long sheath knives, baring teeth as if to make up for their momentary lethargy by a display of ferociousness.

"Do I have to tell you what happens when they board this ship?" Roper gently twisted the knife in the fat flesh.

Frantically Da-chong screamed at the two men clamoring over the rails. They stopped abruptly, but looked across uncertainly, as if wondering whether to proceed on their own. Trembling with anger and frustration, Da-chong repeated his order to retrace their steps, snarling at them when they complied too slowly.

Roper was carefully watching Hock make his way down the bridge ladder. Hock was the unknown factor in his plans. The knife at Da-chong's throat gave him absolute control over every individual subject to the Chinaman's orders; from the islanders he had no fear of sudden moves as long as he stood exactly where he was, in a position to cut Da-chong's life short with a single movement of his wrist.

But would this also apply to Hock?

"Fisher!" Roper called. "I want you and your boys to take over below! They'll lose nothing in the swap. Promise them oiler jobs at scale pay."

Fisher got to his feet, his astonishment quickly fading at this turn-about as he saw the need for haste. He asked for no explanations. To his assistants he whispered a few brief words, turned without waiting for an answer, and headed for the *Star's* engine-room hatch. The blacks, whether out of loyalty or as a result of hearing the magic words "scale pay," followed without hesitation. They reached the *Star's* engine-room hatch at the precise moment that three hot and begrimed islanders emerged from it, wiping their oily hands with waste. Before the men had time to realize what was going on, Fisher's big, potbellied assistant had roughly grasped and sent each stumbling toward the rail to join the deck hands looking on helplessly.

Hock had reached the main deck, stepping off the ladder with his sharp brow puckered in a scowl. "Just what do you think you're getting away with, Roper?" He shot a glance along the *Wanderer's* decks, apparently looking for a sign of Murdock. His eyes lighted on Appley and Karen. Appley was sucking on his corncob, witnessing the proceedings with the air of a man playing the impartial observer. Karen stood by him, her face pale and taut as her eyes shifted uneasily from Hock to Roper.

Hock brought his attention back to Roper. "Where the hell is Murdock?" He was obviously as much puzzled as angered.

Roper didn't answer. The hot sun beating down on the back of his neck and the strain imposed on him by maintaining a grip around Da-chong's slimy neck were producing in him a feeling of nausea. He was bleeding again, the rubbery sensation returning to his legs. Fearing that too many words might betray his weakened condition and encourage

Hock or Da-chong to defy him, he silently answered Hock with what he hoped was a mocking grin.

Why the devil was it taking Fisher so long to get moving?

Hock's eyes lowered to Da-chong, sitting stiffly in the canvas chair. He regarded the Chinese with hostility. "So you and Murdock planned on a party with the girl, did you? It's a wonder he didn't laugh in your face. Hijacking a floating gold mine right out from under your nose!"

The twist Hock was giving to Murdock's absence startled Roper. Evidently Hock thought the *Wanderer's* master was backing and covering the entire affair from a place of concealment.

A vibration suddenly swept through the decks as the Diesels below pulsated with life. It was what Roper had been waiting for. His heart racing, he relayed orders through Da-chong for all islanders to board the *Wanderer*.

Hesitantly the men obeyed.

"You're next, Hock! Get off this boat and have those lines released! Karen, come aboard!"

Hock didn't move. It seemed to dawn on him for the first time that possibly Roper alone was taking over the ship. When Appley, after helping Karen over the rails, stepped back to remain on the *Wanderer*, his suspicions were confirmed.

"He's playing this alone?" Still incredulous, Hock asked this of Appley.

The mate's lips curled into a wry smile around the stem of his pipe. "Speaking for myself, I never play long shots."

It was an effort now for Roper to keep his knees from buckling. At any moment he would be sagging against the deck chair. Through clenched teeth he rapped orders.

"Karen, go up to the bridge! Push the telegraph to slow ahead when I give the word. Hock, get moving. Now!"

Hock's answer was a sardonic laugh. He permitted Karen to move by him to the bridge, but then he threw back his head and laughed, displaying his strong white teeth. "Roper, you must be using dream pills to think one man could get away with something like this!" He undid the top button of his coat. A bead of sunlight glittered on the small nickel-plated pistol he drew from an armpit holster.

Roper crouched slightly, using the massive bulk of the Chinese as a shield. "You won't even have time for a prayer once he pulls that trigger. Tell him to put the gun down."

Da-chong grunted the warning to Hock. "Do not be impetuous, Captain. Our time will come. For the present we have no choice but to obey."

Hock indolently moved away from the ladder, smiling easily. "We've got a choice, all right. It's our boy here who hasn't a choice." He advanced slowly, raising the pistol and motioning with it. "Back off, Roper. Play it smart while you've still got a chance."

"No, no, Captain," Da-chong interrupted hurriedly. "Put your gun away. If you fired, my life would be forfeit."

Hock came to a halt. His eyes drew together. "What are you asking me to do? Hand over my ship? How the hell you expect us to catch him once he sails off? With that tub?" A contemptuous jerk of his head indicated the *Wanderer*.

"For the present we must admit defeat. The ship is not important."

"It's important to me!" Hock moved forward, raising the gun at arm's length and sighting over the barrel. "Damn if I'll give up a million in gold this easy. Roper, I'm calling your bluff!"

Roper was far from bluffing. Though his position now seemed hopeless, to permit Da-chong to live after being humbled this way before his own men was unthinkable. Karen would suffer a thousand times over for the humiliation the Chinese was undergoing. It was a dubious choice between having Karen at the mercy of Hock or handing her over to Da-chong, but conceivably she might be provided passage on the *Wanderer* if the Chinese weren't there to object. Roper doubted that either Hock or Murdock would engage in such an unprofitable act as killing the girl.

Da-chong felt his resolution in the stirring knife. He felt it and screamed at Hock, thrusting forth his fat hands. "Back, you fool! *Back!* Do as you are ordered!"

Hock cocked the pistol. His eyes steadied over the sights. "I'm not dumping a year's work down the hatch for any man." He fired, the pistol twitching in his hand.

Roper felt the stir of air over his head, heard the ricochet of a bullet careening off the poop bulkhead behind him. He knew it had been deliberately aimed high to unnerve or call his hand.

"Cease!" the Chinese screamed. "Hock!"

The whine of another bullet was Hock's answer, still aimed high. Instead of approaching closer, he started moving sideways, with the intention of circling the hatch. A smile twisted his mouth when he saw Roper's indecision. "Last chance, Roper. I *thought* you wouldn't have the nerve to follow through!"

"Your boys," Roper muttered to Da-chong, who was shivering in his grip. "Tell them to stop him!" He pressed the knife, burying the tip deeper in the heavy jowls. Immediately the Chinese shrieked with pain, roaring in Chinese.

From the deck of the *Wanderer* the two Mongols leaped into action. They came over the rails of the ships, scattering the deck hands aside.

Once again their blades came out.

When Hock saw the two men converging on him, the smile faded from his face. No doubt the Mongols had drawn their knives from force of habit, and the mere act of lowering his gun would have forestalled any violence. But reason seemed to desert Hock. He made for the hatch on the run, his eyes wild.

"It's *my* ship!" he cried. "Mine! Damn your yellow hide!" He fired as he came on, aiming at Roper's head but pulling the trigger so rapidly that accuracy was impossible.

Roper felt the thud of the single bullet hitting Da-chong; the Chinese stiffened as his body arched from the chair. His arms flailed the air as he tried to pull away from Roper. "Imbecile!" he gasped. "You im—" The breath exploded from him as he mouthed a final order to his guards. He slumped back, his head rolling forward, the faint final sounds of death seeping from his lips.

They were on Hock before he could fire again. The first man to reach him drove his blade downward, into the side of Hock's face, ripping the cheek open to the jawbone. Hock blubbered a scream as he went down on his knees. Then the two men were hacking at his face and neck, turning it into a mask of torn flesh and spurting blood. A vicious chopping stroke almost severed Hock's wrist as he blindly tried to bring his gun to bear on his assailants. The gun fell clattering to the deck. As he attempted to pick it up with his other hand, a Mongol drove his blade squarely into the back of his skull.

Hock's body jerked upright, his head flung back, his eyes bulging as if to look for a last time at the hot tropic sky overhead. He tried to speak, was seized by a spasm of coughing. He fell forward, his bloodied face sliding along the rough steel deck, fingers opening and closing convulsively.

Roper's eyes swung to the gun lying on the deck near Hock's hand. Before the two Mongols could bring their thoughts on this key to final victory, he casually lowered himself from the hatch and picked up the weapon. Authoritatively he motioned the men back.

"Get those carcasses off the ship. Step it up!"

For a few seconds the men blinked up at their dead leader slumped in his chair. When it finally penetrated that there would be no further orders from this direction, they meekly went about the task that had been assigned to them.

Roper stood back from them, half leaning, half sitting on the control box of the aft winch. He was still bleeding, but was without any pain. His waist felt stiff and numb. Whether from the excitement of knowing he and Karen were now in the clear, or from loss of blood, he began shivering, seized by a chill. There was no feeling in his legs. It was as if they were packed with sand. A murmur sounded in his ears. Suddenly the faces of the islanders and the *Wanderer's* hands gazing at him from the rail blurred, like a badly focused group snapshot.

"Johnny!"

Calling on all his strength, he managed to bring the ridge wing into hazy perspective. Against the deep blue of the sky Karen's face appeared an oval of gray.

"Johnny, I know I should come down and kiss you, but I think I'd faint if I moved.... You're hurt!"

"Stand by where you are!" he ordered, his senses suddenly sharpened by the sight of Appley swinging a leg over the *Wanderer's* rail. He wasn't forgetting that this mate had a big stake in the *Star's* cargo, that having it sail away was removing a fortune from Appley's pockets. Trickery from this quarter was not improbable. "Where do you think you're going, Appley?" he called.

Appley looked at the gun being pointed unsteadily at him. "With you, mate." He turned his head and barked orders for the coolies to let the lines go.

"Get back aboard!" Roper snarled, gripping the winch controls with his free hand to hold himself upright. In a minute, he thought, I'll be flat on my face. But in a few seconds water would separate the two ships. Just a few seconds more and the *Star* would be under way.

Appley gazed over mildly. "I wouldn't cross you, mate. Seems to me you're going to need me to sail this vessel anywhere."

"G-et back where you belong, Appley!" From the corners of his eyes he saw the last line being taken in by a hand on the *Wanderer*. He nodded up to Karen without looking that way. "Push that telegraph to slow ahead! Let's get out of here!"

"Look, mate," Appley said quickly. "I know I didn't stick my neck out when you needed help. Guess I'm not the hero type. But I'm also guessing you pinned Murdock in one of those pits."

"Guess who else is back there," Roper said bitterly. "Or maybe you want me to tell you how they looked after the rats had been at them?"

"I figured that, too," Appley said humbly. "Roper, there's nothing in this neighborhood for me anymore. Listen, mate...." The *Star* had begun moving; Appley swung his other leg over the rail and prepared to jump.

"As soon as you hit this deck I'm letting you have it," Roper said evenly. "If you don't believe me, it's going to be your own tough luck." He shook his head to clear the mist wavering before his eyes. He couldn't afford to trust Appley. He would have liked to, but he had no way of knowing whether the man was sincere, or whether Appley would attempt to take over the ship.

Appley appealed frantically, "Chum, you're going to need help getting that ship to port; you're going to need some doctoring. Also ..." He hesitated a long moment, his eyes on the gap widening between the vessels. When a good three feet separated them he made the leap, caught the railing of the *Star*, and climbed over onto the deck near Roper.

"Also, chum, that gun of yours is empty. Couldn't say so and have you prove it while our friends still had time to rush."

Roper opened his eyes to pale darkness, the sound of the night wind, and a gentle motion tuned to the retreating wash of the sea along the hull of the vessel. Turning his head slightly brought the western sky into view, long ribbons of orange and purple on the dusky horizon. A gull hung near the rail, a gray shadow gliding with the ship.

He was lying on a cot, facing the bridge house of the *Star*. On the wing he saw the head and shoulders of Appley outlined darkly against the night, a wreath of smoke drifting from his pipe. His voice came down faintly as he turned to the wheelhouse.

"Steady it at one-two-nine."

Roper closed his eyes, trying to reconstruct the events prior to his passing out. That he had passed out was certain; but he had not done so immediately. He recalled ordering the *Star* to circle the *Wanderer* until the islanders walking aimlessly about on the decks there were made to understand they would find Murdock in the stern. Then Appley had asked their course. He couldn't remember answering.

There was a movement behind him. He started to turn his head when a pair of soft arms slid around him.

"Will you stop scaring people?" she murmured against his cheek. "I thought you'd never wake up."

"Tough hide," he said, surprised at the weakness in his voice. "Who have we got at the helm?" His hands touched his middle, finding bandages and tape there.

"One of Fisher's men. Darling, don't you worry about a thing. Appley is attending to everything. He's in a very good mood after listening to some of the things you were mumbling while you were unconscious."

"What was I saying?"

"Well, you certainly sounded like a larcenist, threatening all sorts of things to your old firm. Something about claiming salvage and making them pay a tremendously large sum of money before they can set foot on the ship. Appley said you could, too."

He thought about this as he gazed up at the tropic sky, at the silver dust flung across the dark heavens. It was true the *Equatian Star* had been reported as abandoned, so technically he was in a position to place a salvage claim against the vessel. Concocting a plausible story and tying up both tin and ship to await the decision of a salvage court would certainly cause East-West to come running with a checkbook. Even a shaky claim against something worth five or six million would find the stockholders reluctant to see it in court. The nuisance value alone would be worth a hundred thousand. With that kind of charter money he could step out on his own with a small ship, small but his own.

"Temptation?" she asked.

He admitted it was. "But we'll play it straight from here on in, Karen. East-West won't need much coaxing to figure I've had a bum deal from the beginning. Well, not too much coaxing. If they take care of the men aboard and hand me the *Victorian* again, we'll call it square."

"With three years' back pay for Captain Roper."

"It's an idea."

"And widening the stateroom so his wife can keep an eye on him?"

"You're beginning to sound like a larcenist yourself."

"I'm just a practical woman, dear—and I'll have you know that if they and we can't see eye to eye, we'll put a chain across that gangway and then we'll get a lawyer."

He laughed and reached back to pull her closer. They didn't need the world on a silver platter. Together they had a great deal. The rest, he knew, would all be velvet.

THE END

Barge Girl

By Calvin Clements

Chapter One

Hauling coal barges from Mill Basin up through the Hudson River is a long monotonous run for a tugboat skipper. After five hours behind a wheel the dilapidated coaling hoppers upstream at Hoboken were always a welcome sight.

I got off the stool, shook a cramp from one leg, and played the wheel, easing the tug to bear on the distant Jersey piers—slowly, though, to avoid swinging the barge into the small Chris-Craft coming up on the port side.

Spatola, sitting on the rail below me, broke off rehashing his latest female conquest to comment on the traffic ahead. "If business is bad, you can't tell it none by these waters, Joe." He turned his head to leeward, a stream of brown fluid erupting from his grubby mouth. "Gettin' more crowded every day."

He had something there. The river was jammed, the Hudson's wide expanse swarming with tugs, both burdened and unburdened. Here and there, crossing the wakes of the tugs, steamed the lumbering New York—New Jersey ferries, the green river water creaming at their bows as they held to their fixed courses. In midstream an array of freighters was coming down, a few being assisted to open water by powerful tugs.

Instinct drew my eyes to one ferry that was clearing her Weehawken berth and really piling on the speed. She came about fast, heading in our direction, her thousand tons looming authoritatively, her whistle shrieking that she intended passing to port.

"Bet Degon's behind that wheel, Cap." Spatola got up from the rail to eye the approaching ferry. "You could be totin' six barges and that old bum still wouldn't give you a break on the right of way."

"You can't argue with size." I brought the wheel back and yanked on the whistle cord, notifying the Chris-Craft, now cruising just ahead of me, to wake up. She did and scurried out of the way.

As the ferry swept by, less than thirty yards of water separating us, a group of girls standing on the upper deck began waving at Spatola. The gestures served to recall his favorite subject as he sat back on the rail.

"Now, there's some tomatoes with an eye for a real man." He spat to leeward again. "Like this dame on South Street. 'It ain't the looks that count,' she says—"

"Another time, Romeo. Better stand by those lines." I pushed the wheel over to port, easing the throttle.

Along the line of Hoboken piers a railroad tug was cautiously working two car floats into the river. Another tug coming out with four lighters, attempting to shape upriver and caught in the strong flood, was frantically whistling at a towering grain elevator for sea room. As the grain elevator obligingly backed for the lighters, I slipped in between them—ignoring scowls from both skippers—and shaped up on the coaling slip that marked the end of our run.

In a few moments we were squeezing past a barge lying at the head of the dock. Spatola paused in the coiling of his line to gape at something on the barge's deck. "Hey, Joe, take a look at that!"

I kept my eyes on the business at hand, easing the throttle further and steadying the wheel. We crept up the slip, and as we moved in under the hoppers Spatola came into the pilothouse. "Gawd, Joe, d'ya get a gander at that babe aft?"

You can take just so much of Spatola's raving over his water-front blowzers. I shoved him aside, cut the throttle, and spun the wheel to midships. "Get that brass finished below before we get relieved. You've been dodging that job all day."

"You *gotta* catch this one, Joe. Hell, she's showin' it right off!"

I waited until the dock hand got a line on the barge, then I turned to see what Spatola was talking about.

She was standing at the cabin end of the coal barge, which was secured up the slip, a tall chesty girl hanging wash on a clothesline. She had sandy-blonde hair that blew loosely in the wind and a pert suntanned face, which from that distance looked rather pretty. An attractive dish, all right, but what had got Spatola excited was the sleeveless, tight-fitting dress she wore. It was made of some cheap material through which the late sunlight was filtering. The way she was standing, bare arms lifted and her long legs spread, her body was etched so sharply you could tell she wasn't wearing a thing underneath.

Spatola let out his breath, and with it a faint smell of whisky. "Ain't that somethin', Joe?"

"That brass below—finish it?"

He shook his head. "Jees. That's what I call something to—"

"If it's not finished, what are you doing up here? That stuff don't shine by itself."

He pointed a blunt finger. "Jus' came up to show you the hunky dame." He looked like he'd just bitten his tongue. "Jeez, Joe, sorry. Meant nothin' personal by it, guess ya know...."

I reached for the log. "Get started on that brass. I don't want it left for the next man."

He made for the door, stumbling over himself. "Gettin' right to it, Cap! Gettin' right to it."

My final entries for the day took only a few minutes. Then, to kill time until Johnson, my relief, arrived, I picked up the binoculars and trained them on the Manhattan shore, where some activity was going on at Pier 40: Two Diesel tugs, both laboring with squat stacks belching and sterns trembling over boiling wakes, were coaxing a large red-hulled freighter, heavy in the water, from its berth. Just above it an excursion boat was backing furiously, its skipper apparently caught napping by the freighter leaving the slip.

I held the glasses on the excursion boat until the danger of collision had passed. Then I remembered the barge girl.

She was still busy at the clothesline when I focused the glasses on the barge. She was solidly built, and it was a tantalizing thing the way the sunlight from the river continued to silhouette her long shapely legs. As I watched, she lifted her arms to hang up a stocking, her dress stretching tight and bringing her thrusting bosom into prominence.

My eyes shifted to the name of the barge: *Sand Point*. That rang a bell.

I put the glasses aside, got the log out, and looked up the night schedule sheet. The entry for the evening run was there. Johnson to tow the *Sand Point* from its Hoboken coaling pier to Mill Basin. Then I remembered that this barge was among the four that Hackett Towing had bought last month.

I checked my watch, saw that Johnson was late and would be pressed for time. I gave the whistle cord a yank.

Spatola came along the deck, cramming a small bottle into his hip pocket.

"At it again?"

He wiped his mouth; grinning sheepishly. "Jus' a snort, Joe."

"You're going to snort yourself out of a job someday. Throw 'er off. We're moving."

"Ain't we gettin' relieved here?"

"We're securing the *Sand Point* for towing. She's moving out tonight, and it'll save Johnson a little time."

He squinted up the slip, then rolled his eyes slyly back to me. "Sure, Cap. I getcha!"

The Hackett *Junior* was a tug you could spin on a dime—when her engines weren't coughing out. I backed her away from the hoppers, spun the wheel, and kicked it hard ahead. For once she came foaming around without a hitch, her whiskered nose heading for the *Sand Point*. I cut and let her drift. We eased up the slip toward the barge.

The girl was rummaging in the clothesbasket at her feet. She gave us a brief glance as we came alongside, then went back to the basket.

Close up she wasn't the beauty I'd thought, but then, neither was she homely. Her blonde hair had a soft natural sheen and a well-brushed look. Her tanned cheeks were freckled, her mouth full and red and a little sulky.

She wasn't wearing a wedding ring.

Spatola looped the line over a cleat on the barge and secured us. He parked himself on the rail, looked over at the girl, and cleared his throat.

"How about those towlines?"

"Aw, Joe, gimme a break...."

"Get aft before you blow a fuse."

He gave me a reproachful look as he got up, but he went aft. I lit a cigarette and rested my arms on the window sill. She was still leaning over the basket; fishing for a particular article of clothing, and from where I was standing, some ten feet away and a little higher, my gaze couldn't help traveling straight down that neckline. She was a big girl.

Her head came up at that same moment, and two insolent blue eyes gave me a frosty stare. "Don't strain your eyes, mister!"

That rubbed me the wrong way, both the remark and her crisp tone. It never fails; they wear next to nothing, and then rear back if a man looks them over.

"When you want privacy, sis, you pull down the blinds. When you don't, you leave them up. *Capeesh?*"

For a brief moment her mouth hung open. Then she closed it and slowly straightened, put one hand on one shapely hip, rested her weight on that side, and coolly considered me. "I don't recall asking for your advice on how to dress, mister."

"No charge, sis."

Her eyes darkened to a frigid blue. "You *could* go somewhere else, you know. You don't *have* to be breathing down my neck!"

"I can't go anywhere until my relief shows up. And I am not breathing down your neck. I happen to be in the only spot where I can keep one eye on that rumpot aft, to make sure he doesn't louse up those lines and leave you adrift when you're halfway down the bay. Satisfied?"

She brushed a wisp of hair from her cheek and reached into the clothesbasket. "Try putting both eyes on him." She started pinning a piece of wash to the line, then suddenly hesitated, her sun-browned face clouding with uncertainty.

The reason for her hesitation was a pair of pale-blue panties, the net type with some frilly lace around the bottom. She had one clothespin on, the other in her hand, and it was apparent she was mulling over the wisdom of displaying something so intimate with me around.

The opportunity to really take her down a peg was too good to let slide. "They must be the kind with plenty of stretch."

When her eyes snapped up at me, I was reflectively dragging on my cigarette and gazing at the firm curve of her flanks.

"That, mister, is what I call a cheap crack!" Her steady look and tone were contemptuous. "And just about what you'd expect from a smart aleck tug jockey!"

I gave her a grin then, satisfied that I had finally got one in under her guard. "Suppose we call it quits, sis, and start off on the right foot. O.K.?"

Her answer was another withering look. She stretched out the panties with a defiant yank and viciously jammed the clothespin on them.

"If it will make you feel any better, that remark was strictly on the kidding side."

"Lose yourself, mister. Kid somebody else." She started to take something from the basket, then hurriedly pushed it back out of sight. She lifted out a pillowcase instead.

"Of course, sis, there's one way to look at it. A man has to work up some kind of interest to kid *anybody*."

"You don't say." She pinned the pillowcase to the line and smoothed it.

"We're working for the same outfit, so maybe we should be introduced. My name is Baski. Joe Baski."

She picked up another pillowcase. "I was dying to know."

Instead of being annoyed, I found myself liking her snap. No coy clinging vine here; both feet on the ground. She'd give a man a tussle, all right.

Worth a try. "Couldn't we take that chip off your shoulder, Miss ... Miss ..."

"Murk. And it's not Miss, It's Mrs." She turned to face me, her cheeks dimpling in a sweet, smug smile as if a final victory of some sort were hers.

I put on a long face to play along. Actually, I didn't care whether she was in circulation or not. I take what's offered and lose no sleep over what I can't get.

"My luck again, sis. That's the way it goes."

Johnson suddenly appeared on the wharf from behind a coal chute. He hopped onto the barge, a stumpy weathered man who'd been pushing tugs long before I was born. "Evening, Stella. How's the cutest thing this side of heaven doing?"

She gave him a saucy look to show she was pleased with the compliment. "Still flirting, Pop? And at your age!"

He threw her a kidding leer. "Thirty years younger and I wouldn't be wasting time with words. I'd be breaking your door down."

"Such talk!"

Johnson grinned and boarded the tug. He climbed up the ladder and came into the pilothouse shaking his head. "Surprises never cease—a young handsome lad like you chewing the fat with Stella and her hubby not around? Murk must be slipping."

"She needs watching that close?"

"Wouldn't say she *needs* it. It's just that he never seems to be more than five feet away when there's another man within smelling distance. Ha! Speak of the devil ..."

A man had come out of the barge cabin, a short chunky guy in his fifties, wearing thick glasses. He was completely bald. He was holding his jaw. "Where's them tooth drops, Stella?"

"In the medicine closet, I guess. Where'd you leave them?"

"They ain't there now, they ain't!"

"Well, they're where you last put them. I certainly never touch them."

"'Bout time you had the meal on, ain't it?" He kept holding his jaw.

"Get to it in a minute."

"Well, you should've had it on. Be cooking all this time, it would've. You know I like to eat proper hours."

"O.K., O.K. It won't take me long." She picked up the basket and went into the cabin.

He came over to the edge of the barge and peered up at me. "Want something, do you?"

He was the kind of guy you disliked on sight. "Yeah. We're leaving here in ten minutes. Get the lead out of your lard and shape those lines up!" I stepped back and pushed the window closed before he could say anything.

Johnson was pulling his fatigues on. He grinned at me. "He don't like that 'lard' stuff. Kinda sensitive about his weight."

"He got me, growling for his grub like that."

"He gets everybody. Cheap as they come, too. Kills him if he has to spend ten cents on his wife. Nice kid, that Stella."

"How come she ever hooked up with him? He must be two, three times her age."

"Three is closer. The 'how come,' I dunno. She was about seventeen, I understand, strictly an East Side product, and maybe she saw a chance to swap the tenements for some elbow room. Bet she's not too happy about it now, though. You'll catch her sitting out and looking at the moon some nights, like any young girl might who hankers for a bit of romance. Murk's kind of lax in that department, they say. Checkers are his passion.... Joe, Hackett gave me a call." He got up and slipped into his leather jacket. "Says for you to drop in at the office tonight."

"O.K." I turned in time to catch Stella peeking up at me through the curtained cabin window. She quickly jerked her head back. "Drop me off at the Battery, Pop?" As soon as I made the request I felt foolish.

He nodded, without looking too puzzled. "Sure thing, lad. Anywhere you say."

I ducked down into the bunkroom behind the pilothouse. I stripped and washed, still feeling slightly ridiculous for not going ashore and taking the tube to New York. Johnson had wondered why. I elected to stay aboard a slow-moving tug, and now I was wondering the same thing. Was it to get another glimpse of a piece of fluff—married, at that—who had simply taken a second look my way?

If so, how silly can you get?

I dressed in street clothes and went up to the pilothouse again. We were under way, bearing diagonally over to Manhattan. The *Sand Point* was alongside, its deck empty.

Far downstream, in the vicinity of Ellis Island, a huge black-hulled liner was coming into view, her fat stack encircled with red, white, and blue, which helped to identify her as the *United States*. On either side, acting as escorts for the climax of her record-breaking crossing, were a score or more tugs, Coast Guard cutters, and police boats, their whistles and horns setting up a discordant din. Three fireboats, also attempting to keep pace, were sending saluting streams of water high in the air. You couldn't see the fireboats, just the misty veils descending about them.

On the lower Manhattan shore traffic had been brought to a standstill. The West Side Highway was choked with cars slowed to a crawl, and down along West Street trucking had halted to watch the new queen of the seas make her bow. Ticker tape was fluttering from skyscrapers, the offshore breeze bearing some of it out over the river. Even the ferries, the ferries you could almost set your watch by, were backwatering, their whistle blasting a welcome, their passengers waving handkerchiefs.

The commotion finally brought the girl out on the deck of the barge. She stood near the edge, shading her eyes against the late sunlight, the breeze molding the thin dress to her curvy back. It was the kind of full, firm curve that made you restless if you kept looking.

I kept looking. "How long they married, Pop?"

Johnson, sitting on a stool beside the wheel, glanced down at the barge. "Stella? Five years, there about. Say, you two have met before, haven't you?"

"First time today."

"Never met her over at your boat shed? I know she's taken a morning walk over there from the basin once or twice when Murk was napping."

I stared at him. "What the devil does she want over there?"

He shrugged and brought the wheel over slightly. "Guess I mentioned that project of yours while I was talking with her one time. Probably went over for a look at something nobody but a crazy Polack would even start."

Right then I lost all interest in the view on the barge. "I can see I'm going to have to padlock my place when I'm not there. All that has to happen is for some dumb cluck of a dame to leave a cigarette lying around!" The mere thought of a fire at the shed made my legs weak.

Johnson shook his head. "She doesn't smoke, Joey." He took out his pipe. "Calm yourself where she's concerned. There's good sense in that pretty head."

"That padlock's going on just the same. First thing tomorrow."

His faded eyes twinkled as he filled the pipe. "The smart thing would be to padlock it after she's in, lad. Then you'd have something worth working on."

"You're getting to sound like Spatola. Listen, Pop, drop me off over there, at Pier Fifty. I'll grab the subway at Fourteenth Street."

"Fifty it is."

With a practiced ease that was a pleasure to watch, Johnson approached the Manhattan line of piers. He played the wheel, slipped between a derrick and a lighter, and slowed to drift along the head of the pier, where a freighter was being loaded with tractors.

I went down on deck, stepped off on the dock, and gave him a wave. "See you in the morning, Pop." The girl, I noticed, had disappeared into the barge cabin.

"Don't forget about seeing Hackett tonight."

"Right." I went up the dock, skirting darting Hi-Lows being worked by sweating longshoremen, and picked my way through the West Street traffic to Fourteenth.

A subway, then a bus took me over to Brooklyn's Mill Basin, where Hackett's office was located. The basin itself was a reedy tortuous inlet off the westerly end of Jamaica Bay, its tenants a few coaling hoppers, a line of weather-peeled bungalows with their small boat slips, and some rickety fishing wharves. Off the head of the first wharf stood a lone shanty, and this served as Hackett Towing's one and only office.

Our outfit was strictly a one-man setup, with Jud Hackett spending twenty-four hours a day worrying a living out of the three shallow-draft tugs left to him by his old man. Each of these tugs was rigged for pilothouse control, and so they got along with only a skipper and a deckie—no engine-room men. This meant cheap running, about the cheapest you can get for barge hauling, but Hackett stayed awake nights trying to come up with gimmicks to make it cheaper. Monthly pep talks to the skippers was one of these gimmicks. In a way you couldn't blame him for attempting to cut corners where he could; the big outfits are always trying to strangle the runts. Hackett had to keep on his toes, or fold.

He waved me to the chair by his desk when I walked in, riffled some papers, and worked a soggy cigar to the corner of his mouth. He was a heavy guy with a bulldog jaw and nervous hands. "Sorry to take your time this way, Joe. Thought if something's been on your mind, talking about it might get it off. Can't maneuver a boat with your mind elsewhere, you know." He kept riffling the papers and chewing on the cigar.

I just looked at him, wondering what he was talking about.

"Well, take damage money, Joe. You haven't collected any for three months. Why?" He sat back, pointed the cigar at the ceiling, and blew a cloud of smoke in the same direction.

Damage money is the forty a month added to a tugboat skipper's salary for coming through thirty days without damaging a guardrail or the bulwark of a barge he's handling. It's quite a trick when you consider you work mostly in close quarters when maneuvering around slips, and a tide setting you against a barge can split a rail just like that. There's no such thing as trifling damage to a boat. Yardwork starts at a thousand dollars, just for laying the boat up; and this doesn't include the cost of being idle. With insurance rebating only part of the premium for non-claims, it pays the owner to ante up to his skippers for extra-careful handling.

Believe me, you keep a sharp eye out and make less like a cowboy rounding into slips when you figure an extra forty may be found in your envelope.

Hackett knew the reason I hadn't been collecting. He knew it as well as I did, and it got me a little sore. "You tell *me* why I haven't been collecting."

"Eh?" The cigar leveled and swung my way.

"That dough. That forty a month. I haven't been collecting it, and that's right. What do *you* think the reason is?"

He fooled with the papers again. "Well, that boat of yours *has* got tricky engines. Handicapped in a way, Joe. Got to admit that. Fair to give you the benefit of the doubt, so we'll let it slide. Yeah, we'll let it slide. But this other thing, Joe. Schedules. Got to try for faster running time."

"'Tricky' is a lousy word. Those engines are a menace to shipping and to the boat itself. The last time those reversing cams stuck on me I damn near got cut in two by a tanker. It's been pure luck getting away with minor wrap-ups these past few months. Pure luck!"

The cigar nodded. "Tug's a problem child, all right. Not your fault she doesn't behave. Like I said, we'll let it slide. About this running time—"

"No problem child. She just needs new engines. Maybe there *is* something on my mind, at that. That damage money. The way I figure it, it's coming to me. Those crumby engines aren't my responsibility. O.K., you haven't the dough for new ones, but why penalize me every time they balk and I bang into something?"

He looked sorry he'd brought the subject up. He had wanted to open the pep talk with me on the ropes, but it had backfired. "We'll forget it, Joe. Know you're on the ball. You're a good skipper."

"Forget what? The damage, or damage money?"

He took the cigar from his mouth and looked at it. It was a mess. He dropped it into the ash tray. "Three months makes it one-twenty."

I agreed.

"Meet me halfway, Joe."

"Sixty bucks, then." I hadn't figured on collecting a dime.

"Tommy!"

Miss Thomas came out of her cubbyhole, giving me an impersonal smile. She was a small, shapely brunette leaning to tailored suits, mannish bobs, and a faint trace of a mustache. We'd had one date before I found out she liked everything on a Platonic level—at least with men. We had killed the rest of the evening bowling.

"Make out a check for sixty dollars to Baski, Tommy." He clamped his jaw around a fresh cigar and beat a thoughtful tattoo on the desk with his big fingers. "Digs the hole a little deeper, but I guess we'll manage."

The crying towel was all part of the act. I went along. "The barge deal tough to handle?"

He shrugged. "Mortgaged to the hilt to pull it off. Good insurance, though. Whatever happens, our boats now have four barges to move, and it's nice to be able to count on that steady piece of business. But it's rough going, Joe. Going to stay rough until they're paid off."

"Seems to me you're running a fouled-up schedule—at least where the barge *Sand Point* is concerned. It was lying in that Hoboken slip all day. Makes the daily basin run, doesn't it? Why not send it out with me mornings?"

He thought about it. "Don't know, Joe. Running time would be slowed with two barges. The *Junior's* not built for that kind of towing."

"Work it this way: On the ebb, double up on my tows coming down to the basin; on the flood, double them going back. That way, where I'm running with the tide, the time wouldn't be too much slower. You'd have to use two boats bucking the tide, sure, but using just one part of the time would show in your books at the end of the month. I'll bet it would show plenty."

He worked on the cigar and thought some more. He shot me a quick look. "You giving me a slow rub just to get near that chassis on the *Sand Point*?"

That angle hadn't occurred to me, and I said so.

He gazed at the tip of his cigar. "They say he plays checkers with her every evening." He roused himself and went back to chewing on the cigar. "All right, we'll try it, Joe. Means shifting the coaling schedule, but we'll try it. You'd better take tomorrow as your day off so you can fall in with it. Mind?"

"Suits me."

Tommy brought the check over. Hackett signed it with a flourish. "Coming along with that yacht of yours, Joe?" He handed me the check.

"Never miss a day on it. I'll beat it over there now, if we're finished here."

"Wait a minute, Joe." He reached into a drawer and came up with an envelope. "I've got two tickets for the annual Propeller Club shindig at the Astor tonight. Dinner and heaven only knows how many speeches. How about us taking in that dinner and forgetting our cares for one night? The speeches we'll skip—bend a few at the bar instead."

"Sounds good."

"Be a late affair, so we'll take a room for the night." He took the cigar from his mouth and gave me a big grin. "Maybe two rooms. Think you can turn that charm on a couple of dolls with damn little will power?"

"I can try." I grinned right back at him. He was a pretty good skate when he came out from behind that desk.

Chapter Two

About this boat of mine: You're going to say it couldn't be built by one man, by me. Well, in a way you'd be right. Back in '43 at Pensacola a man named Ralph Creelman played a part in it, a big part.

In civilian life Creelman had been a hosiery manufacturer with a fanatical passion for boating. When the war broke out he traded his fifty-foot motor cruiser *Delta* to the government for a jg rank and a patrol-duty assignment aboard the boat. There was nothing shady about the deal, because it was unlikely that the government would ever have called on the services of either Creelman, who was close to sixty, or his boat. For a duty concession, the Navy was getting both a patrol boat and someone to run it, with everybody satisfied, and Creelman, a tall wiry guy, walking around with his gray head in the clouds.

He was looking for a quartermaster who knew the Florida Keys and the Bahamas, when I spotted his cruiser buoyed in the bay.

Now, you either like boats or you don't. I do. To me, the ultimate goal in anyone's life should be ownership of a cabin cruiser large enough for coastwise travel, large enough so you can move away from the river and bays if you have the urge. But this is quite a goal. You don't buy deep-water cruisers on a tug captain's salary. You can look at them and swallow the ache in your throat, as I often did, but you don't buy. And if you don't understand about that ache, no amount of explanation will make you understand. As I said, you either like boats or you don't.

Creelman didn't have to look any farther for his quartermaster. I took one look at the lazy *Delta* sitting out there in the bay with silver glints of sunlight flashing from her chrome ports, got an armload of charts, and fed Creelman a line that I'd been sailing those waters for ten years. It didn't take him long to discover that my nose had to go into those charts for just about every move we made, but by that time he also found out that I was as nutty about boats as he was, and that made everything O.K.

That fifty-foot cruiser of his was really something out of a boatman's dream. For outward beauty its long, graceful hull was finished in white porcelain, its awninged decks in a black Russian mahogany that must have cost a dollar a running foot or more. Below, it had been designed with a sharp eye for room and comfort. It slept eight, or ten in a pinch. Every inch of space had been carefully planned and utilized. The main cabin even included a built-in bar, and forward of the galley the flooring had been dropped to make room for full-height tile showers. A top designing job.

I loved that boat, and Creelman knew it.

"Did I ever show you the drawings for the *Delta*?" he asked me one day.

He brought out two thick volumes that must have weighed close to five pounds. Everything was there, from an over-all sketch right down to detailed specifications for the type and size of wood screws to be used on the bunks.

I studied those drawings—the intricate designing that had been broken down to an a-b-c simplicity. It was a crazy idea that began forming in my mind. Crazy, and yet not crazy.

"Mr. Creelman, I'm going to build a twin to the *Delta*."

He smiled. "Do you happen to know her final cost?"

"Sixty thousand?"

"Close enough. And you're in a position to lay that out?"

"You're going to say I'm nuts, but I can see myself putting this together for eight or nine thousand."

"That, Baski, you have to show me."

"O.K., take these plans. Do you mind if I have photostats made?"

"Not at all."

"That's my start, twenty bucks' worth of pictures. Now, this is no yard boat. Everything in and on it was cut and assembled by hand. Nothing standard that you can buy from the factory, except maybe the panel instruments and engines. O.K., that's labor with a capital L. High-priced labor. For every dollar's worth of material you put into the *Delta*, you paid another dollar for labor. Right?"

"Go on."

"I'm building this boat with my hands in my spare time. Cost of labor, zero. Sure, it'll take me five or six years, but it can be done. And I won't have to pay any thirty thousand, for materials, either."

"How do you figure on cutting it?" He was trying to conceal his amusement.

"These, engines are Seafarers, two-fifty horse. What'd they set you back? Eight thousand? What's wrong with rebuilt GM's, half the horse, for a thousand? Sure, sure, the speed is cut a third, but tell me, Mr. Creelman, when did you last cruise above eighteen? And just look at this interior woodwork! All top fancy grade, costing a third more than a plain serviceable run-of-the-mill wood. Couldn't that mahogany paneling in the cabin be spruce or white pine, stained and grained? Where's that thirty thousand now?"

He tilted his head thoughtfully. "Well, you've got the drive, Baski. Perhaps you'll do it." He paused a moment. "If you do, I want you to bring your boat to Creel Haven. You might construct a bungalow at the south end. Use it as a place to hang your hat and shake the sea from your legs."

I was familiar with Creel Haven, the cay he had bought in the Bahamas. It was a beauty of a spot, about fifty acres of high, fertile ground partly developed with fruit-bearing tropical trees, and entirely surrounded by sloping beaches having dust-fine sand that was always cool to the touch. Most of the cays in the Bahamas are nothing more than clusters of reefs and rocks. Those that are privately owned and developed into estates are about as difficult and expensive to buy as midtown Manhattan plots, and I couldn't see Creelman handing over squatter's rights on his.

He saw my skepticism. "I'm not joking, Baski. You can have that south end. Show me a man who can build another *Delta* by hand, and from scratch, and I'll be happy to have that boatman as a neighbor. I hope you succeed. But, in any event, you've given yourself something to dream about for the duration."

But I did more than just dream. Instead of trying to support the local bars, I socked every penny away, and I studied those plans. I read every book in the base library on boat construction. Two years later, a Normandy casualty and lying on a hospital bed in Dundee, I could close my eyes and see each step that would be taken. In my sleep I drilled framing, sawed flooring, glued and hammered.

The one big worry on my mind was the boat shed. You don't build a twelve-ton, fifty-foot cabin cruiser in somebody's backyard. But, as sometimes happens, the thing you worry about most becomes no problem at all once you work on it. The very first day back on the job with Hackett Towing, and wheeling one of his tugs up Jamaica Bay, I saw where the *Delta's* twin could be built.

It was about two miles from Mill Basin, in the heart of the Jamaica marshlands, a desolate area overgrown with shoulder-high reeds and brush that parted for a small winding creek fed by the bay. Back along the south bank of the creek were three clapboard bungalows, long abandoned because of seepage undermining them and now sitting at cockeyed angles. Accessible from the basin by a single footpath through the marshes—which meant privacy—one of the bungalows had a full attic, giving me the height needed for my boat shed. The clincher for me was the shanty in the rear, containing a gasoline generator that had been used as a common source of power for the three buildings.

The old guy who owned the place thought I was crazy when I offered three hundred, but he took the money. It took me six months to lay out, cut, and assemble the keel and rib structure, and by that time every penny I'd saved during the war was gone. But I was on my way. I brought Hackett over one day to show him the start. He looked through the plans, studied the photographs of the *Delta*, and then walked up and down the shed, frowning at the half-completed hull.

"Joe, you're nuts. Wheeling a tug all day and working this at night? You're nuts. Take you five years."

"That's what I figured."

"Where's the dough coming from?"

"What you're looking at is the three grand I saved in the service. I'll be putting fifteen hundred a year of my salary in her for the next five years. Pay as I go along."

"Ten thousand?" He shook his head. "Been away too long, Joe. A buck isn't a buck anymore. This thing will run fifteen. More."

It turned out he was right about the buck. It didn't go far. But I partly solved that by scavenging around the harbor for interior bracing, partitions, and stuff like that. A two-by-four here, some tongue and groove there, and I managed to cut costs.

All the way it was hard, backbreaking work, but in four years my cruiser was no longer a dream. It was a solid reality, with hull, decking, and compartments built, and the most difficult fitting jobs behind me. Even the engines were installed. And no rebuilts or conversions— these were brand-new Grey marines, two hundred horse, and represented the happiest moment in my harbor scavenging. I took them from a sixty-two-footer that had piled into a sand bar off Barren Island during a blow. The insurance adjuster, who had paid off in full to the boat owner, asked fifteen hundred for them and then settled for an even thousand when I threatened to dump them back on the sand bar at high water.

I sent Creelman snapshots of the construction from time to time, and then one day I received a snapshot from him. It was a view of southern Creel Haven. In the foreground was the beach, and in the background, standing under some dark palms, was a small ranch-type bungalow. On the back of the snap he had written that it was only four walls and a roof, just some stuff they had left over after building his place, and if it would make me feel better, I owed him nine hundred for the native labor.

Really tickled that he was carrying out his word to give me a piece of the cay, I wrote and thanked him, setting a date three months away when I might be arriving. Three months, I thought, would be plenty of time to complete the boat. That was the same day I wangled sixty dollars' damage money out of Hackett, plus the Propeller dinner, which turned out to be strictly an all-night drinking affair.

It was almost noon the next day before I arrived at the boat shed, and it wasn't until I stepped through the door and saw Stella sitting on my workbench with my cat on her lap that I remembered I hadn't bought the padlock.

She was gazing dreamy-eyed at the varnished, well-rubbed flying bridge that towered into the rafters, and absently stroking the cat's back. The sound of the door closing snapped her out of it. She put the cat on the bench and stood up, looking confused and embarrassed. She was wearing a black linen dress that was belted tightly at the waist, accentuating her high bosom and rounded hips. In white high heels she made a smart appearance.

She made a show of smoothing her dress. "I'm sorry. I thought you were working the tug today."

"Is that why you're in here? Because I'm supposed to be somewhere else?"

She looked more confused. "Well, that does sound—"

"Listen, sis, that happens to be the time you should stay out of here. If I'm around, O.K., you're welcome to come in and look things over. But when I'm pushing a tug I don't want to be worrying about what might be going on here."

Her chin went up, the familiar frost gathering in her blue eyes. "You talk almost as if I were a thief. I can assure you all I ever did was to sit and admire your work. This is the largest boat I've ever seen being built, and I found myself intrigued."

Picking her way through the odd pieces of lumber on the floor, she came over and stood in front of me. She cocked her head to one side. "You happen to be standing in front of the door. If you'll move to one side—"

"Perhaps I shouldn't have put it just the way I did. The boat means a lot to me and I worry about fire. While it's under construction the insurance rates are so high I can't handle them." I was revising my estimate of her. Even though you couldn't call her beautiful, she was so nice to look at that the difference was hair-splitting.

Her blonde hair was tied back with a red ribbon, and the way the freckles spread across the bridge of her nose and onto her cheeks gave her a wholesome girl-next-door appeal. Her eyebrows were thick and dark, her full mouth a ripe red.

"Well?" She was waiting for me to move away from the door.

"We seem to be two people with a knack for getting off on the wrong foot every time." I tilted my head to the boat. "Been inside yet?"

She hesitated, her eyes lighting with sudden interest, but her tone was that of a martyr. "No, but I don't think I'd care to—"

"Sure you would. I'll get a lamp and show you around the staterooms." I went over to the workbench and got the battery lamp. She didn't leave, as I half expected she might. She had moved over to the stem post of the boat and was gently touching it. Her eyes, somewhat mollified, traveled down the long white hull that ran the length of the floor, then lifted in admiration to the superstructure.

I had caulked and painted, then sanded and repainted until the hull had taken on the bright, smooth appearance of baked enamel. The superstructure and flying bridge had been stained and rubbed to give it a rich redwood tone. Six coats of varnish had been used on that wood, each one oil-rubbed until a natural luster appeared. "Like it?"

She nodded. "It's beautiful. I've never seen anything so beautiful. Never."

"You sound like you mean it."

"I do. I really do. And it seems so unbelievable that one man could build all this."

"Every plank by J. Baski. Every last single plank. And I don't mind bragging about it."

She smiled at that. Her teeth were small and even, startlingly white against her tanned skin. "Nobody would blame you for that, I'm sure. This may sound like a silly question, but how on earth do you plan to get it out of here without tearing down the whole bungalow?"

"If I did tear it down, it wouldn't matter. It'll never be used again. But I'm going to knock out just those front walls and run it down on those rails there, at high water. She'll draw less than three, so we'll make the bay easily enough."

"And when will that be?"

"Few months. She could go into the water now, but her interior is still rough—not too rough, though. Come aboard and I'll show you around. Up this ladder here...."

The amount of space and headroom in a cabin cruiser is always a surprise to those unfamiliar with small craft. They appear cramped until you're aboard and walking around, and then you're amazed at the room you have to move in. So it was with Stella. And she was really surprised when she stepped into the master stateroom aft.

It was the one compartment I had completed. The overhead was painted a dark bottle green, the sides a lighter green, and covering the flooring was a thick broadloom rug, also light green, one of the few luxuries I had permitted myself. Against the side bulkheads were fitted twin bunks that I had made by hand, with drawer-chests fitted into the space beneath. Separating the bunks was a large bureau. Cream-colored Venetian blinds were in place at the side windows, and all that was needed was bedding, a chair or two, and perhaps a painting over each bunk.

She sighed as she looked around. "Do you call this rough? It's the most beautiful bedroom I've ever seen."

"Well, hardly that. But I don't mind hearing you say it."

"And you can even stand erect in here. Now, isn't that something?" She shook her blonde head in admiration.

"You don't stoop on any boat worthy of its name. Watch your footing here...."

We went forward to the main cabin. Here, my dinette nook had been fashioned from an old oak kitchen set that I had refinished. I described how, with convertible sofas on each side, the cabin could serve as an additional bunk room.

"My! A couple could live on board forever, couldn't they? It's really a home."

"It is that. They could live and travel. And a lot more than a couple. You could raise a family here."

She gave me a casual side glance. "Is that what you're planning to do?"

"It's not on my mind. I wanted a big boat for two reasons: one, so I wouldn't be restricted by every little blow that came up, and two, it's easier making a living in the Keys and the Bahamas. That's where I intend to go. Down there you can hire out faster and for better money with a comfortable boat. You get charters by the week from vacationers with dough, and when they're satisfied they come back looking for you.... Here's a place that will interest you."

We moved past the forward stateroom, where I had four Pullman berths in place, and then into the galley. None of the galley equipment had been put in, but all the framing and plumbing were completed. Now it was simply a matter of buying and installing the stove, sink, and refrigerator. "I'll admit a boat galley sort of crowds you, but then you save steps. Evens things out."

"I don't think it's small at all. Just right, I would say." She stood on tiptoe to inspect the interior of the cupboard.

We were standing pretty close, almost touching, and whatever kind of perfume she had on, it was doing to me what perfume advertisers claim it does.

"Everything is lovely." She closed the cupboard door. "It's such a tremendous amount of work, I wonder how you could even bring yourself to start."

"Well, when you want something bad enough you don't think too much of the work involved. You ask yourself can it be done, and if it can, you go ahead and do it. I wanted this boat and I knew I could build it. To me, it's kind of a Noah's ark to freedom."

"I certainly envy you. Hoboken to Brooklyn—that's the longest trip I've ever made. You'll be able to go anywhere, even cross the ocean."

"That would be a bit risky. But the entire North American continent will be my own personal stamping grounds, and I'm satisfied with that. First, I'm heading for Creel Haven. The name means nothing to you, but come topside and I'll tell you about it."

Above, in the flying bridge, I showed her the control board and the ease of operation, and I told her about Creelman, and how I had first decided to build the twin to his boat when I saw his plans. As I talked I kept smelling her perfume, and wishing to hell Murk was an uncle of hers instead of her husband.

She thought I was kidding about the island Creelman had bought and the bungalow he had built for me. "An entire island, just for himself?"

"Well, it's smaller than the island you picture. They call them cays down there. There are several thousand of them throughout the Bahamas, the larger ones cultivated as private estates. Generally they run from about twenty to several hundred acres. Creel Haven is about fifty or so, small but as pretty as any of them."

"Sounds lonesome—small islands with only a few people."

I didn't answer immediately. For some reason there flashed into my mind a picture of the basin as I had passed it on my way over to the shed. The Hackett *Junior* had been tied up about fifty yards astern of the barge *Sand Point*, and was to remain there until evening, when Johnson came on duty. Stella couldn't have missed spotting that idle tug. Therefore she knew I was not out working tows, and that in all probability I would come over to the shed some time that morning.

She knew, and she had come; and here I was gabbing, wasting time like a big clown.

"Lonesome, Stella?" I said in answer to her comment. "Well, yes and no."

She was standing at the wheel, her back to me, looking out over the bow. I reached around her, putting both my hands on the wheel, imprisoning her. I casually turned the wheel back and forth, as if testing it. "If it's lonesome, it's a comfortable kind of lonesomeness. You pick the kind of company you want, and when you want it, not just any Joe who happens to be your neighbor. And whether you have people around or not, you couldn't get lonesome in Bahama waters. At least, I couldn't. Ever see them?"

She shook her head without turning. "From Hoboken to Brooklyn. Remember?"

I remembered, and I was remembering she was married to an old guy who'd rather play checkers, so it figured that she'd do some back-alley prowling: She saw me, liked me; she primped, powdered, and came over—and I'd need more than a hole in my head to ignore that kind of invitation from a girl like Stella Murk. "Well, you've missed something, Stella. Just look over there...."

I moved in closer and pointed ahead, out over the bow of the boat. Her soft hair was about two inches from my nostrils. I wasn't smelling the perfume now. Just her. "Forget that attic window you see. Out there are the waters, but you wouldn't see them as just one color, as you do in New York. There's purple-blue and bright green and splashes of brown and red, the color varying with the depth of the water. Half the Bahama area runs shallow, and the sun reflects the bottom. When you spot threads of dark blue running between those brown and red splashes, that's your deep-water channels. Those colors are something you never tire of looking at while you're cruising.

"Take a look down here, over the side. Look at those wood shavings on the floor—at that box of nails reflecting the light. In the Bahamas that's exactly how plain and detailed the ocean floor looks. The water's so clear you can sail for days on end and almost believe you're moving across liquid glass. Four thousand square miles of it. Drop the hook anywhere, put on a diving mask, and walk around down there, and Stella, you'd think you were in the Garden of Eden. It's like somebody had gathered together every possible color and combination of colors in the world and splattered them over a vast rock garden. Feel like collecting shells for a hobby? O.K. they're all down there, every type, shape, and color. Spear fishing? You can load the boat in an hour with the best eating fish in the world. Does being lonesome that way sound so bad? I'll take it every time.

"And you don't take the subway home to a crowded flat. Your home is right ahead of you, that ridge of white water merging with the pink coral sand of the beach and the olive-green foliage stirring above it."

"It sounds wonderful." She turned, her blue eyes dreamy. "You make it sound like para—" She saw then that she couldn't move any farther because my arms were still on each side of her, my hands on the wheel.

"You knew I'd be over here today, didn't you, Stella?"

"No, of course not. I—"

"You're a liar."

Her eyes began to frost up. "Of all the egotistical—"

"When you left the basin, wasn't the *Junior* tied up astern of your barge? And didn't you say you thought I was out with it?"

Her eyes wavered, the red creeping up under the tan of her cheeks. She looked like a kid caught with her hand in the cookie jar.

"You're not a very good liar."

"No, I'm not. But I didn't want you to think what you seem to be thinking."

"Then why did you come here this morning?"

"To see the boat, of course."

"I said you weren't a good liar." I leaned forward and kissed her lightly on the mouth.

"Is that included in the fifty-cent tour?" She looked up at me calmly, or attempted to.

"Stella, I generally say what I mean, and ask for what want. Maybe I haven't the time for beating around the bush. I want you."

"Well, that's frank enough. Now if you'll drop your arms ..."

"You came over here to see me today."

"Lord, the conceit—"

I put my arms around her waist and drew her against me. She squirmed to free herself, her hands pushing against my chest. "You seem to be forgetting I have a husband!"

"He's easy to forget." My mouth found hers. She stopped struggling, but her lips remained unyielding.

"Joe, let me go."

"From 'mister' to 'Joe' is quite an improvement." My face went into her hair, my arms tightening around her, molding her against me.

A tremor passed through her. "Joe, please ... let me go," she whispered in a breathless way. "Please...."

Suddenly I saw where there was nothing tough or worldly about her, that her language and manner of the previous day had apparently been just an act, a defense used against the towboat men who were constantly about and making passes. She seemed very young now, and very frightened, completely adrift in a man's arms. Still, she had come to me.

"You don't want me to let you go, Stella." I could feel it building up in her as my mouth went up her smooth cheek, then down to her throat. Her pulses beat against my lips, her breath quickening.

"You came over to see me."

"Yes."

"Why?" My mouth moved back to her cheek. Her eyes were glazing, heavy-lidded.

"To talk, I guess. It's a lonely life on a barge. But not for this, Joe. I didn't come for this. You must believe me. Joe, please don't! You mustn't ... you ..."

On the fourth kiss her arms encircled my neck. She strained against me, her fingers digging into my neck.

Then she pulled back, trembling, her eyes dark with fright. "Joe! I didn't mean that— No, no, let me go!" She broke away.

I didn't follow her down the ladder. I hadn't the strength. From the flying bridge I watched her hurry out the door without looking back. Then I picked up a chisel and sat down.

I sat there with the chisel in my hand, remembering and savoring that sudden bolt of passion that had flamed through her.

Murk?

The hell with Murk.

Chapter Three

The basin was in its usual hustle of morning activity when we tied up to Murk's barge the next day. Loaded coal barges were being brought into the basin, the tugs backing and filling, their skippers cursing from pilothouse windows at the jam of empty barges tied along the bulkhead that were not being moved fast enough to suit them. Up along the bulkhead itself, trucks were waiting their turn to be loaded, the drivers standing in groups and smoking, kidding the young office girls as they passed by on their way to work. Farther up the basin two fishing sloops were gathering their dried nets, taking on provisions and fuel, completing last-minute jobs before heading for their fishing grounds.

When Murk came out on deck in answer to my whistle, he was grumbling about the new schedule changing his day off, but he went aft to arrange his lines when I ignored his beefing.

She came out then, carrying a bucket with a line on it. "Morning, Stella."

She acknowledged my greeting by nodding slightly, but not looking up. She tossed the bucket over the side, holding onto the line. It didn't hit the surface right and floated.

"We're not talking this morning, I see."

She yanked on the line to bring the bucket over on its side, so it would fill. "We haven't anything to talk about, Baski."

"From 'Joe' back to 'Baski'? I've slipped, it seems."

She glanced down the barge toward Murk, who was fussing with an oily line. "Let's forget about yesterday, Joe. We do crazy things sometimes."

She was wearing a cotton dress with a flared skirt and a square neckline that permitted the slope of her full bosom to disappear just in time. With the morning sunlight putting a golden glow on her long blonde hair and highlighting the smooth bronze of her face and shoulders, she was so completely feminine I wanted to jump down on the barge just to be near her again, to touch her. Murk or no Murk.

"Coming to the boat shed again, Stella?"

"No. Of course not." She drew the filled bucket up, hand over hand, giving me a cold look. "That's a fresh question."

I leaned out the window, keeping my voice low. "Stella, you'll think this is fresh, too, but one of us is going to come to the other. We can spar around from now until Christmas, but that's the way it's going to be, and I haven't the time for sparring."

That took the snap right out of her. She looked frightened. "Joe, don't talk like that."

"Here comes the boy friend."

Murk apparently caught the last remark as he came up the barge. "What you two talking about?" His weak eyes glinted suspiciously.

"I was just telling your wife the company owes you time under this new system. You'll be working this Sunday and won't have a day off until the next Wednesday. That's a ten-day stretch without a day off."

"They should make it up to me, they should."

"You bet they should. I'll see Hackett and mention it. Maybe I can get you a full day's pay out of it. That'd be even better than getting the time."

He blinked, as if suddenly seeing me for the first time. "Well, that's obliging of you, Cap."

"Think nothing of it." I watched the undulating movement of her hips under the cotton dress as she carried the bucket over to the cabin and disappeared through the door.

"Can I see you for a minute, Cap?" Murk was looking up at me, rubbing his jaw.

"What's on your mind, Murk?"

He glanced at Spatola, who had just come forward to coil the lines. "Well, it's kind of personal, it is."

"O.K., come on up."

The lines were off and we were lying a good six feet off the barge. Before I had a chance to touch the throttle and close the gap, Murk made the jump.

Spatola gave him a disgusted look. "That ain't a smart trick, pal. You slip and bang ya head and maybe you just don't come up. You go gurgle-gurgle an' that's it."

Murk came up the ladder and into the pilothouse. "Never missed a jump yet. I look heavy now, but I'm still in good shape, I am. I once had gland trouble. That accounts for the weight."

"What's on your mind?"

He stepped over to the rear bulkhead, shaking his head in admiration at the model motor cruiser on the shelf. "That sure is smooth, Cap. This the one you building? Heard about that, I did. Takes a talent to put together something as pretty as that. You carve the model, too?"

"Yeah. But what's on your mind, Murk?" I didn't like being buttered up for a favor, and I could see that was what he wanted.

He reached up and ran a finger along the hull of the model. "Well, Cap, I got to go to the dentist, I do. I got a cavity and it's been giving me fierce trouble, it has." He looked at me, as if he wanted some encouragement to go on.

"So why don't you go and have it taken care of?"

He took off his glasses and inspected the lenses. He cleared his throat. "I thought if you could see your way a little, you wouldn't mind giving me a slip, you wouldn't...." He let it hang there.

"Health slip to the Marine Hospital? But you're not working for this tug. I sign slips only for my own men."

"I figured you might stretch a point, you might." The point he wanted me to stretch was a big one. The government provides free medical and dental care for seamen working aboard documented vessels. Tugboats come under this classification. With a health slip from the master of the vessel, a seaman gets all the medical attention he requires—and it's good attention, the best. Strictly speaking, barge captains are not entitled to this service, but are generally admitted under their own signatures.

"What's wrong with signing your own slips, Murk?"

"What I did last time. Then the feller says I'm not a master, he did. Two hours I was there, waiting, and then I had to go home. I figured getting one from you would put me through sure, it would."

"That means I'd be testifying to something that's not true."

He looked uncomfortable. "Well, in a way it does. Save me some trouble, though, it would."

Murk was one guy I couldn't see going out of my way to help. I was on the point of giving him a quick brush when Stella came out of the cabin. She put up a folding chair in the shade of the cabin, sat down, and opened a magazine. When she crossed her legs to support the magazine her skirt slid up along a smooth solid thigh. Mechanically she tugged her skirt down, and in the time it took her to do that I had it thought out.

"I don't know, Murk. I don't know." I reached over, lifted the log from the shelf, and took out a pad of health slips. "We got to be pretty careful about handing these things out. They've been recognizing barge captains over there in the past, but if the policy has been changed it could get me in trouble."

He watched me anxiously. "I'd sure appreciate you calling me one of your hands, Cap. It costs plenty these days to go to the regular dentist, it does. *Four* dollars, they charge now." He made four sound like four hundred.

"Yeah, I guess you got it pretty tough making out on a barge captain's salary."

"You can say that again, you can. Know what I paid for grapefruit yesterday?"

"Couldn't even guess."

"Five cents each." He waited for me to get over the shock.

"Imagine that. Five cents each."

"And they're from the market, they are. You can just figure what they'd cost at a regular store."

"Maybe six?"

"Oh, more than that. Even at the A & P they're more."

"That so." I took out my pen and started filling in the form. "Albert Murk?"

"That's right. The Albert is from my mother's side, it is. Named after my—"

"Age?"

"Fifty-nine." He looked as though he wanted me to say he didn't look it, so I said it.

He looked pleased. "I take care of myself, I do. Always have. No smoking, no drinking, no vices."

I filled in the rest of the slip, signed it, and handed it to him. "When are you going?"

"This afternoon."

"You expect to get treated this afternoon? Hell, the Marine Hospital is on Staten Island, in case you didn't know. It will take you two hours to get there. Then you have a wait."

"But I didn't figure on going to the hospital. I'm going to the clinic on Hudson Street, I am. Much closer."

I'd forgotten about the clinic.

He carefully folded the slip and put it into his pocket. "See, we have shopping to do in New York, and it will be killing two birds with one stone, it will."

"We?" I stared at him.

"Stella and me. She's going looking for a dress, she is. Being price-conscious, I sort of tag along."

"Well, it's your teeth. Go to Hudson if you want to. Saves a little time, I guess. Want some advice, though, I'd go straight over to the hospital. Tell you why, Murk. They got regular dentists at the hospital. Sure, it takes you longer to get there; and you have a wait, but you get a job. A good job. No aching tooth for months afterward that you can't locate because it's filled and looks O.K., like one guy I know that went to Hudson Street."

He was impressed. "You don't say. That happened to someone, it did?"

"Sure did. When they finally figured out which tooth it was, they had to yank it, and then cut out the abscess that got into the bone."

He was impressed. He began to look worried.

"Cost him about two hundred for a specialist before he was through, too."

That rocked him. He rubbed his jaw, frowning. "Thing is, Cap, I got no time to go to the hospital. Take a whole day, it would."

"Go tomorrow morning. Meet us at Hoboken when you finish."

"But who'd handle the barge?"

"Leave that to us. Mrs. Murk's being aboard covers your pay in case Hackett comes snooping around. We can say she's handling the lines so he can't complain. I'll have Spatola doing it, of course. We'll work together on this, Murk."

"Well, that's white of you, Captain. Sure is." He thought of something. "It's going to cost me more, it is. The bus fare in Staten Island."

"Leave here early and walk it. It's not too far from the ferry."

"And there's the ferry fare, now that you mention it."

"That, Murk, I wouldn't swim."

He saw it as a joke and smiled. "Well, thanks again, Cap. I'll try to pay the favor back sometime, I will."

I had a hunch we'd be even before he was sitting in the dentist chair.

That night I took in a show and watched Humphrey Bogart blow smoke in some redhead's face for an hour, then I went back to the shed and tried to work. I couldn't. I stretched out on the bed and stared up at the ceiling for a while. In the morning I'd be picking up the *Sand Point*. It would take about four hours to haul that barge to Hoboken, maybe five, depending on the tide. And Murk would be as good as a million miles away.

Four hours.

Maybe five. With Stella.

"We're taking it alongside, Spatola. Shift those lines."

He gave me a dumb look. "Alongside? All the way?"

"That's right."

"Wouldn't it be a lot better—"

"Just do as you're told." I went up the ladder and into the pilothouse. He threw the line off and I kicked the tug around and laid it broadside to the *Sand Point*, stern to stern, so the barge cabin was aft.

I was leaning out the window, watching a small ketch attempt to free itself from the mud flats at the neck of the basin, when Stella came out wearing jeans and a shirt and heavy gloves. Even in the rough jeans her shape was enough to have Spatola stumbling over himself. He waved her away. "'Sall right, Mrs. Murk. We'll take care of it."

She nodded her thanks, studiously avoided looking at me, and went back inside.

Spatola drew a deep breath. "A month's pay, Joe. That's what I'd pay. A whole month's pay!" He saw me scowling and beat it aft.

We took it easy going out of the basin. It was a warm, sunny day, perfect cruising weather, and the place was cluttered with sailboats and motorboats in addition to the morning tows.

I stayed at the wheel until we cleared the Marine Parkway Bridge and were bearing on Coney Island channel, then I called Spatola up. "Want to take it a while?"

"Sure, Joe. Glad to. Any time."

"Watch the small craft. Don't be afraid to give them a blast if they go moping off in front of you. Any grub left below?"

"Some lamb, maybe a pie, I think. Yeah, a couple of pies."

"I'll have a bite and then go aft. Want to get a little sun. Don't leave the wheel. If anything comes up you can't handle, give me a blow."

"Figured you might be able to use this pie we had left over. They're always loading us with more grub than we can use." Before she could take it from me, I walked past her and put it on the kitchen table. My hat went beside it. I saw she had changed from the jeans to a strapless sun dress. Her tanned legs were bare.

All barge cabins are rigged the same, a combined kitchen, sitting room, and bunk room, furnished with stuff from the Year 1 that a junkie wouldn't give you a nickel for. This one differed in that it had twin bunks with a blanket hung between them for privacy. "Hey, you got a neat place here! Not bad." I went over to look at the pot-bellied wood stove. "Don't remember the last time I saw one of these. Throws plenty of heat in the winter, though, I bet."

She slammed the door shut. "That's enough of that, Baski!"

"Eh?"

She put her hands on her hips, her blue eyes chilly. "Don't be so condescending! I know what you must think of a barge cabin."

"Hey, look, I didn't mean it that way. Hell, you can't do much with a barge cabin. This is fixed up neat with what you got here. No kidding. You should see some of the cabins around. They don't even bother putting curtains up."

"I do the best I can." She smoothed her skirt.

"And it shows. Certainly does. This looks comfortable." I parked myself in the huge overstuffed chair near the window. It was about as comfortable as sitting on a bag of coal.

"Tell me that monstrosity feels good, Baski, and you can get right out of here!" She almost smiled.

I grinned at her. "Well made, anyway. They really believed in enough springs in those days, didn't they?"

She came over to the table, a few feet from my outstretched legs. She picked up the pie. "Hmmm, apple. My favorite. Shall I cut you a piece and make some tea?"

"I don't want either pie or tea, Stella." I took out some cigarettes and lit one.

"Joe, you'd better go." Her voice was low. She put the pie back on the table and stood looking at it.

"Want me to? Or is that the easiest thing to say?"

"It's best if you go. Now."

"I had an idea you weren't kidding yesterday."

"I'm sorry if ... if I led you on. I didn't mean to. I really didn't."

"Ash tray?" I held the cigarette out to her.

She reached to take it. I grabbed her wrist and pulled her over, onto my lap. I flicked the cigarette over to the sheet metal under the stove.

"Joe, let me go!"

I pulled her low in the chair, against me, both arms around her so she couldn't move.

"Joe, please." She made no attempt to struggle. "I know what you must think, but—"

"I don't think anything, Stella. I'm just nuts about you."

"Please, you must let me go. You *must*."

"Afraid of me—or yourself?"

"Joe—"

I kissed her hard, holding it. Her arm finally crept up around my neck. "Joe, this is wrong."

"Not a big wrong. Just a small one."

"I do want you to leave. I'm not strong enough to stop this."

"Why should we stop? You're not married any more than the man in the moon. You've got the license to show for it, but what else? Any pleasure, any fun? Any love?"

"Please let me up, Joe."

"O.K., we'll sit here and talk for a few minutes. I'll go then."

"You said we'd talk. Please...."

Her head dropped wearily on my shoulder, her eyes smoky blue and half closed.

Her arm moved restlessly around my neck. Suddenly it tightened. "Hold me, Joe. Hold me close."

Then her face was hot against mine, her lips hungry....

"I want to tell you something, Joe, and I hope you believe me. I'm not a tramp that's just looking—"

"I never said you were a tramp, Stella."

"You don't have to say it. I know what you're thinking—what anybody would think."

"I'm not thinking anything of the kind. Not that. Listen, get this straight. I don't think it at all. If I did I wouldn't be here with you."

"Not much, you wouldn't."

"O.K., I mean I wouldn't be here this long. You know what I mean by that?"

"I believe I do. But Joe, we won't let this happen again. It's not right. We both know it."

"Murk doesn't count with me, Stella. He just doesn't count. As far as I'm concerned, it's just as if you weren't even married."

"But I *am* married. And we both have to be sensible. We were carried away and we have to forget it ever happened."

"Funny how just the sight of him rubs me. But then, all guys do when they squeeze nickels for no reason."

"Oh, he's not so bad. Really he isn't. He gets grouchy sometimes, and he's thrifty, perhaps to an extreme. But he's got his good side. You'd be sur—"

"Thrifty, eh? Oh, brother. 'Know what I paid for grapefruit yesterday? *Five* cents, I did, I did, I did.' Thrifty's hardly the word."

"Stop that, Joe. Money is just one of his bad points, and it's not nice to mimic or talk about anybody like that. He just can't help himself and that's all there is to it."

"He can't help himself? That's a laugh. Listen— Oh, O.K., Stella. I'm sorry. We'll talk about you."

"I'm a woman, so I won't object to that."

"You're a woman, all right. I've never met anybody like you before."

"My, what an original line!"

"No line, Stella. It's true."

She snuggled against me, sighing. "Where are we now, darling?"

"Off Bedloe's. From 'Baski' to 'Joe' to 'darling.' I'm really making time."

"We'll be in shortly, won't we?"

"Another half hour. We're bucking the ebb now, so perhaps a little longer."

"Shouldn't you go up and relieve Spatola? He'll be getting suspicious— if he doesn't actually know. Gosh, I hope he doesn't."

"He knows from nothing if his eyes are where they're supposed to be. That dress is certainly a mess. How much did you pay for it?"

"Not much. Three-ninety-five, I believe. Why?"

"Just wondering how much that tooth is costing him."

We both got a kick out of that one.

Chapter Four

He was waiting at the dock when we pulled into the Hoboken coaling slip and his chin was hanging down to his chest. They hadn't time at the hospital for more than a preliminary examination and had given him a return appointment. He griped for ten minutes straight.

"Couldn't walk to that place, neither. Three miles, it was."

"Three miles? Didn't think it was that far. Figured it a mile at the most."

"And they said I should've gone to Hudson Street. Said they had the same kind of dentists over there, they had."

"Guess there's been changes made since I was there last. What day is your appointment?"

"Tomorrow morning. Two days it's taking me for just one tooth. Figuring the fares and everything, I'm not saving much, I'm not."

"Ask for a cleaning at the same time. That'd be the same as saving another two, three bucks."

"I never thought of that."

At eight o'clock the next morning Murk left for his dental appointment. I picked up the *Sand Point* after it was loaded at Hoboken and another coal barge at Jersey City, and headed down the bay with one on each side.

Below Governor's Island we ran into a fog bank, the soupy kind that occasionally rolls into New York to foul things up for an hour or so. This one held visibility to zero, a milky-gray wall that broke into clammy tentacles clutching at the railing of the tug as we pushed into it. We reduced speed and Spatola came up to take care of the whistle, sounding a blast every minute or so.

I fretted at the wheel as we crawled along, debating the wisdom of letting Spatola take over. Nothing had been said, but I knew Stella would be waiting back in the barge cabin.

The distant deep-throated growl of a freighter moving up the channel decided things. I reduced speed further and stayed at the wheel, silently cursing, begrudging every minute away from her.

"Big baby, Joe."

"Sounds like it. Yank that cord more often."

The unseen freighter was prompt in answering. As the sound of her shorter-spaced blasts drew near, it began to seem like two kids were having a great time tooting to each other. But it was all serious business. In narrow channels with a fast-running tide you either keep track of each other at all times or else.

"She's movin', Joe. Comin' up fast."

"Probably on radar."

She loomed out of the grayness ahead, slightly to our port, a huge freighter, her sides scabby with rust, her deckhouse a grimy white. Her screw churned the water as she went by, not slackening speed.

Spatola enviously eyed the swinging radar cage on her foremast. "Now, if we had one of them things we'd chop-chop into the basin in no time."

The last thing I wanted to do was to get home in a hurry this day.

"Think you can handle it alone from here on if I go aft for a snooze? We'll slow it down more if you like."

He studied the fog blanketing us and scratched his cheek. "Guess so."

"Yes or no?"

He kept scratching his cheek. "Well—"

"Forget it." In disgust I pulled a stool up to the wheel and straddled it. "By now you should be able to make this run blindfolded."

When we cleared the Narrows and rounded the Norton's Point bell we broke out of the fog bank. Hot sunlight danced across the calm waters of Coney Island channel, a welcome sight to me for more than just navigable reasons. Two precious hours had been wasted.

"I'm going aft for that snooze. Keep your eyes open."

"Sure, Joe. I gotcha."

"What side you going to favor when you line up the bridge?"

"Rockaway. Right?"

"Right." I patted the pint bottle in his rear pocket. "If I see you tilting this at the wheel, I'll drop you off at the nearest dock and have your check mailed."

He gave me a weak smile. "You know me better than that, Joe."

"I know you, period."

"This was me at ten—or was it eleven? No, ten. I was still wearing pigtails."

"Scrawny, but kind of cute."

She flipped the page of the album. "Here's Pop. Looks fierce with that handle-bar mustache, but he was always gentle as a lamb. Swell guy."

We were stretched out on the bunk, on our stomachs, the morning sun slanting through the window warming our backs. Outside, the engines of the tug were working smoothly; we were making good time. Worse luck.

"This one is my mother."

"Young-looking. And pretty."

"She was the apple of Pop's eye. He was crazy about her. In fact, they were both really wrapped up in each other. Having each other, they had everything, even though they had nothing. Know what I mean, Joe?"

"I know what you mean."

"I think losing her killed him. He was a dock builder, and that's one job you can't drink on. He got in the way of a swinging pile less than six months after she passed away."

"Tough. Who's the sour-puss dame—the one there on top?"

"My aunt. She's the one who took me in."

"Was she as mean as she looks?"

"Well ... looking back, no. I mean, it wasn't so much her fault. She was a janitress for two buildings on Grant Street. They were like those big

East Side tenements you see, and keeping them clean was quite a job. We lived in the basement of one.... Joe, did you ever have a rat crawl over your face while you were sleeping?"

"No, thanks."

"Well, I did. And from that time on, until I married Albert, I was never able to sleep a single night through. Every evening when I went to bed it would take me an hour to get to sleep, and then, every so often, I'd wake up and listen to the rats scurrying between the walls and wonder if one would come out and over to my bed."

"I begin to get the picture. Murk came along and looked like Prince Charming."

"Well, Albert has never looked anything like a Prince Charming, but he was a lot thinner then."

"So he said. His glands, wasn't it?"

"That sounds like a sarcastic remark."

"He said it. I didn't."

"I know. He's always saying that. But he isn't so bad when you get to know him."

"Stop it, Stella. Stop building him up, and start telling yourself the truth. You grabbed him to get away from those rats. But at seventeen you should've had sense enough to simply move away and leave that aunt of yours. There's no wall around the East Side. Why didn't you just pack up and leave?"

"Joe."

"Yeah?"

"I was fifteen."

"Good Lord!"

"Albert didn't know, of course. I was always a big girl for my age."

"But your aunt knew, and she gave her permission? She should've been lynched for a trick like that!"

"I was very definite in what I wanted, so you can't blame her too much."

"At fifteen, who isn't definite in what they want?"

"That's true, but you still can't blame her. I said I'd run away if she didn't agree, so what was she to do?"

"Fan that behind of yours."

"Such talk! I was bigger than she was, even at fifteen. Joe, you don't know how it affected me—the harbor, I mean. Every evening I'd go down to the piers and watch the boats, the tugs and barges; the cleanliness of everything in comparison to the streets and tenements. All I wanted then was to be free of the dirt and the rats and the drunken yelling that went on every night over my head. Anything, *anything*, I thought, would be better than the way I was living at the time."

"And you're satisfied with what you have?"

"I think so."

"You know damn well you're not!"

She turned and kissed my cheek. "We can't have everything, Joe."

"*You* have nothing."

She pushed the album aside and rolled over onto her back and closed her eyes. "Let's not talk about it."

I watched the sunlight from the window play across the soft curve of her cheek a moment, then pushed my face into her hair. I just couldn't stay away from her. "You smell delicious."

Her arm held me tightly. "This will be our last time together, Joe. It wouldn't do either of us any good to let this go any further, even if we had the chance."

"What does that mean?"

"I told you yesterday. We just can't have it go on. We'd be found out in time. I know we would."

"Suppose he gets another toothache?"

"He won't. But it would make no difference if he did. Do you know this is the first time in five years we've been apart for more than one day?"

"It's a wonder he doesn't put you under lock and key."

"Perhaps it would have been better if he had."

"Yeah. Perhaps."

"Sorry?"

"You know I'm not."

"How much time have we got, Joe?"

"Be another hour. Tide is setting and we'll be bucking it from here on in."

"Want me to make some tea?"

"You crazy? I've got better plans than drinking tea for the next hour."

That was Monday. The following Friday Hackett called me in and said he was pleased with the new schedule and was letting it stand. "Bound to show in the books, Joe, like you said. There'll be a few extra dollars in your envelope when the pressure lifts. Say in two months."

"O. K."

"I'd do it sooner, but you know how things are."

"Anything else?"

"Look, Joe, your idea was good but it's not going to make me a millionaire. I'm giving you a few extra bucks—an even twenty, we'll make it. What's wrong with that?"

"Nothing is. Who's complaining?"

"You are. You're not complaining, but you look put out."

"I'm not. I'm satisfied."

"Sure?"

"If I wasn't, I'd say so."

"Well, O.K. But any time you're dissatisfied or figure I'm giving you the wrong end, you just come in here and we'll talk it over. That goes for any of you boys. And Joe …"

"Yeah?"

"Don't like that business of leaping from barge to dock that Murk does. What does he think he is, a jack rabbit?"

"Showing off, I guess. Maybe habit."

"Well, I don't want that business going on around my equipment. The number-one rule around boats is to watch your footing, and if he doesn't know that by now, he should. You tell that guy to find some other way to impress his wife, if that's his idea of showing there's life in the old boy. When lines are too slack I want him to take them in instead of jumping five feet and even more to the dock. You tell him that."

"I'll tell him."

"How are you coming on with that boat of yours? Don't see you going to the creek nights anymore."

"Knocked off for a while."

"Short of dough?"

"I've enough to keep going."

"And you're not working it? Hey, you sick? Don't answer that. Can't afford to lose you right now."

It's a screwy world. You can't figure it. You lie on your bunk at night and try to figure it, but you can't. Blondes, brunettes, and redheads, most of them young and shapely; and quite a procession over the years when you come to think about it. But an hour, or a night, perhaps a week end, and you withdraw into your small private world that does not include permanent room for any woman. Then one comes along and you're walking around feeling like you've been punched in the belly. You wake in the night and remember how her soft arms slid around your neck, and then sleep is gone. You sit up and smoke, and remember how her warm lips felt against yours, and your cigarette is tasteless. You keep remembering, and you can't figure it. You know you'll never stop wanting this one particular woman, but you can't figure it. She's become a part of you, and until you're together for good you know it's going to hurt, and hurt, and keep on hurting.

"Stella, you get rid of him Wednesday. Tell him to beat it for the day and take in a movie. Tell him you've got a headache if he tries to take you somewhere. Just get rid of him."

"Joe, please. It's finished. I told you that. Besides, you know he wouldn't leave me alone for a day."

"For a day? Hell, he hasn't been five feet from you since he's had that tooth fixed! Stella, I've got to see you again. I've got to. We'll talk. That's all I want. Just a chance to talk to you alone."

"He's coming!"

We were standing on the barge, Stella hanging out some wash. The tug was tied alongside, and Spatola was up on a ladder propped against the stack, repairing the whistle connection. I had stepped down on the barge and stood next to Stella, as if for a better view of what Spatola was doing.

"Make sure the play is completely out of that!"

"Sure, Joe. Jus' what I'm doin'."

When Murk came up the deck he halted beside me. He leaned on the broom he'd just used to give the barge a sweepdown. "Trouble up there, Cap?"

"Lever was bent a bit."

"We're a little late shoving off, we are."

"Let *me* worry about that, Murk!" I snapped at him.

He looked surprised. "Just commenting, Cap. Just commenting, I am." He went into the cabin.

I waited until the door closed, then moved a few feet along the clothesline where she was working.

"Joe, he might be watching."

"You get rid of him this Wednesday. You hear, Stella? *Get rid of him!*"

"I can't, Joe. I can't. *Don't* keep asking."

"Stella, I can't sleep nights. I can't do anything anymore. It's like that with me." I stood right behind her, so close I could smell the warm freshness of her hair and loving her so much my belly was tied in knots.

"Please, Joe. Don't keep standing there. He may come out."

"Stella, baby, you're more than just another woman to me. I've got to talk to you. I've *got* to."

She put both hands on the clothesline and bowed her head. Her voice choked up. "Joe, stop it. *Stop it.* You'll drive me mad. Nothing can come of it, so stop!"

"This Wednesday. Chase him off by himself. I'll take the same day off."

"No."

Wednesday Murk took Stella on a sight-seeing boat ride around Manhattan. Somebody had given him a free ticket for the ride, and rather than waste anything worth a buck, he spent an entire afternoon traveling over waters he must have seen ten thousand times.

A barge captain and his wife taking a boat ride.

That part of it was funny, but when I found out that same afternoon that he had been willing to go alone, and had suggested Stella visit her aunt for the day, I didn't do any laughing. She'd had it thrown right in her lap—a chance for us to be together for a whole day. She hadn't taken it.

At that moment I could have slugged her and enjoyed it.

That night I had dinner on South Street and ran into Stevens, an old ferry skipper, at the Seamen's Institute We shot two games of Eight in the poolroom, sharing the pint he had brought along; then we went out and bought another bottle. This we polished off on Fisherman's Wharf, sitting on the edge of the stringpiece and watching the East River traffic, the heavy car floats struggling against the strong ebb, a battleship en route to the navy yard and inching cautiously beneath the Brooklyn Bridge, its mast just clearing the underside.

"Joey lad, let's see what's going on at Flo's."

"Guess not. Not tonight, anyway." I tossed the empty into the river and got to my feet.

"C'mon, boy, perk up!"

"You go. I'll see you 'round, Stevens."

"Look, you damn Polack, you coming or do I plant one?" He lurched away from me, put up his hands, and tried to square off. I grabbed to keep him from falling into the river.

"Aw, c'mon, Joey, no fun alone."

"O.K. I'll keep you company. But you try to take this joint apart again and I'll hammer your head in."

"Good ol' Joey!"

Flo's was a spaghetti place on Greenwich Avenue, but if you walked right through the dining room and up the back stairs you ran into Flo's big bosom, a hug, and a garlic kiss.

For Stevens she had only a cold eye. "You old snake in the grass, you behave yourself this time, d'ya hear?"

Stevens gave her a silly grin. "Sure, Flo. Just heard you had some new girls, so I figured on getting acquainted."

Her black eyes widened in mock surprise. "You mean, darlin', you didn't come to see *me?*"

Stevens wrinkled his nose. "Gawd help me. I ain't that hard up!"

She cuffed him for that one, and then hustled us inside. "Make yourselves miserable and I'll call the dearies down."

They came down wearing the thin, knee-length negligees Flo had designed to speed business along. The slim redhead evaded Stevens' grab and came over to the sofa where I was sitting. "O.K. with you, honey?"

"I think you're in for a disappointment," I said. "I'm just here for laughs."

She didn't like that. "What kind of a sense of humor could *you* have?"

"Well, maybe we could dance."

"Maybe we could."

The jukebox in the corner was like any other, except it called for a quarter a record. I put two of them in. The redhead did her best to give me my money's worth.

"Do I bother you?" she asked.

"Nope."

"You must be hard to bother."

"Could be."

Flo came waddling in. "Well, ain't this cute! Like two lovebirds." She whacked the redhead across the behind with a big hand. "Time's awasting, dearie. Get on with it."

"The man says he's not interested."

"What's the matter?"

The "matter," I figured, was by now sound asleep on a barge tied to a Hoboken pier.

Chapter Five

How many sewers empty into the Gowanus Canal and its vicinity is anybody's guess, but just about anything you can name can be found there. For instance? Well, a lot of people say they wouldn't be caught dead in the Gowanus, but a lot of people are. The canal seems to be a catchall for the harbor's floaters, and by the time a police launch picks them up they have been crushed between barges, chewed by passing propellers, and basted with oil dregs under the hot sun for many hours. Occasionally the cops pick them up in one piece.

The point is, the Gowanus exudes varied and peculiar odors twenty-four hours a day, and it's no place for a guy with a big head, an uncertain stomach, and his mind on a sweet-smelling blonde. But I was there the next morning on a do-or-die selling job. It was either convince Old Man Walsh of Walsh's Sand, Gravel, & Hoisting not to cancel the derrick towing contract we had with him or Joe Baski was going to find himself working a Hackett tug on a day-to-day basis in Newtown Creek.

Hackett had been apologetic about it. "Hate to do it, Joe, but in seniority you're low man among the skippers, and you'll have to give up the coaling run. The creek will give you some split time, and that means a small pay cut for a while. Slow you down on that boat of yours, I know, but just one of those things we have no control over."

But it wasn't only the boat I was thinking about then. I needed a steady income to keep going on it, true, but that had become secondary now. The boat could wait. What came first was Stella, and buried up in Newtown Creek I'd be as good as a million miles away from her. That I didn't like. I had already made up my mind that this girl was eventually going to be my wife, but I knew I'd have a job convincing her. I couldn't do it from Newtown.

"Mr. Hackett, I need that coaling run. I'll have no time for my boat if I spend three hours' traveling time just getting to the creek. I don't care about the money too much, but three hours a day adds up to a lot of time."

"Know it, Joe. Damnit, I know it. And I'm not kidding when I say it hurts me more than it does you. That derrick tow has been grossing some four hundred a week for the past seven years, and it knocked me flat when Walsh phoned and said he was giving it to Soboy Tugs." Hackett got sore then. "When you toe the line with union help you have a right to expect protection against parasites like Soboy, who undercut! With the boozers and misfits they hire, who couldn't afford to knock off thirty dollars a haul? But can I? Damn right, I can't."

"Did you talk up that point with Walsh—that you have good men—"

"Frankly, Joe, I said nothing. I was so burned up to think that chiseler would ignore seven years of efficient service at the lowest rate in New York that I was afraid to trust my voice, afraid I'd tell him to shove the derrick and all future work. When I stop to think of all the fat jobs I've had to pass up because our *Credenda* was at *his* disposal—"

"Suppose I take a crack at him, in person—give him our side of it."

"Go ahead. But don't eat humble pie, Joe. Get you no place. Walsh's heart is strictly a cash register."

I was willing to eat more than humble pie to keep the *Sand Point* and what it carried on the end of my hawser, but I didn't say so.

A cab dropped me off at the Ninth Street slip, and I saw Walsh's derrick tied up at the end of the pier, its towering steel crane rusted and badly in need of scaling, neglected like the rest of his equipment. Secured on the outboard side was a Soboy tug. It was an old-fashioned wooden coaler that hadn't seen a coat of paint in ten years and probably wouldn't for another ten.

Tied up nearby was Hackett's tug *Credenda*, Johnson glumly framed in the pilothouse window. I called up to him. "Hi, Pop. Where's Mr. P.

Aloysius Walsh, the P for you know what?"

He tilted his weathered head in the direction of the derrick. "Under the housing, killing the fires. Looks like I'll take up and write off a day's pay."

"Stick around. I'm going to cry on his shoulder, make him see the light. After all, we've done the job since the war."

Johnson snorted. "Only because he couldn't find anybody to do it cheaper!"

"I'll try some buttering, anyway. Might work."

I found Walsh in the shed of the derrick, killing what remained of the boiler fires. He was in his sixties, a runt of a guy with a gray, wrinkled face and small quick eyes that seemed to look everywhere at once. He wore a faded blue serge that he would probably be buried in and an old-fashioned bowler that his ears seemed to be supporting.

"Give you a hand, Mr. Walsh?"

He jerked his head around, sweeping me from head to foot with a rapid glance. "Eh? Oh, you, Baski. No, no, I'll handle it. Gave my watchman the day off. Mother's sick."

This was pure malarky. He never used a watchman when the derrick was secured at the canal. A guy with a million bucks dirtying his hands to save a few more.

"Mr. Walsh, about this towing job. I wonder if you've considered the dependable service you've been getting. I'll bet you don't recall a single day a delivery hasn't been made on time. Fair weather or foul, we've—"

"Made up my mind, Baski. Made up my mind." He straightened, brushing dirt off his hands with quick little motions. "Losing money left and right on this piece of equipment. Got to make it up on cheaper towing."

"Now, that's exactly what Mr. Hackett asked me to see you about."

He looked interested. "Well, if he'll meet the Soboy bid, we can talk over a renewal. Don't see how he can do it, though, the high wages he's paying."

I fought down an impulse to heave Mr. Walsh into the Gowanus with the rest of the sewage. Twenty-one-fifty a day might sound high, but come up with an idle day or two and a tug captain begins scratching for a buck to take home.

"He can't do it any cheaper, Mr. Walsh. I didn't mean it that way."

"Didn't think he could. Nothing to discuss, then. I'm in a hurry, Captain, so if you'll excuse me ..." He clamped his bowler on tighter and hurried out the door

I followed him out on the derrick's deck, shoving my hands in my pockets before they did something I'd be sorry for, and waited for him to complete his instructions to the bleary-eyed, red-jowled skipper on the Soboy tug before I moved in front of him.

"Mr. Walsh, Hackett asked me to relay some information before you actually canceled his services. Number one, he wanted to remind you he can handle that derrick cheaper than any outfit in New York, and once the contract is broken he can't guarantee he'll be available at the same price." I drew a picture of Hackett being besieged on all sides for his small-crew, shallow-draft tugs. "Number two"—Walsh was impatiently studying a nickel-plated watch he'd pulled from his pocket— "Hackett wanted me to warn you of the swindle these Soboy people are getting into. You know how Hackett is—always a guy who gets upset when an old friend may be nearing a shoal—"

"Swindle?" He pushed his wrinkled face closer to mine. "What swindle?"

I managed to look surprised. "Mean you haven't heard of the Jersey mob organizing the nonunion towing outfits in South Amboy? Why, they're in—damn near, anyway. That means the rates will be going up, and a damn sight higher than legit outfits on this side."

He chewed on his lower lip, his shrewd eyes searching mine. "News to me. Never pay much attention to union business, though." His face tightened, as uncompromising as a fist. "Well, that won't bother me. On a daily basis I can go elsewhere as soon as Soboy ups their price. Maybe Newark. Good day, Baski. We've got some rush work in Princess Bay. It's a case of on time or work forfeited."

Silently cursing myself for not having made up a better story, I turned and walked over onto the pier. Make a buck today, let tomorrow take care of itself—that was it, Walsh's motto.

And he had a million proofs it was a good one.

Johnson was sitting on his stool smoking when I boarded the *Credenda* and stepped into the pilothouse. "No luck, lad?"

"None. There goes a good piece of change for the boss, not to mention the split time I'm shackled with in Newtown Creek. I'm losing that *Sand Point* haul."

"Maybe you're losing more than that." He relighted his pipe, eying me over the flaming match. "Maybe you'll be losing a package of trouble."

I instantly knew what he meant and didn't bother sparring. "Hearing things, Pop?"

He shook his head. "Just a word dropped by Spatola that you took the *Sand Point* in tow alongside those two days Murk wasn't around. Spatola maybe can't add two and two, but I can. Trouble, lad. Forget her. When they wear a ring, don't go back for seconds and thirds. Never get in so deep you can't pull out quick."

"You got this wrong, Pop. I'm going to marry that girl."

"And what does she say?"

"She wants to end it. That's what she says, anyway. But I know she doesn't. We've only seen each other a few times, Pop, but this thing is solid. She'll come around."

"Lad, you take this Newtown job without a murmur."

"Pop, I said I'm going to marry this girl. Nothing you can say will change my mind. If I stick around close by, I know she's going to see it my way. She won't see me alone, when I'm off the job, so I've got to keep that tow." I leaned out the window, watching the Soboy tug whistle the lines off. Its grimy stack belched black smoke as it moved slowly into the canal with the derrick.

As I watched them come about and head for the mouth of the Gowanus, something in the towing setup struck me as wrong, but it was something I couldn't put my finger on. The tug's lines were out and snug, the derrick clasped tightly alongside. All according to the book. Still …

Johnson shook his head when I mentioned it. "He's rigged properly. What about Murk, lad? Do any thinking about how he'll take it?"

"Murk I don't care about. He'll be losing a cook, not a wife." I continued watching the tug and derrick, and it wasn't until they were passing from sight around the bend that I suddenly realized what was wrong.

Old Man Walsh had been sitting on a bench out on deck, sunning himself, set for a relaxing three-hour run. The Soboy skipper was sitting alongside the wheel, as though he had no intention of budging from that spot on the long haul to Princess Bay.

"Pop, has that Soboy junk heap ever towed Walsh's derrick before?"

Johnson pushed back his cap and scratched his white head. "Couldn't say. Probably not. Before we took it over Moran had it, before that Eastern."

"How old would you say that tug is? Old enough to have only one bilge pump, no suction? Her fire pump a rigid connection to the hull?"

"Probably, but what would—" He got it and his jaw sagged. "Well, I'll be damned! No suction lines stretched, and the old bum sitting there as unconcerned as can be!"

"Sure he's unconcerned. He's taken the pumping for granted for so many years that he thinks it automatically goes with towing, like bacon with eggs."

Johnson grinned, his bony hand yanking down the whistle cord. "Tail 'em, lad, and watch the fun?"

"We'll do more than watch. Let him get halfway down, then we'll pull a Rover Boy rescue and see about that contract."

Johnson's deck hand, Olson, a big strapping Swede, came lumbering forward to cast off. We backed from the slip, came about, and headed up the canal. Near its narrow mouth a sanitation tug had snapped the lines on a garbage scow, the scow swinging across the waterway and blocking it as effectively as a cork in a bottle. On the other side an oil barge, waiting impatiently to enter the canal, was having words with a city-owned tug, and they only cut it short when Johnson leaned out the window to roast the both of them for holding things up.

The delay by the scow cost us ten minutes, but within another twenty we were halfway down the upper bay and threading our way between anchored freighters, finally creeping up to within a mile of the derrick tow. Johnson idled speed to stay that distance astern.

Now, the one thing Walsh had not taken into consideration when he was getting another tug was its ability to take suction and pump a hull dry if it had to. Every wooden-hulled piece of equipment needs pumping, but generally it's sufficient to have it done weekly. Not Walsh's derrick. It needed a caulking job badly. While the derrick was working on a job, with an engineer on board and boilers in operation, its own bilge pump was forced to work continuously. When it was being towed, with its boilers banked and no engineer in attendance, the towing tug would run a suction into its bottom and keep it afloat that way.

A slip-shod way to keep a fifty-thousand-dollar piece of equipment? Sure, but don't forget about that million bucks.

We trailed the tow through the Narrows, Johnson and I taking turns with the glasses to watch the derrick's freeboard decreasing, very slowly, but still decreasing. It was apparent the Soboy skipper had no knowledge of the condition developing, because he set a course down the wide lower bay without hesitation.

"Run 'er alongside, lad?"

"Not yet. We'll wait until he reaches the Roamer Shoal, point of no return for Mr. Walsh."

A light mist settled over the bay as we drew abreast of West Bank, and we were forced to close distance in order to keep the derrick in sight.

I was wondering how long it would take Walsh to discover his derrick was sinking when he suddenly appeared from behind the housing, waving his arms at the tug skipper. Through the glasses I watched the dumfounded expression on the skipper's face as Walsh kept gesturing that the derrick was taking on water. Then Walsh stopped gesturing and froze, as if shocked by the skipper's answer. When he mopped his face with a handkerchief and leaned weakly against the derrick's housing for support, Johnson had to laugh. "He's just been notified all tugs can't take suction."

The situation would have seemed funny to me, too, if so much did not depend on the contract renewal. Also, my mind was occupied with a new angle for getting rid of Murk for a few days. With Murk out of the way a while there would be time for leisurely talks with Stella, time to state my case. On the long coaling hauls we'd be bound to reach an understanding.

"Climb up on him now, Pop, but don't stop. Make like we have urgent business at Sandy Hook."

It was almost pathetic, the relief on Walsh's face when he spotted the *Credenda*. The lower bay is a big place, some hundred square miles of open water. With the exception of an awkward dredge under tow and a lumber schooner being given an assist through Swash Channel, there wasn't another tug in sight to take over the derrick.

I thought Walsh would break an arm signaling as we went by, kicking our wash over to him. Johnson brought the wheel over to come around. "Serve him right if we did keep going. That Soboy doesn't carry any phone, and he'd have to run the derrick over a shoal if he couldn't get help."

We headed back and I ordered Olson not to pick up any lines or show any sign that we intended to tow Walsh. Johnson cut the throttle, and we drifted up on the outboard side of the derrick.

Walsh was now losing his temper in a running verbal battle with the Soboy skipper. But the skipper came out on top with the last word. He advised Walsh where to put his derrick, ordered his deck hand to cast off all lines, and jerked his head my way to indicate it was our baby.

Walsh angrily turned to us as the Soboy tug pulled away. "The stupidity of it! The stupidity!"

"Didn't he know you owned the crumbiest equipment on the East Coast?"

Johnson's crack brought him up short. He swallowed and hauled in his sheets. "Fortunate you happened by, Captain. Fortunate indeed."

"Where do you want it beached? On Roamer Shoal?" Walsh's jaw dropped. "Beached!" His small eyes darted to the distant Roamer Shoal lighthouse, barely visible through the haze. He saw clearly, though, the ominous dark blue surrounding it, the quick water lapping at its concrete base. He swallowed again.

Johnson barely managed to keep a straight face. He leaned out the window. "We'll beach it for you and notify a salvage tug to pick you up. We're late, Mr. Walsh, else we'd do it ourselves. Any particular salvage people you like to do business with?"

Walsh's shriek cut him off. "Pump it out! Don't stand there. Get lines over and pump it!"

Johnson shook his head regretfully. "Take an hour or more. We got a rush job that might turn into something steady."

"Wait!" Walsh pulled out a handkerchief, removed his bowler, and mopped his wrinkled head. "You don't understand. This Princess Bay work is a bonded job. Whatever they lose by delay I'll be forced to pay. It'll cost me ..." Whatever it was going to cost him seemed too horrible to put into words. He gazed up at Johnson and me in despair.

I nudged Johnson and held my voice to a whisper. "Cut it short before another tug shows up, or the joke may be on us. This contract is in our hands, so start grabbing."

In a stage whisper that could be heard thirty yards Johnson wondered which was more important—our Sandy Hook job or saving Mr. Walsh's hide? Of course, if Mr. Walsh gave his work to Hackett we'd have something to show for ignoring the Sandy Hook work....

Much of marine work is sealed by verbal bonds, and even a man like Walsh wouldn't dare break one. So when he affirmed that the derrick was ours, and fixed a one-year term, Olson broke out suction lines and went to work laying them. Within five minutes we had the derrick in tow and were heading for Princess Bay.

"So you've made up your mind on it, lad? It's going to be you and this girl?"

"She's my woman, Pop. It may be corny to say we were meant for each other, but that just about states it."

"You feel Murk has no rights in this case?"

"Not a one. I'm going after that woman until she's mine."

We were on our way back to the basin, the bow of the tug plowing through a shimmering ribbon of orange that the full moon had laid across the bay. It was a clear night, and far to the north the lighted skyscrapers in lower Manhattan rose like a fantastic crown of glittering jewels against a background of blue velvet. Across the wide stretches of the dark bay crawled brief strips of lights, the ever moving ferries, which appeared like so many luminous worms inching their way through the night.

I lit a cigarette, leaned on the sill, and watched the phosphorescent wash rush astern. "Here's the way I feel, Pop. Murk is married for the sake of convenience, to ease the boredom of a barge cabin more than anything else. He's got a cook and a woman who'll keep things clean and neat. What does it cost him? Peanuts. Would he want a wife if he worked ashore and had to maintain an apartment for her? I doubt it. His expenses would be tripled over what they are now, and Murk's not a man who'd pay that for the comfort of a woman. When I step into the picture he'll lose nothing but convenience. Look at it from her side. Has she had any kind of a life with him? He's lived his, but has she ever had a chance at hers? She was fifteen, Pop. Think of it. Married at fifteen. She hasn't lived, and she never will on that barge. I'm going to make her understand that."

He didn't say anything for a while, leaning over the wheel, puffing on his pipe. Finally he shook his head.

"I'd say you're headed for trouble, Joe. The ingredients are all there. Murk likes the way he lives, so he won't give Stella up easily. She happens to be a girl with a streak of loyalty, so neither will she give in to you easily. If she loves you—and probably she does—she'll be torn between her marriage vows and her love; Murk pulling on one side, you on the other. That spells trouble—for somebody. I know you won't take this advice, Joe, but if I were you I'd complete my boat and get out of New York just the way I'd planned."

"I can't do that, Pop. I can't leave alone. Not now."

"Let me finish my say, Joe. You can't leave alone? Well, then, maybe you won't leave at all. Wait. Wait, now. I'll tell you why. You're a lad with a dream, Joe, and dreams are generally empty things. Yours, you've made real, almost. Not many people have believed you could do it—put a boat in the water that you couldn't hope to buy in a lifetime. But you have done it, almost. I've lived a good many years and seen a good many things accomplished, *almost* accomplished. Time and again we set out to do something big, something that will change our lives, give us our dreams, and time and again we fail at the last minute. Why is this, lad? Why does something stop us from gaining complete fulfillment? I don't know the answer and neither do you. But it seems you can't reach for too much. Lad, I don't care one way or the other about Murk and his wife. I wish them both luck, her a little more, and I let it go at that. I care about you, though, and what you started out to do. Finish that boat of yours, Joe. Go down to your island, to the life you've dreamed of. Don't reach too far or for too much. You'll fall flat on your face. By reaching I mean trying for something not really meant for us, in your case a married woman who feels she should stay with her husband. Intrude in this marriage—that's what it amounts to, an intrusion into something joined by God, smile if you will—intrude in this marriage and something will knock you flat. You'll lose everything. Don't ask me what it is that will make you fail. I don't know. But something will. Call it Mr. X, but up he pops when you reach for too much. He always does."

"Superstition, Pop." I flicked my cigarette over the side and watched it disappear in the black water. "Only two things are important in my life, Stella and my boat, and I intend to get both. And, frankly, I can't see what completing the boat has to do with convincing Stella she'll be better off as Mrs. Baski."

He knocked his pipe against the wheel, emptying the bowl. "Neither can I, lad. But none of us can see the future. We can only attempt to predict some of it by what we've seen in the past. I'm not a talker, neither am I a very smart man. But I've seen Mr. X work. He won't let us reach for too much."

I had an answer on the tip of my tongue on this business of not reaching for too much, but I kept my mouth shut. After forty years behind a tug wheel Johnson had nothing. He never reached, so he didn't get. Or maybe he did reach out for something but didn't put up a fight.

I intended to do both.

Chapter Six

"If you can use it, Murk, you're certainly welcome to it. This butcher friend occasionally pushes the stuff on me for past favors, and I can't do much else but give it away."

Murk accepted the large boneless ham, his eyes popping. "Use it? I'll say I can. Hey, wait till Stella sees this. The price of meat being what it is, we don't have one of these often, we don't."

"Don't know very much about meats, but this guy gives me the best."

"I'm obliged, Cap. I sure am."

"Think nothing of it. Glad you can use it. Wish I could. I don't have the facilities for cooking meals. That's one thing you miss being a bachelor—a good old-fashioned home-cooked meal." I waited.

"Guess you do. Young fella like you should get married." He kept pinching the ham. "Real firm, it is. No waste. Don't know how to thank you, Cap."

I was beginning to wonder if it had been wasted money when he finally got around to it. "Don't figure you'd like a meal with us, would you? Sort of help put this away?" He looked like he wanted me to say no.

"I could be coaxed."

"I'll tell Stella to set another place, I will. About seven o'clock?"

I was there at six-thirty and found her alone, standing by the oven and basting the sizzling ham. She wore a frilly apron over a blue polka-dot dress, and with her cheeks flushed and her blue eyes sparkling, maybe from the heat of the stove, she looked cute enough to eat. I told her so.

"It's a wonderful ham, Joe. Thank you."

"I wasn't talking about food. Where's the boy?"

"He went up the street for some coffee and things. He'll be back any minute."

"I figured that part. He's always coming back in a minute. Enjoy that boat ride Wednesday?"

She slipped the ham back inside the oven and closed the door. "Oh, yes. It was very nice."

"You're a liar. You were bored stiff. Listen, this coming Friday you and I have a date. Coney, maybe. Dancing, hot dogs, and a moonlight swim. Sound good?"

She gave me a look. "Joe, why do you talk this way? You know very well—" She turned back to the stove.

Murk came in carrying a bag of groceries. He stopped short in surprise, looking from me to Stella, then back to me. "Wasn't expecting you so soon, Cap."

"Heard you played a mean game of checkers and thought we'd have a round or two before supper."

He relaxed. "Heard about that, did you? You sit down there and I'll get the board, I will."

We played two games. He was pretty good, and took both of them. Then he put the board away and went over to carve the ham Stella had placed now on the table. It was a pretty tasty ham, and it should have been because it had cost me enough, but Stella did nothing but toy with her food.

"You sick?" Murk frowned.

"No. Not hungry, that's all."

"You don't eat much lately, you don't. Maybe you ought to take something." He hesitated. "No sense in seeing a doctor, but you ought to take something, you should."

"I don't need anything. I told you, I'm just not hungry."

"How's that tooth, Murk? Do a good job over there?"

He shoved a large slice of ham in his mouth, chewed a moment, and nodded. "They did that, they did. One thing I can say for them people, they treat you good."

He waved his fork at me. "You fellows sure are lucky. I was talking to a couple of old seamen who'd been there close to three months getting treatments for ulcers. Three months in a hospital and not a penny charged against them! One even had a hernia taken care of and a new set of false teeth put in during that time, he did. He was telling me he figured it would've cost him two, maybe three thousand dollars if he'd had it all done by a private doctor in a regular hospital."

"Guess it would, at that. They do take care of you and that's a fact. A man's wise to take advantage of those facilities while he has the chance. I went over there—think it was about three years back—feeling out of sorts and wondering why. Not sick, mind you. Just feeling out of sorts. Now, you know how it would be going to a private doc? He'd look you over, maybe give your chest a jab, and then hand you a bottle of pills. Pills, hell—he'd hand you nothing! He'd prescribe those pills and you'd go out and buy them. Well, not those docs at the Marine Hospital. No, sir, they do it up right. They got me in a room, kept asking questions until they knew my medical history from A to Z, and then when they saw nothing wrong, *apparently* wrong, they gave me a three-day observation treatment to make sure. You know what that treatment would ordinarily cost?"

Murk blinked. He shook his head.

"One hundred dollars—not counting the room and board a private hospital would charge you. Believe me, Murk, when those babies got through I left there knowing I was A-one from head to toe, and it was a nice feeling for a guy to have. You leave there with a spring in your toes when they get through with you."

"But what'd they find wrong?"

"Nothing at all. Not a thing."

He put his fork down. "And they weren't mad at you? I mean, all that trouble—"

"Why should they be mad? That's one of the functions of the Public Health Service—improving the general health of seamen. Mad? Why, the doc in charge slapped me on the back, said I'd live to be a hundred, and wished more guys would come in for a checkup—especially the old-timers, the guys who pass fifty and strut around brimming with health. Those are the birds, he said, who won't come over until it's too late, until they begin to feel something is wrong, and then have to go under a knife. If they would only come in earlier for a checkup they could avoid all that. That means less work for the docs, too. Figure it out. All around everybody is that much happier."

"Common sense." He nodded slowly. "That's common sense, it is."

"Certainly it's common sense, but how many guys do you know personally who won't go to a doctor until they can barely walk there? And how many do you know who would go to a hospital only when they're at the point where they have to be carried?"

"That's right. That happens, it does."

"Would you care for some cake, Captain Baski?" Stella eyed me coldly. She had caught on and didn't like it.

"No, thanks, Mrs. Murk.... You bet it happens. The sad part of it all, this doc was telling me, the older you get, the less susceptible to pain you are and the longer it takes you to find out something is wrong. Now, take that tooth of yours. Did the drilling hurt? I mean, did it hurt as much as when you were a younger man?"

He thought about it. "Now that you mention it, it bothered me some, but not like years ago. Years ago a drill pushed me right down in the chair, it did."

"That proves my point—not *my* point, but the doc's. Nature, he says, is a wonderful thing. When you get old—and naturally more things go wrong with you—your nerves aren't as sensitive as a young man's, and you don't feel the aches and pains as strongly as you might. But, by the same token, this doc says, nature is making a mistake, because if an old guy had *severe* pains when something went wrong, he wouldn't put off going to a doc until it was too late. Like this one guy that came in with a tumor the size of— Hey, maybe I shouldn't be talking like this at the table."

"No, no. Go on. Stella don't mind."

I didn't look at Stella but went ahead and described a tumor as big as a baseball that this guy was supposed to have been carrying for years and feeling nothing more than a gas pain every so often. Healthy guy, too, as spry as Murk. Of course, by the time the operation came off, it was too late.

While Stella was washing the dishes we played another game of checkers. Murk lost. We played another and he lost again. He kept gazing absently at the board all through those two games. We got a third game under way, and he started shifting restlessly in his chair and clearing his throat.

"Cap, I guess I never got around to thanking you for that health slip. I sure did appreciate it, I did."

"Eh? Oh, that. It was nothing, Murk. Glad to do it. Barge captains rate that service as much as any seaman. King me."

He did, and then started drumming on the table with his stubby fingers. "I sure would never say anything to anybody about you signing for me. I keep things to myself, I do."

"Wouldn't have given you the slip if I didn't think so. Your move."

He made his move and walked right into my trap.

"That seems to be it. Guess I'll call it a night, Murk. Thanks again for the meal, Mrs. Murk. You know how to cook. I'll say that."

She was sitting in the corner, mending some stockings while we were playing the last game. She lifted her eyes long enough for a glance that said it wouldn't work and if it did she wouldn't play ball.

It took Murk until Thursday to get up the nerve to make the approach. When he did he was feeling a little achy and was wondering if he could see one of the hospital medics and get a checkup at the same time. "Hate to ask you, Cap, but if you could see your way clear—"

"I can't, Murk. I'd like to but I can't. A tooth is one thing, but hospitalization is another. You can see that, can't you?"

"Guess I can. It's a lot I'm asking."

"Well, it is in a way. You see, Murk, every time I sign one of these things for anybody but my crew I'm liable for fraud.... Oh, the hell with it. What's the sense in having friends if you can't get a little help from them when you need it? Just one thing, Murk: When you go over, tell them you've had internal pains for several years. That'll clinch an observation. And don't you worry about being docked any pay. We'll handle your barge so you just stay on there as long as they want you to."

When Murk left for the hospital the next morning Stella went with him. She didn't return until ten that night. When she came into the barge cabin she found me sitting in the dark, smoking and waiting, and ready to tear something apart. "Where have you been?"

"Where do you think I've been, and just what business is it of yours?" She glared defiantly at me from the doorway.

"You knew I'd be waiting."

"Listen to him! He's been waiting. Well, you do your waiting somewhere else!" She stepped to one side and motioned me out.

I snubbed out the cigarette, walked over, and grabbed her arm. "What are you sore about? It's me that should be sore. We had a date and you knew it!"

She twisted out of my grip. The half-light from the door revealed the angry glints in her eyes. "You listen to me, Joe Baski. I told you before we couldn't go on with what we started and I meant it. What do you think I am, anyway? That all you need to do is get my husband out of the way and I'll come running? Well, you can just stop your conniving because I won't!" She moved past me and went over to the window and stood there, grimly looking out at the night.

"It's not me you're sore at, Stella."

"I'm not sore at anybody."

"You're sore at Murk, at the fix you're in. You want out, away from Murk and this barge. O.K., get out. Leave him."

"I don't want to leave him. You're taking a lot for granted when you say that. Joe, you'd better go."

"I'm not going anyplace." I went over and stood behind her, but didn't touch her. "Stella, the first time I came in here I was after just one thing from a good-looking woman. You were married and I thought that was fine, too. No complications. A little fun and we could both forget about it. It didn't work out quite that way, Stella. Not for me. It didn't even start slow. I walked away that first time crazy in love with you, but not really sure, because with me that kind of feeling was something new. I knew I wanted you, and not for just a few hours, but I didn't know why. It took me a week to find out. I know now, Stella. Maybe it sounds pretty slushy to say I'm madly in love with you, but that's it. You've got me walking around and thinking about you day and night, going nuts just watching you on this barge and not able to touch you. Stella, I've stopped being a smart guy about women. I don't want just anyone for a time anymore. I want you, and only you, and for good. I love you, Stella."

For a long moment she kept looking out the window, then her hand came back, reaching for mine.

"You feel like that, Joe? Really?"

"I can't throw you a line, Stella. Not you. Not now. I'd choke on the words."

"No one ever said that to me before, that they loved me. It's nice, Joe. Nice to hear it. Say it again."

I said it again. Her hand squeezed mine. "That's nice, Joe."

I slipped my arm around her waist, drawing her against me. She turned her head and rubbed her smooth cheek against my mouth. "All day I've been feeling so cheap, Joe. After I left him at the hospital I stayed in Staten Island, just walking around and feeling like some piece of baggage being waited for."

"It isn't like that, baby. It never was. Is he staying over the week end?"

"Until Monday. I'm calling for him then."

"We have a lot of things to talk over before then."

"Let's not talk too much, Joe. Let's just go out and have fun."

"I'm your boy. Just name the place."

"You mentioned Coney?"

"Suits you, suits me. Let's go."

To me the Island with all its hokum and come-on plays had always been strictly sucker bait, but that night I found myself having a good time. It was who you were with that made the difference, a big difference. Like any high-school kid, I found myself showing off at the shooting gallery, knocking off clay pipes until I'd won enough coupons for a rag doll. That doll was worth maybe a buck and cost me about three to get, but when she said she'd never seen such a cute one before, that made it O.K. We took in the rides, the scooter cars, the parachute, and then the Cyclone. On the Cyclone dips she would wrap her arms around me and squeal, and we went around four times. When I tried to pay for a fifth ride she pulled me out of the car, threw her arms around my neck right on the platform, and hugged me.

"There, that saves you the price of another ride." The crowd along the rail got a kick out of that.

We got frozen custards and sat on the sand near the edge of the surf to eat them. It was almost midnight. There was plenty going on around us, and it wasn't too dark to see.

"Have you a hankie, Joe?"

"Let's see. Nope. Mouth sticky? Come here." I pulled her over and licked her lips. "How's that?"

"Hmmm, good. Except *you're* sticky."

"Well?"

She did the same for me. "Now you be good, little boy. We don't happen to be alone."

"I'm the only one being good, though. Look around."

"I don't want to look." She turned, wriggled herself into position, and stretched out on the sand, her head on my lap. "Talk to me, Joe."

"About what?"

"Talk to me about yourself, about— Joe Baski, give me that hand!" She grabbed it, kissed it, and brought up to her cheek. "You were in the Navy, weren't you?"

"Not by choice. I had an invite, like a million other guys."

"And what ship were you on?"

"No ship. Pensacola for two years and Liverpool for one."

"Somebody said you were there when they invaded the French coast, and you were given some medals. Tell me about that, the part you played."

"No part. I was one of the first casualties. Bing, bang, and I was on the side lines, a total loss to Uncle."

"Oh, come on. Tell me. There's more to it than that."

"There isn't, though. Sums up my total war effort. One minute I'm sitting in a landing barge, with the French coast getting bigger all the time and me getting more frightened, and the next minute I'm in a hospital with a little Scotch nurse giving me a bath. Some French general came in later with a boxful of medals, and in the confusion I got two."

"Was she pretty? The nurse?"

"When you get a piece of steel in your ribs, anybody that's healthy looks pretty."

"Was she?"

"Too flat."

"You *would* notice that."

"I was wounded, not dead."

"Give me that other hand, Mr. Baski. Now, go on. You were saying?"

"You're the sweetest thing on two feet."

She reached up, pulled my head down, and lightly kissed me. "Your reward, darling. But tell me more about yourself, how you became a tug captain and so on."

"More or less born into that. My old man used to push a Hackett tug around, and every chance I got I'd play hooky and ride with him. Before I was twelve I was standing at the wheel with him behind me, and getting my skull cuffed every time I made a wrong move. By the time I was fifteen I was a little punchy from those cuffs but I was a boatman, and ready to sit for a master's license, if I'd been old enough. The old man was pretty proud of that. I think the one thing he was looking forward to was the day I'd be hanging my license in the pilothouse beside his, and then he'd be able to bawl me out whenever I relieved him late. That would have really tickled him."

"I can understand his pride. He was drowned, wasn't he?"

"So was my mother. Both of them went down in an overloaded fishing boat off Sandy Hook. Hackett's old man had been a good friend of the family, and the first thing he did was to hire me as a deckie. As soon as I got my master's license he put me behind the wheel, and I've been there ever since. Nice guy, that Hackett Senior. He was like his son Jud—cry on your shoulder about how lousy business was, and then take you out for a dinner. Hey, you're shivering."

"Turning cool." She sat up and moved back against me. "Put your arms around me."

"Glad to."

"*Around* me, dear."

"How's this?"

"I see I'll have to buy something to keep your hand occupied."

"I'm doing all right."

"Better than all right, if you ask me."

"Which reminds me I've put something new on the boat. What say we run over there and I'll show you?"

"What is it?"

"Oh, just a little surprise. Something that finishes off that master stateroom you admired so much."

"We'd better make it tomorrow, Joe. It's late, and I'm getting sleepy."

"We'll take a cab to the basin. You can catch a nap on the way."

"Well, all right. But your surprise better be good after walking me across those marshes this time of night."

"You devil! Walk me two miles just to show me bunk mattresses."

"Mad?"

"Furious. Come here."

She slept with her head on my chest, breathing deeply. I lay there, stroking her warm shoulders, looking at the dark green overhead, at the bulkheads, at the faint glimmer of light showing through the blinds at the side windows. This was my home. I had created it and I loved every inch of it, but now, for the first time, I realized how cold and empty it would have been without Stella.

She stirred sleepily. "Darling, are you awake yet?"

"Haven't been sleeping."

"Awake all this time?"

"Lying here and thinking."

"About what?"

"Us. We have a lot to talk about, hon."

She turned her head and pressed her lips to my chin. "Let's not spoil this night by talking, darling."

"How would that spoil it? Straightening things out would make it perfect, it seems."

"Just say you love me."

"You know I do."

"Say it."

"I love you, Stella."

"There, now that's all the talking we'll do. It makes everything perfect. Tomorrow we'll ... we'll talk."

"Come over here tomorrow night?"

"All right, and I'll bring a picnic basket. But you must do some work on the boat. I'll just sit by and watch. You're falling behind in your schedule, you know."

"The schedule doesn't matter."

"Of course it does. Or do you mean it doesn't matter as much as I do?"

"Not a tenth as much. You're everything, and that's what we're going to talk about."

She rose slightly, propped herself on one elbow, and leaned over me; her hair was tousled and her eyes looked sleepy. Her lips gently brushed mine. "Darling, I love you. You'll never know how much. Remember that first day we met and you were standing on the tug and looking down? You were *looking*, too."

"You have something to look at. What about that day?"

"Well, that wasn't the first time I had seen you. Oh, I know you never noticed me, but I used to watch you steam past in your tug many times, standing up there at the wheel and frowning, looking so serious all the time. I thought you were just about the handsomest thing I had ever seen. Then, that morning, when you came alongside, I felt exactly like a silly schoolgirl, as if I'd start blushing the moment I looked up at you. I became so nervous I talked fresh to hide the way I felt."

"You did come to the shed that second day hoping to meet me?"

"I did, and I was done for as soon as you kissed me."

She pressed her cheek against mine. I drew her against me. "Stella, baby, when are you going to tell Murk?"

For a moment she was silent. "Joe, let's not talk about it. It's been so grand I just don't want to talk about it."

"But look, baby—"

Her hand went across my mouth. "Please?"

"Tomorrow?"

She relaxed against me again. "Tomorrow, darling. It's been such a perfect night, I don't want to think of anything else."

The next day I towed Walsh's derrick to Yonkers and didn't get back to the basin until after dark. The reason for the delay was a squall that blew up as we were coming down the Hudson. We were just passing under the glittering span of the George Washington Bridge when it hit, and within five minutes the river had boiled up into a tidal race. We headed full speed down to the Weehawken Barge Terminal, getting there just in time to pick up the gravy that a high wind occasionally offers tugs. Almost a dozen barges had broken their moorings and were adrift in the river. For thirty minutes Spatola and I were busy, grabbing a barge here, another there, pulling them into the shelter of slips and tying them up. For each barge we threw a line on, fifty dollars automatically went into Hackett's pocket. That's the usual fee a tug receives from a barge company for grabbing its equipment before it goes aground—or worse, before it smashes into a pier, making the company liable to a damage suit.

All told, we got seven barges, and then an eighth that a fireboat slipped us on the q.t. For the city-owned boat it was emergency work that had to be performed gratis, so its skipper was only too happy to hand the barge over to us, knowing there'd be a little something coming from Hackett in a few days by way of appreciation.

From Weehawken I phoned Hackett and told him the registry numbers of the barges and where we had tied them up—four hundred dollars' worth of business completed in less than an hour. He was delighted, and promised he wouldn't forget about the fireboat.

It was almost nine when I arrived at the shed. Stella was already there with a basket of fried chicken and cold beer. We finished the chicken and most of the beer, and then I unwrapped the package I'd brought along.

"My, that's pretty paper."

"It's gold leaf, not paper. I thought I'd letter the stern tonight, and perhaps put a border around it."

"Then you've decided on a name?"

"I have. You just sit there and watch. Not there, where you can see. I mean sit and *don't* watch. You stay over here by the bench."

I broke out the can of varnish-kerosene mixture, got the lettering brush, and went back to the stern. It had all been marked and blocked out three days before, so it was a simple matter of painting the mixture within the lines and placing the gold on.

"O.K."

She came back and looked at it. All she saw was a dozen sheets of gold leaf plastered haphazardly—or so it seemed—across the reddish wood of the stern. "What on earth is that?"

"That's how a gold-leaf job works. You paint your letters with a thin varnish, then put the leaf over them. Just slap it on any old way. In say an hour, when the varnish is fairly dry, you take a dry paintbrush and brush lightly across the gold leaf. What isn't held by the varnish crumbles off. Simple?"

"When you know how. And what's the name?"

"Top secret. You have to wait. Any more beer?"

"One can. And I think you're mean."

We shared the last of the beer between kisses. "Stella, honey, I'm leaving New York in about three months. I told you that before. You know my plans, where I'm going and what I want to do. And I think you know by now that you're included in those plans."

She lowered her eyes. "It's not that simple, Joe." She moved away from the bench, keeping her back to me. "I wish it were, but it's not. I've been thinking about it. In fact, I've been doing nothing but think about us. And it just isn't a simple matter of doing what we please."

"You love me, Stella, so you're coming with me. It's that simple. There's nothing that can stop us."

"There's more to it than that, Joe. Lots more."

"I'm listening."

"Well ..." She turned and faced me, her expression wooden. "Joe, it can't work out. It can't and that's why I didn't want to speak of it last night. I didn't want to spoil the happiest moments of my life."

All along I'd given no thought to the possibility that she would refuse to leave Murk. Now, it scared me silly to realize my hand was not a pat one, that I wasn't exactly a prize package. But then, was Murk?

Suddenly it made me sore, that she could even weigh Murk against me. "What do you mean it won't work out? What's there to prevent you from telling Murk you're leaving?"

"Joe, please. You don't break up a marriage just like that."

"Give it to me straight. Do you or don't you want to leave him?"

"I ..." She clasped her hands, shrugging helplessly. "I just can't, that's all."

I lit a cigarette and leaned back against the bench.

"Joe, don't glare at me like that."

"You expect me to be smiling? Listen, Stella, you're pushing us into a silly situation. You don't love that character and you do love me. At least, you say you do. Why won't you leave him?"

She moved slowly over to the door and stood there looking out at the night, at the dark marshlands. She jumped back, startled, as a streak of lightning ripped across the eastern sky. "It's going to rain again, Joe."

"Yeah, it's going to rain." I went over to her. "And I'm waiting for an answer."

"But we have a long walk across the marshes."

"Cut it! Give me a flat, sound reason why you can't leave Murk."

Her shoulders lifted. "Call it loyalty, Joe."

"Loyalty, my— Stella, listen to me. Just listen. What has he given you? Not one thing. Look at it this way: You've given him a home. At least, you've made a home of where he lives. You work, cook, and ... and sew for him. What have you received in return? A roof over your head? Sure, but he doesn't pay for it. Food, a few dresses? O.K., but can you name anything else? He's laid out damn few bucks for what he's got these last five years. Damn few!"

She shook her head. "You talk as if I've had to work hard, Joe, and go without things. That's not true. I've lived comfortably, compared to what I had before."

The rain came suddenly, a preliminary sprinkle pattering the dry brush outside. Thunder rumbled in the distance.

"All right, Stella, I'll put it frankly. He's had *you*. He's had you these past five years. In exchange for a bunk on a crumby coal barge he's had a woman. Whatever you think you owe him is paid. Paid twenty times over, believe me."

"You're wrong there, too. He ... he's not too interested in that."

"I won't say I'm sorry to hear that, because I'm not. And it's just one more reason to leave him. Stella, if you walk back to the stern of the boat and rub that gold leaf off, you'll find 'Stella B.' remaining. The B is for Baski."

I placed my hands on her shoulders and gently turned her around. She was blinking tears from her eyes. "Stella, honey, look up at the boat. It's all yours. Ours. Up there on that bow is where a kid is going to be playing someday. Our kid. He'll ..."

Her eyes widened, darting to me as if she were suddenly frightened by what I had said. Then she quickly turned away, looking out at the marshes again, at the rain falling more heavily.

"You want kids, don't you, Stella? If you don't, we'll—"

"Yes ..." She whispered it softly. "Dear God, yes."

My arms encircled her waist, my lips nuzzling her neck. "We'll have a dozen, honey. Run 'em off on a production line."

"No, Joe, no!" She choked up. "And I won't talk about it anymore. I won't. And you must stay away from me." She broke away and ran down the steps into the rain.

It was coming down hard, a warm but heavy rain that had her dress clinging to her back before she had gone fifty feet down the footpath. "Stella!"

She kept running ahead, and was swallowed up by the brush and the night. I set out after her.

Heat flashes flung yellow streaks across the black sky, momentarily lighting the marshes. Stella was about thirty yards ahead, stumbling in the face of the driving rain, her wet dress plastered against her back and looking like no dress at all but wrinkled skin. She stopped suddenly, glanced back over her shoulder, and saw me. Then she turned to the right and disappeared into the brush, in the direction of the basin.

She was taking a short cut, but it was a way that was almost impossible to make in the daytime, let alone at night. The ground was firm enough, with layers of decayed brush forming a bed over the marsh, but the meshing of high reeds and brush made impossible barriers that could keep you wandering all night trying to get around them to the basin.

I turned off at the same place she had, pushing ahead through a brush opening that quickly narrowed. It was like forcing a path through thick jungle growth that slapped at you when you tried to pass. When I had gone less than thirty feet I stumbled over her.

She was down on her knees, her shoulders shaking with wild sobs, her head bowed, her wet hair hanging in front of her face. I bent down beside her, pushed her hair hack, and pressed my face against hers. I was so choked up could hardly talk. "Baby, whatever it is, it can't keep us apart. Nothing can! Just us. You and me. Stella, baby, don't ... don't cry like this. Honey, listen to me...."

She shook her head and kept crying. I put my arms around her and pulled her against me. I kissed her face and suddenly her mouth was on mine with kisses and love words and she kept crying and kissing me and saying she loved me, and that's when I began crying and saying she was so much a part of me that nothing mattered except our love. She lifted her head. "You sure nothing would matter, Joe? You love me that way, so much? So very much?"

"More than life, baby. More than life itself!"

Her eyes brightened, glowing feverishly as her hands gripped me. "The way I love you? Something deep inside hurting?"

At that moment it was tearing my heart out and I said so.

"That's it, Joe! That's how I feel now. It hurts terribly, so terribly...."

The driving rain; lightning darting through the night; the thunder crashing; brush rough against wet skin; her mouth hot.

"Always, Joe? Always?"

"Just you and me, baby."

Lightning smashed across the heavens. The earth shook.

We crept down the road and over to the barge, both of us crouching against the rain and laughing like a couple of kids at the way we looked. We were both drenched and muddy, our clothes torn by the brush. But we didn't care.

Nothing mattered anymore.

In the cabin we took off our things in the dark and dried each other. She put coffee on then, and we put a pillow in the lumpy overstuffed chair and sat there, Stella on my lap, a blanket across us while our clothes were drying.

"Tell him tomorrow, Stella?"

"Give me time, Joe. You can't rush a thing like this."

"O.K., break it to him easy. But break it."

"And Joe, listen. I'm not going to say anything about us. About you, I mean. I'm simply going to ask for a divorce. He doesn't suspect a thing, and to hear I wanted to marry you would lead him to think things had been going on behind his back. Not that they haven't, I know, but I'd rather he didn't think so. In fact, I insist it be that way."

"O.K., honey, any way you want it. But let's get everything settled."

Chapter Seven

Murk came back the following Monday morning looking like the condemned man. They had examined him, all right. They had given him the works and found a small kidney stone. Nobody is ever as sick as the guy who claims never to have been sick a day in his life, and Murk turned out to be a lulu. All he had to do was to take some medicine after each meal to dissolve the stone and he'd be O.K., but to hear him talk, he was just about at death's door.

I saw her alone for a moment the next day. "Tell him?"

"I can't, Joe. Not yet, Not until he's up and around again."

"He's still in bed?"

"Most of the day. He gets up an hour or two."

"But what the hell's he doing in bed? He's not that sick."

"The medicine makes him dizzy."

"And so he's got you waiting on him hand and foot. Listen, you tell him, and tell him today."

"Joe, be sensible. I'll talk to him as soon as he's feeling better."

Three weeks later I was on the verge of going in and throttling Murk. He not only stayed in bed most of the day, but when he did appear on deck he would be in bathrobe and slippers and acting sorry for himself.

"What seems to be the trouble, Murk?"

"When I walk I get dizzy, I do. Real strong stuff they gave me. Makes my head go round."

"Stop taking it if it makes you dizzy."

"They'd operate, then. I don't want that if I can help it, I don't."

"None of my business, but I'll give you a tip. Hackett's worrying. He's wondering if you're getting too old for this work."

"Old? Fifty-nine, I am."

"Yeah, but he's plenty worried. You'd better show your face around in work clothes and look alive for a while."

"Bosses!"

"They pay the money."

She was alone when I walked in on her the next morning. She gave me a cold stare. "That was dirty, Joe. He's stopped taking his medicine."

"Tell him?"

"You don't even care, do you? He's just a nobody that you push around."

"Look, Stella, I'm not pushing anybody around. All I want is for the ball to start rolling."

She put the last of the dishes in the cupboard, closed the door, and took off her apron. "I asked him for a divorce, Joe."

"So?"

"He wanted to know why. I said I wanted a change. To live differently."

"Good reason."

She moved over to the window and adjusted the curtains. "We had a long talk. Last night we had a very long talk."

I didn't like her tone. I waited.

"He said he would never hold me against my wishes, but asked that I wait a while. He ... he said he'd like the chance of being a better husband." She kept fooling with the curtains.

"Very touching. But it doesn't mean anything to us. Or does it?"

She looked at me. "Joe, I can't hurt anybody. I never could. What is a simple matter of saying the right words with you isn't so with me. I'm just not built that way. What I'm trying to say is that I can't leave him. Not just now. It's not fair to walk out on him. So quick, I mean. Later, perhaps, when he thinks it over—"

"Wait a minute, baby! Wait a minute. Remember that thunder and lightning? Remember? You and me. That was all that mattered then. What changed that? What gives with all this fairness?"

"Joe, listen." She drew a breath, then wearily shook her head. "I'm so confused. Perhaps it's the rushing—"

"Hooey! Don't hand me that. Your marriage is no good. It's one-sided, so it's no good. Stella, there's something else. I know there is. It just doesn't add up. You want out; you walk out. Nothing to it. Murk owes you nothing; you owe him nothing. Or do you?"

"All right, Joe. All right." She folded her arms and leaned back against the bulkhead. "Now, I'll tell you. I'll tell you something I never thought I'd have to. You think Albert is just an old grumpy tightwad, don't you? Well, he is, Joe, but he's something else. Deep inside he's kind and thoughtful, tenderhearted when someone's in trouble. Does that surprise you? That someone like him could have another side but keep it hidden? He's close with money, but that's nothing more than habit. He gets grouchy often, too, and complains. But that's habit, too. Perhaps it's because he's always led a hard life. But he has feelings, Joe. Feelings for other people. Remember I told you about my coming down to the docks and sitting there and watching the boats? And meeting Albert there? Well, Joe, the day I met Albert I wasn't watching any boats. I was crying and asking God for help. Can you guess why?"

She dropped her arms and straightened. Her face was suddenly pale, the skin tight. "I was going to have a baby, Joe. And I wanted to die. For me the world was at an end when Albert sat down beside me and held my hand and talked to me."

My legs felt weak. I hadn't expected it. I sat down at the table and lit a cigarette. I said nothing. So this was it, the thing that tied her to Murk.

"You despise me now."

"I don't." I growled it at her. "So he showed up. So?"

For a while she was silent. "He was willing to marry me, Joe. He carefully explained he had nothing much, but he could give me a name and a home. To me it was heaven being offered. He was giving me my life back. I found out later he had seen me a few times sitting on the wharf and had been quite taken with me, thinking, of course, I was much older. Joe, you may not understand this. I know you're not very religious—for that matter, neither am I—but when we were married I thanked God and said I'd be Albert's as long as he wanted me. With you, Joe, I get carried away. Perhaps I've said things, made promises. Well, I meant them, and I still do. But when Albert asks me to wait I can't simply walk out. Later things will change. I know they will. He'll think enough about my wanting to leave and he'll talk it over with me again."

"How long do we wait?"

She made a vague gesture. "I don't know. If we just wait, things will work out."

"You know they won't, don't you? Maybe if he knows about us—"

She stiffened. "No! Never. Never, Joe. I could never tell him."

"I could."

Her eyes were steady. "I'd hate you for it, Joe. I told him there was no one else. I'd hate you for it."

"What happened to the kid?" I snubbed out the cigarette, then lit another.

She moved over to the window again. "It was never born."

"Who was its old man?" The cigarette tasted lousy. I crushed it out.

She kept staring out the window. "This won't put me in a good light…. I didn't know."

That hit me right below the belt and knocked the wind out of me. An affair is one thing, but when she couldn't figure out who the father was—

I lit another cigarette, my fingers shaking.

"Joe, it wasn't as bad as it sounds. I was only fifteen."

"So you said before. Only fifteen, but you sure were getting around!" My nerves were jumping and a sickness was rising in me, choking me.

"Joe, let me explain."

"You came down to sit on the docks and watch the boats? Was that your story before—? What was it, a lineup?"

"Stop it!" Her eyes were blazing, her cheeks turning livid. She clenched her fists. "You—you get out! Get out! Get out, do you hear?"

I got up but I didn't go. I stood there, sick at the thoughts that kept crowding my head and sick at the things I had said. I wanted to tell her I was a big dope with a filthy mouth but I just stood there, my belly twisted in knots, the words refusing to come. I wanted to go over to where she stood glaring at me and get down on my knees and apologize, but I didn't. I turned and walked out, and when I climbed over onto the tug I could hear her crying.

Three days of it was all I could stand. The few times I tried to talk to her on deck she refused to even so much as look at me. I went in one morning when Murk was over at the office getting his check.

She was up to her elbows in baking dough.

"Stella, you know I didn't mean a word I said that day."

"Didn't you?" She lifted the dough out of the bowl onto a board and began flattening it. She looked tired.

"It just hit me hard, that's all. The things I said didn't mean anything. What happened before we met doesn't matter."

She gave me a level stare. "Sure about that? Even if there was an even dozen in that line-up?"

"Baby, don't say it."

"You said it, not me."

"I could cut my tongue out for making such a crack."

She gave the dough a vicious whack with the pin and began rolling it. "Maybe it was the truth."

"Don't rub it in, Stella. It hurts plenty now."

"I guess it would—seeing you were such an angel all your life." She looked up, her mouth grim. "You men make me sick. You flop in strange beds as regularly as you eat, and then you're shocked speechless if a girl admits one mistake. Yes, *one*, if it will make you feel better." Her lips trembled. "Just to set you at ease, it was at a party. My first. There was liquor. I couldn't handle it. It got late and I passed out in a room. Someone—I never found out who—but someone came in there. That's all I ever knew, that someone had been in there. One mistake? And it wasn't even a mistake."

"Stella, it doesn't matter. It doesn't." I wanted to go over and take her in my arms, but I knew it wouldn't help. She was too worked up against me.

"You mean *now* it doesn't? Now that I've explained it, everything is much better?" She went back to rolling the dough. "You'd better go. Albert will be back soon."

"You're not going to leave him?"

"I've thought it out very carefully. I'm staying with him."

"For good?"

"Yes."

"You say that because you're sore at me."

"That has nothing to do with my decision."

"You still love me, Stella?"

"Go 'way, Joe." She set her lips.

"Honey, I haven't worked on the boat. I haven't done anything. You've got me walking in circles—"

"Please go. I don't wish to talk to you anymore."

That night I did something I'd never done before in my life. I got loaded to the ears, so loaded it came up. Then I drank some more, trying to ease the leaden ache from my belly. That's the way I showed up on the tug in the morning, dead drunk and with an extra bottle in my pocket.

Spatola had never seen me in that condition. He treated it as a joke, pushing me into the bunk room behind the pilothouse. "I'll take 'er out, Cap. Jeez, what a snootful!"

"Get your hands off me!"

"Take it easy, Cap. The boss may be 'round. Take it nice 'n' easy, now...." He went out grinning, locking the door behind him.

I sat on the bunk and cursed him, and then cursed myself. Half a bottle later I got around to cursing Stella, but I couldn't put my heart into it so I took to cursing Murk. There I did a good job. I started on his ancestors, worked up to him, then went back to his ancestors. I fell asleep praying he would break his fat neck barge-leaping someday, and dreamed that he did. It was a pleasant dream.

When I woke up my mouth felt as if it were stuffed with cotton. Spatola was standing there, watching me admiringly. "Jeez, Cap, you sure done it up right."

"Where are we?"

"The basin. Be leavin' in a while."

"What's holding things up? We were ready to leave when I came aboard." I sat up, grabbing my head to hold it together.

He grinned down at me. "That was yesterday, Cap. Been to Hoboken an' back, ready to go out again. Murk is up gettin' some grub an' that's holdin' us up. Jeez, do I see that other bottle empty?"

"You got any aboard?"

"Nary a drop. Stayed sober as a judge while I had the wheel. Not so much as a sip in twenty-four hours."

"You deserve a medal." I pulled a bill from my pocket. "Go up the street and pick up a bottle."

After he left I washed and changed into fresh clothes. I wasn't feeling any better when I went up into the pilothouse. It was a hot humid morning, the basin blanketed under a muggy haze. Up the street a bunch of kids were diving off a makeshift springboard. My head ached with each whoop and holler they let out. The *Sand Point* was secured alongside us. No one was on its deck.

When Spatola came back and climbed aboard I ordered him to cast off.

"Murk is still up the street, Joe. Should be along any minute."

"We're not waiting for Murk." The mere sound of his name was enough to put a sour taste in my mouth.

Spatola shrugged. He threw off the forward line. "Ain't this him now, Joe?"

He was ambling down the dock, carrying a bag of groceries in his arm. He saw we were ready to shove off and quickened his pace.

"Kick it ahead, Joe, and I'll tie it up again."

We had drifted about four feet from the stringpiece. With the barge alongside and in towing position, our bow was the only means Murk had of climbing aboard. Spatola coiled the line for heaving.

"Never mind that. The fool likes to jump, so let him!"

Spatola hesitated, then dropped the line. "You say so." He patted his side pocket. "Got the stuff here when you want it."

"That's yours for good behavior. But get up here out of sight before you do any sampling."

He came up, happily cutting the seal of the bottle. "Much obliged, Joe. Maybe I'll save it till after lunch." He shoved it into his pocket and leaned on the throttle box. "Don't think he's goin' to make this jump."

Murk had stopped at the stringpiece, out of breath. "Sorry, Cap. Sorry I'm late. Had to wait, I did. Them markets is getting more crowded every day." He looked at the gap between the stringpiece and the bow of the boat. The distance was now about five feet. He looked up at me. I was lounging across the wheel, lighting a cigarette, waiting for him to say something. One word and I was prepared to bring the boat in—after giving him a few growls to relieve my feelings.

As if he had guessed my mood, he said nothing. Shifting the groceries to his other arm, he scratched his chin, studying the widening gap between boat and dock. He gave me another hesitant look, finally decided it was now or never, and prepared to jump. He crouched slightly, gauging the distance as his weight leaned forward. Suddenly he saw he'd never make it. He floundered, trying to regain his balance, his eyes dropping to the oily waters eddying below, where he would have to fall.

At that same moment—purely a reflex action to move the boat in and save Murk a wetting—Spatola slammed the engine throttle to full ahead.

In less time than it takes to tell it I saw the bow surging in, the frantic expression on Murk's face when he realized he might drop between the bulkhead pilings and the crushing weight of an eighty-ton tug. I swore, shoved Spatola out of the way, and yanked the throttle back to astern.

The engines stuttered, coughed, then quit cold. The bow moved in.

Stella screamed first. She must have come out of the barge cabin just in time to see Murk falling squarely against the stern of the tug a split second before it hit the bulkhead. Then Murk screamed. He was out of my line of vision, pinned somewhere near the water line, screaming in a peculiar high-pitched womanish voice. His bag of groceries had fallen on the rail of the boat and split open, the contents rolling on deck. A bottle of ketchup had broken and was mixed up with a head of cabbage; it looked like a pale, bloodied head rolling down the deck.

For a moment I was too dazed by the swiftness of the accident to move from the wheel. I kept looking at the bloodied head rolling, and listening to Murk screaming. My fault? Damn right it was!

"Joe! Joe!" Spatola's face had turned a dirty gray, and his teeth chattered. "I w-was only trying to help. You know that, Joe! They'll hang me for this. They—they'll say I'm a drinker, I was drunk! They'll blackball me out of the boats! Joe, I got too many strikes on me."

Only then did I become aware of the whisky fumes filling the pilothouse and realized that somehow Spatola had dropped and smashed the bottle he'd brought aboard. To anyone coming into the pilothouse it would mean only one thing. I straightened up fast.

"Clean up this mess as quick as you can. And keep your mouth shut. You were just sitting here and doing nothing. Savvy? Just sitting here and talking to me."

"But they'll ask—"

"You don't know a thing! You had nothing to do with it. I was at the controls when Murk jumped. Keep your mouth shut about everything else and your hide will be safe. I operated that throttle. *I* did, not you!"

Chapter Eight

"Terrible thing, a terrible thing. Really a terrible thing...." Hackett kept shaking his head and crumbling a cigar between his fingers. Stella sat between us, silently looking out the cab window as we sped up the street, no expression on her face. Only her hands, clasped tightly in her lap, the knuckles showing white, betrayed her intense emotions.

Ahead of our cab the ambulance maneuvered through the heavy Flatbush traffic, its siren wailing. Murk was in that ambulance, his left leg covered with blood from the hip down. How badly his leg was injured we didn't know—and neither Hackett nor Stella knew that it had been Spatola's hand that pushed that throttle forward.

Spatola had been right when he'd said they'd hang him for handling the throttle. A deck hand touches a vessel's controls only under direction of the skipper. I had been at the wheel, therefore he had no business interfering. Even if he beat the Coast Guard rap, it would be a cinch he wouldn't be able to board another boat as a deckie, and that was the only kind of work he knew. Rummy, yes, but Spatola had the sense to realize that once he was off the boats it wasn't far to Skid Row.

The fact that the *Junior's* engines had stalled might count for little in this accident. Why were they full ahead in the first place to move a boat five or six feet? That was quite a question. And only my opinion as a reputable skipper that it was necessary at the time would suffice for an answer. An error in judgment on *my* part, a licensed master, was one thing. On the basis of my past record and experience it would be acceptable. An error in judgment on Spatola's part would be attributed to wits dulled by liquor.

But the main reason I was shouldering the blame, if any should fall, was that I had baited Murk into making that jump. Spatola's action was wrong? Sure. So was Murk's. And the faulty engines had contributed their share. But I had baited Murk into making that jump. It was a fact I couldn't get away from. I couldn't have a poor slob like Spatola paying through the nose for something for which Joe Baski had laid the foundation.

"Joe." Hackett turned and cleared his throat. "Did you tell Murk not to jump? I mean did you notify him the boat was coming in?"

"Never had a chance. Happened too fast."

He looked as if he wanted to say more. But he simply nodded and settled back again. "Bad habit, jumping on marine equipment. Very bad."

Stella said nothing. Suddenly I wondered how much she had seen, if she knew I was lying, concealing the truth. Or was she blaming me for not having the tug up against the bulkhead to begin with? Another thought struck me.

Was she thinking I had *deliberately* run Murk down? Ridiculous. She couldn't think that.

At the hospital we were ushered into a small room, to wait for the doctor's verdict on the extent of Murk's injuries. Hackett immediately began pacing the floor, stopping now and then to take a soggy cigar from his mouth and look at Stella, who wasn't looking at anything except her hands folded in her lap. He'd shake his head, jam the cigar back in his mouth, and resume pacing.

Not once during the time we waited did Stella so much as look my way.

I had a pretty good idea now what was going on in her mind. I wanted to walk over and tell her it wasn't so, that I would never deliberately set out to hurt Murk or anyone else.

Then why push the throttle full ahead?

I was still trying to come up with an answer when Spatola entered the room with a uniformed cop. The cop stayed by the door, leaning back against the wall, his eyes on Stella's legs. Spatola came over and sat down beside me. "Is he bad, Joe?" he asked nervously.

"Don't know yet."

He looked guiltily in the cop's direction and lowered his voice. "Told the cop I was in the engine room. Figured it'd look better if I wasn't topside at all. O.K. with you?"

"Good idea. Stick with it."

"Standin' right by the engines, I told 'im. Ahead, then back they went. One, two, like that. But no backin'. They fizzled right out." He dropped his voice to a whisper. "I cleaned out the pilothouse good, Joe. Nobody came up there, so we're all set on that."

That relieved my mind somewhat. Liquor on board a tug, of course, is nothing new. It's pretty well taken for granted that tug hands consume plenty, but it's also known they're a rugged lot and can hold plenty. Nothing much is ever said—until something happens. When something does happen and somebody gets hurt, if they can prove liquor was aboard the captain is liable for criminal negligence. Before a tough board of inquiry his ticket becomes a scrap of paper.

Hackett came over. "Joe, I'd like to straighten out a point. If the engines had operated efficiently, would the boat have stopped in time?"

I weighed my answer carefully. The accent on the cause of the accident could be placed on the engines or on judgment. If I made a big thing out of the *Junior's* engines, Hackett would be on the spot. Possibly the tug *could* have stopped, then again possibly not. "The blame is mine—part of it, anyway. Let's say half. I should have let him fall into the water. I know those engines. I've worked with them long enough."

He shook his head. "I don't think you can even share part of the blame. Murk placed you in an awkward position by his carelessness. But *could* the tug have stopped if the engines had performed properly?"

"I doubt it very much."

He sucked on the cigar to conceal his relief. It was apparent he had been worried about the possibility of Murk's bringing suit for a sum of money far above what Hackett Towing carried in the way of liability insurance. He turned in Stella's direction, half apologetic.

"To speak so bluntly of responsibility at a time like this may seem harsh, but in protecting my company I am also protecting the livelihood of a score of people and their families. I am not a rich man, Mrs. Murk, so forgive me if my mind dwells on the interests of the company. Lord knows my sympathies are with any man who's injured or crippled—and let's pray such will not be the case now...." He stopped as Lieutenant

Delaney walked into the room.

Delaney was a harbor dick, and I don't know whether I was glad to see him or not. You wouldn't want a squarer, straighter-shooting cop, but he was a stickler for pinning a rap where it was supposed to be pinned. With Delaney, when a guy crossed the law, it was something personal. If you were some poor slob who stepped out of line and were in need of a break, you got it. But heaven help you if you were wrong, knew it, and wanted to play it that way.

He glanced briefly around the room, then began speaking in low tones to the uniformed cop and studying the notepad the cop held. Delaney was a tall, stoop-shouldered guy in a rumpled gray suit, wearing a perpetual frown on his long bony face. He dismissed the cop with a nod but kept frowning at the notebook he'd taken from him.

"Spatola."

Spatola got up, looking uncertain.

Delaney's frown deepened. "We've met before, haven't we?"

Spatola shifted his feet. "Guess so, Lieutenant. Maybe a little disorderly conduct on pay night, maybe." He smiled sheepishly and scratched his nose.

"You're the engineer of the Hackett *Junior*?"

"Jus' a deckie, Lieutenant. The *Junior* don't carry no engineer."

Delaney eyed his notebook. "Oh, yes. But you were in the engine room at the time of the accident?"

Spatola nodded. "I was ... I was standin' right there."

"You couldn't have seen any of the accident, then."

"Didn't see it, but I saw the engines and how they fizzled out when Joe, here, tried to reverse them. Full ahead, then back, except they didn't back."

Delaney's eyes lifted, flicked to me momentarily. "Full ahead?"

Spatola nodded, then looked confused. "Well, they was revvin' up like they was full ahead, but only for a second. Just enough to get the boat movin', then back they went. But like I said, they didn't back. They just fizzled."

Hackett got to his feet. "Perhaps I should explain about those engines, Lieutenant. I want to be completely fair about this. My name is Hackett. Jud Hackett."

Delaney tilted his head. "Go right ahead. This is merely my preliminary report, but I must warn you, it can be used by a defendant in a civil court."

"I understand. I quite understand. But we've nothing to hide, I can assure you. Those engines are not the best and I readily admit that. They are old and under constant repair. But—and it's quite a big 'but,'

Lieutenant—Murk should have known better than to make that jump." Once again he glanced apologetically in Stella's direction. "From habit, perhaps, I don't know, but Murk constantly made jumps of that sort, and it was only a question of time before he misjudged his distance or lost his footing. I sympathize with the man, but, as I've already explained to Mrs. Murk, I must also protect my company."

"You say Murk was in the habit of jumping from dock to the boat?"

"Or to the barge. That fact is well known. And not just a foot or two. He's been known to hop six and seven feet. Mind you, Lieutenant, I admit the *Junior* does have faulty engines, but I am going to maintain that a barge captain with Murk's long experience should have known better. Oh, yes. One more thing—Baski. There isn't better skipper in the harbor. I want that on the record."

Delaney closed his notebook. He shoved it into pocket, then glanced at Stella. "Mrs. Murk, did you see the accident?"

Stella nodded slowly. She didn't look up. She took a gentle breath, as if she'd been holding it for some time. "But not very much of it. I mean, I came out of the cabin when he was falling onto the tug. He screamed...." She paused and swallowed. "I screamed, too, I think, and turned my head away. I—I didn't want to look."

Delaney nodded sympathetically. He turned to me. "And you're the tug skipper, Joseph Baski?" He broke off as the doctor entered the room.

In crisp tones the doctor diagnosed Murk's injuries as dislocation of the hip, a torn thigh muscle, and multiple lacerations. "On his feet in a month, perhaps less. A sturdy man for his years. But lucky, very lucky."

A tremendous load slipped from my shoulders. I looked across at Stella, and when I caught her eye I smiled. She didn't smile back.

Delaney was over near the door in a huddle with the doctor. The doc shook his head a few times, then shrugged. "One minute. But no more than that."

Delaney looked at me. "Mind stepping outside with us a minute, Captain?"

I got up and followed the two of them into the corridor. Delaney let the doc go on ahead and fell in step beside me as we walked down the corridor. "Been behind a wheel long, Baski?"

"All my life."

"Ten years as skipper, say?"

"Off and on, yes."

"How far were you from the dock when you started your engines?"

"Five feet. Could have been six."

"You were easing it ahead when Murk jumped?"

"He jumped first. That is, he started to. He caught himself and tried to fall backward."

"Then you eased in?"

I saw what Delaney was driving at. "I opened the throttle wide."

He nodded, his frown deepening. "Your deck hand, Spatola, said that. I wondered why. Is that the usual thing? To throw your engines full ahead to move five or six feet?"

The doc broke it up by stopping at a door and turning. "I hope you'll make it brief, Lieutenant."

"One question. Nothing that will excite him."

Two nurses stood by the head of Murk's bed. One was checking a bottle of some clear liquid being fed into his arm. The other was wiping the sweat from his forehead. Murk's eyes were closed, his breathing heavy. The room smelled of antiseptics.

I stood at the foot of the bed, blocking off some of the bars of sunlight slanting in through the window blinds. The bars reminded me that criminal negligence was no trivial charge. Murk might be out of the woods, but Spatola wasn't—nor, for that matter, was I—until Murk gave his version of the accident. Had he seen Spatola at the throttle?

Delaney leaned over the bed. "Mr. Murk, we would like to ask you a question. Just answer yes or no."

Murk opened his eyes. Whether he heard Delaney or not I don't know, but his glazed eyes focused unsteadily on me. He gave me a weak smile. "That's one time I should've waited, Cap. I thought I could make it, I did."

I didn't say anything. His words absolved me of any negligence as far as Delaney was concerned, and I stopped thinking of Spatola and myself. I was thinking of Murk, of a guy being disliked because of a few faults that had never really hurt anyone. Who was perfect, anyhow?

"Sorry it turned out this way, Murk. Anything I can do, just let me know."

The doc gave me a significant glance. I turned away from the bed and went outside to the corridor. Delaney joined me in a few moments. He pulled some tobacco from his pocket and started to hand-roll a cigarette. I offered him one of mine.

He shook his head. "Trying to cut down, and this seems to be the only way I can. Too convenient to pull out a ready-made." He licked the edge of the paper smoothed it, and stuck the cigarette in his mouth.

"Where were we? Oh, yes. I can't understand that, Baski, that last point we were discussing. I'm getting on and off police launches every day. If someone gunned his engines full ahead simply to move a few feet, I'd hardly consider him a competent boatman. Would you?"

"A tug is heavier than a police launch."

"But has more powerful engines. That evens that, no? Did you think you'd be able to get in there fast enough to catch Murk before he fell?"

"Maybe that was on my mind."

"Maybe?" He touched a match to his cigarette, dragged deeply, and exhaled through his nose. "We'll pass that for the moment. You must be pretty upset about this business. That girl in there, Mrs. Murk. Pretty young for an old duck like Murk. They get along?"

"So-so."

"How well do you know her?"

"We say good morning."

"And that's it?" He took the cigarette from his mouth and made a face at it. "I wish I could quit."

"Look, Lieutenant, what are you getting at? We say good morning, it's a nice day, things like that. Just because she's stacked is no sign she's a—"

"Tut-tut, Baski. I didn't say she was. I don't know a thing about her. That's why I'm asking questions. You say she's straight, she's straight. What was Spatola doing in the engine room?"

He threw this last question at me so fast I stared at him openmouthed for a moment. "Just standing there, I guess."

"Seems I recall him as somewhat of a boozer. Does he take a load on when he's working?"

"Not too much."

"Do you?"

"Never on board." I fumbled for a cigarette.

He dropped his cigarette on the marble floor and put his heel on it. "O.K, Baski. This case is pretty much cut and dried. Murk isn't too banged up. I'll write it off and in case you're worried about the drinking angle, I won't go into it any deeper. Your license is your bread and butter, and I don't like to fool around with anything like that. But if I were you I'd keep a bottle of cloves handy in that pilothouse. You could use some right now."

Chapter Nine

That night I waited for her on the barge. I waited and smoked, watching the gray fingers of light at Floyd Bennett Field sweep the sky south of the basin, and wondered a hundred times over if she really thought Murk's accident was a deliberate attempt on my part to hurt him.

At midnight she still hadn't shown up, so the question remained unanswered. I left the barge, walked up the street to the corner bar, and put in a call to the hospital. Murk's condition was still the same, good; he was resting well.

I had a couple of straight drinks at the bar, watched TV, the last of a night game being fumbled away by the Dodgers, then went back to the barge. Stella still wasn't there.

I waited another hour, then walked across the marshes to the shed, fed the cat, and tried to make a go of sleeping. At dawn I succeeded and wished I hadn't. Talk about a guilt complex. I was getting a bad one. I dreamed of Murk again. The stern of the tug had him pinned against the street bulkhead, and he was staring at me with eyes popping and tongue hanging out. I had the throttle down hard and was cursing more speed out of the engines, Murk being squeezed ... squeezed....

The cat was licking the sweat from my face when I woke up.

"So much for that. Now, here's the picture when Murk takes the stand—I don't say he will, mind you, but you can never tell when some Shylock feeds him telephone figures and gets his name on the dotted line. So if it goes to court and he takes the stand, here's the picture: We throw it at him. We slam it to him. Isn't jumping across marine equipment dangerous? He knows it? Well, well! How long has he been doing it? That long? But why? Why jump when you know it's dangerous? Why, why, Why? No letup. Slam it to him until those twelve jurors get the idea that only a moron leaps across to a boat or barge when one slip can be your last. Get him to admit it's silly to take chances year after year, and he won't collect three cents in damages!" Coletti leaned back in his chair, smiling, his sharp black eyes shifting from Hackett to me.

Hackett didn't say anything. A black cigar was clamped in his heavy jaw, and his fingers drummed steadily on the desk. He had been listening to Coletti for twenty minutes; and occasionally he removed the cigar from his mouth as if it was turning sour.

I didn't blame him for feeling that way, either. After hearing this Coastal Casualty representative rig an airtight case against Murk's collecting damages, I also felt the need for fresh air. When you think of an insurance representative you generally picture some quiet, unassuming old duck who is ready to give a fair shake to a claimant. On marine policies they generally lean over backward to give a fair deal, especially when a man is hurt on the job.

Not Coletti.

He was a dark little man with a razor-thin mustache above razor-thin lips. He wore a checked suit, a pale maroon sport shirt, and a porkpie hat. He smelled of cologne. And from the way he talked I gathered his only purpose in this life was to close each of his indemnity cases with the suckers signing for peanuts. When he managed to write a case off with no check from Coastal being made out, it became a supreme triumph. He really got a bang out of it. And he never, *never* paid off on a shaky claim. Too smart. Too sharp. He didn't mind telling you so, and in the same breath he'd tell you how dumb you were.

When he walked into the office that morning he pulled up a chair, helped himself to one of Hackett's cigars, and proceeded to bawl Hackett out for leaving word at the hospital that all bills were to be sent to Hackett Towing. Never assume even a fraction of the responsibility; always get tough right at the start. Then he launched into a discussion on how thankful he was that Murk hadn't lost his leg, that a man coming into court on crutches would have a fat judgment in his pocket before the case started. Better off dead. According to Mr. Coletti, you're better off with a childless widow on the stand than a one-legged man. Cuts the judgment by a third. Captain Baski will have to remember that, in case he ever runs into another man; and Coletti smiled, showing me a mouthful of sparkling white teeth that I was tempted to ram down his throat.

"Now we have a question: Are we still going to keep Murk in our employ?"

Hackett eyed him coldly. "Do you mean *my* employ?"

"Yes, because if you do, that's a club we have over him. Make him think twice about a lawsuit. The man's not young. Barge captain is the only type of work he knows. You fire him for negligence and who'd hire him? Nobody, of course. So we give him the word that if he gets any funny ideas he'll be walking the streets. If he's a good boy he can keep on being a barge captain." He smiled again. "Case closed before it starts."

"Mr. Coletti." Hackett's voice was a whisper, a sign he was burning. "Mr. Coletti, I don't fire men injured in my employ."

Coletti nodded. "Sure you don't. We just say that you will."

"Mr. Coletti …" Hackett's lips barely moved. "I don't threaten an employee with dismissal for injuring himself. Would you mind changing the subject and completing whatever business we have here?"

Coletti got it. He shrugged. "Well, that's about it. I'll brief Captain Baski and this Spatola on their lines if it ever goes to court."

"How much would you pay Murk for signing a release?" I picked up a letter opener lying on top of the desk and toyed with it.

Coletti looked at me in surprise. "Pay? Pay? Baski, we've just discussed that. Nothing! Absolutely nothing. Not a thin worn-out dime."

"Isn't it a practice with insurance companies to make small settlement in cases like this? A few thousand to smooth feelings all around?"

"Not when Coletti takes the case, Baski." He pushed his porkpie hat farther on his head and leaned across the desk. "When I go on the job the claimant is lucky to get the right time. I've built my rep on filing my cases with no liability. I've spent weeks on a case that could be settled for a few hundred smackers, *weeks* just tying it up tight for the legal department. But it never gets that far. When I take on a case where Joe Blow thinks he has some dollars coming, that case is worked over until Mr. Blow is thinking in terms of pennies."

"You must be quite the fair-haired boy at your office."

He puffed up immediately and began giving me the tails of a specific case that had had his company worried and that he'd settled for a few dollars by bringing in a phony witness.

I threw down the letter opener in disgust. "Mr. Coletti, I'm going to advise Murk to make a court suit out of this. Furthermore, on the stand, as a chief witness, I'm going to stress the fact that Murk took that jump to save time, that he had our company's interest—the running schedule—in mind. He knew I was late and didn't want to inconvenience me by making me bring the tug in. I'm going to stress the fact that he had every right to expect no danger from my tug, that if he had merely missed his footing a ducking would be the worst he could expect. You're right, though, this doesn't have to go to court. Offer Murk a small settlement, say three or four thousand, and I think your company will be getting fair treatment and so will Murk."

Hackett looked pleased. "Yes, why not? You make it thirty-five hundred, Coletti, and I'll add another fifteen. Let's be completely fair in this case. Five thousand isn't too much for the pain and inconvenience Murk has undergone. I'm perfectly willing to chip in fifteen hundred, sharing some of the liability."

Coletti looked far from pleased. He was glaring at me. "Do I understand, Baski, you'll be testifying in favor of Murk if I refuse to offer him a settlement?"

I nodded. "I've known seamen to collect a lot more than that on injuries received on the waterfront. I'm willing to bet your company has statistics on this sort of thing that will prove thirty-five hundred is a reasonable settlement."

"On cases of self-negligence?" He said it through his teeth, a muscle jumping along his jaw.

"On cases where the company has no witness to testify it was self-negligence. Where a doubt exists, say."

"Baski, you can't ..." He paused and stared at me. "What's the score? Why pull something like this?"

"I don't like to see a man pushed around the way you seem to push people. That's all. Simple?" I stared right back at him, my temper going up. "You're over a barrel, Coletti, and you belong there. Your company would never let this enter a courtroom with me on Murk's side, and you know it. You also know any adjuster would be tickled to write this off for thirty-five hundred."

"But I'm not just *any* adjuster!"

He got up, his thin mouth tightening. I suddenly had the feeling Coletti was a first-rate neurotic, a bug on keeping the dough flowing one direction. Maybe, just a bug.

Without saying another word he turned and walked out, slamming the door. Hackett grunted his disgust. "Next time I'll know better than to sign my liability with a two-bit outfit. You were right, Joe, on settlements being worked out on a give-and-take basis. Murk's got something coming and we'll see he gets it. Coast Guard show up yet?"

"Haven't seen anyone from there. They'll be around, though. I telephoned a report this morning."

"Suppose we keep the *Junior* in the basin for a day or two. You stay aboard until this is cleared up."

"Good enough." I got up and stood there a moment. "See Mrs. Murk around? I didn't get the chance to tell her how sorry I am about this mess."

Hackett swiveled in his chair, calling to Miss Thomas behind the glass partition. "What hotel are we putting Mrs. Murk up in, Tommy?"

"The Travers, on Bedford Avenue. It was the closest I could find to the hospital."

She tried to close the door. I got one foot there in time.

She eyed me through the narrow opening. "We have nothing to say, Joe."

"I have, if you haven't. It'll only take a minute. Mind if I say it inside?"

She hesitated a moment, then adjusted her robe and opened the door. The room was tiny, a bureau and a chair facing the bed with one window overlooking Bedford Avenue, but it certainly beat a barge cabin. I moved over to the window, for some reason feeling ill at ease. I lit a cigarette. "How does it feel, living ashore?"

She remained by the opened door. "All right."

I dragged on the cigarette, blew smoke through the window, and watched it curl away over the hot street. Below me a cop was tagging a double-parked car. "Stella, let's say it was partly my fault. That I'll admit. But not all my fault, as you're thinking. Coming, as it did, on the heels of our ... our argument, it looks bad, as if I were trying to get back at Murk some way—take out on him something that wasn't his fault.

It wasn't like that, Stella."

"Perhaps it wasn't." She spoke quietly, her arms folded, and leaned back against the wall. Her robe was a pink woolly affair, and with her blonde hair pulled back in an upsweep she looked cute.

"But you had been drinking, Joe. And I wonder if an accident would have happened to someone like Johnson if he had jumped. Or would you have been more careful, knowing something could always happen to your engines? I've seen you bring the tug in for Johnson, many times, the tug barely moving if he was standing there and was likely to step across. You're a good captain, and a careful one. Why was your boat moving so fast yesterday?"

I shrugged. "One of those things, Stella."

"Why not admit the truth? You just didn't care about him. He was someone you hated, someone that didn't matter."

"O.K., he was. He isn't now." I flicked the cigarette out the window. "I don't hate him, and I don't think he's someone that doesn't matter. Right now, I feel sorry for him. If it were possible to change places with him, I'd do it. Stella, you've got to believe that."

"It doesn't really matter what I believe, does it?"

"To me, it does." I started over to her. "Stella, honey—" I stopped short as she flinched back against the wall, drawing the robe tighter about her.

"I'm just a boy with dirty hands now, is that it?" I was beginning to get sore.

She lowered her eyes. "It's not that. It's ... well ..."

"Tell Murk when you see him not to sign any papers for any sort of settlement until he sees Hackett. Tell him the insurance adjuster is a first-class creep, but the boss will carry the ball for him. See you around."

I went out, slamming the door behind me. I stood in the hall near the elevator, wanting to go back and explain that Spatola had been at the throttle. But would she believe that now? On second thought, why even tell her? If she couldn't accept the fact that I wouldn't—

"Down, sir?" The elevator door had opened and a young colored kid was looking at me impatiently. So were two heavy-bosomed women.

The hell with her! Let her think what she pleased. If she didn't know me any better than that—

"Going down, sir?"

I got in and stood facing the door. One of the heavyweights behind me whispered something about gentlemen removing their hats in the presence of ladies.

I glared over my shoulder. "I always do!" I kept my hat on all the way down.

The hell with all of them!

It took me two hours to get rid of the Coast Guard investigating officer. He was an old duffer of a commander who believed in crossing each *t* and dotting each *i*. He went over the tug, checked its equipment and papers, asked a hundred questions, and wrote out a hundred answers in longhand. Then he had me maneuver the tug in the basin. When he closed his book he gave me a clean bill, wished the injured man luck, said I looked tired, and hurried off the pier.

I was tired, all right, dead tired, but I snapped right out of it when I opened the door to the boat shed and saw Mr. Coletti standing with his hands behind his back, gazing reflectively at the boat. He wore a brown sports jacket, cream-colored flannels, and gray suede shoes. His smooth black hair was parted dead center and looked oily.

"Mind if I come in?"

The sarcasm didn't bother him. He smoothed the fuzz on his upper lip, still gazing at the boat. "Takes a cutie to put something like this into the water. No job for a knucklehead. No, sir."

"If that's a compliment, thanks. Now, mind telling me why you're trespassing on private property?"

"Trying to make the picture clear, Baski. Get it into focus. After talking with that cop Delaney, and then Spatola—routine stuff for the reports—I found myself smelling something. A slight odor." He turned and smiled. "Please don't suggest it might have been me."

"Get to the point. I'm hitting the sack." I thought I knew what Coletti's point would be, that somehow he'd found out there'd been drinking aboard the *Junior* before the accident. It certainly wouldn't alter a contested court suit in favor of Coletti's company, but I didn't need a crystal ball to spot the trouble he could make for me.

He went back to studying the boat. "The point is this, Baski: This morning I had an accident brought about by stupidity of two men. Most accidents are the cause of someone's stupidity and this one was no exception—or so I thought. Murk was stupid to make that jump, we'll both agree: I accepted that. Why not? A barge captain is nothing more than a night watchman with a fancy title, and a watchman is hardly a man you'd expect to find overly developed in the brain department. Then we have you, a tug captain, smarter than a barge captain, but—in my book—not too much so. I accepted your stupidity—and if you don't call depending on unreliable engines with a man directly in front of you just that, I don't know what stupidity is. Naturally, I made no point of this before. My job is to better my company's position, ignoring everything else."

"So just what are you driving at? Get to the point."

He moved over to the workbench and picked up a photostat. He held it up to the light for closer inspection. "An accident caused by stupidity, yet everywhere I turn I find Baski is reputed to be a guy with savvy, a real cutie, known for his sharpness and ability. He's even building a fifty-grand boat on a hundred a week. Not only a sharp apple, but a guy with big ideas. A picture distorted, get it?"

I didn't. I was listening and thinking Spatola wasn't a guy to open his mouth. Who else would talk about the liquor I'd lapped up the preceding day? Stella wouldn't. Neither would any of the basin hands.

He picked up another photostat, examining it absently. "Just one thing puzzles me, Baski. The setup itself was perfect. You knock off the old man, your sweetie collects a big piece of change, and the both of you make tracks after a few months. That's perfect. A gem. Who ever heard of a murder being committed with a tug? A D.A. would tear his hair out trying to prove anything but negligence." He turned suddenly and looked directly at me. "The thing that puzzles me, Baski, is changing your mind at the last moment. What made you do that? Cold feet? Another moment later under full power and that tug would've sent Murk on his way. What made you kill those engines when you were so close to twenty-five, maybe fifty thousand?"

I could only stare at Coletti, shocked speechless at the twist he was giving the entire affair. An attempt to kill Murk for the damages the widow would receive! I would knock off Murk, Stella would sue ... Good Lord!

Coletti was mistaking my expression. He smiled. "You're wondering how I uncovered this little plan? Simple, Baski, simple. I took one look at that dame, couldn't see Murk satisfying that much woman, and thought why not you? One thought led to another. But no matter who I talked to, Hackett, Spatola, Johnson, the answer was the same. Stella was a nice little homebody. And no one seemed to think you ever so much as talked to her except from the pilothouse. You'd think I'd have given up then, wouldn't you? You hardly knew the girl, so how could you two have been friendly long enough to hatch out a bright future over Murk's cold body? So I kept scratching for a lead." He grinned. "The next time you work something out like this, don't get ahead of yourself and christen your boat with the name of your intended until she's a widow. *Stella B*. Nice name. Except Murk didn't die, so she's still Stella M. But tell me, Baski, what made you turn chicken when you almost had a load of dough in one hand and that broad in the other? Now, wait a minute!"

He tried to pull away but I had a firm grip on his fancy jacket. "This way, bum!"

I dragged him to the door. With the assist I gave him he cleared all four steps, landing on his face in the marsh seepage below. It was soft stuff and a bit smelly, and when he came up on his hands and knees, spitting it out of his mouth, his eyes were slits of black ice. "You wise guy! Figure there's no proof, so you're safe, do you? Well, I'll get proof!" He got to his feet, spitting more mud. "With or without it, let's see how you take to mud, Baski. You and her together—"

I went into the shed and shut the door. Coletti, as far as I was concerned, was a study for psychiatrist, a case of frustration who was doing his best to make the rest of the world as unhappy as he was.

I stood looking at the gold lettering at the stern of the boat: Stella B. In a way, I could see why Coletti thought he had stumbled into something. Those seven letters *did* appear incriminating once you let your imagination run.

I went into the bunk room, put some milk out for the cat, and stretched out on the bunk. So what could be done about it? Coletti would no doubt take his findings to Delaney, and the cop would be on my neck with a million questions. Nothing could come of it, of course, but the dirt would fly thick and fast. And plenty of it would cling to Stella.

Would it hit the tabloids, with Stella's face on page one?

I fell asleep with a headache, thinking about that part of it, wondering if there was a way to protect Stella from the scandal.

Chapter Ten

"Sit down, Joe, before you collapse." Hackett motioned me into the chair by his desk and pushed the cigars my way. "What are you doing at night? It can't be sleeping."

"It isn't." I sat down and took my cap off. "Need a rest, I guess. A change. I don't know."

"Accident still on your mind?"

It wasn't, not the way Hackett meant, but I nodded. In the three days since I had thrown Coletti out of the shed I hadn't slept more than an hour or two a night. I had expected him to go to Delaney immediately, ask to have the accident case reopened, and then sit back to enjoy the juicy details. He didn't. Why not? It was the waiting that was wearing me down. Where was Coletti? Was he playing a cat-and-mouse game, waiting until I worried out every last shred of the situation before handing it to Delaney? It looked that way. The crumb.

"Tell you what, Joe." Hackett leaned back in his chair and unwrapped a fresh cigar. "Take a break. Week. Two weeks. You got it coming. Take it now, go someplace and relax. Murk will be on his feet in a few weeks and you'll feel better when you see him walking around."

"Johnson's due to go, isn't he?"

"He won't mind waiting. You take a break. And stay away from that boat of yours. Relax."

"Seen Coletti around?"

He looked at his cigar distastefully. "Yesterday. Says he'll see Murk in court before he pays a dime."

"He'll lose the case. Bound to cost him more."

"Doesn't seem to think so. He's got an idea you may swing over to his side."

"Did he say that?"

"Not in so many words. You seem to be his pet hate, by the way. Anything further happen between you two?"

"Nothing worth mentioning." So Coletti had the idea I'd be coming over to his side. Did that mean he expected a visit from me after I had time to think things over? If so, how long would he wait for me to make up my mind? Certainly the colder the case got, the less effective any smear campaign against Stella and me would be. Once Murk was on his feet, it was hardly likely Delaney would give official recognition to information that would only blacken the characters of two people and serve no other purpose. Suppose I disappeared for a couple of weeks? Was that the answer? Let Coletti wait, maybe let him believe—

"What's it going to be, Joe? Want that vacation now?"

"O.K. I'll start it today." I reached over for one of Hackett's cigars, feeling pretty good about the answer I had come up with. "Suppose Coletti will be dropping by here again?"

"I'm not looking forward to it."

"Listen, when you see him will you mention I was a little worried when I left; that I was wondering if it wouldn't be better to testify solidly in favor of the company and let it go at that?"

Hackett looked puzzled. "Why the change of heart? You wouldn't be perjuring yourself by giving Murk a break. He'd simply be getting the benefit of the doubt."

"And he'll get it. But I want Coletti on the fence a while. Let him think it's going to work out in his favor, then we'll yank the rug out. He might decide to settle then, rid his hands of the whole thing."

"Well, I'll mention you're wavering, if you want it that way, but I'd just as soon he stuck his neck out in court. I've already handed Murk a check for fifteen hundred, and my lawyer tells me that puts Coletti up a tree immediately."

While he was making out a check for my vacation pay, I had an impulse to tell him I was up a tree, too. The more I thought of the possibility of Stella's being questioned downtown, with the likelihood of the newsmen making a field day of the old triangle, the more determined I was to try to keep Coletti's mouth shut. However, I wasn't going to do it at Murk's expense.

Hackett handed me the check. "That cover it?"

I looked at the figures and handed it back. "Two weeks' pay? I'll take the time, but I've had a week with pay earlier this year. You only owe me for one."

"The other is for bringing Walsh's derrick back under our wing. Now beat it and stay away from your boat. Put some calluses on your fanny instead of on your hands."

That afternoon I packed a bag, locked the boat shed, and grabbed a cab to New York. At Grand Central Station I got out and stood on the sidewalk, getting in the way of people, wondering what I was doing there. For the first time in five years I had time on my hands that I wasn't using on the boat. And I didn't know what to do with it. I'd forgotten how to relax.

"There's the station there, Mac!" The cab was still at the curb, the cabbie with his head out the window. "You go inside for trains."

I went back to the cab, and got in.

"Travers Hotel."

"That's in Brooklyn, Mac. We just came from there."

"So we're going back."

"Your dough."

Whatever made me think I could leave town without seeing Stella I didn't know. I had to see her, if only long enough to tell her about Spatola's part in the accident. She had to know that much before I left.

We made it to the hotel in record time. The cab driver didn't push the flag up when I got out. "You want me to wait, maybe?"

"I won't be long."

She was just leaving her room when I got off the elevator. She started walking down the hall when she saw me and stopped. "Oh—Joe."

"Guaranteed not to bite if you get too close."

She didn't smile as she came on and stood by the elevator. She watched the floor indicator. "I'm just on my way to the hospital."

"How is he?" Her manner was too impersonal to suit me.

"The doctor says very well."

"Will he walk O.K. when he gets on his feet?"

"He may have a limp. They can't tell yet."

We got in the elevator and went down. On the sidewalk I tried to steer her to the waiting cab. "I'll drop you off."

"I thought I'd walk. Visiting hours start at three."

"What I have to say won't take long, but it's easier said in the cab." She hesitated a moment, then got in.

We didn't speak rolling down Flatbush Avenue. The driver cursed when he got tied up in a traffic jam. He caught himself, threw back a muttered apology to Stella.

I took out some cigarettes. "He'd consider that language pretty tame if he heard a basin hand sound off."

"I suppose he would." She was looking out the window, watching a red-necked perspiring cop directing a huge trailer-truck that was holding up traffic.

"Visit Murk every day?"

"Yes."

"Pretty short answer, even if a guy is in the doghouse."

She didn't say anything.

When the traffic cleared we continued crosstown, and I decided to bring the subject up. I had held off purposely, hoping she would speak of it herself, possibly mention that she now understood the accident was just an accident, and she wasn't blaming me.

"Stella, you recall the day Spatola handled the tow for me? Well, I was sleeping off a load of liquor. I had been dead drunk."

"I know you were." She said it without any emotion.

"But I wasn't drunk the morning of the accident. I felt lousy, sure, but I had all my senses." I went on to explain in detail what had happened, leaving nothing out. "And it was a pretty sure bet Hackett would have fired Spatola for making a move like that when the skipper was at the wheel. Spatola is well past the stage of getting the benefit of the doubt as to whether or not he was drinking at any particular time."

The disbelief was reflected in her eyes as she turned. "The accident was *not* your doing?"

"I'll put it this way: If Spatola's hands had been in his pockets at the time, Murk would have done nothing more than fall into the water."

"But I *saw* you at the wheel. *You* were there ... *alone*. I didn't see—" She broke off and went back to looking out the window.

"You didn't see Spatola? Well, maybe you didn't. He was leaning on the throttle box, on the other side of me. From where you were standing, down on the barge—"

"Joe. Please." She shook her head impatiently.

"Please what? Listen, Stella, I wouldn't lie to you. He *was* there, even if you didn't see him. You don't think I'd start making something like this up simply for your benefit?"

But she did think so. She kept staring out the window at the passing traffic, her mouth set.

"Now you're calling me a liar."

"Have you always been truthful?"

"Where you were concerned, yes."

She didn't say anything.

"Cabbie, pull over!"

He did. I picked up my bag and got out. I dropped a ten on the front seat. "Take the lady where she wants to go."

The cab pulled away and I headed across the street to a bar without looking back. The hell with her.

The hell with all of them! Had I said that before?

Well, this time I meant it.

"I dunno, pal. Makes quite a few. Maybe you oughta taper off now. How about some coffee?"

"Shove your coffee! I said hand over that bottle."

"You know how many you had, pal?"

"I don't like guessing games. Do I get that bottle or do I go somewhere else?"

"O.K., pal, O.K. You look steady enough, so I'll serve you. Don't know where you put it."

"Yeah, yeah, yeah, yeah, just pass it over and save the other!"

The fourth place? the fifth? I hadn't kept track, but the guy's name was George and he owned it all, a tiny tavern off the Sound, set back among a lot of trees overlooking Glen Cove inlet. Inside the tavern a small circular bar was ringed by dimly lit wall booths, a window opening off each booth. From where I sat I had a view of the tree-fringed shore, the dark shapes of motorboats at their buoys, and here and there the larger, expensive yachts that are a dime a dozen along the North Shore.

Over a cup of black coffee I was vaguely recalling a cabbie impatiently telling me it was the only place he knew where I could drink and watch the boats I kept mumbling about, and would I please get out now and let him go home to his wife?

A snootful, all right, and it didn't make me feel one bit better when I discovered I had exactly ninety bucks left out of the two hundred Hackett had given me. Talk about your drunken sailors.

George came over with another cup of black coffee. "Use it, mister?"

"Spike this one up, will you?"

"Sure thing." He put the coffee in front of me. When he came back from the bar he had a bottle and two glasses. "Mind if I drink with you?"

I did, but I said I didn't. He was a big dumb-looking guy with sparse reddish hair, and he had kept up a running line of chatter since I'd rolled in. He owned the place; it wasn't always so deserted; on Mondays after midnight you never got a crowd; come to think of it, you never get a big crowd out here, but what there was was pretty fair; it was strictly a whisky and cocktail trade with five- and ten-dollar tabs and good tips, etc., etc.

"I like to sit with a drink or two before I close up, and I don't like to drink alone." He slipped into the seat opposite me, poured a stiff drink in my coffee, then filled his glass. "Now, if I bother you by sitting here, you just say the word."

"You don't." I sipped the coffee, made a face, and pushed it aside.

George tilted the bottle over my glass. "Like I was saying before, it's a living here, enough to support the old folks and myself. I don't use help so I get along in the slack summer months, too. Once, I recall, I tried having a night bartender to help out. It didn't work. You'd be surprised the way profits disappear...."

He went on but I wasn't listening. Through the window I was watching a powder-blue Cadillac convertible pull to a stop on the gravel drive outside. Two girls got out, one a redhead, the other a brunette, both dressed in white shorts and tight-fitting candy-striped Basque shirts. Aside from the difference of hair they looked enough alike to be twins, with sun-browned tough-looking faces, small firm bosoms, and shapely hips.

The redhead, who had been behind the wheel, sauntered over to the path leading to the ladies' room. The other came around to the front of the car, put one foot on the bumper, and inspected her knee. Apparently nothing was radically wrong. She straightened and, still with her foot on the bumper, yawned lazily and scratched herself, slowly and luxuriously, where no lady would think of scratching in public, certainly not directly in front of a bright headlight.

Suddenly she caught sight of me at the window. Her hand froze. But only momentarily. Deadpan, she continued.

"Them two again!" George broke off whatever he was saying and snorted in disgust when he saw what was holding my attention. "I sure hope those tramps keep going!"

I turned back to my drink. "Troublemakers?"

"Around here they call them the Gold Dust twins. Both of them have more money than they'll ever be able to spend, but they're doing their best. The things they do you wouldn't believe. The redhead is the worst of the pair."

She was coming back along the footpath, buttoning the side of her shorts. She airily waved at the window, "Hi, Georgie boy!"

George lowered his voice to a whisper. "What do you think of two girls who'll stock up their motorboat with provisions and stay out on the Sound night and day? *Night* and day, they stay out. Once they were gone for a whole week."

Both girls were standing by the car, discussing whether to drive someplace or telephone.

"And dirty mouths? Listen, mister, you'd think you were listening to a couple of sailors, only I don't think sailors know all the words them two do. They're coming in! Darn them! Darn them, anyway." He hurriedly got up and headed for the light switch by the door. They walked in before he could snap off the lights.

The redhead patted his cheek. "Georgie boy, be a honey and call Archibald for us. We ran into a squall off Sparrow Point, and now the boat putt-putts along like it had a barrel of lead up its—" She saw me sitting at the rear booth and broke off. She was slightly taller and heavier than the brunette, who had gone behind the bar and was inspecting a row of bottles.

George was shaking his head: "Can't call Archie at this hour, Babs. He works all day in that marine shop, and he wouldn't get up this time of night."

"The hell he won't." She kept studying me with bold green eyes. "Tell him who wants the job done and he'll come running."

George shook his head again. He was eying the bottles being taken from the shelf and placed on the bar by the brunette. "Besides, his wife'd answer the phone, and I know she wouldn't disturb his sleep."

"Where's the phone?"

The brunette turned from a row of bottles she was inspecting. "Georgie boy, we'll take these six. Put them on our bill like the sweet boy you are."

He nervously ran a fat hand through his hair. "Toni, I'm not supposed to do that. You know I can't sell stuff by the bottle."

He moved behind the bar. When he attempted to reach around Toni to pick up the bottles, she blocked him off by arching her back and pushing her rounded flanks against him. "Can you be coaxed?" She smiled over her shoulder as she slowly undulated her hips.

He hastily backed away, his face reddening. "Now, Toni ..."

The redhead paused in her dialing of the phone at the other end of the bar to throw the pair a smirk.

I poured myself another drink, enjoying the play, my own troubles forgotten.

George's face was flaming. Determination suddenly tightened his mouth. He attempted to get at the bottles again, but Toni quickly seized two of them and backed off to the end of the bar, holding them high above her head.

"Do I drop them, Georgie boy, or do I buy them?" He threw up his hands in defeat, and came out from behind the bar muttering, casting a see-what-I-mean? glance at me.

The redhead was still at the phone, arguing with somebody who was evidently Archie's wife and couldn't see waking her husband to fix a boat engine at this time of night.

I poured myself another drink, feeling warm and clearheaded again, then nearly choked on the liquor when the redhead, in a soft sweet voice, told Archie's wife that her hubby was a lousy fixer anyway, and not just on engines. Then she slammed the receiver down and turned on George, who was standing in the middle of the floor passively watching Toni fit six bottles of liquor into a large paper bag.

"Georgie boy, make up a couple of containers of coffee to go. No milk, light on the sugar."

He stood his ground, but uncertainly. "I'm closing. Right now. And I'm not—"

A crash interrupted him. Behind the bar Toni had taken another bottle from the shelf and was holding it daintily by its neck. "I'll count to ten. One, two, three, four and six are ..."

George hurried into the kitchen, mumbling curses under his breath. The swinging door had no sooner closed behind him than Toni let the bottle drop. It bounced once, then smashed. "That, you crumb, is for swearing in the presence of ladies!"

His groan could be heard all the way from the kitchen. The redhead laughed, adjusted her shorts, and turned to face me.

"Maybe you know something about boats? You look like the rugged outdoor type."

I drained my glass, no longer amused. The bottles the brunette had dropped might mean only pin money to her, but certainly they would mean a lot to George, who was just getting by.

"Well, do you or don't you?" She eyed me impatiently, hands on her hips, her toe tapping the floor. She wore red sandals, a gold slave bracelet around one trim ankle.

I poured another drink, put the bottle down, and picked up the glass. "I know something about them."

"Then could you help two girls in a spot? We were supposed to pick up a—a friend in Bridgeport tonight, but all we can get out of the motor is coughs and grunts. Could you fix it?"

"When does it act up, in damp weather?"

"That's right. Every time it rains or it's humid it—"

"Simple enough to fix."

"Gee, that's swell. The boat is 'way over near Sparrow Point, but our car is right out—"

"But I'm not going to fix it."

She frowned. "We'll pay, of course. Archie would've charged us fifteen dollars to come out at night. We'll give you thirty. That's double."

"The money doesn't happen to be it."

"What is?"

I sat back and lit a cigarette. "Maybe I don't like bottles being dropped—or people who drop them."

Toni came out from behind the bar. They both stood there eying me thoughtfully. "The gentleman doesn't like us, Babs?"

Babs tilted her head and tried a cute act. "I guess we've been bad girls, Daddy. We're sorry. If we pay for the liquor, will you come with us and fix our engines?"

It was on the tip of my tongue to give them a short answer until I thought of my depleted bank roll. Who was I to turn down thirty bucks for an hour's work? I said O.K. and got my bag, and we all went out to the car. I started to get in the back when Toni grabbed my arm. "Up here, darlin'. You'd get lonesome back there."

Babs had the car in gear and rolling when George opened the front door and held up two coffee containers.

"Hey, you forgot these!"

"In a hurry, Georgie boy."

"But what'll I do with 'em?"

That was asking for it, and he got it. I dropped my head on the leather back of the seat, closed my eyes, and listened to the answer being chorused by the girls, explicit instructions loud enough to carry half a mile down the road.

As we turned onto the main highway that paralleled the shore, Toni rested her head on my shoulder. "Name, darlin'. Or should I just keep calling you darlin'?"

"Joe." I was watching the speedometer climb to seventy, the night wind singing gin my ears.

"She always drives like this, Joey, darlin'."

Tires screeched as we took a sharp turn. We shot by a line of terraced mansions, overtook a lumbering trailer truck, and swung around it. The speedometer reached seventy-five.

I was about to lean forward and switch off the ignition when Babs let up on the pedal and told Toni to open one of the bottles that had been rattling around on the floor.

She brought one up and inspected the label. "White Horse. Not bad.

Joe can do the honors."

I slit the cap with my knife and handed the bottle back to Toni. She immediately tilted it to her mouth, the Scotch whisky gurgling its way down her throat. I waited for the explosion. None came.

She wiped her lips and handed it to me. "If you're a man you'll do as good."

I proved I was a man, then passed it to Babs, who immediately brought the car to a halt at the side of the road. "Never drink when I'm driving." She leaned back in the seat, upended the bottle, and let it flow.

The bottle was passed back to me with a polite hiccup. "If you're a man you'll do as good."

I proved I was a man again, and on the fourth round Toni tossed the empty into the middle of the road, where it broke. She promptly opened another and offered me first licks.

When Babs started the car with a lurch the bottle slipped out of my hands and onto my lap. I recovered it with a half pint or so soaking into my trousers, but I didn't care. I was getting loaded again and it felt fine. It felt fine not to be able to think clearly. Two gold-plated tramps, one on each side and both playing kneesy, a half-dozen bottles on hand. What more could you want?

"Come up for air, Joe. Babs, it's this next left turn. *Left*, you goof!"

Babs recovered, and took it with tires screeching, bouncing onto a rutted dirt road. A gleam of water showed through the trees ahead as she drove more slowly, low-hanging branches and brush scraping the sides of the car.

"This is it." She cut the motor as we rolled off the path and onto a narrow sandy beach. It was cluttered with driftwood but otherwise deserted. Near the edge of the water a dinghy had been drawn up on the sand. Out on the water a forty-foot white-hulled cabin job was riding at anchor, the moonlight displaying her long expensive lines.

Toni got out of the car, staggered, turned completely around, and flopped on her bottom on the sand. She sat there giggling while I transferred the bottles to the dinghy.

When I got back to the car Babs was trying to shake her awake.

"Passed out?"

"She'll come to in about ten minutes, feeling as chipper as ever. Always does. She can hold her liquor."

"You don't do so bad yourself. Listen, the coil is probably shot on your boat. Wet or sticky weather will do that. I figure on swiping the car's, and you can send a mechanic out tomorrow to put another back in. That O.K.?"

"Anything you say." She pushed back her thick red hair, fluffing it with both hands while her bold green eyes traveled over me. "She'll be out for ten minutes so ... anything you say."

"I'll sleep for twenty minutes if you like." Toni sat up with a giggle.

She squealed as Babs spat out a dirty word and kicked sand over her.

It took me an hour to put the new coil in and clean the plugs. A valve job was badly needed, but that was for their shop to worry about. Once the engines were ticking over we sat in club chairs in the saloon, eating anchovy sandwiches and drinking cold beer. After the beer we went back to the Scotch, and about halfway through a bottle we were singing something about three souls being lost and wasn't it a damn shame. After that they got into an argument about somebody in Bridgeport they were opposed to pick up and to hell with the pint-sized bum, wasn't Joey darlin' right here and wasn't he the sweetest and biggest thing you ever laid your eyes on? The cigarettes they had were long, king-sized, and the sweetish smell of them filled the cabin.

"Have another, Joey."

"No. I'm dizzy from the other one."

"That's because it's the first. Here, puff on this. Take it in deep. Inhale. Hold it. Now exhale.... How do you feel now?"

"Like a bird."

"Should we move the boat away from shore? Perhaps anchor it in the middle of the Sound?"

"I'm your boy."

"Say, you sure get sent, don't you?"

"I think I'm coming in for a landing. Pour me a stiff drink."

"You need a smoke, Joey. Here, share mine."

"I need that drink first."

"Then try smoking with it. Don't land, Joey dear, don't land. It's too bumpy on the ground. We'll share this one together and I'll fly off with you. The two musketeers."

"Reminds me, where's the third?"

"On deck sleeping. Who cares? God, it lifts, doesn't it? I feel like a feather. You man. You beautiful man."

"Hey, you wanted the boat moved, remember?"

"Not now, Joey dear. Hold me or I'll float away."

And then there was the dawn and the sunlight on the Sound with the radio blaring above the roar of the engines, and the laughter of the two dancing nymphs on the foredeck, their squeals in the sharp sting of the spray. And then the nights, a cigarette, a drink, and through the haze of smoke a soft curve, a laughing red mouth. Another day. Another night. Time forgotten. Little remembered, except for a walk up a yachting pier, arms loaded with provisions, the well-dressed people drawing back, contempt in their eyes. Hell with 'em. Hell with 'em all. Back to the smooth waters of the Sound again, the cigarettes, the dreams ... the one where the man and woman were clinging to a capsized fishing boat, supporting a dazed and half-drowned boy between them. Somehow the man had found a life jacket, and he fitted around the boy after an exhausting effort. When the man and woman surrendered, the choppy seas wrenching away their fragile holds, the boy could only watch and cry his helplessness. Two lives being given that he might live—that fifteen years later he might keep a date at a reefer party.

I woke from that dream trying to spit something from my mouth that wasn't there, but which tasted exactly like the sour breath coming from Toni sleeping beside me, her dark head in the crook of my arm, her mouth open, and the lipstick smeared across her lips like a bloody gash.

It was morning, and a gray, dirty light filled the cabin. Rain beat against the ports and drummed on the deck overhead. Babs was across the room, sprawled in a club chair, her long legs outstretched, arms hanging over the sides of the chair, her head back. She was snoring. She wore exactly what Toni was wearing, nothing.

I got up, climbed over Toni without disturbing her, and looked out the port. We were in some sort of inlet; a line of trees was visible through the heavy drizzle sweeping the water. Long Island? The Jersey shore? I didn't know. I didn't even know what day it was.

I started looking for my clothes. Shoes and socks were by the sofa, my hat was hanging on a wheel spoke. I went aft to the stateroom and found my shirt crumpled on the floor. No trousers. I swore, but not too loudly. All I wanted to do was leave without waking them up, go ashore and forget there ever were two tramps named Babs and Toni. I'd had enough for a lifetime.

Finally I located the trousers on the lounge in the cabin, under Toni. As gently as I could I rolled her over. She mumbled something but didn't wake up.

The rain had stopped when I finally put the dinghy over and rowed ashore. I pulled it well up on the bank, leaving it in plain sight so they wouldn't motor away without it. Only then did I remember I had left my bag aboard the boat. But even if I had wanted to I couldn't have rowed out there again. I hadn't the strength.

I got the shock of my life when I decided to wash up and caught sight of my reflection in the water. It was as if some bearded character had died there and was staring back with sunken cheeks and dark hollows for eyes.

That beard! A week's growth? Two weeks'?

When I walked into a small village store near the eastern tip of Long Island I discovered it had been eighteen days. The gray-haired woman tending the store hovered nervously around the cash register while I was at the phone. I didn't blame her.

Miss Thomas answered the phone. "Joe? Where— It's Joe Baski."

Hackett's voice boomed over the phone. "Where have you been, boy?"

"Look, boss, I didn't mean to put you in a spot by taking a few extra days—"

"I'm not in a spot, Joe. You are. You get over to the Flatbush station house as fast as you can. Your girl friend's down there sweating it out, and don't play coy by asking what girl friend."

"Wait a minute! Slow down! What are you talking about?"

"I'm talking about Coletti tipping Delaney off on the business going on between you two. He's also come out with some nonsense on that accident. A murder conspiracy, he calls it. I don't know how much stock Delaney is putting in that part of it, but Mrs. Murk's been there two days now, answering questions."

Chapter Eleven

"Nobody's pushing me around, Baski! You, Coletti, or anybody else!" Delaney moved in front of me, hands on hips, his bony face brittle. "I had a job to do and I did it, in my own way. Rushing in here like a madman isn't going to do one bit of good. Now, calm down. Calm down and listen!"

"That miserable—"

"O.K., O.K.! You said that before. He's that and maybe a case for Bellevue. But he threw me a hot potato that I couldn't drop."

"All he wanted was to jam it into me! He didn't give a damn who was hurt."

"Shut up and let me talk!"

We were in his private office, where he had hustled me as soon as I showed up. All the way back from Long Island it had been building up in me, a rage against Coletti. When I walked into the station house I was ready to tear him apart. He couldn't have waited more than two weeks to go to Delaney and still seriously believe his charges had any foundation. His delay proved, at least to my way of thinking, that he was using the influence of his position to dirty two people.

"Are you ready to listen?" He sat down at his desk.

I settled back in the chair and lit a cigarette, dragging the hot smoke in deep. "But first, Delaney, let me tell you you're being used to settle a grudge. You and the newspapers. Coletti no more believes—"

"Baski, I don't give a damn what Coletti believes, and I'm not interested in grudges. When a man drops some questions in my lap that require answers, I go looking for the answers. Don't tell me you and that girl are in the clear. I know it. *Now*, I know it. After forty-eight hours of questioning." He glared across the desk at me, openly hostile. "You knew this was going to pop up and you took a powder."

"Vacation. And I didn't know anything of the sort."

"Coletti didn't tell you he was going to look into it further and bring his findings to me?"

I couldn't remember. "Maybe he did. I don't know. Look, if that guy is making the charge that we—"

"No charges. He brought me facts. You and the girl were like that. Murk had no intention of giving her a divorce, yet you two had everything set but the license. At least, the name of your boat indicated you did. Baski, if Murk had been killed this case would have been out of my hands and on the D.A.'s desk Monday morning when you failed to return to work. The fact that Murk is alive and still says you were bringing the boat in for him has held it to a routine investigation."

"Delaney, if I give you some information that will clear up a point, will you keep it under your hat?"

"Yes, if there isn't a felony involved."

"There isn't. It's a Coast Guard rap if it comes out. And a man's job."

"Let's have it."

"Spatola was handling that throttle. He got excited and thought he was doing the right thing."

Delaney swore under his breath, glaring at me. He had a tough time controlling his temper. "Spatola said he was in the engine room."

"That's right, but actually he was standing beside—"

"Also, Stella Murk said she saw you at the wheel, alone."

"From where she was standing she did."

He leaned back in the chair. "And all that, Baski, is on the record. Do you think for one minute a switch in Spatola's testimony, if you were facing a serious charge, would carry much weight? Not when another eyewitness thinks she saw you there alone—an eyewitness who is definitely on your side. Covering Spatola was not a smart trick, Baski. You're lucky it hasn't backfired, that this case is being cut short. And listen...."

He pulled a bag of tobacco from his pocket, staring across at me. "That dig you gave me when you walked in, about me being used to settle a grudge. *Nobody* uses me, Baski. Get it out of your head we're a bunch of jokers down here. We get thousands of letters, complaints, and what have you during the year. Sometimes it's a big name that somebody is hoping will land in the papers and be left holding the dirty end of it with bad publicity—guilty or not. But we don't go off half-cocked here. I've had three men on this case for two days, and the only one who knows more now than he did before is your boss, whom I questioned personally. A lot of people have been asked a lot of questions, but none of them know anything more than that you were involved in an accident that we're still working on."

I lit another cigarette, feeling easier now. The one big fear in my mind had been the newspapers. New York tabloids with their cheesecake photographers have a field day when a shapely blonde is involved in anything more serious than a speeding charge. "Where's Mrs. Murk now?"

"You mean Stella?" He scowled over at me again. "Don't start being cute now. She went home a few minutes before you came in."

"The case is closed?"

He crumpled the cigarette he was attempting to make and dropped it into the ash tray "It was never more than half opened. Nobody was hurt, except Mrs. Murk. Sit down! She was hurt, but not in the way you think. The rubber hose went out the window with the dime novel, Baski. It's just that she's a nice kid and the questions hurt. Or rather, the answers she was forced to give."

"Remind me to toss Coletti in more than plain mud next time I see him."

He looked squarely at me. "Want a tip, Baski? Leave Coletti alone. He doesn't like to play the fool. It's my opinion, despite what you think, that he honestly believes you and that girl were plotting funny business. I don't think you've seen the last of him. He'll hurt you if he can."

"I'm not worried about him."

"You're dumber than I thought, then. When a man wants your scalp, worry. It keeps you on your toes. Now beat it so I can catch up on the work that's piled up on my desk because of Murk versus Baski."

I had the door open before I thought of something. "Delaney, just what made you so sure Coletti wasn't right, that something funny hadn't been plotted under your nose? You didn't know about Spatola,"

He looked up wearily from the desk. "How much is that boat of yours valued at?"

"I don't know. Over fifty thousand as she stands, I guess."

"When does a guy with fifty thousand dollars carefully plan to murder someone for an uncertain twenty-five or thirty? A bum with a buck will murder for a hundred. A guy with a hundred for a thousand. It's all a matter of percentage. The odds have to be there. Where murder is planned for profit, the odds must always warrant the risk. Catch?"

It made sense.

To Hackett the whole thing had been a mountain made out of a molehill. He dismissed it with a wave of his cigar, advised me to stay away from married women, and promptly put me back on the *Junior*, relieving the tug captain he'd hired during my vacation.

Neither Spatola nor Johnson made any mention of the affair. Spatola was only too happy to forget the whole thing. The only comment from Johnson was not to forget about Mr. X.

Murk, I learned, was now out of the hospital and living at the hotel with Stella. I sent a brief note to Stella, saying I was sorry she'd had a rough time, but made no attempt to see her. From now on it would be Baski and his boat, and to hell with everything else.

That resolution lasted until one rainy night when I sharpened a scraper and started to remove the gold lettering on the stern. After one letter I had to stop. I felt as if the chisel were scraping across my heart. I threw the tool aside, went over to the basin and up the street to the bar. Then I changed my mind about a drink and called the Travers Hotel instead. Murk answered.

"Oh, hello, Cap. Nice to hear from you."

"How's it feel to be on your feet?"

"Real good. Real good, it does."

"Leg stiff?"

"I favor it a bit, but I can walk all right, I can."

It went on like that for a while, then I asked how Stella was.

"Well, she's a little upset, she is. That feller, what's his name, Coletti? He's been coming around with those darn fool questions of his."

Coletti again. Damn him anyway! "What does he want?"

"Don't know, Cap. I won't talk to him anymore. Since that day he came to the hospital and started telling me I should lose my job, I should, he knows better than to talk to me. I got mad, I did, and told him—"

"Where's Stel—your wife now?"

"She left just a while ago, she did. Said she wanted to tell you to watch out for this feller, that he's going to go to the government and say you were drunk and that's what caused the accident. Something like that, it was. She was talking to him in the hall so she'd know more—"

"How long ago did she leave the hotel?"

Murk thought it was ten minutes.

I thanked him and hung up, and then went inside just in time to see a cab pull up near the corner and Stella get out. She was fumbling in her purse when I handed a bill to the driver and took her arm. "What's this I hear about Coletti bothering you?"

She seemed glad to see me. "It's not me so much, Joe. It's you he's after." The concern in her voice really gave me a lift.

"What did he have to say?"

"Can we talk about it over some coffee? How about in that tavern up there?"

"What they serve is barely drinkable, but it'll be hot. Come on."

She wore a pink transparent slicker, the hooded type, and looked like a golden-haired queen as we entered the bar. In my eyes she did.

At a table in the rear, away from the noisy crowd at the bar, we ordered coffee, and then she told me of Coletti's latest work. On a hunch he had checked the liquor store near the basin and had found out Spatola had bought a pint bottle of rye just prior to the accident. With that he had gone to Stella, ready, as he put it, to make a deal. If she would talk Murk into signing away his rights, he would drop the whole thing. If she refused, he would ask the steamboat inspectors to revoke my license.

"And that's what had you worried?"

"Well, after all, Joe, if they take away your license you won't be able to go into business with your boat. It had me worried."

"Listen, baby, forget about Coletti. The steamboat men are mostly ex-shipmasters who know the score. When they close the books on an accident, it takes more than a complaint from a guy with an ax to grind to reopen it. Let's talk about us."

"Are you sure, Joe? If he can injure you in some way—"

"He can't. Forget him." I reached across the table for her hand. "Look, honey, a lot of things have happened between us that never should have happened. Now, I don't think this Coletti business brought you down here tonight. Well, maybe it did, but I'm hoping it wasn't that alone. I'm hoping you've decided to forgive and forget some of the things this clown has said. Stella, what's the chances of us making a fresh start?"

She pressed my hand, smiling gently. "I think I've been a bit of a clown myself, Joe. That afternoon in the taxi, after you left, I cried. I was so ashamed of myself for the way I acted, I cried."

"Well, you were hardly to blame for thinking I was using Spatola to crawl out from under. It did look funny when you were right there at the time and never saw him."

"But I should have believed you. Once, I started to write to tell you so, but then thought it better not to, that we'd only be back where we started and still not able to solve anything. Joe ..." She smiled again as she squeezed my hand tighter. "Joe, I have grand news. He's giving me a divorce!"

Happily dazed from the sudden announcement, I sat there holding her hand while she quickly explained that Murk had been dropping hints ever since the day it appeared certain he was getting five thousand dollars for his leg injury that he might retire in October and live with his spinster sister in Vermont. Maybe Stella wouldn't like it up there, big lonesome house, cold climate, and so on. If she wanted to stay in the city, that was O.K. with him.

She was beaming. "When I asked point-blank about a divorce he hedged a little. It was only today I discovered he was worrying about who would pay the cost. When I said I'd take care of that, he became quite agreeable."

A guy couldn't be any happier than I was at that moment. I felt like ordering champagne but settled for martinis. "He's quitting in October? Why then? Why not now?"

"He'll be sixty on the second and some annuity will be due. It seems he and his sister have been paying into some combined policy that pays them a certain amount when he reaches sixty. When he receives the settlement from the accident, he's going to mail it to her to hold. They have one of those joint accounts, too, so between the cash they've put away—"

"You mean you've been scrimping these years so he and his sister can sit back in ease? Oh, brother!"

"Joe, listen. I don't care about that. It's not important. The important thing is, in October we're parting."

"What's wrong with your leaving now? Let him work the barge himself."

She sipped her Martini and shook her head. "He needs somebody around for a month or two. Especially on the barge."

"Listen, baby, I'd rather hand him a couple of months' pay than have you go on living on the barge with him."

"You can't do that, Joe. He still doesn't know about us. I'm going to break it to him easy that we're friends, and ... well, that we might become serious. Anyway, he wouldn't take the money."

"Guess not. He loves dough, but I can see him rearing back at a handout."

"Everyone has some pride."

The potbellied bartender brought refills and removed the empties, his eyes lingering on the off-the-shoulder blouse Stella wore. He waddled off whistling tunelessly.

I grinned at her. "Can't blame 'im, hon. Exactly the way I feel every time I look at you. Reminds me, there's something new on the boat I've got to show you."

She smiled sweetly, not buying it this time. "*That*, dear, will have to wait until October. We're turning over a new leaf."

We batted that back and forth for a while over another drink, then I paid the check and we took a walk arm in arm up to Flatbush Avenue in the direction of a cab stand.

"Joe, I was thinking how thorough that policeman Delaney was in his questioning."

"He's a good cop. Maybe you think you had a rough time, but if it had been another cop it would've been rougher. Some guys would have been tickled to call in the papers and keep the pot boiling for two or three weeks."

"Suppose Albert had been killed, Joe?"

"Hey, we have more pleasant things to talk about than that!"

"No, seriously. If Albert had been killed, would Delaney have taken our affair so lightly?"

"Been worrying that one out?"

She admitted she had. "It's silly, Joe, I know. But you read so many times where evidence is circumstantial, where people are tried and convicted on slight clues. In our case, the jury would have heard such awful things. They might've thought we were just awful and were capable of anything."

"You keep your mind off such things, hon. Two months from now we'll be cutting out past Sandy Hook, heading south to our island. We've got the world by the tail now and we're going to hang on."

During the short ride to the hotel we discussed the divorce plans. Florida seemed the best bet for that, unless Stella could work an annulment in New York on child-marriage grounds. But either way we would ready the boat and leave the first week of October. Murk had asked not to let their separation be known until they actually parted. Stella cautioned me on this, because Murk was afraid the basin hands would rib him.

We said good night in the back of the cab. We were feeling good, and why not? On the way back to the basin the cabbie brought me out of the fog by announcing we had been tailed on the way to the hotel. I twisted around and glanced out the rear window. The dark street was deserted except for a bus lumbering behind.

"Not there now, pal. He was, though. I wasn't sure until we stopped at the hotel. He did, too. Parked about a block behind while you was smooch—saying good night."

"Police car?"

"Cab."

I settled back and dragged on a cigarette. I was pretty sure it was Coletti who had done the tailing. But what could he hope to gain by verifying what he already knew, that Stella and I were in love? Was it simply that he liked to play detective? I worried it out all the way to the shed but couldn't come up with an answer. I knew Delaney was right, that it would be foolish to underestimate a man in his position.

Damn Coletti! The one dark spot in an otherwise sunny picture.

Chapter Twelve

The answer to Coletti's shadowing came the next day. Delaney gave me the story. Coletti's company had ordered him to settle with Murk for thirty-five hundred, unless the tug captain, Joseph Baski, could be expected to testify in favor of the company, and they had given Coletti a week to clear matters up. He had used the time instead to keep tabs on how often Stella and I were seeing each other, and then went to the steamboat inspectors with two charges against me. One was having liquor aboard; the other, that I'd unlawfully associated with a female passenger, Stella's official status when I had charge of the *Sand Point*, and that I was still doing so.

Coletti struck out on both counts. The steamboat inspectors had pulled out the records on Murk's case, noted an investigation had also been conducted by Delaney, and promptly called him. After he finished giving them an earful of Coletti's motives, that he was only interested in character assassination, they told Coletti to bring in affidavits from Albert Murk detailing the complaints and they would take action. Murk, they contended, was the sole interested party. *He* was the one injured, not Coletti. They had showed Coletti the door when he had started talking a bit too loudly.

I told Stella about Coletti's final efforts to get back at me. She wasn't amused. "Joe, I'll never forget that man when he came into Delaney's office while I was being questioned. He said the most horrible things."

"Yeah, he would. But look, we're through worrying about Mr. Coletti. Let's worry about this boat. Come in here for a minute." I led her into the forward stateroom. It had been painted and was ready for occupancy. "This place will be for paying guests. The master room aft we'll keep for ourselves, of course. The question is, where's the dough coming from to make up these upper berths? The mattresses on the lowers cost sixty smackers each, and I'm running short of cash."

"Do you really need them? There's the sofas in the cabin."

"Sleeps two there and these two make four. But I figured on six berths for paying customers right at the start. Hate to go into debt now after being in the black five years."

"We'll just give up our room temporarily."

"Hate to do that, too.... Well, it's only temporary, as you say. How do these bunks feel to you? Soft enough?"

"Just fine."

"Stretch out flat. Think our female customers will have any complaints?"

"I should say not. They're as soft as ... Mr. Baski! We made plans to wait, remember?"

"Lady, you have no heart."

Murk came back to work a week later. But all he did was to use the barge for living quarters and draw pay. Hackett's orders were that he wasn't to handle lines and could come and go as he pleased. This all suited Murk fine. He no longer tried to keep Stella on a leash, the only thing on his mind being his kidney stone. Should he undertake an operation before October, or attempt to get rid of it by continuing with his medicine? He was really in a stew about it, because after October he would be footing the bill for an operation. If the treatments failed to work, he wanted to find out as soon as possible and get that operation in for free.

That's when he began doubling up on his medicine, staggering around like a drunken sailor from the effect it had until Stella finally persuaded him to stay in bed. This meant she was waiting on him hand and foot again, but I didn't mind this time. I was plenty busy, spending four to five hours a night on the boat, planning to have it a hundred per cent complete when it was launched. By September I had the galley completely rigged and both heads tiled. I was on the last lap with deck fixtures and odds and ends to be installed—no more than three weeks work.

Occasionally Stella would come to the shed to sit and watch me while I worked. Whenever I would discuss our home on the Bahama cay she would simply smile and shake her head. She didn't like to talk about it. To her it was the stuff dreams were made of, and she was afraid that speaking of it too much would make it disappear.

Although I said nothing to her, I was feeling somewhat the same myself. Two years of planning and five years of work added up to seven years of waiting for the day my boat would be launched. Each night before I turned in I would walk around the cruiser, touching its finish here and there and wondering if it was a dream, if this could really be mine. Twelve tons of gleaming beauty that I'd fashioned with my own hands. I'd look at it and touch it, and little fears would chase up my spine that perhaps it wasn't meant to be, that something would surely happen to it and dump me back into the world of reality where monotonous hours over a tug's wheel would continue indefinitely.

I got so jumpy I finally got around to padlocking the boat shed during the day. Another precaution I took was to clear the reeds and brush fifty feet in all directions from the bungalow to create a fire break. The autumn dry spell had made the marshes as dry as tinder. You occasionally found tramps bedding down beside fires, and they were never too careful.

When the usual fall pickup in coaling deliveries put the barges on a twenty-four-hour schedule, the tug crew began working eight-on and eight-off to keep the basin hoppers full. This overtime during my last two weeks was a godsend because I was down to my last buck and wondering where the dough would come from for the long trip to the Bahamas. Everyone else welcomed the overtime for the Christmas-shopping money he could put aside. All the basin hands were walking around in a cheerful mood. Except Murk.

As October drew near he was grouchier than ever. He was still drinking the stuff the hospital gave him, doubling and tripling the doses, trying to hurry a decision from the doctors on whether they would have to operate or not. He even hinted he might stay on a month or two longer if necessary, and he was a little put out when Stella told him flatly she was pulling out on schedule, and that he'd have to take care of himself if he remained.

So as far as Stella and I were concerned, things couldn't have been rosier when I pulled into Mill Basin on my last night as a tug captain and made fast to the *Sand Point*.

She was standing at the far edge of the barge, her face a pale blur in the moonless night. Spatola ringed the barge cleat and called out to her, "All set, Mrs. Murk. You don't have to touch anything yourself."

She moved nearer the cabin door, then halted as if uncertain. "Albert's asleep."

Spatola signaled to me that he was set. "Sure. No need for him to come out, neither. He ain't supposed to do nothin' but play watchman, anyway."

My hand hit the throttle while he was still talking, and I worked the tug forward to line up the bridle. In a matter of a minute we were under way with the barge astern and lines being let out.

Settling down to the mechanical routine of steering on a long haul, I kept thinking about Stella's words to Spatola and found them odd. She had said Murk was asleep. But Spatola didn't ask where Murk was, so why even mention it? Besides, no one expected Murk to handle lines. He hadn't so much as lifted a finger to help since the accident; he was seldom even on deck when his barge was prepared for towing.

Out through the Rockaway Inlet we moved past the lighted buoys that winked in the dark. After safely clearing two dredges anchored for the night, I stepped out and glanced aft, at the barge astern. Stella was still standing out on the foredeck, her dress a vague gray against the blackness of the cabin.

It was a warm night; nothing wrong in staying outside a stuffy cabin, but still ...

A southwest wind pushing choppy swells across Coney Island channel settled the matter. When I spotted her still on deck, not moving away from the spray breaking over the barge's bow, I yanked the whistle cord.

Spatola came hurrying forward, tucking something in his rear pocket. I couldn't see it in the dark, but I could easily guess what it was.

"We'll take it alongside. Let your lines slip as I back and we'll grab it coming around."

"Right, Joe."

The tow lines had been arranged with no bites on the barge, so all the handling could be done from the tug. It took only a few minutes for Spatola to take them in, and then I cut around in a sharp circle, coming up alongside the barge. She disappeared into the cabin as our lines went out.

"Come up and take it, Spatola."

He came into the pilothouse shaking his head. "In this chop we should leave it astern."

"Skip it. Watch this wheel so you don't get pushed into that Coney sand ledge."

She had been expecting me. Before I had a chance to knock on the door she opened it. In the dim light coming from the single oil lamp on the kitchen table her face was that of a stranger, a woman with taut sallow skin and colorless eyes.

I stepped inside and closed the door. "What in the name of—"

She was in my arms, trembling, sobbing hysterically. "Joe, I called! I called! You couldn't hear me over the engines. I didn't want to say anything with Spatola there. Then the lines were out. Joe, I called! I—"

"Wait a minute! Stella—"

Then I saw him. Murk. Sprawled by the stove, one arm outflung, the other across his chest. One side of his bald head looked black. Dried blood. There was more of it on the worn linoleum beneath his head. His eyes were open, his mouth too. His teeth showed, as if he were smiling at us. Only Murk never smiled. Not when he was alive.

"He ... he ... The medicine, Joe. He got up. He fell against the stove, reaching for the poker."

I took a deep breath, shaking off the shock of it. "O.K. O.K. Take it easy, baby." I patted her shoulder. "He should've known better than to take so much." I suddenly grabbed her arms and held her away from me. "You said he was asleep!" My fingers bit into her arms as I shook her. "You told Spatola he was *asleep!*"

Helplessly she nodded. "I—I didn't know what to say. I wanted to t-talk to you first."

"But Spatola thinks he was alive when we left the basin! An idiot could see he's been dead over an hour! They'll wonder why you tried to cover it up. Good God, they might even think you hit him!"

I caught her as she collapsed in my arms, in a dead faint.

Chapter Thirteen

"Let's take it slower, Stella. Just when did he fall?"

"Almost the same instant I heard the tug approaching. I—I saw the way his head was and knew he was dead. Then I saw that poker there. See, lying beside his head, blood on it? Joe, it struck me how awful everything looked, how violent his death appeared. That's when I became panicky and thought of what Coletti and Delaney would say."

"What do you think they'll say now?"

"I know, Joe. God, I know...."

"Drink this." I set a glass of water on the table. She wearily pushed her hair back from her face and picked up the glass. She put it down without drinking.

"It's crazy, Joe. It's all so crazy the way it happened. When I rushed out and saw Spatola there I became tongue-tied. All I could think of was how they'd say it looked funny, that perhaps we finally finished what we had set out to do. I wanted to tell you what happened before anyone else knew."

"It wouldn't have changed things any."

"Joe, I know! I knew it then, the moment I told Spatola he was asleep. But before I could say anything else you were moving the tug and the lines were being let out. I called. Joe, I kept calling, screaming really. The engines drowned me out." She buried her face in her arms. "They'll say I did it! They'll say I did it! Oh, my God—"

"Stella, we can't be hysterical about this. You've had a bad time, but we'll have to take it easy and think it over calmly. One thing is sure— Murk died *after* we left the basin. It's got to be that way. You said he was asleep back there and asleep he'll have to be. Five or ten minutes either way in his death isn't going to make any difference in the autopsy, but it's going to be a lot easier not to have to account for telling

Spatola he was asleep."

I lit a cigarette and stood there studying Murk's body. The poker he had intended to use was lying beside him, one end in the pool of blood on the linoleum. I stepped over for a closer inspection and saw no blood on the sharp edge of the stove that had broken his skull. Apparently he had fallen away from the edge almost immediately.

Looking down at Murk, with that poker lying near the bloody crease in his head, I couldn't blame Stella much for not being able to think properly. It did look as if someone had slammed it across his head.

"Stella, did you mention to anyone that Murk had consented to a divorce? Or did he mention it?"

"No. *I* didn't, and I'm sure *he* didn't."

"And Hackett doesn't even know." I was talking to myself now, but she caught the drift.

"You mean they might say we had an argument about it, and that I hit him in anger?"

"That, or that we planned it this way. At least, Coletti will be coming up with some fancy theory. Oh, the hell with him!" I went over to the window that was outboard of the tug and pushed aside the curtain. We were rounding the Norton's Point light and would soon be in the Narrows. In the distance, past the point, the lights of the Belt Parkway along the Brooklyn shore looked like a string of pale amber beads. I turned away from the window. Stella was sitting at the table and staring dully at the glass of water near her hand.

"Look, hon, we'll be in Hoboken in about two hours. You'll have a lot of questions to answer. But I'll get Delaney right over and it won't be so bad."

"What makes you think it won't? Suppose he doesn't believe us? Suppose ..." She shivered and her voice broke. "Joe, suppose he doesn't? Suppose it looks too—too bad? Then maybe he doesn't have the right to believe us. Maybe there'll be others ... detectives who will find out in some way that he was dead in the basin, that he died before we left there. Maybe ..." She rested her head in her hand. "I need a drink."

I was beginning to need one, too. Was it possible that Murk's death could be ballooned into a sensational murder case? Would Coletti feed the fire, perhaps backed by the outfit he worked for? Would it leave Delaney's hands and be picked up by headline-happy dicks who'd squeeze the last drop of publicity from it? And what guarantee did we have that a murder indictment couldn't be got, and that a trial wouldn't end in a conviction?

Could we prove Murk was *not* murdered?

Right then, I began sweating. All along I had been looking at it from the viewpoint of an innocent bystander; tough on Stella, tougher on Murk. Now, looking at it closer, I could see that either side of the case was going to be difficult to believe. For one thing, could anyone believe this thing had happened to Murk right on top of his other accident? A guy lives fifty-nine years, plodding along, then like a one-two punch he gets hurt, then killed. Hard to believe? Sure, but could you believe the other side of it, what Coletti would be screaming? That a guy and a gal muffed one attempt at murder, then pulled it again two months later with more success? Could you believe any two people could be that stupid?

But then, there are a lot of stupid people in this world. Maybe in the eyes of the New York police we would just be two more.

I sat down across the table from Stella and lit another cigarette, trying to think clearly. She wearily raised her head. "I'm so frightened, Joe. Everything seems frozen inside me." The tug's whistle cut her off, two shrieking blasts.

I hopped up and went out the door on the run. We were moving through the Narrows, the upper bay stretching out before us with its darkness punctured by the quick flashes of the channel buoys. Dead ahead was another light and not a marker. It was sliding across our bow, a tow cutting over from the starboard side of the channel, where it had a right to be, in order to give Spatola enough room.

Spatola's head appeared at the pilothouse window. "It's O.K., Joe. Jus' figured on slippin' by on his left but guess he got scared."

"Why are you over on this side?"

"Jus' tryin' for better time."

"You working on that bottle?"

He sounded hurt. "Now, Joe, you know when I'm at the wheel I don't—"

"Yeah, yeah, I know. Keep your eyes open up there and stay on the right side of the channel!"

I was back in the cabin, the door closing behind me, when I thought of it. I began swearing.

"What is it, Joe?" She half rose from the table.

"I've just shoved both our feet in a bucket, that's all. I was talking to Spatola and said nothing about Murk when it certainly would be the most natural thing in the world to mention his death. What do I do now? Walk out and say a little matter slipped my mind? That Murk is in here with his head bashed in?"

She sank back into her chair helplessly. "That will look bad, too."

"It won't look good when they question him. Damnit, I need a drink! I'm going up and get his bottle."

The distant sound of a brassy orchestra came drifting into the cabin. It was a night excursion boat passing by. Somewhere to starboard a bell buoy announced itself on the job. The muffled drone of the tug's engines also drifted in, reminding me that time was growing short.

I poured Stella another drink, gave myself the last few drops remaining in the bottle, and pushed it aside. It was her third drink, but she was still a bundle of nerves. I had tried to convince her that all would be well with Delaney on the job, but she wasn't convinced. Neither was I, for that matter. The more I thought it over, the more clearly I could see the criminal proceedings, with the two of us right in the middle and holding the dirty end of it. I had been thinking of something else, too, a way out of the whole mess. It would be a simple thing to accomplish. At least, it seemed so. Murk died by accidentally striking his head, didn't he? Suppose we had him die again, this time in plain sight of Spatola?

Might work.

It *would* work.

"Listen, baby, listen closely. I want you to go up into the pilothouse with Spatola. It's a warm night so you say you're up there for a little air. Mention that I'm in the engine room, that I've discovered the engines overheating. That's all you're to say about me. Stay with Spatola and talk about the weather. Anything. That's your part. Now here's mine...."

When I got through explaining what we would do, she didn't like it. The plan itself seemed perfect; she objected only to Murk's body going into the bay.

"He's getting a sea burial, Stella. I know it's without the ceremony, but it's nothing more than a sea burial. At least, we've got to think of it like that."

She still didn't like it.

"O.K., baby, this choice will have to be yours. Play it my way and there'll be no reporters, no scandal, no cops waiting at Hoboken. We'll be guilty of nothing—except burying Murk at sea. Stella, we've got to play it this way! Johnson once predicted a package of trouble for me if I reached too far. He said I'd be knocked flat. Well, maybe this is it. Maybe this was meant to be the final K.O. for my plans. And it will be if we don't put up a fight. But it's up to you. Do we climb up out of this hole or do we face the D.A. tonight?"

"I don't know, Joe. I—I'm too tired to think."

"We haven't much time."

"All right. But it seems ... well, sacrilegious." Maybe it was. Maybe the way I was going to handle Murk was a brutal and callous thing to do. But time was limited. I couldn't think of another way out. In a matter of an hour or so we would be in Hoboken and the play would be out of my hands unless I acted fast.

The first thing I did after Stella left to keep Spatola company was to take the poker lying by Murk's head, wash it, and then stick it into the dying embers of the coal stove for a thorough cleaning. Then I wrapped Murk's head in a towel, completely covering it, to prevent any trail of blood while I was moving him. I propped him up near the door, scrubbed the blood from the linoleum, and then spotted that and the area around the stove with coal dust.

I extinguished the oil lamp. Through the cabin window I saw we were passing the midway point of the upper bay. A heavy overcast had the bay gripped in total darkness, disturbed only by the occasional flash of a channel marker and the side lights of a passing vessel. I was thankful for this darkness, even though from the tug's pilothouse neither the afterdeck of the barge nor its outboard side would be visible to Spatola, the coal bulwark cutting off his view of anyone crouching on that outboard side.

When I opened the door and moved out on deck Murk was across my shoulders, all two hundred pounds of him. Any one of a dozen things could have happened while I was lugging his body along the outboard side, and I sweated out every one. Suppose I tripped and fell over the side with the body? Suppose a distant tub threw its searchlight across the bay, a pair of binoculars following it out of boredom? One man crawling along the side of a barge, a body across his shoulders, would make a pretty picture.

But nothing happened.

The sweat dripped down my legs. My heart pounded as I inched along the bulwark, but I reached the point I wanted without mishap, directly beneath a wooden stanchion. Here I put Murk down, beneath the stanchion, his back resting against the bulwark. Then I removed the towel from his head and tossed it over the side. After making sure his feet were firmly wedged against the deck cleat, I crawled back and got a five-inch mooring line from the afterdeck. This I faked down by Murk, putting some twenty feet of it in his lap for ballast to make sure he wouldn't roll overboard after a ground swell. Now for step number three.

I headed for the tug's engine room.

In the gloom of the pilothouse both Spatola and Stella were two vague forms, Spatola by the wheel and gabbing away on why he had never married as I walked in. "Hi, Cap. Jus' sayin'—"

"How are you on these Diesel jobs? Know much about them?"

He started scratching his head. "Not much, Cap. Mrs. Murk mentioned you had trouble down there, but I can't hear it from here. Perkin' right along."

He heard it then, a misfire, followed by the mixed beat of a sick engine. "Hey, she's coughin' out, all right!"

Just then the engines stopped, as I had known they would. "Those injectors might be fouled, Spatola. Want to take a stab at them before we call for another tug?"

"Well, I seen a guy loosen them once and clear the air, sorta. Maybe—"

"Give that a try. If you have no luck we'll phone for another tug." I took over the wheel and waited until he left. "Feeling O.K.?"

She stirred from the window. "I feel terrible."

"How are your nerves?"

"Joe, I'm frightened. Terribly frightened."

"Take it easy and listen. We're doing fine. Now I want you to go down and talk to Spatola in the engine room. Ask questions, any kind. Keep him busy at the engines. If he starts to give it up as a bad job, ask him what he meant when he spoke about loosening the injectors. Keep him puttering around."

I needed just three minutes for what I had to do. As soon as she left I went down on deck, leaped across to the barge, and went around to Murk. It wasn't necessary to crawl behind the bulwark to keep out of sight now. The engine room was below the level of the main deck of the tug, and as long as Spatola remained there I was out of his view.

It took only a moment to prop Murk up on his feet and place his right arm around the stanchion, jamming his weight in against the bulwark. With the five-inch mooring line I took three crossing turns around Murk's heavy middle, then lowered the rest of the line over the side, into the water.

The principle I was using was simple enough. Once the tug's engines turned over and the barge moved, that mooring line would drag in the water, throwing its full weight on Murk, dragging him over the side. The line would then slacken and the rope about him would fall away as he sank.

Man overboard! Happens all the time.

But Spatola had to be a witness to it. That was step four, the final one.

"Find the trouble?"

Spatola straightened and shook his head. "Got 'em all loosened and don't see nothin' cloggin' 'em." He indicated the four injectors he had pulled from their sockets.

"Try the main fuel line." I lit a cigarette and moved over by the ladder, where Stella was standing. I started to talk about the weather, keeping one eye on Spatola as he uncapped the line I had jammed with cotton waste.

With the cupful of oil that poured out into his hand came the waste. "Well, I'll be damned!" He held the dripping waste up. "Must have fed all the way through. Hey, I wonder if this is the thing that's been chokin' the engines out all the time."

"Could be. Cap it, bleed the injectors, and start it up. We've wasted enough time."

He got the main feed back on, shoved the switch, and pulled the starter. When oil spouted at the injectors he cut the switch and tightened the fittings.

He looked pleased with himself. "Regular mechanic, I'm gettin' to be. Ought to hand Hackett a bill for repairs."

We went up on deck, and I followed Stella into the pilothouse. Over on the outboard side of the barge Murk's head and shoulders were faintly visible above the bulwark, a dark shape in the night that would be unnoticed unless attention was called to it. Spatola was about to seat himself on the railing when I did just that.

"Is that Murk standing over there, Spatola? Give him a yell to come aboard. We'll all have some coffee." At the same moment I did two things: shoved the throttle half ahead and grabbed Stella's arm in a warning hold.

She sucked in her breath when she caught sight of Murk, apparently standing on the barge and gazing at the water.

Spatola moved down the deck for a better view of Murk, craning his neck as he looked over at the barge. He finally spotted the rear of Murk's head and shoulders, one arm hanging around the stanchion as if for support. "Yeah, there he is. Hey, Murk!"

I shoved the throttle full ahead.

Almost immediately the drag of the line began to pull Murk free of the bulwark, half turning him as his arm held momentarily at the stanchion. It appeared exactly as if he were turning around in answer to Spatola. Then his head and shoulders disappeared, the sound of the splash as he hit the water coming distinctly over the throbbing of the Diesels.

"*Joe, he went over!*" Spatola came up the deck on the run. "Gawd, Joe—"

"Get that lighted buoy over! The aft one, too!" I turned to Stella. "Go over on the barge. Stay on deck a few minutes helping us search. Then go into the cabin and stay there."

In a few moments carbide lights were burning on the water, lighting a hundred square yards of the bay with a golden light. Spatola used the searchlight as we rounded to, sweeping a wider area. Over the phone I asked the dispatcher to send out a police boat. He did. Two of them. By the time they arrived, a Moran and two Tracy tugs had been attracted to the scene and were helping in the search. But it was all routine. When a man goes into the swift current of the bay he either swims or goes down for a few days. It looked good, though, all this activity on Murk's behalf.

When the marine cops decided to give it up they took all the information, name, age, company, and so on, and headed back to their berths. They didn't even bother to question Stella; but then, why should they bother a woman just widowed?

Spatola couldn't get over it. All the way to Hoboken he kept talking about it. "Jeez, there he was, jus' standin' there. I call him, bang, he's gone!"

"He started to turn around when you called. Probably twisted his ankle and fell. Tough. He was all set to retire."

"Sure is. I never liked him much, but holy smoke, so quick! He's there one minute 'n' then he's gone. I feel like I was to blame, almost, for callin' him."

"You can't figure it that way, Spatola. We go when our time comes and there's nothing we can do about it."

Before we landed at the coaling docks Spatola had Murk actually throwing up his hands with a yell before going over.

"He did yell, didn't he, Joe? Seems I heard—"

"You called, then he turned. Whether he said anything before he fell I'm not sure. Wait.... Sure he did. He yelled something out as he fell. Didn't hear what it was, though."

Why not? It takes a live man to yell out.

Chapter Fourteen

It was an open and shut case.

Delaney came down the next morning, and it took him less than ten minutes to write it off. At first he was a bit on the skeptical side, though he tried to conceal it, as he listened to my testimony and then Stella's. It was when Spatola gave his version, and swore he heard Murk answering at the very moment he slipped and fell, that Delaney promptly offered his sympathy to Stella, tagged Murk as a hard-luck guy, and headed back to his office.

The steamboat men didn't even bother to send an investigating officer down. They accepted my report and filed it. Hackett, Johnson, others in the basin, all accepted Murk's death in the same manner—tough, but one of those things.

Stella took a room at the Travers again, putting barge life behind her for good. But she wasn't too happy the following days. Not that she didn't enjoy living ashore. She did. It was the waiting—waiting for Murk's body to appear. Usually a body will come up in the harbor within three to five days, but when Murk's body still hadn't appeared at the end of ten days, she became moody and spoke of it as something hanging over our heads.

This wasn't exactly true. The longer Murk was in the water, the less chance there was that a medical examiner would have anything to examine. Of course, I made no mention of this to her. She felt bad enough as it was that Murk had not had a funeral with all the trimmings.

One thing I hadn't counted on was her reluctance to marry too soon after Murk's death. I was all for tying us together immediately and leaving for the South, but she held firm for a waiting period, even if only as a formality. We finally compromised on two months, but I did talk her into going ahead with the blood tests and obtaining the license.

As far as I could see, it was to be clear sailing from here on in. I went ahead, working on the boat, but taking it easier now. With some six weeks' time on my hands, there wasn't much point in rushing it into the water until it was a hundred per cent complete.

Johnson commented on this when he visited me at the boat shed one evening. "Time schedule a little off, I see."

"A little. No sense in launching it as long as I can find work to do on it. Easier working on it in the shed."

"When is the launching date?"

"I figure November, first week or so. We're getting married then, Pop. In case you didn't know." I grinned at him. "You probably do. You seem to know everything."

"Working out pretty well, eh?"

"Well, Murk passing out of the picture the way he did put a damper on things. Outside of that, things couldn't be better."

He squatted down beside me, beneath the counter where I was resanding. "Since you quit I've had Spatola decking for me occasionally."

"He's O.K., Pop. Keep him down to a pint a day and he'll do his work."

"Quite a chatterbox when he gets a few under his belt."

"In one ear and out the other. Just ignore it." I dropped the sandpaper, straightened, and dug into my pocket for a smoke.

Johnson also rose, nodding. "I ignore it, but I think somebody else might not be only listening, but buying some nightcaps to keep him talking. Maybe you've heard of him. Coletti." Johnson made a pretense of stepping close to the boat to inspect its finish.

My hand suddenly shook as I lit my cigarette. As sure as I was that we had clear skies, there's nothing like a guilty conscience to make the imagination come alive. Spatola talking? About what? Had he had time to think things over and come up with some unanswered questions? I had told him to call Murk over for coffee—but I had never bothered being too friendly with Murk. So why my sociability at that moment? Or why didn't *I* call Murk? Or why hadn't Stella called? Why did I send him to the engine room to clean the injectors? Why didn't *I* do it, as long as he was up at the wheel?

Quite a few whys, when I started to think them over.

"Go on, Pop. You've got something to say."

He shook his head. "No, lad, I haven't. But I have an idea Coletti is thinking you and Stella are somehow pulling a fast one, that you went after Murk again and this time got him. The way he's pumping Spatola, you can see it's an obsession with him, that you're a smart potato who intends to get a pocketful of change at his expense."

"Pop, he's way off base! Murk wasn't involved in an accident this time. He was, but it wasn't due to faulty equipment or anybody's actions. Stella certainly wouldn't take this to court. No reason. First she couldn't collect, second she wouldn't want to."

"Joey, you're forgetting that five-thousand group policy Hackett Towing has on its personnel."

I had forgotten that. "O.K., Stella will get five thousand. So you think for that kind of dough she'd plan to kill Murk?"

"She wouldn't, not even for ten thousand, which is what she's getting. But that's not small change, and to Coletti's way of thinking—"

"Wait a minute. How does five thousand suddenly become ten?"

"The group policy calls for five on death from natural causes, double that if killed on the job, regardless of whose fault. Thought you knew that."

I hadn't. Ten thousand bucks, tax free, was a nice bundle of dough any way you looked at it. It could even be seen as a motive for knocking Murk off if somebody was looking for a motive—as Coletti was.

"What did Spatola tell Coletti, Pop?" I studied the tip of my cigarette.

"Don't exactly know. Coletti kept buying him drinks and asking about the happenings that night. Kept him going over it. Seems Coletti claimed he was writing up marine accidents for a book or something, and wanted to get all the details of this one from Spatola's angle." He eyed me shrewdly. "Could Spatola hurt you any by talking over that accident?"

I went to the door, tossed my cigarette outside, and came back. "Pop, Murk died an accidental death that night. No matter what happens, what Coletti says or does, I want you to know that. I wouldn't lie to you. I may not always enlighten you if it suits my purpose, but I wouldn't lie to you."

"I know that, Joey. I know that. There's plenty I don't know and don't want to know, but you play a straight game and that's good enough for me. Get me some of that sandpaper, and we'll go to work on a more pleasant subject."

We worked for a while, talking about the boat and leaving other things unsaid. I would have liked to ask him more about Spatola and how often he had spoken to Coletti, but decided the less said, the better.

Near midnight we knocked off work. I broke out a few cans of beer and we wandered through the boat drinking them, Johnson inspecting my work with a boatman's critical eye. He had nothing but praise for the entire job, saying there was a good chance of the boat's outliving me. His tone was envious.

"Makes a man think, Joey, makes him wonder what he's done with his life. Every man should have something to call his own after a lifetime of labor. I have nothing. A few hundred in the bank, a hall bedroom, an alarm clock that tells me I have to begin another day behind a tug wheel. Another day ..." He shook his head. "Just like all the rest. I'd give my right eye to be leaving with you, Joey. It would be like being born all over again—a new deck to walk, new skies, new waters. Guess you wouldn't have need of a mate, would you?"

He smiled as if he were joking but I knew he wasn't. He was reaching an age where he was able to count his remaining active years on his fingers. A less demanding job than a tug skipper's could lengthen those years. As if to save me the embarrassment of an answer, he quickly changed the subject. "Long as you're going to be around a while, Joey, why not stay on Hackett's pay roll? Pick up a day's pay now and then?"

"May do that, Pop. Could use the dough."

"I'll say good night. Hard day ahead of me tomorrow and I've got to get my rest at my age."

From the doorway I watched him move down the path, his stooped figure fading into the marshes. There was little doubt in my mind that he had put a feeler out on coming to the Bahamas with Stella and me, and I felt a little guilty for evading an answer. There had been many a night he'd given me a hand when a particular fitting or heavy lift required two men. Add those nights together, over a five-year period, and Johnson had put in the equivalent of two or three months' work on the boat. Also, he'd always been a good friend.

What made my silence all the more awkward was the fact that he knew as well as I did that I'd need a hand on the boat, perhaps two. But I intended to get them as I needed them by hiring native boys from the islands. To have Johnson around would seem too much like sharing the boat, lessening the privacy I wanted for Stella and me. Selfish attitude? Maybe. But you don't take a third party along on a honeymoon, and that's how I felt about my boat and Stella. Our lives were going to be long perpetual honeymoon. I'd certainly try to make it one, anyway.

"But that's impossible, Joe! Ten thousand dollars insurance? It can't be." She shook her head unbelievingly, "So much money—"

"It's true, hon. And it's all yours. No strings attached."

We were having dinner in a chophouse near the basin. The lights were low, a cute slant-eyed doll was softly playing a piano in the center of the room, and there was a diamond in my pocket that set me back more than I could afford. I was saving that for the right moment.

Instead of being elated by the fat check Hackett was forwarding, she began to pick at her steak, a tiny furrow appearing between her eyes. "Joe, it's almost ... well, it's almost as if we're going to profit from the way he died."

"That's not so, Stella. You'd be collecting regardless. This is a company policy, financed partly by the union and partly by each marine outfit. The double-indemnity clause covers deaths from any cause that actually occurs on operating equipment. It's your dough automatically. The widow is beneficiary unless another person is designated."

She continued toying with her food. "I'll bet you'd call me a dunce if I didn't accept it."

"Not at all. I was hoping you wouldn't."

She looked up in surprise. "You wouldn't? You're so practical in other matters, why not in this case?"

I shrugged. "Tough to explain. I've thought it over. Maybe I like to work for everything I get. I always have, I guess. Nothing's ever been handed to me on a silver platter and maybe it's a habit now of valuing only what I personally produce. That money is yours and I'm telling you right now it's only common sense to accept it. If you do, fine. Stick it in the bank. Someday you might want to use it. But as far as I'm concerned, it would only be so many figures in a bankbook."

She leaned forward, tilting her head to one side, a smile lighting her face. "Mr. Baski, I think I'm going to be crazy about my husband."

This seemed as good a time as any, so I brought out the ring. Her squeal of delight had every head in the room pivoting our way.

"It's not *that* big."

"It's beautiful! Joey, it's just grand!" Eagerly she slipped it on her finger, then quickly drew it off. "You're supposed to do the honors."

I signaled the grinning Chinese waiter for the check. "I need a place less public to do that. How about coming over to the shed?"

"So much privacy simply to put a ring on a girl's finger?" She smiled mischievously. "I wonder why."

I grinned at her. "You'd blush if I told you in actual words."

She blushed anyway.

When we came in sight of the shed a figure got up from the steps. It was Delaney. Stella's hand was in mine. I felt it tremble as we stopped in front of the steps.

"Waiting for me, Lieutenant?"

He nodded. "For a talk. Mind?"

"Not if it's over a drink. Come on inside." I unlocked the door but didn't snap on the overhead lights, just the shaded bulb over the workbench. This kept the rest of the shed in shadows. Stella needed those shadows. She was visibly nervous.

Delaney commented on this when she left to get some beer from the refrigerator. "I think that's one reason Coletti keeps getting in our hair downtown." He tilted his head to the rear of the shed where she had disappeared. "Every time I see that girl she seems to turn a bit pale. Struck Coletti the same way."

"What do you expect after that grilling you gave her while I was on vacation?"

"Questioning, Baski, not grilling."

"Same thing. What's this about Coletti? He still around?"

He rolled a cigarette before he answered. "Around and making a pest of himself. Let me give you the picture of the tie-up between a guy like Coletti and our department."

Stella came back with two glasses of beer. She handed Delaney his. I took the other, silently telling her everything was O.K.

"You probably know, Baski, an insurance concern will spend any kind of money to break a fraud case. They'll spend ten thousand to save a hundred, their idea being, of course, to discourage other cases of the same type."

"Where do you get the idea there's any fraud—"

"Wait! Hold it." He shook his head. "Don't go running off in that direction. I'm here to explain something and ask a couple of questions, not to start an argument."

I sipped my beer and kept quiet.

"As I was saying, they'll spend all kinds of money to break a fraud case. Naturally the police will co-operate with them. Many times they're a big help, other times their investigators are a pain in the neck. But it's a department policy to accept co-operation and nurture it. We'd be silly not to. And on an individual plane a single cop like myself would be more than silly to take a position where my commissioner might receive a letter from a top insurance executive complaining I was refusing to co-operate on a legitimate matter. I like the waterfront beat. I wouldn't like supervising the clerical staff in a traffic court or some such nonsense. So I play along and listen to Coletti."

He stopped to finish his beer. "Not bad."

"Have another?"

He shook his head, leaned back against the bench, and started to roll another cigarette. "To get back to Coletti. He's been dropping in on week ends, filling my ear with every kind of theory imaginable on this Murk business. I don't mind listening to him, but I have to send a man out on anything that needs clearing up. For instance, Coletti claims this deck hand of yours—or rather the one that worked for you when you were still on the tugs—changes his story every time he speaks to him. Not a radical change, but just enough so that no credit could be given to any part of his story. One day he's a whiz on engines so you always depend on him if something goes wrong. Next time he speaks about it he forgets he's a born mechanic and brags he doesn't know a wrench from a screw driver and wouldn't want to."

"A lot of seamen do that, Lieutenant. They take a pride in deckwork and disclaim knowledge of work below deck, as if it were beneath their dignity. By the same token, you have your engineers doing the same, proud of being crackerjack men below deck and disdainful of labor above deck."

He nodded, his long face frowning at the crumbling cigarette he was attempting to smoke. "I know that. I think Coletti does too, but he's seizing on every point he can to keep this Murk case alive. He also says Spatola now is not sure if Murk spoke to him the night he went overboard. He's not sure of your whereabouts at the time, either."

"I was in the pilothouse, handling the wheel, when Murk fell. If he can't remember that—"

"He does, Baski. He remembers you were there then, but he's not sure where you were *before* that time."

"I don't see where that could be important."

"Better let me finish. As I said before, I didn't come here to argue any of the details. If there's anything I want cleared up I'll ask in the form of a simple question. I just want you to get the picture of what's going on. We can't ignore Coletti when he comes in asking us to double-check anything, no matter how crackpot it may seem. About two years back he was sent to settle a case in Allentown—filling in for the regular adjustor, I think—and instead of settling the case for cash as ordered, he came up with some evidence that put the claimant behind bars. That made him a big wheel around his office for a time and probably accounts for his ability to keep dropping in to New York on this case."

"What does he hope to prove, his old theory that we tried to do away with Murk?"

"Not that you tried. That you *did*." He started rolling another cigarette. "He believes Murk was murdered in the barge cabin while he slept, taken out on deck while Spatola was in the engine room, and propped up in a position where he could be tumbled into the bay by starting your engines and throwing the wheel over hard."

Stella's gasp was distinctly audible. She was standing over by the boat and her hands quickly covered her mouth as if to suppress a scream.

If Delaney had noticed her reaction he didn't let on. "His theory is good up to a certain point; then it falls apart. If you did prop Murk up in some way so that he couldn't fall—so that Spatola could see him clearly—you would have no guarantee you could dislodge him by merely starting your engines and swinging the tug against the barge. Then, too, Spatola is positive you did not bump the barge at all."

I was glad I hadn't put the overhead lights on. There was a slow trickle of sweat running down the back of my neck, and I could feel some more on my forehead.

"Any more beer, hon?"

Delaney's eyes followed her as she walked to the rear. "Murk's death *did* solve your love problem, Baski, but you're—"

"It complicated it! Murk had agreed to a divorce. Don't pin *that* motive on us!"

He looked at me. "When had he agreed to a divorce?"

"Right after his first accident." I went on to explain, in a voice I tried to keep steady, why Murk wanted Stella to stay with him until he was ready to leave for his sister's place in Vermont, why he had asked that it be kept a secret.

"And who knows about this agreement, besides you and Mrs. Murk?"

"No one. I told you, he wanted it kept quiet."

He nodded thoughtfully. "Well, as I was about to say, you're not the type to murder for a woman. Neither is she the type that would consent to disposing of a husband. Physically, that is. But back to Coletti." He smiled wryly. "Seems we can't get away from this gent. Well, yesterday morning I got a little fed up and asked him point-blank if he wanted to bring up Murk's original accident and make something of it again. He said he did. That told me something I already knew but wanted to verify for my report. Though he's convinced of your guilt, he's out primarily for personal injury. He knows as well as I do that nothing could come of it except some publicity. Good for him, bad for you. He's not interested in bringing a criminal to justice, or even in saving his company money. He wants just two things, personal publicity and your neck, or at least your hide dirtied. That's what he wants. But as Guinan, the assistant D.A., says, he's not going to get it."

He nodded at my surprised look. "That's how much furor Mr. Coletti has kicked up since Murk fell into the bay. Even went after the D.A.'s ear with his theory of how Murk could have been murdered."

Stella had come back with another bottle of beer. She stood near the boat again, as if waiting for Delaney's next words. I had exactly the same feeling she did, that he had been building up to something.

He looked in disgust at the cigarette he'd just rolled. He dropped it on the floor and started rolling another. "Naturally Guinan told me to keep the case open. Fine thing if Coletti made fools of us all by coming up with something. But what could he come up with? Spatola saw Murk fall. That much of his story can't be changed. And it's apparent he's telling the truth. O.K., what else have we to work on? Murk's body, when and if it surfaces? What would that tell us? According to Coletti, something must have pulled him over the side. Would Murk's body tell us something when it came up? Well, today we got our answer."

I knew what was coming then, and so did Stella. She drew back in the shadow of the boat as he gave it to us.

"Murk was picked up at three o'clock this afternoon in the Gowanus Canal." He looked at me, his bony face tightening. "Why did you do it, Baski? I still don't believe you killed him, but why did you rig that weight on his body so a movement of the tug and barge would pull it into the bay?"

I almost fell for it. For a brief moment I felt as Stella did. Her face had whitened as she leaned against the boat for support. But Delaney wasn't watching Stella. He was eying me, and that was his mistake. I was giving him a blank look, having quickly realized from the way he worded his question that it was a shot in the dark. If he had picked up Murk with a Manila line wrapped around him—and it was almost impossible that that line could have been found anywhere near Murk— he was seaman enough to call it a dragline, not a weight. He had been talking for ten minutes so matter-of-factly, I'm on your side, bub, that he expected instant recognition if his accusation was anywhere near correct.

"Delaney, you're lying!"

The furrows in his brow deepened. "You don't believe we found Murk?"

"Not with a sea anchor or anything like that attached. If you did, somebody around the Gowanus has a lousy sense of humor."

For a long moment he looked at me, his face expressionless. Then he grinned. "O.K., Baski, I had to give it a try. Maybe I'm getting dizzy from too much Coletti, but I had to give it a cop's try before I closed this case. It's been established that Murk died from an injury to the brain, apparently from a fall. Nothing was found connected to the body, as Coletti's been insisting."

He turned to Stella. "Mr. Hackett has made identification so it won't be necessary for you to come down to the morgue—unless you want to." He waited.

Stella shook her head, her face still pale. "I—I can't. I ..." She closed her eyes and breathed deeply. "Why do you say such things? We didn't kill my husband! I didn't love him, but we didn't kill him. He fell, that's all. He fell—"

"Delaney, why don't you beat it?" I deliberately cut her off before she could go on. Another few seconds and Delaney would have the whole story, and we'd be in a cell with the law taking its due course.

He looked uncomfortable. "I'm sorry, Mrs. Murk. With examination of your husband's body complete, the case is now closed. I couldn't resist trying for a reaction on Coletti's theory. I'll say good night. Once again, I'm sorry."

"Joe, I'm certain we'll be found out."

"We won't. It's over, Stella. You heard Delaney. The case is closed. The only thing that held it open was Murk's body being missing. As Delaney says, they'd look like fools to have closed it before that, and then find Murk floating around with a bullet or a knife sticking in him, or that weight around him that Coletti was talking about. That was the only thing holding it open. Now that they have the body in their hands and no way to prove he died a violent death, there's nothing they can do."

"But I feel guilty, so dirty."

"Baby, listen, we're not guilty of anything except protecting ourselves. Murk died from a fall. We're both innocent of any wrongdoing. Maybe it's a violation of the sanitary code to dump a body into the bay, but we've got clean hands otherwise. Now forget it."

"Can you? I mean, really?"

"Listen, Stella, I've got an idea that could take your mind off the whole thing within twenty-four hours—marriage. You and me at City Hall tomorrow morning, like that, man and wife. We'll launch the boat at nightfall and take off for the South. Wait a moment, honey. Don't tell me it's too early yet. That's too easy to say. I'll take you back to your hotel now and call for you in the morning. Then we can either walk around Brooklyn and brood over every unpleasant thing that's happened, or we go over to the Hall and make a fresh start as Mr. and Mrs. Sleep on it, baby. Give me your answer in the morning. Make it yes, and by this time tomorrow we'll be speeding along the Jersey coast. You'll have the wind and the sea in your hair and you'll feel like a million."

Chapter Fifteen

She met me in the hotel lobby early the next morning, smiling, her answer in her right hand. A traveling bag.

She laughed as I swung her off her feet. "People are looking, you dope!"

"Who cares? Let them look, and drool."

That's what the clerk and bellhop were doing when she checked out, and you couldn't blame them. She was dressed simply, in a navy blue suit, white blouse, and white gloves, but the color was high in her cheeks and her vivid blue eyes radiated a zest for living. She had never looked lovelier.

An hour later we came down City Hall steps as man and wife, and having our first tiff. A small one, though. She was all for spending our wedding day together, celebrating. I couldn't see it. I wanted to put the boat into the creek at high water, and that meant a full day's work, preparing it for launching. I stood fast for leaving New York behind us that very night, really making it a new beginning for both of us. It would be a great day to remember, I argued. Looking at it that way, she finally agreed to shop for supplies while I went ahead with my work at the shed.

At the basin I found the *Junior* was still in, with Hackett, Johnson, and Spatola sweating over the balky engine. They all promised to be at the shed that evening, and Hackett said he'd supply a bottle of champagne for launching and maybe a few bottles for the launchers. Nobody seemed surprised when I announced that Stella and I had just been married. They kidded me about the swiftness of the move, of being an eager beaver. Then they wished me luck and said they'd be kissing the bride at launching time.

At the boat shed I didn't waste a minute. Within two hours I had my power tools knocked down and stored in the boat along with the rest of my belongings. Then I went to work on the front wall with a sledge hammer, mocking out the frames and boarding. That took the rest of the afternoon.

The boat itself was on keel and bilge blocks. While it was still light I jacked up the keel, inserted pipe rollers, and eased it onto the railway. It was now only a matter of knocking off the chocks and slacking the restraining cable, and the *Stella B*. would be sliding into the water. That, of course, would have to wait until the others were present.

Somehow I couldn't believe it as I sat down to rest, with a can of beer and a cigarette. It was hard to realize it was over. Seven years before it had been twenty dollars' worth of photostats, and now it was ready to slide down the railway, fifty feet of sturdy boat that could carry me anywhere I chose to go. It was a great moment for me, with the best yet to come—the launching.

I was in the process of tidying up, shining one of the chrome ports, when Coletti walked in. He was dressed as nattily as ever, in a brown pin-stripe suit, pale yellow shirt, and green tie. The side brim of his tan fedora was turned down, sharpy style.

"Who invited you here?" I dropped the rag and climbed down the ladder.

"Baski, I'm here to do you a favor." He stood his ground. "Let's not argue, mince words, or beat around the bush. Only by leveling with each other will we get anyplace. Now, I'm going to start off by being frank with you. I don't believe you murdered Murk."

"Took you long enough to get around to not believing that. But—and this is frankly speaking—I don't give a damn what you believe. Hightail it out of here, and fast!"

He didn't move. "I wouldn't talk that way, Baski. I said I'm here to help you. Just give me your side of it, how you found Murk dead in that cabin and the reason you feel you have to protect that girl. We'll go over it together, smooth it out, and make it sound good. Wait a minute, Baski...." He backed away as I started for him. "That stuff will get you nowhere. Everything is known. The cleaning the blood off the poker, the cotton waste you plugged the feed line with, how you timed the action of the engines while calling Spatola's attention to Murk standing on the outboard side of the barge—*apparently* standing, I should say. It's all known, Baski."

I stopped short, the breath slowly leaving me. I suddenly felt a hundred years old. It was down too pat to be a wild guess.

He smiled with satisfaction at my deflation and started describing everything that had happened that night from the time the tow left Mill Basin until Murk went over the side. He had it down to a T. A numbness crept over me as I listened.

"All correct, Baski? Of course it is. But one part of her story I don't believe: that *you* beat Murk to death with that poker. It just isn't logical—"

"*Her* story?" I snapped out of it then. "What are you talking about?"

He spread his hands. "I'm trying to tell you. That woman is putting you on the spot. She's down there now at Delaney's office pinning it all on you. But listen, Baski, I have an idea you're simply a fall guy, a sucker for a trim ankle. Now you give me the truth, a signed statement how you went into that cabin and found Murk with his head hammered in, and I'm throwing my weight on your side. How about it?"

I stared at him, bewildered by the double talk. Stella giving Delaney the true story was one thing. I could accept that, though I didn't like the idea that she had done it on her own. I could accept the fact that she must have thought it over during the day and decided to tell everything instead of constantly worrying about it. But having me—or anybody else, for that matter—hammering in Murk's head was another thing.

"Well, Baski, what'll it be?" Coletti shifted his feet impatiently.

Suddenly I smelled something fishy in the twisted version of Murk's death. Was Coletti down here trying to break Stella's story? Play me against her in the hopes his version was the correct one? "She's up there now? Confessing, as you put it?"

He nodded, glancing at his watch. "Every detail, except she's accused you of the actual killing. When I bumped into her this afternoon on the avenue I took the trouble to remind her Coastal Casualty had branches all along the seaboard, that she might possibly see me again operating out of the Florida office. She looked so upset on hearing that, I tried a long-shot hunch, and asked if she wouldn't like to go to Delaney and relieve her mind."

"So that explains it. *You* again." I had a job keeping my hands still. "And now you want a confession ... from me?"

"A statement, not a confession, Baski." He approached me eagerly. "They're on their way down here now—Stella, Delaney, and the assistant D.A. But you're not guilty of anything except protecting her. I can see it clearly. When you walked into that cabin you found Murk with his head beat in. She had done the job while the tow was under way. She even admitted it, didn't she?"

"Coletti, isn't it about time you gave up? I'm in a jam, sure, and so is she. But you're beating up the wrong channel. I know exactly what Stella must have told Delaney."

"Baski, Baski, I'm out to help you! Nobody blames you for shielding her. Women with less looks have made fools of men. We make allowances for that sort of thing." He jabbed me in the chest with a manicured finger. "I've been checking her past, Baski. She's rotten, clear through. She even put one over on Murk when she married him." He kept jabbing me in the chest, oblivious of the fact that I was ready to explode.

"Listen, boy, nobody blames you for being taken in. I'd be tempted to keep her from being sent up myself."

He bowed from the waist, choking on his wind as I slammed my right into his belly. I wanted to kill him, but settled for picking him up bodily, carrying him to the front of the shed, and tossing him in the marsh seepage.

He landed flat on his back with a splash, his mouth still open, gasping like a floundering fish. To make the job a thorough one, I rolled him over and jammed his swarthy face deep in the soft mud.

"Chew on *that* dirt, Coletti!"

I went back inside, washed, and changed my clothes. Coletti was nowhere in sight when I put the lights out and left the shed. But Delaney was there, and Stella, both standing in the path and looking back toward the brush, puzzled. With them was a stout gray-haired guy wearing silver-rimmed glasses who immediately walked toward me.

"Baski? My name is Guinan, D.A.'s office. Just stand where you are, don't speak to your wife, and briefly relate what actually happened the night Albert Murk died."

I knew this was the showdown, that it was a story-against-story check. I lit a cigarette and slowly and carefully went over the details. I made it plain that Coletti's bounding had made Stella so frightened that she was unable to think clearly the night Murk fell against the stove. When I finished Stella came forward and started to tell me her reasons for revealing the truth, but I knew what they were and said it was all O.K. And it was. I could see that clearly, now that everything was in the open. You can't run away from anything hanging over your head. You can't and feel free.

"This boat of yours, Baski ..." Guinan removed his glasses and toyed with them, squinting past my shoulder into the gloom of the shed. Delaney stood in back of him, scowling at me. "This boat of yours. Where did you raise the money to build it?"

"Saved a couple of thousand in the service. The rest of it came out of my pay as, a tug captain."

"I hear it's more or less a yacht, valued perhaps at sixty thousand. From what I see there, it could run even more."

"At today's prices, I guess it could."

"That come out of your salary? A sixty-thousand-dollar boat?"

I saw what he was getting at. "Listen, Mr. Guinan, if you're thinking of building up a thievery case, take another guess. I have an account book and can prove every penny that went into that boat."

"Suppose we take a look at it." He moved past me, snapping on the lights himself as he entered the shed.

"Lord, it's certainly big enough!" He paused a moment, looking at the boat.

While Delaney stood on the railway, still scowling at Stella and me holding hands, Guinan walked around the boat several times, then climbed up into the flying bridge. When he came down you could see he was impressed.

"Five years on it, Baski?"

"Lacking a few months."

"It's a tremendous effort, and vouches for your character. More than you are probably aware. That's a point I wanted to clear my mind on." He turned to Stella. "Mrs. Baski, to go back to finances. That check your husband—your former husband—received for his leg injury—he forwarded that to his sister?"

"Yes."

"You have no control over that fund they owned jointly, the money going to the survivor?"

"I believe so. But even if I did have something to say about it, I wouldn't want to."

"And this group policy Hackett Towing has on its employees—what was your reason for refusing that? Ten thousand dollars is a great deal of money."

"I know it is." She went on to explain she simply disliked profiting by Murk's death, or anyone else's.

Guinan glanced over at Delaney. "Any questions?"

"Just one. How can a smart guy be so stupid?" He snapped this at me, still visibly burning.

Guinan nodded, removed his glasses, and fiddled with them. "Well, Baski, that just about sums up my attitude. It's a mystery to me, and always will be, why citizens immediately think in terms of handcuffs and a prison when through fate they become involved in something like you did. However, that's neither here nor there. I'll tell you exactly what I told Coletti earlier: I'd be beating my brains out if I tried to convict you two of anything more than dumping a body in the bay. There isn't a single shred of evidence to convict you of murder. All you would have to do is keep quiet in court, and we'd have nothing to offer to even start a case. Your wife came to us voluntarily and submitted the purported true facts of Albert Murk's death when the case was completely closed, and that would outweigh any arguments of mine that she deliberately plotted against Murk's life. A defense attorney would instantly crumble the only motive I'd have to offer, profit, simply by displaying those checks canceled by Murk's sister. All I have is testimony freely given, and I'd he playing the fool to build a murder case out of that. You're off the big hook. However ...” He put on his glasses and carefully adjusted them. “You’re still on a small one, a misdemeanor, which I’ll leave in Lieutenant Delaney’s hands.”

Both Stella and I were so happy that Guinan was dropping the case that it was few moments before we realized he had left the shed and Delaney was coldly eying us. “O.K., Baski, about this little hook you’re on. You’re getting no charity from me. I’m booking you tonight.”

“Delaney, could you make it tomorrow? This is our wedding night.”

He snorted. “By tomorrow you’d be three hundred miles down the coast. Nothing doing. And don’t try to give me your word you’ll remain in New York. You, I’ve stopped believing!”

I couldn’t blame him much there.

On the way across the marshes Stella managed to pry from him the opinion that I’d be getting sixty days. When she looked ready to burst into tears he cut it to thirty, then added I’d probably be only fined if he put in a word for me—which at the moment he didn’t feel like doing.

“By the way, Baski, was that Coletti stumbling off just as we arrived here?”

“Yeah, he came over to the shed wanting to make some crazy deal with me. I was supposed to say Stella did it and I was led on to protect her. Some such stuff.”

Delaney stumbled into a mudhole and swore. “That’s the same angle he wanted Guinan to try. Keep you two apart and have each believing the other was doing some singing. He left the office before your wife got around to the fact that you were married, although even that little item probably wouldn’t have stopped him—” He halted suddenly, his head coming up, sniffing the night air.

Stella grabbed my arm. “Joe! Joe, *look!*”

At first I thought I was looking at a series of crimson banners wildly waving in the dark sky over the east end of the marshes. As the banners rose higher, spreading into an orange lake that moved in the direction of the creek, the truth hit me. Fire!

For a moment I was frozen motionless, feeling as if a cold steel rod had been rammed into my stomach. “Joe, the boat!”

I broke into a run, crashing southward through a maze of brush, attempting the short cut. It was probably a mile that way; it seemed ten. Some places I had to crawl on my belly, the reeds and thick brush forming almost impassable barriers. My face and hands became raw from the cutting brush, but that didn’t matter. The entire marshland now lay under a thickening blanket of drifting smoke, and all I could think of was the firebreak around the bungalows. I prayed that the flames wouldn’t jump it before I got there. Ahead of me I could see a leaping crimson wall moving toward the creek. My legs seemed packed with sand as I crashed on through the marsh.

An eternity had passed when I stumbled into the clearing, my lungs choked with the heavy smoke. Hot sparks flew in my face from the roaring flames that were swiftly skirting the clearing, casting a furnace wave of heat ahead of them.

All three bungalows were untouched!

I thought, Thank God. Then it blew—the generator shed with its tank of gasoline. From behind the bungalow a sheet of white, bluish-tipped flame shot into the night, curving in all directions like a huge beach umbrella opening, showering burning gas over the entire clearing.

I went flat on my belly, my coat over my head, crawling toward the boat shed, which was erupting smoke as if it had only been waiting for the additional burst of heat from the generator shed. My coat was smoldering when I reached the entrance, my hands blistered and pocked with burns from the splattering gas. Taking time only to empty the contents of one of the fire pails over me, I raced to the rear in search of the sledge to knock out the chocks on the boat.

I never made it.

I could only guess what caused the next blast. Perhaps the bungalow facing to the north, boarded up, the way it was, had heated internally to create a vacuum, sucked in the roaring fire around it, and then blew outward. Whatever it was, the rotted planking on the rear of the shed gave way. A blast of smoke, sparks, and hot air charged in to knock me flat, cutting me off from the rear. I rolled under the keel of the boat, beating the flames from my hair, then crawled out on the other side with a sob at my helplessness. Flames were now climbing up all the walls, sparks and searing embers dropping from the overhead. The smell of, burning plaster and paint filled my nostrils. In the dirty swirls of smoke I saw the white enameled hull of the boat yellowing, moist bubbles appearing on the rich varnished curves of the flying bridge.

Too late.

It was too late. As firmly as if it had been imbedded in concrete, the four-by-four chocks and the releasing cable held prisoner my dream, my future. In a few minutes the *Stella B.* would become a roaring torch. A mass of smoking ashes would be my dividend for five years of labor.

I think I went crazy. I was like a madman, smashing myself against the chocks, a human battering ram, beating at the supports with my bare fists, burning lathe and plaster continually falling around me.

"Joe! Joe!"

A bucket of cooling water hit me full in the face, and then Stella was there, working alongside me, her shoulder at the last chock. Together we lifted. It gave way and the boat quivered on the railway, free of its side supports, waiting only for the restraining cable to be released.

But we had failed.

The cable in the rear of the shed was now hidden by crackling flames reaching for the stern of the boat. Stella started toward it, then shrank back from the savage heat. I threw an arm around her and we stumbled toward the front of the shed, where, through the smoke, I saw a group of figures, Hackett and Spatola among them. Hackett took Stella from me.

"Joe! Pop Johnson ran in there! He's in there now!" someone shouted.

Later, they told me how I was towed out by the moving boat, one arm holding the limp form of Johnson, my other wrapped around the propeller of the boat as it slid down the railway, plowed a path through flaming timbers, and skated into the waters of the creek, carrying Johnson and me with it. I didn't remember any of it. I remembered only the agony of my burned hands and face, of lifting Johnson off the releasing mechanism that he had managed to operate before passing out, of blindly reaching for the stern of the boat as it began to slide, locking one arm around the screw as its twelve tons slowly gained momentum, dragging me with it. I remembered nothing more.

I came to on the bank of the creek, my head in Stella's lap. The first thing I saw was the boat, her bow jammed into the reeds at the far side of the creek, Hackett on the flying bridge barking instructions to Spatola, who was wading waist-deep in water to remove the launching cable. The boat sat like a black shadow in the creek, its paint and varnish scorched from stem to stern.

But I'd never seen anything so beautiful. My happiness was an ache I could feel right down to my toes just to see it safely afloat. I turned my head to Johnson, who was sitting beside me, his smoke-reddened eyes on the boat. He looked like the end man in a minstrel show, his white hair so many dirty scraps of cotton pasted above a blackened face.

"She's not bad, Joey, not bad at all. Those half-dozen coats of paint you sanded into her saved her. Nothin's been touched 'cept the paint, and you can leave the fixing of that until you put in at your island."

I tried to put into words my gratitude, but he shook his head, protesting that I had evened the score by dragging him out. I knew that I hadn't, and then Stella leaned over me and whispered something in my ear that I should have thought of myself.

"Pop, in a month or two, I don't know when—"

"Baski, you fight too hard!" Delaney squatted down beside me, sucking on a crumbled cigarette between his lips. "The picture of you behind bars, or even in a court, doesn't jell. Maybe I like a fighter, maybe I'm getting soft. Anyway, you're clear as far as I'm concerned. Guinan will go along, so don't worry about him."

"Lieutenant," I sighed in the luxury of Stella's happy embrace. "Lieutenant, this Creel Haven I'm going to is a great spot for a cop to spend his vacation."

He grinned. "You must be a mind reader. Saves me from asking. Maybe I'll be dropping in for a week's fishing."

I reached over and touched Johnson's arm as he was about to rise. "Pop, I started to say something before that I can put differently now. Tonight I'm sailing on open waters. How long will it take you to pack?"

He didn't believe me, and then when he saw I was serious he was too choked up to speak for a minute. "Figure you might need me as mate, Joe?" He gazed over at the boat, swallowing his feelings.

I said I did, really getting a lift out of what I was doing. "Can you make it in an hour, Pop? It's O.K. if you can't—"

"Half the time, Joey! Half the time!" He got up and went up the path like a kid just out of school.

In the darkness ahead the pinpoint lights of Sandy Hook winked at us. The spray, lifting at the bow in cloudlike formations, whipped back over the flying bridge. Stella was at the wheel, with me behind her, my cheek against hers. We could hear Johnson below, whistling as he prepared a midnight snack for the three of us.

"He certainly is happy about coming along, isn't he, Joe?"

"Pop? He's tickled pink. And so am I. He's a nice guy to have around."

"Think he'd mind baby-sitting once in a while?"

"Hell, no. He loves—" I got it then, and pulled her close, her cheek against my lips, too happy to say anything. Together we watched the dark shadows ahead ebb and flow across the silvered waters, the yellow moon rising in the distance over Sandy Hook. There was so much ahead of us.

THE END

Calvin Clements Bibliography
(1915-1997)

NOVELS:

Satan Takes the Helm (Gold Medal, 1952)

Barge Girl (Gold Medal, 1953)

Hell Ship to Kuma (Gold Medal, 1954)

Dark Night of Love (Popular Library, 1956)

SCREENPLAYS
(all TV except where noted):

Wanted: Dead or Alive (1 episode, 1959)

Law of the Plainsman (3 episodes, 1959-60)

Have Gun—Will Travel (1 episode, 1960)

Laramie (1 episode, 1960)

The Detectives (2 episodes, 1960-62)

The Rifleman (10 episodes, 1960-63)

Zane Grey Theater (1 episode, 1961)

The Brothers Brannagan (1 episode, 1961)

Ichabod and Me (1 episode, 1961)

Bachelor Father (1 episode, 1961)

Alfred Hitchcock Presents (1 episode, 1961)

The Greatest Show on Earth (1 episode, 1963)

The Great Adventure (1 episode, 1964)

Daniel Boone (1 episode, 1964)

Gunsmoke (39 episodes, 1964-74)

Wagon Train (5 episodes, 1964-65)

Karen (1 episode, 1965)

Convoy (1 episode, 1965)

Firecreek (movie, 1968)

The Sixth Sense (1 episode, 1972)

Kansas City Bomber (movie, 1972)

Jigsaw (1 episode, 1972)

The F.B.I. (6 episodes, 1973-74)

Dirty Sally (1 episode, 1974)

Attack on Terror: The FBI vs the Ku Klux Klan (TV movie, 1975)

How the West Was Won (3 episodes, 1979)

STORIES
(as by Calvin J. Clements):

The Test (*Argosy*, Nov 1948)

Shanghai Reckoning (*Argosy*, May 1949)

The Captain's Prisoner (*Argosy*, July 1949)

The Black Bag (*Thrilling Detective*, Aug 1949)

Keep Off the Rail! (*Argosy*, Feb 1950)

The Crooked Circle (*The Blue Book Magazine*, June 1950)

Too Clever (*5 Detective Novels Magazine*, Winter 1950)

It Happened in Gowanus (*The Blue Book Magazine*, June 1951)

Duel at Greasewood Flats (*Nation's Business*, Nov 1951)

Money Rider (*Collier's*, Nov 10 1951)

Liar! (*Bluebook*, Jan 1954)

Curse of the Idol (*Argosy*, Feb 1954)

Mr. Martin's Folly (*The Saturday Evening Post*, Oct 15 1955)

Outcast Rider (*Argosy*, Nov 1956)

www.ingramcontent.com/pod-product-compliance
Lightning Source LLC
Chambersburg PA
CBHW071752190726
48292CB00003B/954